THE
OLDEST
CONFESSION

The
Oldest Confession

RICHARD CONDON

A FOUR SQUARE BOOK

For my darling Evelyn
and for Max
with love

First published in Great Britain by Longmans, Green and Company Ltd., in 1959
Copyright © 1958 by Richard Condon
*
FIRST FOUR SQUARE EDITION 1965
Reprinted February 1965

*Four Square Books are published by The New English Library Limited from Barnard's Inn,
Holborn, London EC1. They are made and printed in Great Britain by Love and
Malcomson Ltd., Redhill, Surrey*

PART I

Levantado

The bull is fresh and believes himself prepared for anything. He knows his strength and has great confidence in his ability to conquer anything in the ring. He lunges at the cape with unbelievable speed.

THE small hotel on Calle de Marengo stood back-to-back with a German restaurant whose cooks and kitchens had been flown from Berlin to Madrid by the late Luftwaffe. Prior to that the hotel had been headquarters for the Soviet General Staff in the river of blood of only twenty years before. To those of a romantic turn, like James Bourne, these conditions should have made the hotel seem endemically sinister but the warm press of spring helped to shoo away the sachet of old death. It was still there however but, like a touch of insanity in a well-to-do family, never mentioned.

Off the main hall, in the American Bar, sat Dr. Victoriano Muñoz, Marqués de Villalba; Representative and Mrs. Homer Quarles Pickett (R., Ill.); a bullfighter named Cayetano Jiminez; James Bourne, the American who leased and operated the hotel; and Doña Blanca Conchita Hombria y Arias de Ochoa y Acebal, Marquesa de Vidal, Condesa de Ocho Pinas, Vizcondesa Ferri, Duquesa de Dos Cortes.

Dr. Muñoz carried his cat, Montes, with him as he always did. Muñoz was a tree to the cat. It climbed him continuously when the climbing mood came upon it. It rested upon him, anywhere upon him, when resting suited it. The marqués had named this cat after the pasodoble El Gato Montes. Montes, a topaz cat, was the doctor's only real confidant.

The duchess was an intense, formidably prejudiced woman of memorable, sensual beauty and suspended youth, a tribal yo-yo on a string eight hundred years long, whose pale, blond hair was dark at the root.

She was a most reckless partisan of Spain's royal pretender. In his name she had breached the peace, resisted the law, inveighed against Franco, the Falange and Communism. The Pretender is said to have written to her with considerable urgency from Portugal commanding that she cease and desist in her alarums against the Caudillo and she is said to have replied by return mail that when he commanded her from Spanish soil she would obey, and not until. She had not seen her husband for three years, by his choice. The duchess was twenty-nine years old.

Cayetano Jiminez, whose father, grandfather, and great-grandfather had been bullfighters and whose great-great-grandfather had been a British rifleman who had entered Spain *sin pasaporte* with Wellington at Badajoz, had golden-red hair and milky skin. He was a tall man, not beside James Bourne, but certainly when next to Dr. Muñoz he seemed quite long. The illusion of even greater length came from his slimness which was a good thing because when he fought bulls he went in close, without tricks, and that was no business for a plump man.

Tourists might be confused by the duchess's blondness and Cayetano's golden redness, but the Picketts at least looked quite typically Spanish. She was angularly thin and black with olive skin and large, dark passionate eyes which were then sticky from the sound of her husband's voice and from four absinthe frappés. The bones of her shoulders and back seemed exhausted from having to hold up her large breasts. She was nearly twenty-five years younger than her husband.

Homer Pickett was a billowing man with a census of chins, very red lips and a highly pitched voice. He looked like a receiver of stolen goods or a jolly undertaker, anything in a category at once sedentary and abnormal. His hands touched and fondled his person endlessly, from ear lobe to kneecap, as he talked. He was a prodigious talker. He spoke Castilian Spanish, as did Mrs. Pickett. He could also speak Galician and Catalan, and if the Basque language could have been learned by an adult, Mr. Pickett would have learned Basque. He was between fifty and fifty-five years old.

Representative and Mrs. Pickett, he a prize of Dr. Muñoz' who had read in that morning's paper of the Picketts' presence in Madrid, had met these four new friends exactly fifty-five minutes before. Dr. Muñoz was an art lover, the duchess an art enthusiast, and Bourne an art student, in his way. Cayetano Jiminez was there because the duchess was there.

Mr. Pickett was a world authority on the graphic art of Spain. When he spoke of Morales or Murillo or Valdés Leal with the frequently emotional and always interstitial information he could bring to these subjects, it made Dr. Muñoz narrow his eyes suddenly to keep back the mist which always filled them in the presence of Spain's beauty and made Cayetano Jiminez, a person of clearly defined interests, seem to drink in the duchess's image and breathe more heavily. As Mr. Pickett spoke the duchess would stare at him with protuberant eyes and keep wetting her lower lip with the soft underside of her tongue.

It was not all reverential talk they exchanged. In fact a great deal of the talk concerned contemporary Spanish painters and was pure gossip, much of it delicious. To this part of the feast it was Mr. Pickett who brought the appetite.

Victoriano Muñoz, behind thick lenses and under a third-rate mustache, wearing a tightly fitting suit over his small body which seemed martyred to the broad chocolate stripes over the blue material, and flashing that tiny tic at the corner of his mouth which, like the lock of a dam, released white moisture which he was continually wiping away, resembled a schoolmaster of an older time. His family had lost most of its enormous fortune, the basis of which had been twenty per cent of the Peruvian gold yield of Francisco Pizarro, by too public an alliance with Joseph Bonaparte. They had been that kind of Spaniard. Although the duchess for example would not recognize a title conferred by any Bonaparte, Dr. Muñoz still held a souvenir from the French in that he could, if he chose, which he most certainly did not as he bitterly resented his family's past mistake in loyalties, call himself Comte de la Frontière. His consuming interest was the art of Spain. Representative Pickett was one of his heroes. James Bourne was the other.

His warm devotion to Bourne, an innkeeper and a foreigner, was one of the most discussed puzzles of fashionable Madrid. Because of Dr. Muñoz, Bourne was accepted by everyone in Spanish society. In return, Bourne discussed the Spanish masters with the marqués who was dismayed, awed, excited, fulfilled and engrossed by Bourne's knowledge.

Bourne spoke to the marqués in the form of a lecture or seminar. Otherwise, under any other condition of their meeting or association, Bourne rarely spoke to him directly. He could feel his laughter turn rancid when Muñoz joined in; feeling uneasiness over how long and how well he could continue to conceal his distaste for the doctor. Lack of talk itself was not indicative of aloofness with Bourne. It was a great effort, or he made it seem to be, for Bourne to speak. The duchess and Cayetano Jiminez were perhaps the only exceptions to this rule of silence. He could be nearly garrulous with them.

Bourne either learned by listening or did not bother to listen at all, remembering instead all that he had been unable to understand throughout his life, remaining silent, chewing upon the statement of this fact, staring at the memory of that dream, awaiting some sign of recognition, some association of the words with reality, a sargasso sea obscured by bulbous fronds.

He was very tall; more than six feet four inches tall, a compactly muscular man whose elegant clothes and nervous grace made him seem slender. He had a huge head, though, and small features like cinders stuck in suet. Bourne always sat uncommonly still; uncommon at least for nearly everyone else of that decade, a monument to his own nerves which bayed like bloodhounds at the moon of his ambitions.

Bourne thought of himself as a criminal the way others might think of themselves as lawyers or doctors. In countries where men are introduced as, for example, Engineer di Giorgio or Accountant Scheffler, Bourne to himself would have been simply Criminal Bourne. He had never been arrested. Excepting for his wife and his French associate, Jean Marie, Bourne was not known as a criminal to anyone else and most particularly was he unknown to the police or any other criminals. His account books, kept as meticulously as though he expected any day to have to justify his income tax returns to an examiner, showed that he had earned by criminal methods the multiple currency equivalent of seven hundred and twelve thousand dollars over a period of sixteen years through efficiently executed crime in Pasadena, California; London, England; Des Moines, Iowa; Paris, France; and in the Federal District of Mexico, among other places.

He had had the hotel in Madrid under operating lease for three and one-half years and had been so patient in the development of this Spanish criminal project, patience having been one of his strongest professional points, that he had been invited to play with the Danne String Quartet, a pool of gifted amateurs of great family, in charity concerts at the Royal Palace; he had twice been invited to enjoy the festival of Our Lady of Rocio on the horses of Don Eduardo Miura; he was considered to be the closest friend of the great Cayetano Jiminez and was favored by the duchess as were perhaps two dozen Spaniards, most of whom were of great age. It was all part of Bourne's exquisite sense of composition.

Michelangelo had said that the successful completion of a great mosaic must rest upon the infinite design in the placement of a single tile. One could relate the developmental side of Bourne's crimes to that of the work of any fine artist. He assembled his tiles under demanding standards. He was willing to consume time and capital and to spend weeks at a time away from a new wife of only nine and three-quarter months while he considered the infinite design of his tasks. He did not assign himself to steal property only because it was marked by vulgar display as worth stealing.

Bourne breathed the same air with his victims. He did not sentimentalize. His crimes were indigenous. In moving to Spain he had not known in advance what it was he had come to steal. Bourne always waited for a worthy object to present itself to him. This was not difficult for, by prearrangement and somehow connected with his romanticism, Bourne had always arranged to move among riches.

His counters were in full play as he sat trying to listen to Representative Pickett talk ravenously of Ferrer Bassa, a Spanish primitive painter. Bourne fastened his concentration upon the duchess with the friendliest kind of detachment.

It was only nine o'clock in the evening, maybe a little later. It would be two hours to dinnertime, maybe a little longer.

Congressman Pickett could not remember where he had

last seen Ferrer Bassa's work exhibited. The duchess merely said, "Jaime will know. Jaime?" Bourne heard his name and at once pulled the plastic covers off his expression.

"Yes, Blanca, darling?"

"Where are the Ferrer Bassa, sweet?"

"The altarpieces?"

"Yes, darling."

"Oh. At Pedralbes. You know. The convent near Barcelona."

"Thank you, darling. Do continue, Mr. Pickett."

Pickett shifted quite smoothly into the genius of Bernardo Martorell. It took rather a few words to do but each one was spoken with such authority that everyone listened closely, or seemed to be listening.

Mrs. Pickett looked the most attentive, but she was the most experienced at listening to her husband. She focused her eyes on the bridge of his nose and leaned forward slightly in excited interest, her mouth the tiniest bit opened. With this tribute she freed herself.

Her mind wandered out of the world of art and entered another to consider the gallantry of a man whom she admired beyond all others because after his wife had spent three weeks away from him in a Florida resort he had met her at the Newark Airport on her return with a private ambulance so that he could welcome her warmly and pleasure them both behind an ejaculating siren at seventy-three miles an hour across the Pulaski Skyway and the Jersey Flats. She mulled over it as one of the greatest compliments a woman had ever been paid.

"You would be *astonished,* my dear duchess," Congressman Pickett was saying, "how much Berenson knows about your own neoclassical school. It *is* astonishing, you know. I mean to say I can, of course, *converse* in his field. That is, I am familiar with *something* of Titian. I have, as matter of pure fact, been trapped into lecturing for several hours on the Italians in a dreary *unconvincing* sort of way, haven't I, Marianne?" Mrs. Pickett nodded like The Hanging Judge. "But I mean to say, compared to Berenson in *my* field, I was as ignorant in *his* as—well, as some popular art critic, I suppose. Spain is *my* field. I mean, all of it. I mean I *do excel* with the Spanish quite a few *light* years beyond Berenson because, naturally, it is *my* field where it is *not* his. You see what I mean, doctor?".

"I see what you mean. Yes. But I want to assure you with all the power at my command, Mr. Pickett, I am not interested in Italian painters or in such people who choose to be interested in them. I intend no rudeness by this, please. Mr. Pickett, please clear up one point for me. The Velázquez 'Lancer on a White Horse' which is now in the Metropolitan in New York——"

"Yes, doctor?"

"It was acquired for over two hundred thousand dollars in 1952."

"Yes, doctor."

"Who sold it to them?"

"Uh. Why—uh. Now that you mention it, I—was it—uh?——"

The duchess coughed slightly. The cat Montes leaped from Muñoz' lap to his left shoulder but no one batted an eye except Mrs. Pickett who looked as if she'd like to swipe at the cat's chops with the Ojen bottle. Cayetano pressed Bourne's thigh with his knee. Bourne understood the gesture if not the existence of any question. "Yes, Blanca? Am I missing something?"

"Sweet, who sold the 'Lancer on a White Horse' to the New York museum?"

"You mean the name of the agent?"

"No, no, my dear Jaime," Dr. Muñoz said. "Who owned the painting?"

"Well, it had been bought by the fourth Earl of Lethbridge in Parma in 1803. Most people thought it was a copy with variations of the Prado portrait. I saw it in '45 at the present Earl of Lethbridge's place in Dorset. They found out it was no copy, all right, when it was cleaned up for an Edinburgh Festival. Good heavens, any of us could have told them that. The *pentimenti* around the hat and the face gave the whole thing away. I rather think that Don Julio Vigo, the lancer in the picture, realized that the white horse caught the eye rather than the rider and had the color altered. Nor can one blame him."

"Whew! Man, what a talker. You just never stop, do you, Jaimito?" Cayetano shook him by the nape of the neck laughing. Bourne grinned back at him, but the vault of his

11

lower face had been resealed. His mind left them again. He began to go through the steps of the problem again, leading away from his objective to explore once again each contingency which might, but which undoubtedly would not, arise.

The thought of Spanish masterpieces floating about in foreign lands, being bought and sold with no Spanish hope for control, launched the duchess upon a virulent attack upon the efficiency, aims, progress, permanent collections, influence or lack of it and general shortcomings of the Instituto de Cultura Hispanica, a cultural arm of the Foreign Office and a source of abiding pride to Generalissimo Franco. She chopped away in fine detail, as Dr. Muñoz and Congressman Pickett formed the other sides of the triangular argument.

As she spoke with delicate eloquence and heated partisan fervor Cayetano stared at her. His hands clenched his napkin, annoyed nut dishes, twisted his watch band or played with his necktie. They were long-fingered hands with wire-haired backs. The nails had been bitten so low into the fingers that each finger end was stumpy and bald, each having the expression of blind men.

He watched her, missing no move and hearing no word. His eyes addressed her with the intensity of demand which they were accustomed to use only to address the statues of the Virgin in the chapels of the bull rings in Madrid, Caracas, Seville, Mexico City or anywhere else like that near eternity. Before he knew what or why, he felt Bourne tap him, as the others stood up. The group left the hotel to move diagonally across the street through the gentling night to the *frontón*.

Victoriano Muñoz, carrying the topaz cat Montes like a baby in arms, walked most earnestly beside Mr. Pickett, nodding in continuing understanding as Mr. Pickett fussed at the garments of the Spanish masters with unrelieved syntax.

Bourne gave support to Mrs. Pickett who told him that the bartender at the hotel was in love with her, she believed, and had been serving her double absinthes. She smiled hazily up at Bourne and asked him if he knew just how much of an aphrodisiac absinthe was. He replied that he had had no experience with that sort of thing.

Cayetano walked slowly beside the duchess, twenty yards behind the others. They seemed to have nothing to say which was not being said by the gift of their presence to each other.

12

Their fingertips, as they walked side-by-side, just touched, so that they might swing away from each other at any sudden appearance of vulgarity.

They were walking slowly and without any interest in their destination to the *frontón* because Mrs. Pickett had begun to express her ideas and opinions about bullfights. The duchess had looked to Bourne as though she might become ill, so Bourne had turned the conversation to *pelota* and Mrs. Pickett had insisted upon seeing it played.

Inside the *frontón* the noise was so abusive that the slumbrousness of the instant past seemed unreal. The sound of the crowd was the sound of a pet shop in a fire. The smoke of cigars and cigarettes, some of it years old, settled in billows like damp organdy.

The party climbed to seats in the eleventh row and settled down to the sound of the ball hitting the walls with the sound of a nightstick hitting a shinbone, and to watch the small players make the giant gestures of throwing the ball from the long baskets as Van Gogh might have tried to throw off despair only to have it bound back at him from some crazy, new angle.

Along the bottom aisle the *corredores* acted out the phrase in the prayer at the end of the Mass, seeming to roam through the world seeking the ruin of souls, flinging ruptured tennis balls into the mottled face of the crowd. Bourne had to explain their motivations to Mrs. Pickett.

He explained that *corredores* were betting commissioners. A bettor in the crowd would signal his sporting choice, betting on the changes in lead between the blue or the white team on the court. The agent would stuff a blue and white slip containing the current odds quotation into a split tennis ball, fling it to the bettor who would return it crammed with the cash amount of his bet. He yelled at a *corredore* who had a scar as red as an ambassador's decoration running diagonally and memorably across his face and held up ten fingers. The agent yelled back like a dubbed version of Dizzy Dean and let fly at Bourne's head with the ball. He showed her the betting slip.

He didn't show her the other slip which said QUINN NUMERO 811. He read it and dropped that slip on the floor.

When he threw the ball back to the agent, Mrs. Pickett still didn't understand the game. Within a half hour they stood

13

outside the *frontón*. The duchess decided for everyone, without asking anyone, that they would go to the garden at the Fenix for another drink.

Bourne turned her aside for a moment and excused himself. They agreed that he was to rejoin them for dinner at the German restaurant at eleven o'clock, an hour and twenty-five minutes away. Bourne helped Mrs. Pickett into the Bentley as Mr. Pickett complained that Byron's lines in *Don Juan* were unjust to the Spanish master, Ribera, and Mr. Pickett quoted, "Spagnoletto tainted his brush with all the blood of all the sainted." As the Bentley drew away with Cayetano behind the wheel, and the duchess closely beside him, Bourne could still hear the marqués' answer from the tonneau which promised to be a rather long anecdote concerning Ribera and the bastard half-brother of Philip IV.

Bourne crossed the street, walking slowly. He entered the lobby of the hotel and went to the key desk to ask if the Paris plane had arrived at Barajas. The conserje looked up at the clock and told him that the flight had been on the ground for thirty-five minutes and that any passengers the hotel might expect should be arriving immediately. Bourne thanked him, then slipped around behind the desk and began a thoughtful examination of the room rack. He did not run his fingers down the cards so that neither the conserje nor Gustavo Elek, the assistant manager, who had joined them silently, could discover which card Bourne was interested in reading.

When one moves from airport to airport one can observe the restlessness which has come to the world since Hiroshima. Barajas Airport, which serves Madrid, had prospered in a few short years as the driven people, led by their Father William of a Foreign Secretary, had soared out across the world on a go-now-pay-later basis.

The girl was on the Iberia flight from Le Bourget. Her real name was Eve Lewis, or had been Lewis until she had married. She never questioned why she had changed it illegally four times on four sets of vital documents which had had to be forged.

She was a tall, young woman. She had dark hair, either gray-blue or green eyes and a straight nose. She was tastelessly dressed as though through a fruitless effort to discount

14

her physical beauty which had brought her so much attention in the past that it had eventually led to the business of her changing her name. She walked across the apron of the field like a moving light; refreshing and refreshed. She carried a cardboard tube; two and a half inches in diameter, three feet long.

To comprehend the tastelessness of her clothes it must be seen that they were frumpish and untidy, not loud or vulgar. There was a spot on her hat, perhaps two smudges which could have come from greasy fingers holding a greasy sandwich on a tourist flight. Her skirt was longer on the right side than on the left. The lipstick on the corner of her full, soft, moist mouth was out of registration with the line of her lip. She had the slightly tilted mouth of the secret self-pitier. Her eyes could not be said to pity anyone or anything, but the general lucky expression on her face and the way she carried her full body created excellent diversion from this which, after all, not everyone would have regarded as a shortcoming.

In the *Aduanas* as she cleared Currency Control, after a speechless ritual with the kelly-green passport, the baggage from the flight was just coming off the trucks, jarring the low customs counters. The *duanistas*, in field green with scarlet bursts, ignored the physical manifest of visitors until the last bag had been placed. Then they moved down the lines of cases, touching the cargoes softly, appealing with their eyes, and waiting patiently until the baggage was opened for examination.

She had one large bag and a make-up kit besides the cardboard tube. She propped the tube against the counter carelessly. She opened the big bag. The *duanista* patted the silken contents gingerly. He signaled for her to shut the bag, then chalked it. He chalked the make-up kit without asking her to open it. He asked her, in English, what was in the cardboard tube. She answered, in Spanish, that it was the copy of a painting she had bought in Paris. He smiled briefly to acknowledge his appreciation of her courtesy in taking the trouble to learn his language, and held out his hand. She gave him the tube, then, losing interest, looked away over the heads of the departing crowd, calling *"Portero! Portero!"*

A porter shouldered his way to her. She told him to put her bags in a taxi, not the bus. When she turned back to the

15

duanista he was returning the rolled copy to the cardboard tube. He directed her to the chief of the *Aduanas* whose office adjoined the main room.

She took the tube there and the chief entered a description of its contents in his charge book explaining that this was done to convenience her as a tourist so that she could leave Spain with the same copy of a great painting without red tape and bother, also explaining how absolutely necessary it would be that she be sure to leave Spain with the same article as, in the case of an oversight in this regard, the red tape would be bothersome indeed. She thanked him.

He smiled at her, appreciating her with great delicacy, and staring at her breasts. He asked for her name and for her passport to complete the official forms. She told him her name was Carmen Quinn as she handed him the green book. He reminded her that Carmen was a very Spanish name. He told her how very well she spoke Spanish. She thanked him.

She explained that she had been born Mary Ellen Quinn, as the words under the brutalized picture on her passport showed, but that she adored Spain and the Spanish and that Carmen had been the only name she would answer to since she had been fourteen years old. She told him that she had saved up for many years to come to Spain; that at last her dreams were coming true in that she was about to see with her own eyes the fabled cities of Madrid, Córdoba, Seville and Granada. She told him she had always wished with all her heart that she could marry a Spaniard. She sighed. For an instant it seemed as though he could not look up at her.

"You are married?" she asked softly. He nodded. When he looked up he had finished with staring at her breasts and looked into her eyes. He produced a pen and asked her to sign the form. His face seemed flushed. She signed, spelling her name carefully. He gave her the cardboard tube with a slight bow. He walked with her to the entrance of his office, signaled importantly to the pistoled guard at the outer door to gain her passage through, then smiled at her brilliantly. She wasted no more time on him but left hurriedly to find her cab.

The elevator went up very slowly, Bourne almost filling it. He stared at the roof of the cage as he ascended. He seemed to rest his head on his own back. With his mouth open and

16

his eyes staring fixedly upward into the gloom he had the look of a drowned man.

When the cage halted at the eighth floor Bourne fought the two doors open then turned right in the corridor, fumbling in his trousers pocket to bring out a ring of master keys. He whistled softly which made his heavy chin more prominent and made his mouth look like a bee sting. As he walked his fingers found the individual master key without consulting his eyes. Everything in Bourne's physical plant was trained to move and act independently with maximum economy and without distracting his eyes from their constant vigil. He stopped walking when he came to the door marked 811. He opened the door with the passkey, entered and closed it behind him, carrying a cardboard tube in his left hand.

She was in the chair by the window. She still had the soiled hat on. She was staring, without focusing, out the window, over the top of the Post Office, across the Plaza de los Cibeles and up toward the Gran Via, holding that sentimental look many people get when they are daydreaming about imposssible quantities of money. She didn't hear him until he closed the door, then she turned.

"My God, what's *that* tube for?" she said. Her cardboard tube was on the bed. Bourne propped his in the corner near the door and answered, "You'll have to take a tube along to Seville and so forth and I'll need one for the project."

He walked to the bed and slipped the copy out of the tube Eve had brought from Paris. He unrolled it and stared at it, nodding. He slid it back into the tube then placed the tube across the marble top of the bureau.

"Jean Marie is a marvel," he said to no one but himself to remind himself, perhaps, that he could not do without Jean Marie. Rubbing his hands with satisfaction he went to the window sill and sat down between Eve and her view. He took an envelope printed in two colors from his pocket and dropped it gently in her lap. She held the envelope by the corners, staring down at it with an absent smile which marked her mouth with the stain of secret self-pity. Bourne spoke more quietly than usual. It wasn't a whisper, but it wasn't a conversational tone either.

"You'll have a wonderful time. Córdoba, Seville, Granada, then back to Madrid, all by luxury bus."

Her voice became just as subdued. "You're a smart man, Jim."

"If you say so, I believe it."

"I did everything you said at the airport. The clothes this way were a tremendous help. I said those outrageous things to the chief of customs and everything happened as though it were all part of a play you had written. I don't even bother to worry any more. I just do it the way you rehearse me."

"You are my angel," he said, leaning over to lift her out of the chair by the waist as though she were a tiny slip of a thing instead of five feet ten and a half, as though she were a large stein of beer. He lifted her high enough to place her mouth on his mouth then to bring her down to him, pressed into him. They clung to each other like human flies clinging to a wall of life, like Toynbee's people clinging to their history. She broke the fluid oneness of the still statue they had become by wrenching her heavy mouth away from his and dropping her head to rest on his shoulder, breathing heavily in the silence.

"What painting this time?"

He was breathing even more heavily. "Diego Rodríguez da Silva y Velázquez," he said, "born on June 6th, 1599, of noble, if not aristocratic, parents. Court painter to Philip IV for thirty-seven years until his death in 1660. His work was proud, exquisitely refined and sensitive, gentle, serious and brilliantly intelligent. He was the painter of painters."

"How much will it bring?"

His hands seemed to grow into her back. His eyes, closed in pain or ecstasy, opened slowly. They became compassionate. The compassion congealed. Their protoplasm was transmuted into green polystyrene flecked with gold. "Over a hundred thousand dollars," he whispered. Her mouth soared toward his again. This time she gave up control of herself.

Although Bourne arrived ten minutes late at the German restaurant, he was twenty minutes ahead of his hosts. He sat at the table for six before an open window across from El Retino, ordered white wine upon young strawberries which is not as delicious as it sounds merely because it could not be, and went over his plans for the two hundredth time. His plans were sound because in every over-all sense they remained general plans, going into minute and rigid detail only within the areas of possible contingencies. To remain elastic and yet to be able to move reflexively without the need to think at the moment of stress was a measure of Bourne's excellence in design. Years before he had planned his method of planning.

When the others arrived Mrs. Pickett, who was quite flushed, noticed in a loud voice that Bourne had changed his clothes, but the duchess glossed over that. Mr. Pickett was saying, "—perhaps it looked better above the altar than in the gallery alongside the other paintings. I must say I prefer the charming serious-faced Blessed Henry Suso and Saint Louis Bertram which were designed to hang together. Or Saint Hugh of Grenoble Visiting the Refectory—he had the monks fasting, you know, refusing to eat the meat the cooks had served by mistake." Muñoz, the saffron, inky-eyed cat Montes held in the crook of his arm, insisted upon its being known that his Zubarán favorite was the adorable Santa Marina in the black tricorne hat, black bodice, blue-green gown with red and olive-green bustle, holding a boat hook.

Their prattle caused Cayetano to shake his head violently like a muddled prizefighter. He held the silk scarf of the duchess loosely in his hands. He stared at her, then forced himself to look away for an equal period of time, then looked back at her. The few drinks she had had brought gentle action to the capillaries beneath her fair skin so that she was sublimely rosy and white. Conscious of Cayetano's hungry stare, the duchess was happy.

Mrs. Pickett caught the table captain's attention most discreetly and told him she had heard about a French alcool called *framboise,* something she had been told had been distilled from raspberries, which she would very much like to taste. Equally discreetly, as privately as though they were planning an assignation, the table captain explained that, while *framboise* was delicious indeed when served quite cold, it was an *after* dinner liqueur which, by the way, madame should know, was the strongest of all liqueurs, running, as it did, to one hundred and fifty-three proof. Mrs. Pickett thanked him for all that detailed information and said that since she was only interested in smelling *framboise* to savor its delicate raspberry bouquet she would greatly appreciate his bringing some at once. The table captain sent a man to fetch a bottle and Mrs. Pickett confided to Bourne that her husband was a gourmet who could order for everyone if they so wished.

A waiter brought the bottle of *framboise* in a mound of ice. While everyone was either talking or listening to talk about art Mrs. Pickett poured six tiny glasses full, then offered a glass to each one at the table, with gracious generousness. Everyone refused. Cayetano explained that he was allergic to fruit. The others were checking a point of information with Bourne about a painter named Ramón Casas. Mrs. Pickett said, as though propitiating a god, that, oh dear, now that they had been poured she certainly didn't want to see them wasted so suiting the action to the word she emptied every little glass into her own throat, then settled down with the bottle and a little glass all her own.

They dined extremely well on venison stew, dumplings, apple sauce and other un-Spanish dishes. Bourne was beginning to feel that his pent-up tension would explode through the ends of his fingers, hitting someone and mortally wounding them. Fortunately, years before he had conditioned the reflexes of his friends to the realization that he spoke very little, usually only when spoken to, so that he could sit very still and concentrate upon controlling himself. He was a nervous man to be in such work as high-stakes crime, but there was no doubt that his degree of sensitiveness and imagination had most certainly made him a leader in that field. In his mind, he began a mental drill; the moves he had practiced again and again and again in his own locked room at the hotel. The clock in his head stayed apace with the movements within his imagination. He was relieved to see that he had cut seconds from the operation. This cheered him enormously. He began again from the very beginning to the completion of the task. It was true. He had shaved seven and one-half seconds. Soon he would make the moves in reality, with the reassurance which contact with material objects could bring.

Midway through the meal, Mrs. Pickett began to speak somewhat ramblingly about bullfighters whom she adored. She asked if they had ever met any. She asked each one in grave turn, except her husband. The duchess seemed most puzzled by the question but she admitted that she had, turning to Cayetano with a questioning shrug. Cayetano answered briskly. He had met several toreros he said but he had seen so many newsreels about bullfighting to say nothing of other kinds of motion pictures, that he felt as if he knew bullfighters very well. Bourne said he didn't know many bullfighters but that he had met Ava Gardner. Muñoz listened to her question with a blank expression, answered with a quick, yes of course, then turned to continue his discussion with Mr. Pickett concerning Murillo's "Sagrada Familia de Pararito" with the Christ Child holding the bird in his hand in a perfectly charming manner, to say nothing of that little dog, that precious little dog, looking up at it. Mrs. Pickett explained that although she had never permitted herself to attend a bullfight she absolutely adored bullfighters, then offered the thought that bullfighting was all tied up with the national death wish of Spain, of course, proving how morbid the Spanish actually were.

The duchess had no capacity to suffer such boredom. She said, "Come, come, Mrs. Pickett, I have been Spanish for more than nine centuries and I will thank you sincerely not to explain Spaniards to me. We have a ninety-kilometer journey ahead of us. Eat your food and stop parroting what the ignorant think they think." Cayetano said, "It is rather morbid, you know. I'm a vegetarian myself." Bourne took exception to this, saying that plants were not only living things but that plants made it possible for humans to live supplying as they did the very oxygen in the air we breathe, and that for his part science damned well should come up with a chemical diet, an all-mineral chemical diet because there was nothing morbid about killing rocks. Mrs. Pickett retreated to her private world, pink as raspberries, where she always had a much better time anyway. She slowly undressed a tall, faceless film actor in her mind, then caused him to come running to her pleading for her body. With delicacy and out of consideration of the others, she closed her eyes as she gave herself to him.

They left for Dos Cortes at one-twenty ayem to feast on the duchess's paintings. The duchess and Cayetano drove in a small white Mercedes two-seater. The others traveled in the Bentley. Bourne drove. Mrs. Pickett fell asleep in the back seat, beside her husband, looking rather pretty.

They waited for the duchess and Cayetano for nearly fifteen minues in the great hall after they arrived. The waiting was a burden on Mrs. Pickett who had become extremely sleepy and, through fatigue, slightly irritated. She kept asking her husband if he would for Christ's sake please stop talking about those goddam paintings, for Christ's sake? She inquired as to whether either his throat or Dr. Muñoz' throat ever got sore, that he had been talking steadily and saying nothing for nine goddam hours for Christ's sake and that she, for one, would be greatly cheered and gratified if he would kindly shut his goddam big expert mouth and go to bed, for Christ's sake. Her voice had hidden resources of volume so everyone agreed that the duchess and Cayetano must have had a flat tire, that the hour was late, and that they should go up to bed. They made their way up the niagaran staircase with Dr. Muñoz pointing out, en route, a Goya here, a Zurbarán there, a Morales on the curve, a Murillo above it, an El Greco to the right, a Velázquez beyond that, all of them quite invisible, hanging high in the darkness.

The moment they reached the top of the staircase the duchess and Cayetano entered the great hall below them and called out good night. The others waved back, then went their separate ways, with Dr. Muñoz guiding the Picketts to their apartment knowing that Bourne knew his own way, and with the sunshine-yellow cat Montes leading the entire procession, guiding Dr. Muñoz.

Bourne was enormously relieved that his two friends had arrived. The plan returned to normal. His internal timing mechanism began to function on its own again, constructing yet other negative possibilities. When he was sure that the Picketts and Dr. Muñoz were bedded down for the night, Bourne relaxed as well as he could in a niche in the stone wall waiting for the duchess and Cayetano to ascend the stairs and retire. He was not impatient. He had many things to weigh and consider. He amused himself thinking of the story he would have for Jean Marie if he could get his work done before Mr. Pickett made his talkative tour of all of the duchess's paintings in the morning.

An amateur might have felt that it would be taking needless risk which was nonsense. First off, Mr. Pickett would be so captured by the verisimilitude of the setting, by the legend of the painter, by the monetary worth of the painting, by the proximity of its illustrious companions that he

22

would not be able to judge it objectively or dispassionately. He remembered the surge of elation he had felt when Muñoz had gabbled about how he had succeeded in attracting the great Homer Pickett to view Blanca's gallery and how Bourne must come and listen to such erudition concerning Spanish art as existed nowhere else in the world. Bourne remembered having registered instantly that if a world authority could be swept into pronouncing Jean Marie's copy as a masterwork of a great Spanish painter it would remain a masterwork throughout time as it hung in concealment, high in the shadows above the staircase at Dos Cortes. He knew that Mr. Pickett would never once doubt that he was in the presence of an authentic Velázquez. He would take that for granted because it was hanging in the castle of a grandee of Spain. If through some miracle of fifth sight the man did spot it as a fraud he would not, for fear of offending or embarrassing his hostess, have one word to say concerning the suspected fraud. Furthermore, if a man so totally lacked courtesy, sensitivity or gratitude to so expose such a painting as being fraudulent who could prove how long the fraud had hung there? Who knew but what some ancestor of the duke's, needing a large sum of money, had not sold the whole lot of paintings, substituting copies. That last thought gave Bourne pause for an instant, but he dismissed it quickly as being impossible. To pass the time he began to think about business and what had signaled to bring him here, standing in a niche in stone and darkness.

One day three years before inside the great cathedral at El Escorial he had noticed masterpieces of art hanging high in the darkness, beyond eye level by twice, beyond the sight of priest or communicant, and disclosed entirely by accident by the huge lights of an American film company which had been producing a film about the Spanish War of Independence of 1810.

As he watched the monks and the old priests stare up at the countless masterpieces, seeing them for the first time after a lifetime spent within the walls of the cathedral, some of them weeping as the theatrical lights illuminated all of this deathless beauty, Bourne forced himself to think through something which seemed to be just on the rim of his conscious thought for when the movie maker's lights went out the paintings would disappear again, perhaps forever.

From that point on, it had been simple to decide what his Spanish project would be, for if one could succeed in substituting an excellent copy of a great master for the master's original work hanging on some darkened wall, no one would ever have any means of knowing whether the original had been taken or if it had, no means of knowing exactly when it had been taken.

This consideration led to others such as setting up a suitable Factory, or production facilities to turn out excellent copies under blameless conditions by an utterly trustworthy person. He put that off to the side as being relatively simple compared to the problem of The Market, or how to dispose of such paintings at prices close to their optimum extrinsic worth to a collector who would have to understand that they could never be shown or announced publicly as having been acquired.

He pored over these problems for a number of months while he managed the hotel and continued his studies of Spanish art. He would muddle absent-mindedly through days of a week nibbling away at his central problem, The Market. He reached one set of conclusions that throughout the world there were any number of instantly lucky men who, wishing to propitiate something which disturbed them vaguely, would seek to endow their community with expensive beauty. In this manner rich museums had sprung up at country crossroads in the United States. Bourne felt, as time went by, that if he could bring a "safe" Sánchez Coello for example to the trustees of such a museum through stiffly correct channels The Market could be created.

He turned the possibility over and over in his mind together with the large tax advantages the donation of such a work could bring to stiffly correct channels of donation and began to feel that this method could be made workable because if one of the twenty richest men in a country donated a "safe" Coello to earn a tax profit in a most unostentatious manner to a small provincial museum, who was to demand at the museum that the starting point of the most authentic Sánchez Coello be investigated, and if they did who could say for sure on which dark, dark wall high beyond possible view this Coello had last been hung?

He lost eleven months following this turn then, character-

24

istically ended by solving the problem of The Market quite differently.

Below, in the great hall, the duchess had walked briskly into an anteroom beyond a waiting room, across a common room too large to light, with Cayetano following her. They sat opposite each other on benches with high backs set at right angles to a fireplace which held a roaring fire.

Spain is a walled country where the eyes of the present continually record the manners of the past. The duchess and Cayetano exceeded the past by piling more tradition on tradition. Always, for what the duchess considered very good reasons, she and Cayetano comported themselves as though a large, round duenna sat, stifling belches, within the same room with them.

Their love for each other had left reason behind. They were monomaniacal. They could feel nothing else, think of little else than being together someday. They were tense and strung-up when they sat across from each other like this, with no one to watch them. They were waiting for something to happen. They expressed with every impulsive move they did not make, with every choked cry of joy that they never uttered, that even though they might need to wait seven minutes this side of death before they were joined as one, body and soul, what they would share, when their moment did come, would be mountainous and holy.

The clear fact that their pain and sense of suffocation could be ended by one move by the duchess had no meaning to them because they had accepted wholly and forever the reason for their agony and had found it just. Cayetano could almost understand what she had done to them, was doing to them. The pressure of their emotion could cause implosion if one were taken away before the other had been fulfilled.

They were ecstatically happy, desperate people because the duchess's seventy-two-year-old husband had chosen to journey through the world in the search for greater and more delectable sins. The duchess, to whom the church was a living thing, had sworn to cherish him until death did them part, while she loved Cayetano operatically.

They sat in repose before the fire, finding survival in each other's eyes.

"Where shall we go when he is dead?" asked Cayetano, looking through the cognac in his glass at the fire.

"To bed."

"Assuredly. Then where?"

"To London, I think. I have relatives there."

"I don't speak English."

"That is fitting for a great matador of bulls."

"Luis Miguel speaks English."

"He pretends. You do understand, love, that absolutely no one will mind if you don't speak English? Some of them speak Spanish, after all, and we shan't go about much. We will go to concerts and to the galleries and late at night before we go to bed I will tell you everything everyone has said."

"Then we will go to bed."

"Oh, yes." They were silent for a little while until the duchess decided it would be best to divert such thoughts. "Where else would you like to go?" she asked softly, anxious to continue one of their favorite games.

"Mexico. Yucatan. There are beautiful little islands in the Gulf of Mexico. I have seen them. Yes. After we go to London to the concerts and the galleries and make love whenever we are alone then we will go to an island near Yucatan which I think by God I will buy tomorrow by cable. No one can take anything away, once we are there."

"No one can take away, wherever we go." The duchess's voice was decisive, her policy, instantly formed, was firm, and that was that. "Except death and then to be rejoined."

"I was thinking of politics, my sweetest, darling, little jailbird." He smiled at her deliciously, at all of her and then at just a beautiful part of her, at the lobe of her left ear as it reflected the moving color of the fire.

She purred at him. "You are jealous of Generalissimo Franco?"

"No."

Cayetano thought of the Caudillo in the State Box, draped with flags, at the Plaza de Toros in Madrid or San Sebastian or Sevilla, the crowds cheering him as affectionately as every Spanish crowd has cheered their every chief of state in history, even Ferdinand VII. Twice a year he and the generalissimo exchanged solemn bows across a hundred yards of air as Cayetano *brindised* to the chief of the Spanish

26

state and as the chief of the Spanish state acknowledged the dedication, with the ineffable graciousness of a politician who does not have to depend on votes. During such afternoons each matador would go to the state box, shake hands with the generalissimo, who was a virile and extremely pleasant man on those occasions, and receive a silver cigarette box, suitably inscribed. Cayetano had more of those silver sigarette boxes than he had cigarettes. These exchanges were Cayetano's only brushes with politics from one year to the next. He could not and would never be able to comprehend the duchess's disapproval of the government. He liked Mrs. Franco's taste in hats. He liked the generalissimo's darting movement, forward and across, to explain a fine point of the faena of Antonio Ordonez, say, or the dentist-like precision and efficiency of the kill of Rafael Ortega, to a visiting foreign dignitary. The train held Cayetano's thought for a moment on Ortega. He was at least as emotional as a dentist as he worked the bulls, and Cayetano had always felt he should carry an attaché case in the paseo. But how the man could kill! Ai!

The people cheered Franco when he arrived and when he departed, particularly on the *sombra* side; Franco understood and liked bullfighting, after all the man *was* a Spaniard; and Mrs. Franco wore stunning hats. It was that simple to Cayetano, a simple artisan who earned thirty thousand dollars for an afternoon's work. However, if Blanca preferred to have a king in that box of state, then she should have a king. She had suffered greatly to have a king there.

"You are jealous of the king then?"

He stretched out a little on the bench and touched the tip of her shoe with the tip of his in a small, joshing gesture. "Are there any bulls in the Gulf of Mexico?" she asked.

"I will not have you talking shop. It can only lead to maudlin praise of my work."

"What with my aptitude for politics and your tendency to get gored, we—"

"What with my tendency to get arrested and your tendency to get gored, we—"

"Ah, no. I am adept. I have great art. Ask my manager."

"So they tell me."

"I am. I have some advertisements from the *Digame* which

I paid for myself as a legitimate business expense which tend to prove this."

"Adept enough to have been gored twenty-seven times, twice in the stomach and once in the throat."

"My foot slipped."

"That is a lot of slips."

"In a lifetime!"

"You are only twenty-seven years old now."

"It is a business of some risks. Not many to such an adept, but some. And it is a family business."

"Politics is my family business."

"Yes. But you overdo it."

"For nine hundred years our family's business has been the monarchy. And we've drawn some dandies. What I do has to be done and no one else seems to want to do it."

He leaned forward earnestly. His voice had the material texture of loving. "Tell me, my dearest," he said softly, "why it must be done? What will it change? The same sort of people will continue to be born and persist in dying. I don't have to understand what you know to be the truth, but I want to understand if I can."

She stared at him absently, savoring him, imagining him inside her, knowing exactly what it would be like to be beside him, secure at his side throughout the eternity given to her by God, if she protected God's love by denying Cayetano's while God said she must deny. She talked to him softly, as though she were breathing an ecstatic exhaustion into his chest, held by his arms. "I am a desperate woman who will stay desperate until we know it is right that we be together. We wait and we wait. I think I cannot continue to live while I wait for such transcendence for my body and my soul and my heart which sings to you." She smiled at him, radiantly and suddenly, changing the mood. "When that day arrives I may not be able to assemble enough interest in the cause of the king to remember to mail a letter which could save his life."

They fell into silence and took to staring at the future beyond the fire.

Bourne watched the duchess and Cayetano bow to each other at the top of the staircase and retire to rooms which were situated in opposite directions within the castle. He

28

allowed forty minutes to pass after that. At thirty-seven minutes before dawn, feeling that the preciseness of his calculations might be laughable to anyone not in his business, he left his room with Jean Marie's copy of the Velázquez, and made an efficient job of the highly technical work of transferring the copy of the painting to the bared frame of the original, repeating precisely the various calesthenics and rigorous positionings he had practiced for over one hundred and fifty hours at his hotel, to succeed in removing the original masterpiece and replacing it with the copy in twenty-eight minutes, seventeen seconds; eighty seconds less than his best previous time at the exercise.

He was warmly dressed in a black sweat suit which tied at the wrists and ankles. He wore a black bandanna tied around his forehead at the hairline because it was extremely hot work and it would not have done to have had sweat run into his eyes. He counted to himself through each separate section of the movements. His count accurately represented the passage of individual seconds and the peril of his position in no way pressed him to hasten the cadence. He thought about what he was doing, as he had long ago trained himself.

It was extremely ticklish kind of work, needing a good deal more than physical strength and coordination. Criminality means a lack of herd discipline, yet in its more demanding strata calls for infantile discipline of the kind utilized by a small boy or a salesman who will work to remember baseball batting averages back to Nap Lajoie. It is agreed with a social sense removed because what is there to be taken must be taken by the criminal consistent with his inner resources, eliminating envy, a much smaller sin. Criminality is the grisly, freakish mutation of an artist's horror of keeping the hours other people keep and enjoying the safety other people enjoy for the sake of safety, which in a sense is why there are so few women abstract creativists, and why one post-office wanted poster shows a woman's picture out of every thirty-four. The non-organization man, the abjurer of grey flannel clothing, the comforting agony at rest behind the masochistic mask, all are compounded as practiced by the higher criminal orders.

The most obedient physical discipline is required. It must be as reflexively responsive as a submarine commander's, as each man in an experimental rocket crew. It takes innate timing. It must possess, at Bourne's level, a tactile virtuosity equal to, say, a second-year student surgeon at minimal requirement. The job he undertook that morning called for an acrobat's sense of balance because, working against severe time limitations, Bourne had to lean half-body forward in complete darkness from a cold, stone niche fifteen feet above the great staircase and manage, with relative silence, to dislocate a frame which had been stiffened into position for several centuries, although even the Spanish must clean their paintings sometime. Furthermore, his feet had to depend upon building of the middle ages; the castle had been constructed sometime in the reign of Alphonso VI by the same architect who had done the walls of Avila, which made the present masonry all too unreliable. However, as this occasion marked the third Spanish master he had stolen from the Duchess de Dos Cortes, it was not as though he were utterly unfamiliar with the working area, in the darkness.

Whereas few honest people can understand, Bourne would explain to Eve, why a man would marshal such an organization of faculties and reactions for such an essentially juvenile feat, which it would be if it had been performed under ideal conditions and for small profit, almost any criminal mind would warm to a description of Bourne's accomplishment in the execution of these three jobs over so wearying a course, and be able to elaborate on Bourne's work the way cunning folk refight the battles of the American Civil War by mail and in the way many honest folk are able to extrapolate the complex motivations of the entirely secret lives of their fellows from merely a few and, in most cases, even misleading pieces of gossip.

Bourne was in bed, and asleep, forty-two minutes after he had started. He was asleep when dawn put an eye over the edge of the world and, like many a bright business executive, began again the precise duplication of its own existence.

Mr. Pickett started the morning with the Goya quote, which meant he would make this his text for the day, which went: "I had three masters: Velázquez, Rembrandt and Nature." Dr. Muñoz began his textual counterpoint which was an un-
30

relievedly tedious description of his visit to Fuendetodos, Goya's birthplace.

Mr. Pickett discussed Goya with his accustomed brilliance. Dr. Muñoz listened at first attentively then with growing strain. His right hand, which had been patting the cat Montes, who was a golden bunch on his lap, increased its tempo, stroking the cat faster and faster. The words trundled out of Mr. Pickett's throat with lumbering grace, every fourth or fifth word stabbed treacherously with the pointed end of an italic. "I most *certainly* would say that beginning with 1814 and the restoration of Ferdinand to the Spanish throne. Goya began to paint his most *thrilling,* most *brutal* and *most* exhilarating paintings."

Dr. Muñoz spat.

"Why did you *spit?*"

"For Goya!"

"You spit on *Goya?*" Mr. Pickett's hand rose to his breast as though to ward off an evil spirit.

Dr. Muñoz' dark face was flushed darker by a rush of blood. "Goya is why I am a poor man today. If there had been no Goya I would have had more than you, more than the duchess, more than most in this world."

Mr. Pickett gasped, "How is that?"

Dr. Muñoz poked an insistent finger into his own chest. "My ancestors financed Pizarro. Francisco Pizarro. It brought us twenty per cent of all the Inca gold. I would have had whatever paintings in the world I wanted for my own. They would have been hanging on every wall of every house I chose to build, wherever I would build. You would have had to come to me to ingratiate yourself to learn from me about the Spanish masters. I could have journeyed anywhere to buy back the Spanish masters from the museums, to bring them back to Spain where they belong, in my houses. I would have had more than anyone, more than you. I would have owned more than the Prado, more even than the churches because everything I would have possessed would have gone to the paintings. What do you know of a love of Spanish art? What can you feel of the destiny of the Spanish masters? You read books and you write again what you have read? Can you love the history of our art as Cayetano loves Blanca de Dos Cortes? Can you turn yourself into a Spaniard whose ancient lines employed these masters as one employs a cook? Bah!" He leaned forward as though he were thinking of striking Representative Pickett. "Bah!"

Mr. Pickett was fascinated. True, he had recoiled at first, but this promised, really, to be too much to miss.

"*Well*! You must tell me about it!" he said softly, reeling with the gossip value of what must certainly come, appraising it as dinner conversation with a part of his mind knowing that he would be asked *everywhere* once he had patterned the exact responses effectively and polished the climaxes worth for worth. "Good *heavens*! Goya! I never *dreamed*!"

"Pizarro, for one. In addition to that my family took two merchantmen filled with gold bullion from the British at the time when the king was so indebted to us that he refused to take more than a tithe and protected us from losing too great a share to the church as well. Did you know we controlled one third of the trade in Cuba for one hundred and six years? My family goes back to Pedro. We are over a thousand years old. Look about you. We are here at Dos Cortes. How old are they?" He laughed gratingly and bitterly. "Three hundred and two years!" He had to spin away from his baleful stare at Mr. Pickett to regain control of himself. He tried to speak in a less choked and more measured manner. "This duke is a degenerate. How old is the duchess's line? Only eight hundred and ninety-two years, although they have been a great family, too. But Blanca is the *first*—I say to you that Blanca is the *first*—to show any interest in the art of Spain. She is interested because I have taught her. Yet the walls of this small castle are rich with the masters while my walls are blessed to have paper copies in fractions of size!"

Tentatively, as a naturalist might approach a bird in a garden hoping desperately not to frighten it and see it fly away, Mr. Pickett murmured, "But what of Goya? You spoke of Goya actually costing you this fortune or perhaps should I say this opportunity in art."

Dr. Muñoz had regained control. He was embarrassed. "Really, Pickett. You must forgive me, you know. Really. My conduct is unsupportable. You see, I didn't sleep well last night, at all. I have been so stimulated by our talks and by the presence of the masters on the other side of the very wall of my chamber, and I do apologize. Please say you forgive me."

"Forgive you? Nonsense! There is nothing to forgive. My dear man! I mean, well, you *know* how I would adore to catch such an unknown and unexpected glimpse of Goya. Why, it sounds positively melodramatic, in the best and most goyaesque sense of that overused word I mean, of course. *Please* don't stop now due to some fanciful, impossible reason that you have offended *me*! I am *dying* to hear this entire *saga*. Imagine—Pizarro, pirates, a line of over a thousand years. It is *all* really *too much,* you know."

Dr. Muñoz was distinctly flattered. He indulged in a brief smile. "You see, in a word, Goya was a police spy. He was the lowest sort, really he was, Pickett. My family, for *excellent* reasons, worked from within Spain to bring about the abdication of Charles IV." Dr. Muñoz spoke as though he, personally, were as adjacent to that king as Harry Daugherty had been to the late Warren Gamaliel Harding. "We elected to prepare our country for Napoleon because he stood for a new era. We supported Joseph Bonaparte and progress. Our decision was taken publicly and honorably. Goya's decision was taken craftily and opportunistically. He had a genius for treachery, I can tell you. He pretended to support Bonaparte, oh yes indeed. He even painted his portrait, as you know. He painted an endless succession of French generals. He was the chairman of the committee which selected the group of Spanish masterpieces for Napoleon's collection in the Louvre! Oh, yes. Nothing was too good for the Bonapartes. They were his idols, his rulers, his liege lords! Bah!" Dr. Muñoz paused to spit. He shook his head as though he disapproved of himself for doing such a thing, but the disapproval must have been entirely for Francisco Goya, because he spat again.

"A turncoat, sir! A dog of a rotten turncoat! When Wellington entered Madrid in 1814, Goya's first move, after becoming a police spy and Wellington's fawning portraitist, was to impeach my family, to have us turned out by the British cutthroats, to have our estates and fortunes and world of paintings by the *greatest*"—he waved his arm in a wild sweeping gesture—"Spanish masters confiscated by Ferdinand VII. He was an informer. A cheap police informer. That is why I spit on Paco Goya!" He looked

33

out over the parapet. His face was quite flushed and it appeared that only the greatest effort and grimacing were keeping him from weeping. Representative Pickett respected his distress with soaring inner joy. This was simply priceless! To have this absurd little man, and even though he *was* a marqués and a grandee of Spain he *was* an absurd little man, reach the point of tears of *rage* over Francisco Goya, and to have the absolute *gall* to call him Paco as though he were referring to the Spanish Diamond Jim Brady, was heaven on *toast*! But Mr. Pickett kept a solemn, long face. Dr. Muñoz succeeded in not weeping. He refilled their tiny cups with coffee and spoke in a low, shaking voice. "He was also, of course, one of the greatest masters of painting that the world has ever known and his paintings will be forever treasured into an eternity of glory for Spain."

"You are quite right in *that* connection, my dear doctor," Mr. Pickett said. He put a match to a large cigar and the two men fell to musing silently about art.

The group enjoyed four stimulating days, each in his own way. The first day began, immediately after breakfast, with a lecture tour of all of the paintings in Dos Cortes. Mr. Pickett was enthralled. He said he would have traveled twice round the world to see such Spanish paintings. He reserved special reverence for Jean Marie's copy of the Velázquez which Bourne had placed in the frame so much earlier in the day. Bourne watched and listened with outwardly grave composure. It had been a bad half hour as they had worked their way toward the Velázquez. Mr. Pickett's talk at each other painting had seemed interminable. When he had finally drawn the group under the Velázquez by Jean Marie, Bourne suddenly discovered that he had been holding his breath. As he exhaled, his eyes darted to the group standing on both sides of him, but they were absorbed in what Mr. Pickett was feeling about this particular masterpiece, by what he assured them was the greatest painter Spain, or indeed perhaps all civilization, had ever produced. The humor of Mr. Pickett's extravagance, coming as it did, in his opening remarks, cheered Bourne greatly and permitted him to relax and enjoy the rest of the congressman's authoritative treatise.

After his sweepingly generous opening, Mr. Pickett moved in with some of his famous technical observations; trenchant, omniscient and frequently witty. He reminded them that Dostoevski had called Velázquez "a species of eternity within the space of a square foot." He proceeded to offer them some of it.

"You see the back *only* of that long, lithe body, lissome as a hazel wand and stretching with Andalusian indolence. You'll notice that Velázquez was not the man to distract the beholder with two focuses. He is *simply* and *entirely* engrossed with the loveliness of flesh in light. Ah, *mercy*! Look at the *rhythm* and the *modeling* of that figure! Surely some *goddess* guided that hand which gave us this *utter, utter* beauty. See the transparent shadows that lurk where the lower curves of the back and leg slide into the drapes, glimmering with reflected lights? I am now going to say something to you quite *entirely* conscious of the *solemn* responsibility I hold unto the Spanish nation and the world of art. I will tell you that although I saw it now for the *first* time I will say it *again and again* as long as the Lord preserves me, and I will write it and sign my name to it and cause it to be published wherever art is courted that this Velázquez nude is lovelier than the hitherto *loveliest* of *all* nudes in the history of art. I speak of the Rokeby Venus by the same Diego Rodríguez de Silva y Velázquez, the great and before *this* day in my life, *this red letter day in my life*, incomparable as it now hangs in the National Gallery of London. My friends, before us here today, enriching us *forever* through the riot of memory, I say to you that this Dos Cortes Velázquez is the *greatest single nude* ever painted, across all of the pages of man's great art."

Dr. Muñoz shivered in ecstasy as he heard for the first time a new Mr. Pickett, the parliamentarian Pickett, Congressman Homer Pickett (R., Ill.). The orator's face shone with the glory which would begin with the publication of the article already forming in his mind in *Art, Things And You*. He would cable ahead to the *New York Times*. He would change his plans and arrive by boat, not by plane, so that the reporters could have time with him and the many photographs he would take in a large and comfortable stateroom. What a buzz this would cause and how absolutely just it would be! How could he have waited so many long years through a life devoted to the art of Spain to have finally seen this magnificent, incomparable, enchanting

35

masterpiece? He had a great deal more to say, to which he, himself, listening very carefully, taking notes as it were against the polishing days aboard the ship when he could begin to set the words down on paper. How very, very fulfilling art could be, he thought as he talked. Cayetano grew bored after forty minutes of it. He wandered off to the little bar and poured himself a cognac.

The four days moved with much leisure, culture and comfort. Mrs. Pickett, to her surprise, stumbled over a selection of Spanish brandies which were excellent. She spent much of the four days dabbling and experimenting, then taking her siesta for five hours each afternoon, so as never to be tardy for each evening's program of listening to the others. When she did have a chance to talk she talked bullfighting to Cayetano and Bourne, conceding its exhilarating qualities but frankly stating that she could not abide pointless cruelty which did nothing but underscore, in a shameful way, the essential morbidity of the Spanish people. The men agreed with her gravely.

Cayetano and the duchess continued to express each other with gentle patience although they were seldom closer than four feet to each other, never farther away than five. Bourne thought that if their hands should touch or their shoulders brush by accident or by earthquake those in the room would be eternally blinded by the fire the contact would produce, but Bourne being a criminal, was a romantic, which is to say, under the majority definition, a faulty measure offering ten inches to the foot, or fourteen, but never the standard, accurate twelve.

Bourne still felt the pressure of having concealed his friends' property in his effects and frequently sat up with a start to worry whether a servant might have blundered upon it, then realized that he had it held under a stout lock. What might have seemed to have been sighs were not. He had to take deep breaths, then hold the breaths, as part of the control he sought to maintain. No one was aware of the tension he felt. Rather, perhaps Cayetano was because he was sensitive to Bourne, being his friend, but if he was it was in a most vague manner and therefore nothing he could attempt to correct.

36

Bourne used up the first afternoon composing a telegram in code to Jean Marie who was in Paris. After that he disappeared into the library because, in his specialized way, he was as enthusiastic about books as the congressman was about pictures. The Dos Cortes library was a rich one. On the third day he found exactly what he had hoped to find; a great volume containing virtual inventories of the art collections of small churches and large houses together with set upon set of precise floor plans. He made a mental note to ask Dr. Muñoz about the names. He would surely know these people and through him Bourne could easily wangle week-end invitations. It had been by that identical route that he had met the duchess. He borrowed the congressman's camera and film without mentioning it and photographed many of the pages. The activity made him smile wryly as he remembered a summer, twenty-eight years before, when he had struggled and studied to win the Photography Merit Badge which had elevated him to the rank of Star Scout in the Boy Scouts of America.

That evening at dinner Mr. Pickett had come bursting in wildly excited with news about the Velázquez. Bourne felt the blood strike into his head, he had to grasp both arms of the chair for, although sitting, a dizziness severe enough to nearly send him over sideways rushed into his head with the massive heat of the blood. Mr. Pickett's words cured him.

"*This* is absolutely *incredible!*" Mr. Pickett cried and all eyes were swung into his course as he dashed into the room. "I have been staring at that wonderful Velázquez trying to find out, as a scientist would try, what it was which gave the painting its transcendent glory. I peered. I studied. I *absorbed*. Then, all at once it came to me. I *knew*. I tell you I *knew*. And, because of your kindness in bringing me to the *presence* of this masterpiece, I am going to break a rule of long standing with relationship to my art scoops and share it all with *you*." He smiled at them like the bountiful father in the automobile advertisements. The duchess and Bourne, then the duchess and Cayetano, exchanged quick perplexed glances. Mrs. Pickett stared at the bridge of her husband's nose and thought of a certain shoe salesman who had absolutely fondled her foot in Minneapolis seven years before. Dr. Muñoz quivered. He quivered and blinked. He quivered and blinked and fluttered as he waited for Mr. Pickett to explode the bombshell.

"You will all recall," Mr. Pickett said, a substantial platform manner now assumed, "that stimulating event in the life of Velázquez, the visit of Rubens to Madrid in 1628 and 1629, on a diplomatic mission from the Stadtholder Isabella, which was quite possibly connected with negotiations for concluding peace between England and Spain."

Dr. Muñoz raised his hand. With the slightest show of irritation, Mr. Pickett recognized him and, for an instant, turned over the floor. "May I say in passing," asked Dr. Muñoz, "that a full account of the activities of Rubens in Spain is given by Pacheco in his book?"

"*Well*! I think everyone here knows *that*, Victoriano," Mr. Pickett stated acidly.

"Oh, yes. Of course. Please excuse me. Do go on."

Mr. Pickett sniffed. "It has been said that a change is to be observed in the style of Velázquez subsequent to the visit of Rubens, that brought about a new and all-pervading light and color to his paintings. Now—and *please* bear with me—this is to be a very *very* thrilling moment for each of you and one which you may never forget. There is an entry in the Palace Archives for July 1629 in which Velázquez is credited with one hundred ducats—I quote—'on account of a picture of Troilus which he has made in my service.' The Troilus, as it was colloquially called, was painted under the very eyes of Rubens." Mr. Pickett shot his pointing finger onward and upward across the great hall, in direct indication to the painting by Jean Marie. The official title of this painting was "Nude Spring." He peered at his listeners hypnotically and his flutelike voice went staccato. "Although Velázquez went on to become a far, far greater painter than Rubens, it is to be doubly honored to sit beneath the very painting which contains the divinity of both great men." He sank into a chair, too weak by his discovery to support himself. His voice sounded hoarse. "I am prepared to submit an affidavit which will swear that, in my opinion, my *humble* opinion, that as a cosmic jest, both Velázquez *and* Rubens, rather in the manner of a tap dancing 'challenge contest' of old-time vaudeville, painted that picture. Whatever its value before this discovery, I can assure you, my dear duchess, it has doubled now, which value I am prepared to assess in the article I shall write upon the subject for *Art, Things And You*."

Dr. Muñoz squeaked. The duchess said, "How enchanting!" Bourne stood beside the congressman and patted him gratefully on the shoulder, murmuring that he owed it to the world of art and artists to get that article into print at once.

Mr. Pickett was dazed by what he had wrought. He mopped his forehead and whimpered, "What a day this has been for me! I believe with all my heart that today is my apogee in adventures with the Spanish masters." He stared up at Bourne with troubled, gentle eyes. "Do you believe it would be amiss of me to cause influential repetition of a reference to this painting as 'The Pickett Troilus'?"

"I do not, sir," Bourne responded with hearty vigor. "You have earned that right."

The bond of their glance was broken by what really amounted to an outcry from Dr. Muñoz. Words tumbled from him as though the full consideration had just reached him. As he spoke he advanced upon Mr. Pickett, his arms outstretched, as though seeking some hidden pit. "Do you really have faith in that opinion, Pickett? No, no! I have offended you. Please take no offense. I was utilizing rhetoric only. Think of it! Rubens and the blessed Velázquez in united genius upon one canvas! Oh, what a fortunate thing that you could come here, Pickett! Oh, my blessed saint, what a fortunate thing! We must tell the world of this! The world! And we must celebrate. Come along, come along! We must have some wine. This is so thrilling! I cannot remember when I have been so moved. Oh, we must have wine!"

Some of his words got through to Mrs. Pickett. She clambered to her feet. "Yes. Wine. By all means we must have wine! Oh Homer, you have truly made a contribution today!"

Dr. Muñoz prepared for bed, loosening his clothes then stepping out of them as they fell at his feet. He did not remove his lumpy cotton socks or his old-fashioned camisole of tattletale pink, but dropped a large, muslin nightshirt over whatever did not respond to gravity. The nightshirt was striped as his suits were striped, but not as hideously, in two shades of blue against one of green laid upon what had once been white. Tented, he sat at his dressing table and began the painstaking preparation of his Mustache Nourisher, a long, white

39

piece of woolen cloth, two inches wide at its center then tapering out to strings at the ends which had cleverly patented slots for flat fastening. It resembled a money belt but it held vaseline and a Secret Ingredient which had been developed by a Captain Hugh Fitz-Moncrieff, of London, England, formerly a guards officer who had taken to sharing his secret with the readers of *News of the World* advertisements. Fitz-Moncrieff wore a magnificent mustache, thanks to the Nourisher, which resembled a busby laid crossways across the center of his nearly missing face. Dr. Muñoz, told not to expect overnight miracles from the device, had been applying it nightly to his pencil-line fringe for two months but as yet no intimidating bushiness had shown itself. As he prepared this follicle feeding he spoke to the cat who had curled up on the dressing table, the better to ignore its master.

"What a world, Montes, what a stupid world," the marqués drawled in his fashionable style, "and what braying fools we have as neighbors wherever we go. I use my talents with them like a very great actor in a very silly play or like a pulsating, feeling, vibrant man of flesh and blood who has found himself wandering, without escape, through page after page of a child's repulsive storybook. Ugh! Aaah! Faugh, and other such expressions of distaste, disgust and disapproval. Thank heaven, for you, my friend." He patted Montes who purred in Spanish. Muñoz bowed gravely at the figure before him in the mirror which lifted the white Nourisher to its face. "And I thank heaven for you, my friend, and your exquisite mind, and your beautiful, magnanimous forbearance." He tied the strings at the back of his head in the prescribed, patented manner thus avoiding cleverly any annoying bumps which could disturb a sleeper who preferred to rest on his back.

The week-end visit was not all art discovery and crusading. There was sport. Among them they shot over thirty-two hundred pigeons. The duchess and Cayetano rode a great deal. Before she had met Cayetano, the duchess had been an amateur *rejoneadora* much in demand at *tientas* throughout her own region and Andalusia. It is a talent which transmutes equitation into poetry. Afterwards, she abjured the bulls and everything, but one, to do with the bulls. A Laplander would relate more closely to fighting bulls than the duchess, after she met Cayetano.

Bourne was a prisoner of his own schedule. He knew when Eve had left Córdoba. He followed her, in his mind, through and out of Seville. He saw her in his mind, as she left Granada in the large bus, with a book in her lap. Even though he had found everything he had wanted to the completion of his task in the library, Bourne stayed on in that large, dark comfortable room because Mrs. Pickett had become even more impossible and, of course, a steady diet of Mr. Pickett and Dr. Muñoz was simply out of the question. So, he stretched out on the leather couch, his feet higher than his head, and remained for hours on end in a semicataleptic state, thinking of Eve, thinking of the past, relating himself to the few things which were still important to him.

Bourne had tried to know himself, which is a witless phrase indeed since it implies a psychical status quo, a state which would be irresponsible to the community. He did try to examine the seams of the soul he took off every night and, before it was sent back to the cleaners of forgetfulness, he did check its size against the expanding waistband of his infamy. Bourne could use a word like infamous because he sat in the bleachers with the other people when he measured himself. Try as he might, self-search as he would, he never could retrace his motivational spoor to the fork in the forest where he had become trapped by money.

Bourne had gone to the right college after exactly the right preparatory school. He had received a superior status for his scholarship. He had, because of his strength and physical endurance, been active in sports. Upon graduation with a degree in business administration *magna cum laude* he had entered his father's business where he had become more effective than his father within the first seven years. He had resigned in his eighth year, a full partner, earning one hundred and three thousand dollars per year with handsome expense benefits and an enlightened pension system which he had instituted himself. He could not continue in business because he saw it only as a continual distortion of honesty and material morality. It was as though a grain of glass, one of the slivers of ice from the palace of Andersen's Snow Queen had entered his eyes, then had worked its way into his heart. He had pointed out instance upon instance of dishonest,

41

immoral practices by their firm, by all of their competitors, by all of their friends in business and in the professions which was accepted by all as common practice, and his father was appalled that Bourne could so twist facts to reach such a shocking and unfair set of conclusions.

To Bourne there seemed to be nothing that they did or that was done in their world that was not dishonest, not decadent and immoral. To his father, Bourne was a sick man, a suddenly, rottenly, mentally sick man who had to be helped. Before he could help him, or organize the plot to bring in the doctors to help him, Bourne had vanished. He had taken substantial capital of his own with him and had left a childless wife, who had agreed with his father, behind him. It had been easy to vanish, easy to assume a totally new life, under a new name, in a new country.

He had chosen crime as his career, because, in a manner entirely clear to him, he had known that the only way he could achieve a sense of honesty while doing what he had obviously been born to do, had been expensively trained to do, as had most all other men of his class, that is, to amass money, was to steal it. By the stated dishonesty of stealing money illegally, as opposed to the evaded dishonesty of acquiring it as he had among his father's friends, Bourne felt clean, honest and integrated. It was creative work, in its limited way. It was diverting. He stole from anyone, not merely the rich. Robin Hood was not sentimental. It so happens that criminals do not steal from the poor because the poor have nothing to steal. As for stealing from the rich to give to the poor, Bourne felt that everyone did this nearly every day of their existence. Bourne was plagued by the thought of money although he was grateful to the need for it because that need had made him an honest man in a world he saw as being owned by uncommitted thieves.

He could remember a certain contempt for money when he had first married. Then he had matured to the point where he could read contempt for money as fear of money. He was always stopped there. He could not go on very far beyond that point because he could not see what made him fear money. He had always had more than adequate amounts of it. But after he had recognized it as fear he had fostered the fear by indulging himself in having large sums of money on deposit in several countries, in the event of war in one part of the world, or the possible interruption of communications in another, although he could not think of one object he needed requiring a large amount of money to buy, except perhaps his first wife.

Money was at the root of all of his so-called self-study, so he never got very far with it. His present wife seemed to match her fear of money with his own, point for point at every point. As he knew her more and more he was horrified by the thought, when drunk, of witnessing his own feminine genes in an embodiment of their own. The way she spoke about money, thought about money, dwelt upon money was the way he did all of those things. When he was away from her on business, such as now, he would sit in the hotel apartment in Madrid with a whiskey bottle next to a tape recorder and play back all of the tapes she had not known he had recorded of them. He thought he was analyzing her in this way. He did not realize that because most of his waking conversations with her had to do with money in one way or another, that because she loved him, her answers had to do with money. It was as though he could not hear his own voice, only hers, which was how he had come to believe that she was obsessed with the idea of money and that she was some mortal extension of himself.

Bourne got through the four days in a mild shock of anti-climax after the strain of effort on the first morning. He rode back to Madrid in the late afternoon in the white Mercedes with Cayetano. The duchess waved them off from the parapets in the set ritual of fairy tales. Cayetano was depressed, an unusual state for him.

The Picketts were returned to Madrid in the Bentley with Dr. Muñoz driving. The jonquil cat Montes slept on his left shoulder. The car had not traveled sixty yards away from the walls of Dos Cortes when Mrs. Pickett began to sing the lead role in The Woman's Opera, copyright Year One, by Lady Eve.

"Homer?"

"Yes, dear?"

"Isn't the duchess married? I mean is she a widow or——"

"Of course she's married. What kind of a question is that?"

"Then where is he?"

"Who?"

"The husband. The duke."

43

Dr. Muñoz co-operated, shrugging. "Paris, perhaps. Or Hollywood. Or in a sanatorium in Switzerland. He's a very old man."

"What about Cayetano?" Mrs. Pickett asked mildly.

"What about him?" answered her husband not realizing then or ever that much of the conversation he and his wife exchanged was made up almost entirely by questions on both sides.

"Isn't he awfully young?"

"Young for what?"

"Do you mean to sit here and say that you didn't notice that they were madly in love with each other?"

"Marianne, will you please stop this?"

"Are you going to tell me he isn't wildly attractive?"

"What has that got to do with anything?"

"Is he a gigolo?"

Dr. Muñoz hit the brakes involuntarily, jolting the cat Montes into abrupt indignation, stared at Mrs. Pickett blankly, then recovered. Mr. Pickett swung his massive façade full-rudder to starboard to face his wife and he seemed to rise like a gun turret. "A gigolo?" Mr. Pickett demanded. "He is the greatest bullfighter of his generation!"

Dr. Muñoz made a sharp, repetitious clicking sound of disapproval. "He is perhaps, I will say that he is judged by many experts to be, perhaps, the greatest bullfighter who ever lived."

A copy of the Dos Cortes art catalogue reposed in Mrs. Pickett's lap. Her hand closed over it. Her face had drained white with humiliation. "A bullfighter? Cayetano is a bullfighter?" She took up the heavy catalogue like a truncheon and began to rain blows on her husband's head, cursing cubic oaths, then weeping with rage.

They had left Avila behind. Cayetano took the car too fast down out of the mountains but his co-ordination was so fit that Bourne felt no nervousness. The painting was in his case behind them. He had forgotten Cayetano's earlier symptoms of depression with the press of his own plans. Eve would be at the hotel when he returned to Madrid which would be within the hour. She would leave tomorrow with the merchandise. Once through the Spanish customs, the rest was nothing. The French were not sufficiently interested in Spanish paintings to ransack baggage to search for them and he would see to it that Eve wore extreme décolletage.

Neither he nor Cayetano had spoken since Segovia. Cayetano stared at the road ahead. They left the mountain. The road flew straight ahead of them for miles across the plains of Castille.

Cayetano's smile, ready and willing at all hours of the day and night, was the desperate smile of a man who pleads indiscriminately with everyone to like him. Unsuccessful actors frequently let themselves be seen this naked but actors, compared to matadors, are two-dimensional performers no matter how good their writers are. Matadors, good and bad, have every dimension there is in the show business because flops make them bleed and many times make them die. Cayetano's great art as a torero gave him an especial nakedness because his exalted reputation made the crowd insist that he risk more. This made him increasingly aware that there could be very little time left to be liked and reassured, or disliked and ignored, and he had formed a habit for preferring the former.

His profession had done for him what churches had failed to do for other men. To have a deep faith in the absolute imminence of one's own death is to respect life more. Cayetano's obligation had been stated for him by his great-grandfather, his grandfather and his father. He could have continued on with a solid professional respect for death and an enlarged capacity for life until his turn came to be killed or to retire honorably. Unfortunately, he had met the duchess and they had marked each other for each other. It was unfortunate because she was a victim of so many different varieties of honor.

Life became too much of a familiar to him. His death became too much of a familiar to the duchess. This had continued for six years. She had petitioned for an annulment of her marriage five years before. The matter had been taken by a French attorney as far as an ecclesiastical court in Munich, but several technical reasons had stood in the way. Four years before she had offered to ignore her marriage vows if he would leave the bulls. To the duchess, this was an offer to sacrifice her soul throughout eternity to save his body. Since her soul had far more reality to him than his body, in the sense that he knew it would be possible to avoid the horns but that it would be impossible, if she gave in to

45

him, to avoid damnation, he refused by telling her that the bulls were the only way he knew to live. Two years before Cayetano had decided that he should murder the duke, but Bourne kept him drunk for four days and after that, in his weakness, he saw that would have been the wrong solution. The six years tended to give the duchess a tendency to terrible headaches and a dread of continuing to live. It gave Cayetano a thirst for cognac and a desperate need for relief from the sudden fear of living.

He hit the brakes. The car screamed into a stop. Cayetano gripped the top of the steering wheel and yelled from deep in his belly. He yelled twice like a *manso* bull then put his head forward between his hands and did not move. Sweat glistened thickly on his neck.

Bourne waited for five minutes, not moving or speaking, then he lighted two cigarettes. When Cayetano pulled his head back Bourne passed one of the cigarettes to him and said, "There's a *fonda* a few kilometres along this road. Would you mind if we stopped for a while? I have a thirst."

Cayetano grunted. The car moved along, this time almost sedately. It was a cool, bracing spring evening.

Bourne listened while the assistant manager chatted about the action in the house while Bourne had been away. The assistant manager was called Gonzalo Elek. He was a very small, extraordinarily agreeable, perpetually smiling, pencil-line mustached man with limpid, large brown eyes and the whitest teeth. Years before he had inherited a wardrobe from a suicide in the old Ritz Hotel in New York where he had been employed. It consisted of fourteen suits of the finest weave and cut, comprising a model for every occasion. They had hardly been worn, but they had been styled just before World War I. They ran to four-button jackets and peg-top trousers and whispered elegance. Fourteen suits permitted Señor Elek to wear each suit only twice each month which brought him much joy. He would never wear the wardrobe out if he continued to live into his eighty-ninth year, he had explained to Bourne.

Bourne listened carefully to the report. The principal problem was that the Hotel Peñalver-Plaza had stolen one of their best English-speaking telephone operators, so Bourne went with Señor Elek into their common office and called the manager of the Hilton.

"Walter—Jim Bourne." He listened with restrained politeness to the polite greeting. His hand would have been shaking if he did not have firm surfaces and objects to hold on to. Twenty hours more and they would be in the clear. He must do everything at half speed. He must welcome as much routine as possible. He must be deliberate about every move for only twenty hours more. "Listen, Walter, this is the first and last time I'm going to discuss this with you. As a matter of fact I'm entirely surprised that I have to mention it at all." There was a pause while Walter made clear that he didn't know what Bourne was talking about. "Walter—Walter—listen to me. Either you stop stealing switchboard operators from me after we spend six weeks training them or I'll reply in kind." There was another pause. "What do I mean? I mean I own this hotel, I'm not an employee and if I think it's necessary to embarrass you by hiring away your entire key desk crew and the reception men, on a contract basis, I'll do it if it costs me ten thousand dollars. Can I make it any clearer than that, Walter?" He stared up at Señor Elek and shook his head. He kept trying to decide whether he should waste time giving Eve a cover story if the merchandise should be turned up at the airport. Or, if they were discovered, if Eve were discovered, that is, perhaps he should work backwards through the duchess to arrange clemency. No, it wouldn't do. Eve would have to—no. "Walter, if you say it was a mistake, it was a mistake because I know that you know that I mean what I say. Thank you, Walter."

He put the receiver into the cradle softly and spoke to Señor Elek. "How much does Walter pay his third conserje on day duty? We have to make him understand." Señor Elek told him at once, to the peseta. Bourne rubbed his chin and thought about it. "That's a little more than I thought. Well, offer him the number two spot on the night desk here at no increase. He'll make his own increase."

"What about Isidro?"

"His wife is French and her mother is sick so I arranged through a friend of mine to get Isidro the second day spot at the Elysée Parc in Paris. If he needs any help with the exit permit we'll want to help out all we can. I meant to

47

tell you about that." He left the office, crossed the hall and entered the creaking cage of the elevator.

Señor Elek followed him out. He spoke to the chief reception clerk. "Isidro is going to be second man on the day shift at the Elysée Parc in Paris. Hombre! He'll make his fortune!" The chief clerk grinned happily at the news. Both the men seemed as pleased as though it had happened to them, but Spain is two hundred years behind the rest of the West in everything.

Eve was in six twenty-seven, the two-room suite in the luxury line of the building. Carrying the cardboard tube, Bourne let himself in with a passkey. Eve sat in a chair faced to the door.

"Did you get it?" she yelped and threw herself at him. He caught her without an effort, held her over his head for an instant then kissed her with much ardor.

He put her back into the chair and held the tube in his hands like an infantry sergeant demonstrating a rifle to a new recruit. "This is the new tube," he said. "It looks exactly like the others, but it will hold all three paintings—the Velázquez we just got, the Zurbarán from the time before, and the El Greco from the first time out. The Zurbarán and the Greco surround the inside lining. The Velázquez goes in the way it always did. All three of them leave the country together and we cut the risks by two-thirds."

"And if I'm caught we lose them all at once."

"I didn't plan it for you to get caught. I planned it for you to take all three paintings through."

"That's all right with me."

"Thank you, darling. Now the action tomorrow is simplicity itself. You walk directly to the chief of customs, holding the tube out ahead of you, as though you were taking it for granted that he would want to take it from you. Smile as you walk in toward him and have the scarf slide off your shoulders just as you have rehearsed it. He won't take the tube. It is very important that he does not take the tube because it weighs more than four times as much as the first tube weighed and anyone can remember things they don't have to think about."

"What will I do if he does take it?"

"You mean if he starts to take it. You'll be holding it.

48

Think of it as a baton in a relay race. If he reaches for it you drop it into your other hand and you undo the top. You slide the Velázquez out, just as though it were the copy he had seen when you brought it through from Paris. You do this very slowly while you talk very rapidly about Spain and what this trip meant to you. If he still seems to want to look at the painting you tell him that you met a man in Sevilla. You met a Spaniard. You have never experienced anything like it. That should do it."

"And if that doesn't do it shall I grab him by the pants and moan?"

"Only if you have to," Bourne said pretending that she had not made a joke. "I'm not afraid of his seeing the painting. Jean Marie's copy was amazingly close to this one. He saw the copy and knew it was a good copy and he probably doesn't know anything about art anyway, but I don't want him holding that tube. He knows every smuggler's dodge there is, except the ones I've developed for this which are, after all, more psychological than physical, because that's his business. If he hefts that tube, you're sunk."

"We're sunk."

"That's not the way it works and you know it. If one of us gets the door locked behind him he'll need all the help on the outside he can get."

"I was only kidding."

"I know you were. Now—what the hell have you got that goddam dress on for?"

She seemed astonished by the question. "I thought you'd want to celebrate. I thought we'd go out to Villa Rosa and live a little."

She was wearing a white evening dress which is not a good color for a big woman. The material was satin which over-accents a lush woman. Bourne's eyes had become cold and unpleasant. He was sweating lightly. His forehead shone.

"You did, hey?"

"Jim, we've been married for almost ten months and I see you for two days at a time when I do see you!"

The words of recrimination released all of the tension Bourne had been bottling inside himself and he began to speak in a flat, tight voice. After so much enforced silence it seemed to come out in spite of himself.

"If we are seen together, as sure as night follows day, one

49

of us or both of us will eventually be sentenced to live in a Spanish prison. The customs chief will remember you. We designed it that way. My people in the hotel will remember you and they most certainly know me. If and when the people who once owned these paintings are made to realize that copies have been substituted for them, a relentless search will begin to find the criminals who are responsible. Police are most thorough everywhere. Sooner or later they will talk to that chief of customs. Sooner or later they will trace you to this hotel. If they fix on me as being the only one you've spent any time with in Madrid, or in Spain for that matter, I'll be their man. Spaniards will never give up as far as Diego Rodríguez da Silva y Velázquez is concerned. He is a very important part of their national honor."

He slammed his hand down on the top of the bureau. His movements were spasmodic as he worked on himself toward a wider area where he could launch greater tensions.

"What the hell is there to celebrate? We have three pieces of Spanish national treasure in a hotel room. They're still in Spain. When we get them out of the country the work just begins. Where can you sell national treasure? Where would you sell the Liberty Bell if you could get it out of Philadelphia to Mexico? Where would you sell the British crown jewels or the body of Lenin? Do you have an answer? Could you conceive of an answer to that if you thought for forty years? I have the answer. Only I have the answer. You don't know and Jean Marie doesn't know. He is the factory. You are the delivery girl. I designed the project, I stole the paintings, I invested the capital, I take the risks, and only I can dispose of the paintings! You are a delivery girl, nothing else, nothing more! You are the least important, most easily replaceable person in the entire silly, childish business."

Although Bourne was allowing himself to get more and more recklessly excited and disturbed his voice never rose above that same even tone, two tones below the sound of polite conversation. He glared and he gestured and once or twice he seemed to threaten violence but his voice remained at the same low pitch. He stumbled backward into a chair then covered his face with his hands. She poured him a large shot of whiskey and made him take it, but he did not look up at her. She put an ice cube in a towel and began to rub

50

the back of his neck. He sipped the whiskey slowly. He grasped her free hand and began to kiss it softly. She leaned over and kissed his temple, his cheek and the top of his head while she whispered "my darling, my darling," over and over again.

The night stumbled toward dawn. A single pair of heels, one block away, made sharp, clear, shaved noises. They lay in the darkness motionless, as though if they moved time might start again and pull them toward five illuminated minutes at Barajas at ten thirty-five in the morning when they might be separated forevermore. Bourne lay on his back, swallowing air hungrily, his stomach rising and falling like an exhausted prizefighter's. Eve lay on her side, touching him with her body, her breath coming just as hard as she stared into the darkness imagining the outline of the side of his face, while her fingers held his far shoulder.

He tried to lift his arm to reach a cigarette on the night table beside the bed. Her hand blocked his. She drew it away slowly, stopping for an instant to rest on his stomach then, feeling him strain to breathe, dragged it inch by inch across his chest, freeing his hand. He found the cigarette package and the matches. He rested again then slowly got two cigarettes to his mouth. As he lighted them she saw his face. It was like a marble mask. He passed one cigarette to her, exhaling smoke heavily.

She pulled an ash tray on her stomach. They smoked the cigarettes in silence. When they had put the cigarettes out in the ash tray she slid it off her stomach and lowered it sightlessly to the floor.

Her mouth was soft and her mouth opened to take the kiss as though they had never kissed and needed it to live.

A giant hand, so big it spanned the course of comets, rose up and plucked a star out of the sky, then another, and another. Each night the hand returned and took more stars. The nights grew blacker and longer, but no one noticed for no one looked up any more.

The duchess's eyes burned but she continued to knit. When she was alone she knitted most of the night.

       *   *   *

Mrs. Pickett slept soundly. She lay on top of the bedspread, wearing a slip. Through some oversight she still had her shoes on. Mr. Pickett sat at the hotel desk writing with a four-color French ball-point pen on the thin sheets of the hotel stationery. The writing was so small that it seemed as though thousands and thousands of letters covered the page in four different colors because Mr. Pickett wrote in italics by using contrasting colors to make the particular points of emphasis he required. He put the pen down and began to read the letter through, right from the top. The Pickett Troilus was on its way to world fame.

Dr. Muñoz slept on his back with his hands, lightly folded, reposing on his flat stomach. His upper lip was covered with the white, greased cloth which tied at the back of his head and which nourished his mustache. He smiled slightly while he slept, or seemed to.

Cayetano climbed out of the bed and began to dress slowly. The girl spoke to him and he answered her politely. She pulled at his arm, but he disengaged himself, patted her cheek and continued dressing.

Bourne was in a staff meeting with the chefs and the chief steward, projecting the bimonthly supplies order when Victoriano Muñoz telephoned, twenty minutes after Eve had left for the airport with the cardboard tube. Muñoz had found a new apartment on Calle Fortuny and he wanted Bourne to come to tea the following week to see it, after he had had a chance to settle et cetera, et cetera, et cetera.

Bourne thanked him and told him he would be delighted to accept although of course he knew that Victoriano would understand that they were beginning to move into the tourist season and that the pressure of hotel demands could force him to change his plans at the last moment. This threatened to lead into an interminable conversation with Bourne reduced to repeating the word yes and rolling his eyes pitiably at the chef and the chief steward, but he was thinking about Eve's peril.

After he had hung up he forced himself to write down the note of the appointment with Muñoz, then stood up impulsively, told the two men to complete the work without him and left the room to break all of his own rules by driving to the airport.

Earlier that morning Eve had dressed and packed then had kissed Bourne with zest, then with more than zest because they had decided that once the paintings were safe in Paris and the job over, he would come to Paris to get her and then bring her back to Madrid, officially, as his wife. They had gone through the tiresome but necessary inspection to make sure that the corridor outside the room was clear, then Bourne had kissed her again and departed, telling her that everything was going to be all right, that she was not to worry about a thing. She had smiled at him indulgently and had patted his cheek as he slipped through the doorway.

Nor did she worry. Bourne had thought of everything, she was confident of that. It would be more intelligent to feel some kind of goose-pimples about the next hour or so of her life, she thought, but she felt no more than if she were to move through customs with an undeclared package of cigarettes because of the way he had briefed her. She telephoned for a porter and a taxi.

Two porters came up for the luggage which seemed odd because she had told the operator that she had only two pieces. Not only the two porters but the assistant manager, Señor Elek of the four high buttons, was there to serve.

Bourne managed to come around the corner of the corridor, sailing with that comical self-confidence of a managing director in his own hotel, to bid Miss Quinn a polite good morning in Spanish through her opened door and sail on. The attendance of the three employees startled him as well, but for a different reason. He had let time and usage convince him that only he appreciated how excitingly beautiful she was. He suddenly realized, feeling both alarmed and thrilled, that it was possible that she was beautiful enough to cause the chef, the barber, the doorman, and everyone else employed in the hotel, to want to help her with her bags if they thought they could get away with it.

The two porters put Eve into a cab, but only one porter would take a tip. The other one just grinned, shook her hand, backed away and disappeared. Señor Elek handed her the cardboard tube, wished her a formidably pleasant journey and a quick return so that the hotel would not be too long without the endowment of her grace and beauty, instructed the driver to take her to the Barajas Airport, slammed the cab door, and she was off. Nine seconds later, as the cab turned into Alcalá and started toward the Plaza de la Independencia, the fear began to set in.

The feeling started in her stomach. First it was nausea, then it was like hardening concrete which rose in a column and jammed in her throat. She felt feverish. She pushed the cardboard tube involuntarily and it fell to the floor with a rattle.

The cab turned off Alcalá because of a detour caused by street construction into Calle Velázquez. Each time they passed a cross street she would look up and read that threatening word; *Velázquez* at Villanueva, *Velázquez* at Jorge Juan. She leaned forward to ask the driver if he did not know a quicker way to Barajas. To humor her he turned right at the next intersection, at the corner of Velázquez and Goya. She closed her eyes. She tried counting slowly to herself to blank her mind of the fear, then she tried humming while she counted.

At Plaza de Manuel Becerra, the driver took a short cut along Cartagena to Avenida de America. After that they bowled along past the city line. By that time she was wet with perspiration. She wore a light brown dress and the stains of the sweat were clear in dark, circular designs on that nearly mild spring day. She began by thinking that such an ugliness would repel the chief of customs when she was under orders to attract him and ended by imagining that she would bleed in the same wet designs when she panicked and they found her out and, as she ran away, had to shoot her.

Her hands were shaking badly. As the cab rounded the traffic circle to turn off to the airport approach, she fumbled with her purse and somehow separated a hundred peseta note from the others. She dropped it on the seat beside her. When the cab pulled up at the porters' building she got out, managed to say Air Iberia to Paris, then stood stock-still while the driver and porter took her two pieces of luggage down. She realized that the silent driver was standing beside her waiting to be paid. "It is on the seat," she said. "What is on the seat, señora?" the driver asked. She turned as abruptly as a drilling soldier and walked off to the check-in shack.

The driver made a sound after her to stop her, then he thought he understood what she might have meant. He looked into the cab and saw the hundred peseta note on the seat then was happy not to think about the problem any more.

Eve walked directly past the Iberia desk where the porter was weighing her bags, and handed the porter her ticket envelope without stopping. She walked past TWA and BEA, past the Information Desk, past the newsstand, past the Ladies' Room and into the bar. She asked for a double gin and when it came she sipped it slowly and stared at the floor. As she drank her second double gin the porter found her and explained that the ticket agent would have to see her passport. She thanked him and gave him a ten peseta tip from the change on the bar. Her hand didn't shake.

At the Iberia counter she gave the clerk her passport and the baggage checks the porter had given to her and asked, with a dazzling smile, for her large bag. He dragged it out for her at once and, without a word, she carried it to the Ladies' Room where she took off the dress which had been stained with fear and put on another. She returned to check her bag through again and, with a firm grip on the cardboard tube, passed the *guardia* at the customs gate and moved across the customs room to the office of the chief of customs.

Bourne arrived too late to see her. He moved impatiently through the crowds then through the restaurant to the terrace which overlooked the field. As he came up to the wire fence the Iberia Constellation was loading. He looked wildly about to find her, fearing the worst in a terrifying flash, and when he did see her she was halfway up the steps to the plane, carrying the cardboard tube in her hand and chatting pleasantly with an elderly nun who climbed the steep steps slowly ahead of her. She did not look back.

During his immediately preceding criminal enterprise Bourne had lived in Paris for nearly three years. The assignment he had developed for himself involved an intricately designed and routinely executed insurance company embarrassment which Bourne had decided never to repeat ; not because there had not been enough risk, because he in no way appreciated risk, but because it had resembled, far too closely, the kind of dishonesty he had practiced in his father's firm. To Bourne, the insurance company job had been dishonestly dishonest.

The work had taken him four months less than three years and a certain amout of operating capital but, banishing taxes, as he could in his work, he was able to displace his total outlay of twenty-one million francs for the entire period, with a gross profit of ninety-six million francs realized against a risk of twenty to thirty-five years in prison if he had been caught. He had reinvested two-fifths of his profit in annuities with the same insurance company because he was sure that they had learned a massive lesson and would be extremely alert against any semblance of recurrence. The project itself is of no interest in the Spanish connection but the three years it had given him in Paris had brought him friends and a wife. His friends and particularly his wife had turned out much later to have their own friends and connections within the pervasive art world of the city or, to untangle this maze of words, his friends had indirectly lead him to his wife and his wife had taken him to Jean Marie.

Eve Lewis was what many people might call a reject. While she was working in the market for a fashion magazine in New York it was discovered that she had a tendency to weep without reason in inconvenient circumstances. She had wept once at the rather offhand description of a small boy being sent to camp from Grand Central Station and once at the recollection of a method of fixing dog races with chewing gum. Even though, much later, it was discovered that the tendency was due to her revulsion to drugs and that a doctor had put her on something called dexadrine to enforce weight reduction, it served to mark her with other people as being essentially unstable. Also, she got the shakes regularly, which is to say that she overcompensated for a low resistance to alcohol. Other indications which tend to prove that people like this only get what they ask for by being sensitive, imaginative, creative, frightened and valuable ; such as an abortion, a marriage, and a divorce, in that order, set her apart from the more completely adjusted women at the magazine who understood reflexively that there was no need for feeling either rejected or disgraced by either abortion or divorce. They knew, without getting morbid and overwrought about it, that there were pills for sleeping and pills for waking, and pills for in between which removed all excuses for any kind of shakes. The women around her at that time were enlightened, modern women and she was one of those slobs who were just not able to cope, who were most certainly not able to compete, and if a person doesn't have the spirit or the interest to compete, how can they expect to survive?

Naturally, when one lived under the world's greatest standard of living one had to expect the world's highest cost of living. Wages might not exactly keep up with prices, but The Administration certainly saw to it that credit kept up with prices and when it all resulted in a way of life which had evolved out of world leadership why keep calling the resulting, personal condition debt, or if one had to be old-fashioned and call it debt, why act like there was any disgrace connected with that either? Everyone else lived the same way, but no one could pound that into Eve Lewis' head.

She just didn't have it to survive. Consequently she did what a lot of other rejects had done. Instead of killing herself or going into a convent she let herself out by moving to Europe to live on a year-in-year-out basis.

At first it had been totally exhilarating to live in Paris because it was, in a sense, like being invisible. She could travel anywhere there and not understand one word that people were saying if she stayed out of the Georges V, Le Calvados, and the Louvre. For weeks she envied people with the good fortune to have to wear hearing aids which they could turn on or off so they could select what they heard and not be made old by gabble. Eve, however, was a natural linguist the way Darrow was a natural trial lawyer and Eisenhower was a natural golfer, which meant that the three of them had to study and work and devote almost all of their waking hours for the realization of their gifts.

When Eve had first arrived in Paris she had no anticipation that she would one day speak six languages. After four weeks she had met an improbably handsome Polish fashion photographer who spoke no English and had moved in with him on the third floor of a cold-water flat in the Place des Vosges. In four months she had French at a point where she could massage it into perfection, which she did. In seven months she had Polish, which is more difficult.

Working like this, with one teacher at a time, as good women do, she learned Italian in Rome and Spanish in Spain while working as a feature writer with an American film company on location in Italy and as a stringer and a space-rate "columnist" for the Paris edition of an American paper from Madrid. She learned German working as a publicity representative in Frankfurt which is that part of Germany where the most perfect German is spoken, representing a Chicago public relations firm on a cosmetics account for a former cartel which was now bigger than ever. Each man had, fortunately, been the most exciting thing in her life while she had been with him, which had been the way it should be, and the Spanish language contributor had been, by far, the most acceptable male. She was twenty-six years old; in six years she had Parisian French and bad Polish, but then only Poles would or could ever acknowledge that there was such a thing as good Polish, because the only chance she had had to speak it had been with film people. She had Castilian Spanish, Roman Italian which could have been much, much better if the man she had fallen in love with had only been raised in Siena, and German which was high enough to threaten vertigo. Her English was acquired at Julia Richman High School in New York.

Eve was very clear on being a reject because dozens of friends in the States had taken a great deal of their valuable time to explain to her that she was The Laughable Anomaly, The Impossible Condition, The Citizen Pelican Stuffed Into the System Ortolan. This understanding had once caused her to behave rather extravagantly at gatherings, but Bourne had changed all of that. Bourne had removed that freak feeling just as though it had been done by surgery, completely and forever.

Her names on passports and other documents had been Lewis, Cryder, Sment, Quinn and Sundeen, one of those being Bourne's real name and the others being used to transport the three copies of the Spanish masters across the frontier, each on a separate trip through a separate city of entry. Before the second name change, before she knew that he was a criminal and a thief, he had transformed her into a healthy woman, needed and cherished. By the time she had found out about Bourne being a criminal he could do nothing wrong.

The Avenue de la Motte-Picquet of Paris runs across the foot of the Champs de Mars to the Invalides and is as gloriously bourgeoise as anything either bank of the Seine has to offer. Eve went directly to Jean Marie's studio at Number Eighteen on that street as soon as the cab could bring her from Le Bourget to Paris. Somehow, she jammed herself and the two pieces of luggage into the tiny elevator and, holding the cardboard tube over her head because there was nowhere else to put it, rose like a woman in vaudeville levitation toward the top of the shaft, a millimeter at a time, almost at the speed of a twelve-year-old child growing up, or perhaps at the rate a daisy grows. The *ascenseur,* to be indigenous, was extremely French as was Jean Marie when she finally reached the top floor and rang the bell.

The door was flung open. He pulled her inside, leaving the baggage in the corridor outside, and bussed her wetly on the cheek. She made a half-sound meaning to indicate that she had left her luggage behind her which he immediately understood as though she had articulated a full sentence and reopened the door, permitting her to carry the bulky luggage in while he watched her sympathetically. To do this she had to prop the cardboard tube up against the wall inside the door in the semidarkness. He did not touch it at first but cried out, "Is this it? Are they in there? In the name of St. Joseph, Eve, tell me. Are they in there?"

She closed the door and grinned at him, nodding. He picked up the tube and ran from the foyer toward the studio as Lalu came rushing and shouting through another door.

Lalu looked like a nursery doll. Her voice was higher than a dog whistle. Eve had to stoop way over to kiss her. "Is it Eve! Was it a good trip? How was Jim? Will you move there soon? Did they like Jean Marie's painting?" The sounds she made were like a well filled with drunken canaries. She reached up and took Eve's hand and they trooped into the studio after Jean Marie.

It was an enormous studio with a half-roof of glass and two enormous windows on the corner of the building. It was the studio befitting a man who had had two of the most successful shows within fourteen months that the art press of Paris could remember seeing. The studio looked out over just about everything formidable south of the Seine. The Ecole Militaire had been placed in the right foreground area. The Hôtel des Invalides was in the left foreground. The Eiffel Tower was in the right background, and there were more roofs in view than most North American pigeons had ever seen. Being March and close to spring, it was raining, but things like rain and cold don't matter in Paris; an inexplicable condition.

Eve tried to remember that Lalu was absolutely innocent of the real identity of the project and wished Jean Marie would. He always seemed to be on the verge of giving the entire game away. He had decided to tease her by leaning against the piano indolently and staring. "Why don't you open it?" she asked.

"Why? They will be duplicates of the canvases I painted, nothing more, you may be sure."

"What do you mean, dear?" Lalu asked.

"He is teasing," Eve said. "You see, Jim wasn't able to sell Jean Marie's paintings. The man died."

"Oh, what a pity! For the man, I mean," Lalu said.

The explanation served to remind Jean Marie that he had pleaded not to allow Lalu to know what they were doing and he smiled at Eve appreciatively. Eve smiled back at him feeling happy about paintings, happy for Bourne, happy for Jean Marie, and happier still to be free, to have been saved from a Spanish prison.

Jean Marie plumped himself down on a hassock and began to work the top of the tube open. It came off at once. He whistled and made exaggerated movements with his eyebrows which made Eve and Lalu laugh. It was a wonderful moment and she wished very deeply that Bourne could have been there.

Then she saw the puzzled expression on Jean Marie's face. She saw him turn the tube upside down and pound at the bottom of it.

The tube was empty. There was nothing in the tube. There were no paintings; nothing. The tube was empty. It was really empty because Eve took a pair of shears and opened it up. There was nothing in the tube. No Velázquez, no Zurbarán, no Greek; nothing. She was never to forget the look on Jean Marie's face. He was never to forget the look on hers. There were no paintings, not one painting, in the tube.

During his second year in Madrid, Bourne had spent one four-day week end each month in Paris, leaving from Barajas on Air France on the two-thirty plane and returning on the one o'clock Iberia from Le Bourget. The hotel ran smoothly in the hands of Señor Elek during these short periods of time. In the seventh month of these visits, the month of his second date with Eve, he had met Jean Marie, husband of Eve's closest friend, Lalu.

Jean Marie was a gifted painter who claimed to prefer to copy because he said he had studied art as a business. In the tenth month, the second of their association, Bourne felt that he had prepared the painter sufficiently to reveal his proposal and in twenty minutes an arrangement had been reached.

They sat on the tiny *terrasse* of the Café Benito Reyes on Boulevard Malesherbes. Jean Marie and Lalu had lived on Rue Lavoisier at the time, behind an enormous Félix Potin supermarket. Jean Marie ate potato chips and drank chocolate, a filthy habit he had picked up by watching an American named Charles Moses, a French-Italian scholar of the quarter who studied from opening to closing on the *terrasse* eating and drinking the horrible combination. Bourne watched Jean Marie as though fearful that the man would decide to dunk one of the salty slivers into the sugary pinkish-brown mass.

Jean Marie was an exceedingly happy man by digestion, eugenics, metabolism and circumstance. He had been made even more sappily happy by meeting Lalu and had become even more paretically delirious since she had agreed to marry him. They had been married for eight years and joy had expanded, not diminished. He was an average man in all but talent. His talent could have been genius, but his disposition was too good for that. His painting, in any master's style or his own style, was incredibly good both technically and emotionally. He preferred to paint in any master's style because it impressed Lalu so, and because it brought in certain money. He freelanced, working in all museums, mostly at the Louvre, although he had just put in four straight months at the Delacroix Museum in the Place Forstenberg. He worked by commission, using six well-established dealers as agents and rendering precisely perfect copies, mostly of Rubens, Picasso, and Da Vinci; almost entirely for tourists from Germany and Sweden.

Bourne sipped Danish beer and outlined his project to Jean Marie. The painter listened without alarm, nodding frequently, sipping at the chocolate and staring mostly at the traffic which moved about the Place Saint Augustin.

"That is excellent, my friend," he nodded when Bourne had finished. "For years I have been trying to think of some way of increasing the apparent values of my business, but one cannot play fast and loose in the Louvre, of course, although I am sure, on the other hand, that one cannot merely walk into a great cathedral in Spain and have one's own way either." Jean Marie was a Parisian born and bred and his French was like a beautiful song.

"You mustn't give that part of it a thought," answered Bourne. "All of that is my department and my problem."

"I just paint."

"Right."

"And we divide the profits fifty-fifty."

"I have a formula for that."

"Does the formula call for an equal division of the profits?"

"In effect, yes."

"Explain to me the effect, if you please."

"Do you wish to invest an equal amount of capital with me, as an investment?"

"I have no capital."

"I know that. So, we will divide the net profit equally. Before we divide, I am to be reimbursed in full for all funds necessary to be advanced by me."

Jean Marie was dubious. "I'm not sure I like that. Do you have a breakdown of the items which will require capital?"

"I have." Bourne took a sheet of accounting paper out of his pocket. Under a marching sequence of columns, neat, identified figures had been set down. Jean Marie studied the sheet for some time. While he read the sheet, Bourne finished the bottle of Danish beer he was drinking and asked Henri, the waiter, to bring another. In good time, Jean Marie looked up.

"This is really first class, you know," Jean Marie said.

"Thank you."

"But why do you have me down here for fifty thousand francs a week beginning next week?"

"Because beginning right now you will have to devote full time to research on Spanish masters and to planning and to test painting and so forth."

Jean Marie grinned. "I don't work that way. I look and I paint. It all happens very fast. Incidentally, you must make

62

every effort to get absolutely true, fabulously clear color transparencies of whatever we are going to copy."

"Consider it done," Bourne said. "But nonetheless you must stop this professional copying. We'll want everyone to forget you ever were a copyist."

"What will I do in my spare time?"

"Entertain Lalu."

"I do that now."

"I mean outside the apartment."

"She won't allow me to spend the money, but I see what you mean. I'll stop as soon as I finish this Delacroix I'm on which should be in about three days. He worked big, that one. A Goya derivative."

"Good. Study how you can disappear as a copyist. Stay away from the museums and your six dealers. Move across the river. The Right Bank is no place for a painter anyway. There is nothing which says you can't work on your own paintings. After all, why shouldn't you?"

Jean Marie rubbed his jaw, then chewed on a quantity of potato chips. "Why shouldn't I?" He washed the potato chips down with a gulp of lukewarm dreadfully sweet chocolate and Bourne almost gagged.

They finalized the deal. Bourne's capital investment, repayable to him out of the first monies received, was not to exceed an amount equal to twelve and a half per cent of the total profit projection which they agreed as market value to be appraised when the Market and the market value had been established. Jean Marie and Lalu and everyone they knew in the world of art were to tell everyone *they* knew that Jean Marie had seen a blinding light that all copying was fraudulent and parasitical, that in the future he would only paint to create his own seen images. He was to tell Lalu, who would be shocked at the idea of giving up such a regular income, that Bourne believed in him and would sponsor him at the rate of fifty thousand nonreturnable francs a week, a cool fortune, until he was established. They shook hands on the understanding that he would have a one-man show ready in six months, the exhibition of which Bourne would arrange and finance out of the aforementioned common fund, together with suitable publicity designed to erase forever the memory of Jean Marie as a copyist, and to whatever degree made possible by the quality of his original paintings, to establish him as a serious painter.

It was at that point that Jean Marie made his suggestion. Bourne's immediate reaction demonstrated Bourne's reason for pre-eminence as a criminal. His instant recognition of the main chance demonstrated a lack of rigidity which allowed him to discard entirely The Marketing Plan he had built up so painstakingly over the past fourteen months. It took him not more than seven minutes to hear, digest, and evaluate Jean Marie's information, which had been proffered in a most casual manner, quite indifferent to its possibilities, and in sort of a social acknowledgment of Bourne's reference to the eventual marketing of the merchandise.

A Swiss lawyer, known to be of high character and practice, a client of the most successful Parisian art dealer Jean Marie had ever known, had cultivated Jean Marie over expensive lunches twice a month for three months now, as had Bourne. Using the expanding musical note system the lawyer had convinced Jean Marie that the great dealer believed Jean Marie to be the most gifted copyist who had ever lived. Seeing Jean Marie's immediate appreciation of that observation, the lawyer had proceeded to outline, in most general and entirely academic terms, his point of view.

He had a client. No matter how successfully these chats might proceed the client's name could never be mentioned. The client was a man of exalted tastes in art and a man of not inconsiderable means. He had recognized the lawyer as a man of absolute integrity, as a man who would not consent even to discuss any matter which even seemed to take advantage of the law. He told the lawyer of certain properties which were his by right and which he desired to reacquire. He would pay a fabulous amount to reacquire these, however to overtake these properties the client would need to have exact copies which was the matter which the lawyer would very much like to discuss with Jean Marie at Jean Marie's convenience.

"Did you discuss it?" Bourne asked.

"No."

"Why?"

"He was a crook, that guy. I didn't like the way he put it to me."

64

Bourne left Paris for Zurich that evening, after telephoning ahead for an appointment for the following morning.

Lawyer Chern was bald on top, and so yellow on the sides of his head that he looked painted. He was yellow and pink and blue and white; the last two colors accounting for his clear eyes and strong, square teeth. He was an excessively, even repellently, healthy man whose handshake was too strong, whose voice was too loud, whose laugh was too harsh, whose beam was too broad, and whose every move was so insincere that Bourne decided at once that if he should ever have the chance to recommend it, Lawyer Chern must have a place on his father's payroll.

They concluded their arrangements the following day because Lawyer Chern was duck soup to Bourne. Bourne's father had taught him how to screw chaps like Lawyer Chern before Bourne was out of high school. The details of the agreement were clean. The negotiations opened something like this, with Bourne relaxing and playing into Lawyer Chern's greed, just as his father had taught him.

Bourne said, "It has come to my attention through a painter friend of Margat and Sons that you represent a client who is interested in Spanish paintings."

"What painter friend of Margat and Sons is that?" Lawyer Chern asked.

"Jean Marie Calbert."

"Ah!"

"We are associated."

"Ah!"

Bourne stopped there. Chern being a lawyer and therefore doctrinaire fell back upon the law school instruction of waiting silently while the world spilled out gratuitous information. Four silent minutes passed then Lawyer Chern volunteered that he had had discussions with a principal some time ago who had expressed an interest in reaching an arrangement with a special kind of art dealer who might be able to secure Spanish paintings, but that nothing had developed from the discussions since then and that had been some time ago.

Bourne continued to stare at him. Exasperated, Lawyer Chern finally blurted, "Do you have a quantity of Spanish masters?"

C

"They are available."

"Are any of these available?" He opened the top drawer of his desk. He moved two thin sheets of paper which contained listed typewriting and slid them across the desk toward Bourne. Bourne glanced at the lists without picking them up.

"Some of them."

"Which ones?"

"Later."

"What—later?"

"After I have a written agreement." This pleased the lawyer secretly; agreements in writing are covered with cabalistic signs for lawyers, anything in writing was. One's word wasn't worth spit with lawyers. He began to chew absentmindedly on his thumbnail. Minutes passed. Then Lawyer Chern said, "You understand that the name of my client may not appear in this agreement at any time?"

"My dear man," Bourne told him, "neither may mine."

"You are joking, of course."

Bourne did not bother to answer. They concluded their arrangements that day.

In the place of bona fides, Bourne agreed to post an amount of one hundred thousand Swiss francs in escrow against the delivery of the first of three Spanish master paintings, covered by lists known as Schedule A and B, within a period of not more than two hundred and eighty-one days. At the time of the delivery of the first canvas the deposit money was to be returned in full to Bourne, plus a captive bonus of fifteen per cent of the good faith amount held in escrow, plus the amount of one hundred and thirty thousand dollars if the painting delivered was on Schedule A or the amount of eighty-three thousand five hundred dollars if the painting delivered was on Schedule B. Deliveries of all paintings were to be made to the premises of Traumer Frères, bankers doing business at 46 Rue Balzance, Paris, to Wolfgang Gregory Mandel. In consideration of the good faith shown by Bourne in establishing the deposit under escrow, and realizing the necessity of advance expenses and charges made necessary by the gradual acquisition of the paintings in Spain, and the costs of travel and maintenance to and in and from Spain, it was agreed that a sum equal to twenty per cent of the average valuation of the paintings listed in Schedules A and B or a mean sum of twenty-one thousand three hundred dollars, non-returnable and non-accountable funds, would be payable to Bourne two-thirds upon signing and the remaining one-third upon delivery of the first painting.

At first there had been a good deal of haggling over the Bourne insistence that the client underwrite the expenses of the project and, later on, over Lawyer Chern's insistence that Bourne enter into the escrow agreement. Lawyer Chern said, "But, it is eminently fair, my dear fellow. You insist upon being paid in advance for operating expenses, something which is unheard of in the art field but you are a specialist and I can see your argument, but what about your bona fides? You will not give me your name. I must take you, a stranger, on faith. How is my principal to know that you won't take this expense money, and you are talking about a very respectable amount of money, sir, and disappear. I mean, how are we to know you won't go to Spain and then come back saying you had no luck but that you unfortunately spent all the money? I mean, you are a specialist. If you had suppose, in the past, acquired other paintings or say, some jewels, for a principal in the past in this proposed manner, well I could check on you. I would have bona fides even in your own unusual specialty. Oh, no. No, no, If you deliver the paintings, all right we will pay the expenses but in the meantime it is only sound business to demand that you agree to put a good will deposit in escrow under an agreement which will protect my principal."

"But the money may be tied up for eight months!"

"So?"

"Why should a bank enjoy the interest on my money because you want to impress a client?"

"Are you asking if we will repay you for the idleness of your money?"

"Yes."

"We will not. And that is final."

"Then we have finished." Bourne got up immediately and started for the door.

"One moment—please."

Bourne kept walking. Lawyer Chern yelled, "All right!"

Bourne didn't smile or shrug. He returned to the chair and sat down.

It was agreed that Bourne should sign the agreement under the name of Werner Schrampft; agreed mainly because Bourne had given no other name. Lawyer Chern, on behalf of his client, was to sign as Wolfgang Gregory Mandel. Upon the signing of the agreement each was to open a separate account with Traumer Frères in Paris, London or Zurich in any amount required to be accepted by the bank as a number account, that is a nameless account carried by number and kept forever secret by the bank's officers, in this case the Traumer Frères themselves. Upon delivery of the canvases to Lawyer Chern in Paris identification for contracted payments by the bank would be made by the presentation of the numbers of each account as established by the Schrampft and Mandel signatures as used when opening these accounts.

Bourne and Lawyer Chern finalized the transaction in the bank's Zurich offices. Bourne deposited his check in escrow, under detailed agreement, in the amount of one hundred thousand Swiss francs, the equivalent of twenty-three thousand eight hundred and nine dollars and fifty cents and accepted a cashier's check from the bank, issued upon receipt of a personal check from Lawyer Chern, in the amount of fourteen thousand two hundred thirteen dollars and thirty-two cents. They parted agreeing that when Bourne was ready to deliver the paintings he would cable the word TOLEDO to Lawyer Chern who would proceed at once to the Hôtel Rochambeau on the Rue la Boétie, Paris, for meetings the day following the receipt of the cable.

When he left the bank with the signed agreement Bourne wired Jean Marie to tell Eve and Lalu to stand by for a celebration that evening. They had a wonderful time. He had returned to Madrid aching for another month to go by so that he could see her, hear her and hold her again.

They started the evening at the English Bar of the Plaza-Athénée because that would be an easy place to find a cab after they had worked out the unbelievably complex suggestions as to what they should do with the evening. As they left number eighteen Avenue de la Motte-Picquet a private detective named Sacha Youngstein, loaded with Japanese cameras, took their pictures with a camera having a telescopic lens from an automobile across the street. Youngstein was the true ideal of human life, a hypochondriac who was also intensely interested in medicine for objective purposes, so there was no question of their tiring him out no matter how late they stayed up. He would arrange to have various night club concessionaires take more pictures of them while he simultaneously diagnosed his own twinges and speculated as to the possible ailments of strangers who moved around him. He followed Bourne to Eve's apartment on Rue du Boccador, riding a Vespa at three eighteen in the morning and anticipating a bad cold. When he felt much better three days later he returned to the building and bought information about Bourne from Eve's concierge using the photographs. His client, Lawyer Chern, was a stickler for facts for the total protection of his clients.

Jean Marie and Eve sat in numb silence in an indefectible restaurant called Lucien on Rue Surcouf. Somehow they had contained their consternation in the presence of Lalu. Until the moment of discovery of the emptiness of the cardboard tube everything had gone so effortlessly that neither of the amateur criminals could have foreseen their feelings, and now each one began to examine the small fear that if someone knew enough to steal the paintings from Eve, that someone had been watching all of them for some time which suggested vague peril, past and future. Then Jean Marie began to think of the amount of money his share of the sale would have represented, how much they were being cheated out of, and he became extremely indignant. He spoke bitterly about the kind of criminals who would be low enough to allow them to do all of the work and undertake all of the strain and then just swoop down and carry the spoils away. It seemed to him that Eve had looked at him somewhat sardonically as he spoke of undergoing all that strain so he told her not to get her nose out of joint, that she knew bloody awfully damned well what he meant. He was so incensed that he forgot himself and went as far as sipping a Dubonnet.

"You must start from the absolute beginning," he told her. "Start from the instant you got up this morning." He stared at her expectantly, then his face blanked as though lightning had struck. "Aha!" he cried. "Are you sure the substitution was not made during the night?"

"Yes."

"How?"

"Jim was there. We didn't sleep much."

"Oh. Well, then, start recalling every move you made from the instant he left the room this morning."

"Send a wire to Jim. Tell him what has happened. Why are we sitting here? Send a wire to Jim!"

"Eve, we have to have something to tell him."

"I certainly think we meet the requirements there, my friend."

"I mean we must be able to say something more than that the paintings are missing. It sounds so childish. I mean——"

"Please, Jean Marie. Send Jim a wire. I don't know how to send it or I'd send it."

"It's time you knew. The brother of a friend of mine who runs a Basque restaurant on Rue de l'Université is a betting agent in the *jai alai frontón* across the street from Jim's hotel. His name is Jorge Mendoza-Diaz. Number twenty-three Calle de Marengo." Jean Marie asked a waiter to fetch him a piece of paper and a pencil. When it came he thought for some time then wrote: DIEGO AND HIS BROTHERS DID NOT COME HOME SISTER IS HERE BUT MOTHER WORRIED CAN YOU HELP and signed it MIROIR. He showed it to Eve who told him it would be very clever when he wrote it in Spanish instead of French, and he agreed, translating it at once then suggesting that they send it right after lunch because the post office on Rue de Grenelle was only a block away, on the way back to his studio, but she insisted that he go to the post office at once and send the message at an urgent rate. He agreed and hastened away.

When he returned Eve began the self-recriminations all over again.

"Jim will flip."

"Eve, stop it! There is no one to blame! Who could have foreseen this? You brought the tube through. It isn't as though you had lost the tube."

"But, baby. The way he worked to get those paintings! He was sick, physically, actively sick, the night he got them back to the hotel. He's spent almost three years, and now——" She spread her empty hands out in front of her pathetically and looked as though she were going to cry.

"Please, Eve. Please don't be so upset. Look at me, sweet child. As of this minute I have lost sixty or seventy million francs. Am I crying?"

She smiled at him. "Frankly, darling, you look as though you're afraid to start to cry because you're afraid you wouldn't be able to stop."

He grinned wanly. "In ten years I'll probably look back on today and shoot myself," he said. "But, look here. Jim is a professional. He thinks of everything and he has undoubtedly thought of this and I know we can be of help to him when he starts his plan to get our paintings back for us. We must reconstruct every move you made from that hotel room to my studio so that we may give him an intelligent, detailed accounting so that he may decide what must be done."

"But I can't think!"

"I don't want you to think. I want you to relax your mind utterly and *feel* what happened to you this morning," he said. Eve shivered. "I wouldn't trust a person who could think at a moment like this," he added.

Eve stared at the service plate on the table in front of her and returned, in her mind, to the hotel in Madrid, and began to talk.

Jim left the room. He kissed her goodbye then she looked up and down the hall to make sure that the coast was clear and he left. She put on lipstick then she called down for a porter. Where was the tube, Jean Marie wanted to know. The tube was on the bed. Two porters had arrived. The assistant manager Señor Elek had come in. Jean Marie interrupted again to tell her not to remember with her mind but to feel with her body and her senses what had happened as she had moved and the other people had moved with relation to her. Did she feel anything about the two porters and the assistant manager after they had arrived.

Eve was concentrating with her senses so hard she could have been in a trance. Yes. She felt that the two porters had arrived because they liked to look at her body. Good, good —Jean Marie said, what about the assistant manager?

Lucien, the proprietor of the restaurant, stood discreetly at tableside, the *cartes* ready. Jean Marie looked up at him, shook his head imperceptibly, but lifted his glass to signal for a refill.

71

Eve told him that although it had not registered on her mind then, the assistant manager, a man who, with the rest of the men in the hotel, had always indicated a silent but wholly healthy interest in her body, had not had any interest in it while he had been in the room that morning. He had been his usual friendly, agreeable self, but he had had no interest in what she had always represented to him in the past. What did he do, Jean Marie wanted to know. He bustled about supervising the ludicrousness of two large men trying to make a proper job of transporting one suitcase and one small make-up case.

Jean Marie held up his hand to stop her for a moment and paused to consider the significance of Señor Elek's uncharacteristic uncarnal attitude. He decided it was very important and said he knew that her husband would see it as very important. Feelings were much more to be trusted than logic, he said, because no one had devised a means to argue with feelings. Had anyone so much as touched the cardboard tube through all of this?

She explained to Jean Marie that she had been drilled and rehearsed by her husband to treat the cardboard tube as one might regard a rolled-up calendar. It was an inexpensive, unimportant souvenir ; that was the shape of the action she was to follow. It had been on the bed. On the way out she had pretended to look around and see if she had forgotten anything, then she had picked up the tube, almost as an afterthought, and had strolled toward the door where the porters had gotten into a Keystone Kop jam-up by each trying to take the baggage through at once and everyone had laughed at it. Someone had taken the tube from her hand during that jam-up. Who had taken it? She couldn't remember who had taken it.

We will start again at the moment you felt the tube leave your hands, Jean Marie insisted. You must feel this, now, Eve—you must not think. You are at the door. Where are the porters? They are beside her. No, they were near here, near the door. How far away was the door? Could she reach out and touch the door? No, she had backed away to let them go through. She had backed three paces away. She could not touch the door. Where was the assistant manager? He was—he was standing beside her and talking to her. That was when she felt that he was totally unaware of, and

72

disinterested in, her body. At that moment. She had instinctively pushed her breasts out at him as she felt it, and had reached across his chest to the bureau top to pick up a broken package of cigarettes which she had known to be empty until she needed to reach, but he had remained oblivious to her body. She could feel that now, very strongly. He had taken the cardboard tube from her, as she had reached for the cigarette package, saying something indistinctly about the cab and the front of the hotel. When they had reached the lift the two porters were out of sight.

Going down in the lift they had chatted about the shocking jewelry store robbery on the Gran Via the day before. She had gone to the cashier and had checked out. Had he walked with her to the cashier, Jean Marie asked. No. How long was he away from her? Was he in sight? No. He was away as long as it took to pay her small bill and go to the cab. He had been standing beside the cab when she came out. The tube had been in his hand. One porter had taken a tip, Señor Elek had handed her the tube—no, he had propped it up against the far door inside the cab. When did she handle the tube again? At the airport. Did she feel it was the same tube? She could not feel anything. She was too frightened to feel anything but dread about the tube, but the tube had never been out of her sight or out of her hands from that instant until she was inside Jean Marie's studio, so there was only one possible answer. The assistant manager Señor Elek had substituted an empty tube for the real tube. Jean Marie agreed. He felt she was absolutely right; he felt it, too.

Having cracked the case they ordered lunch. Eve ate scrambled eggs with asparagus tips while Jean Marie explained that the one common course all competing chefs had to prepare for the judges in all international cooking competitions was scrambled eggs, they were that difficult to make well. The scrambled eggs at Lucien's were so good that Eve ordered the same thing again. Jean Marie had snails and a veal steak. The white wine was cold and supporting. Lucien's grandfather's Armagnac was dark and lingering, with the slightest overtone of sweetness. They ate heartily because they felt they had been permitted to return to life again.

Bourne arrived early the next morning. He had made con-

73

nections to Barcelona, then to Nice, then to Paris. He was steady and extremely considerate of their anxious feelings.

The Duque de Dos Cores died in his sleep in a chair at a café in the Piazza San Marco in Venice, out in the early morning of March 17th, although no one in the area observed St. Patrick's Day, and it was not until late that night, as the chairs were being taken up after the concert, that the body had been discovered; his posture, even in death, having been so good. The waiter was sure that the old man had died in the early morning because he remembered, when the duchess's lawyer and the police talked with him later, an American woman tourist pointing at the duke and saying to the waiter, "That old man looks dead," which the waiter remembered receiving as extremely bad taste.

It had gotten very busy at the café almost immediately after that when a motion picture company which had been headed by Miss Bella Carnegie photographed a scene on the terrace of the café not far in the duke's immediate foreground. He had been a man who would have invested any scene, real or cinematic, with enormous atmosphere, alive or dead. His friends all over the world who saw the movie two, three or four years later depending upon the country they utilized to attend movies, were always surprised and delighted to see the dead, old man rotting away in the background, easily dominating Miss Carnegie's clasping and unclasping nostrils as she registered that emotion she could register at will. The film company had moved away to some other part of Venice and the concert hour had arrived and, with one thing and another, no one had noticed that the duke was dead until closing time had come around.

With the help of the police, it took the duchess's attorneys no time to reconstruct what had happened which was most necessary for the report because they represented, out of Milan, the duchess's attorneys in Bilbao, and their instructions had been explicit: things must be quick and quiet. The cause of death was clear. The duke had overtaxed himself. He had died of simple exhaustion.

The facts revealed that he had rented a little boy in Hamburg, contemplating merely one week. Then, instead of going on to Montecatini for baths and rest and massage, he suddenly decided that he would rather spend time with the child. This had meant leaving a large deposit with the boy's owner, and what seemed to be endless haggling. The owner would cry out that the boy was one of his best earners and that there was no way of knowing what price he should charge on a lease basis. Then when the area of price had seemed to be settled the man had wailed that he had no way of knowing whether or not the duke ever intended to return the boy, and so on and on. Money had settled everything.

The child spoke only German and the duke's German was quite poor. The boy had been beautifully trained in his work which, while it makes sense on a piece work basis, was disastrous when stretched out over weeks against the foolishness of a seventy-two-year-old man, no matter how strong, and no one had had the time to instruct the boy differently, the duke having acted so impulsively.

It had killed the duke, of course. The police and the Milanese attorney had found the grave child on a straight-backed, wooden chair in the duke's rooms, staring at the Grand Canal, wearing dejected-looking, long, winter underwear, efficient underwear for a northern port like Hamburg in the winter, but out of keeping in Venice in that season.

They could not find his clothes at first. They had been left by the duke with the concierge so that the child would not be tempted to stray away with the duke's valuables, a policy which had not been directed against this particular boy but which had been formed by years of experience in many of the great cities of the world.

They grouped about the boy, asking questions. The hotel manager interpreted the boy's German. Suddenly, with an expression of disgust at the boy's answers, the hotel manager lashed out with his open hand, knocking the lad over sideways, over the arm of the chair to the floor. The manager realized the injustice of his action at once. The boy was a child who spoke the way he had been trained to speak, and when he spoke it was to court and woo or go without his food. The manager picked the boy up, righted him on the chair, and apologized briefly.

The Milan representative charged his firm two hundred and fifty thousand lira for the disposition of the various problems relative to the sad death. He was a young, inex-

75

perienced man so he made very little profit. The Milan firm
charged the duke's representatives in Bilbao two million eight
hundred thousand lira for having sent the young man to
Venice and back. The Bilbao law firm, with the sentimen-
tality of the last of many such commissions, billed for fees
which were the equivalent in pesetas of twelve million lira,
for they after all had had to place a long-distance call from
Bilbao to Milan.

No one objected. It was simply awesomely wonderful that
the duke was dead. He was buried at Dos Cortes in the
presence of his immediate family and many priests. All wore
mourning but no one wept. The family doctor had had to
give the duchess strong sedatives before the funeral and during the last rites at the grave to neutralize her tendency to
laugh whenever the ceremony directed attention to the casket.

Bourne arrived at number eighteen Avenue de la Motte-
Picquet just too late to see Lalu who had been sent to her
mother's so that Eve and Jean Marie could receive Bourne's
worst, but Bourne seemed to have recovered well. He was
almost tender in the way he spoke about the details of the
loss with Eve. So much so that she became afraid, to herself,
that for the second time in two days she was going to cry.
He stayed with routine. He took her back, in patient examination and cross-examination, from number eighteen to the
airport and gradually all the way back to the apartment at
the hotel in Madrid. When he had finished they all regarded
it as confirmed that Señor Elek was the only one who could
have made the switch.

The conclusion amazed Bourne. "Gus has been with that
one hotel for sixteen years," he said. "I don't mean just
working with me. He was a part of that hotel. Besides, I
just gave him a twenty per cent increase."

"And he was such a sweet, agreeable, childish, little man,"
Eve protested.

Jean Marie shrugged. "The period of Naïvete is declared
over," he said. "What do we do now?"

Bourne told him he hadn't decided. He promised he would
try to have an answer by noon the next day. He and Eve
left the studio. Jean Marie began to paint with philoso-
phical detachment, almost cheerfully.

They sat, Bourne and Eve, on two rented iron chairs in the Tuileries, A beautiful, circular pond amused small boys in front of them; members of the league of the tranquil were all around them. On the left, through the toy arch of triumph, they could see the palace of the Louvre, on the right the Place de la Concorde. There stretched square miles of sky directly overhead, vast because the buildings everywhere were so sensibly low. They held hands. Bourne toyed absentmindedly with the magnificent emerald ring on Eve's left hand which he had stolen many years before in Miami.

"I've never been hijacked before," Bourne murmured to himself.

"You'll think of something." Eve stroked the back of his hand.

"There is really only one thing to do."

"I know."

"I don't know where to begin."

"Think it through. You've got to think it through."

"I have to make Señor Elek talk. I hate it when things work out so there are no alternatives. He's very proud and he's tough and I hate violence."

They watched a beautifully rigged ship sail across the pond. "What kind of violence?" Eve asked.

"I can assure you that a man like Elek will not volunteer information."

"I know," Eve said. "I realize that. But why must one thing lead to another? We're still in control of our own lives. We don't have to turn into gangsters because someone has outsmarted us."

Bourne sighed. "That's my father. I hate it but I can't take it this way. Just the same," he said, touching her cheek and liking it leaning over to kiss it, "don't you go worrying about barbarity and one thing leading to another. I'm no strongarm. I hate rough stuff. But this is too much. I mean, I worked a long time on this job and to think of someone watching me plan and sweat and worry and then send a messenger to walk away with everything well, it's too much. I mean, under any circumstances no one could be expected to hold still for a mocking like that."

"I suppose not."

"Well, think about it."

"I have."

"All right. Okay, then."

"Jim, we're out of Spain. Why go back? We don't need money. I have a terrible feeling about our going back to Spain."

"We have to, honey."

"Bosh."

"I have to anyway. I couldn't live with myself."

"Señor Elek is just a messenger?"

"Of course."

"Why?"

"You mean who. Who hired him? Well, that's what we have to find out. Personally, I think it was the same man who hired Chern. For all I know it may be Chern."

"We certainly don't have to go to Spain to talk to Chern."

"I know. I wired him. He'll be in Paris tomorrow and we'll talk it all over with him."

"Jim—what kind of violence?"

"What d'you mean?"

"On Señor Elek."

"Maybe violence was a poor choice of word. What comes to me is putting him in some pitch-black place for fifteen or twenty days with plenty of water but no food. That can't hurt him. *Then* I ask him. That's a very disturbing experience and if he doesn't want to talk and maybe I threaten to repeat the whole thing—well, he should be ready to talk the second time around. And it can't really hurt him. In fact that kind of abstinence could be good for him in the long run. Gandhi thrived on that kind of a regime. He really did, you know."

"You sound miserable and frightened, to me."

"Well, it figures. I'm new here with the violence bit."

"Please stay that way."

"This is my eleventh time at bat. Lucky eleven and the first time in sixteen years that anything missed. I'm supposed to anticipate these things. I could be slipping, letting myself be hijacked. I've been trained against that since boyhood."

"Was your father a bootlegger along with everything else?"

He laughed harshly. "Better than that. My father's principal business was raiding companies, legal hijacking, then milking their cash and throwing them away. In my family, it has always been like counterpunching. I remember one time standing at the Men's Bar in the Waldorf and hearing a man five feet away telling his friend that Allied Mines and Metals had a book value of six hundred and five million dollars and that the directors were in a fight over how much expansion they should undertake, if any. I never saw him again, and he never saw me at all. I finished my drink and on the way back to the office I developed forty per cent of the plan my father used to take that company over. He completed the other sixty per cent in about three days then we called in the lawyers and the press agents who hyena those kind of deals. In seventeen months we controlled Allied's cash surplus of a hundred and sixty-two million, and the Allied stockholders paid every cent to get it for us. My father made me a partner the way Capone let Dion O'Banion have the North Side of Chicago when people still stole outside the laws of etiquette. Oh, believe me, my father is a master thief, an absolute wonder, and I'm a piker with these silly little Spanish master deals. Pop has stolen millions and they can't lay a finger on him."

He stood up and drew her to her feet. "It's getting chilly. Let's charge into La Florida and have an elegant lunch." He kissed her eyelids. "Your eyes are the color of Paris," he said, "sort of smoky, bluish-gray."

They strolled off across the Rue de Rivoli and went along Castiglione toward Capucines and Rue de Sèze. They lunched elegantly at La Florida including quantities of Chambolle-Musigny '49. After lunch they stared soulfully at dachshund puppies in a store across the street then, as they walked some more, Eve got to feeling amorous and Bourne always did, so they flagged a cab and sped for the apartment on Rue du Boccador. The concierge stopped them on their way in and their immediate plans had to be postponed. She had a telegram for Bourne from the hotel in Madrid. It said that Señor Elek had been found murdered and inquired when Bourne could be expected to return.

The universe which held the constellation containing the planet Earth was so small it was hardly noticeable. This universe with its stars, planets, and suns was one of many which fitted into other, greater universes like wood atoms into a pipe bowl. All together, they were like grains of sand upon a beach which stretched into infinity.

PART II

Parado

After the banderillas have been planted the bull is not so sure of his prowess any more. He is only slightly winded but has settled down and begins conserving his energy. He charges in quick, short spurts and pays close attention to his aim.

A GREAT deal of ritual went into the playacting which followed the funeral of the Duque de Dos Cortes, what with the appreciation of state expressions of sorrow, of Falange expressions of sorrow, of relatives' expressions of sorrow; the need for acknowledgment of the regrets which poured out of the dale of monarchs at Estoril; the various lawsuits which had been instituted from all over the world by young men and women who claimed shares of the estate; the endless masses which had to be said in Rome, in Madrid, in Seville, in Escorial, at Santiago de Compostela, and by the Archbishop Primate at Toledo; masses which the soul of the duke might have sorely needed; the narcotic proofreading of the linotyped fictions about the great man which were to run serially in a daily paper then appear in book form; the exacting analysis of the estate which had been left to the duchess in its entirety and which required four specialists at law to interpret and to present to her involving the ownership of approximately eighteen per cent of the population of Spain inclusive with farms, mines, factories, breweries, houses, forests, rocks, vineyards and holdings in eleven countries of the world including shares in a major league baseball club in North America, an ice cream company in Mexico, quite a few diamonds in South Africa, a Chinese restaurant on Rue François Ier in Paris, a television tube factory in Manila, and in geisha houses in Nagasaki and Kobe.

With the estate in her control the duchess lost no time in increasing her own nuisance value to her community. She had irritated the Spanish aristocracy for such a time that she had done her best to step up a program of annoyance each year to make sure that they got what they were looking for. She established four test co-operatives; two in industry and two in agriculture; which earned her the dread name of socialist. The resultant storm was far greater than it had been when she had advocated compulsory education up to the age of twelve years. The Marqués de Altomarches, in a letter to *Arriba,* the newspaper, stated that had the duchess been a man he would have demanded satisfaction with pistols for this "attempted sacking of Spanish ideals." As it was he would "disdain her with silence" should they ever have occasion to meet again.

She did not telephone Cayetano or take the opportunity to think about him very much until all of the relatives had shuffled back to shuttered houses and all the priests had finished chanting.

Cayetano fought in Madrid on the afternoon of the first Sunday in April where some of the bulls of Don Carlos Nuñez had been assembled. The duchess was sitting in barrera in Tendido 10 behind the matador's burladero. He saw her from the center of the ring as he marched in the paseo. It was the first time he had ever seen her in a bull ring and it made the scene, familiar since his boyhood, seem thrillingly different.

As the bull for Vasquez came out of the toril, Cayetano slipped into the callejon and stood grinning up at her. She said, "I thought we might have a drink at El Meson later."

He blushed like a schoolboy and, knowing he was blushing, closed his eyes and shook his head at the wonder of what was happening. He was trying to think of too many things at one time and it made him heady and made his legs feel weak. He said, "I can have my mozo rush back to the apartment right now and bring my clothes here. They can be here before the second bull." He was wearing a traje of apple green and silver. It contrasted with his golden-red hair and gold-flecked eyes.

"Oh yes."

"If you could wait in the patio de caballos outside the chapel say five minutes after the last bull I might even drive you out to El Meson myself."

"I will. Oh, I will."

Cayetano moved like a sleepwalker back to the burladero.

He played the two bulls like a sleepwalker. He worked them mainly about fifteen yards in front of Tendido 10. His templar moved like a wave of water; accumulatively, slowly and fluidly. All of his work had much art but it was done with absent-mindedness as though he were fighting with his grandfather's reflexes while his mind was employed dreaming of different glories. He made fourteen linked passes with the muleta on the first bull and killed recibiendo. He cut one ear for his first bull.

For the second bull his veronicas seemed to be rooted into the earth and the cape leaden-slow. He handled his own sticks, his long body most suited to give the greatest beauty to the instant he hung in the air, arms high, seeming to come out of the bull's morillo like a fountain as he shot the sticks. The crowd sang with an ecstatic voice.

For his faena, Cayetano gave them statuary and plastic friezes with that second bull. The odd illusion of extreme slowness plastered him and the bull together as one figure, no light showing through anywhere; two friends who had taken Sunday afternoon to be together and who seemed to stop in mid-flight so that the bull, whom the man had drawn slowly up to the level of his lips with a pase de la muerte, could cock an ear closely and hear the promise of death.

When he killed, going in, his elbow line had passed both horns. He seemed stretched out along the bull's back with casual grace, while his right hand seemed buried to the wrist in the bull's withers and his left hand solicited the bull's attention, holding the crimson muleta beyond and below his right knee. They stayed together in this attitude for an eternity of truth then the still picture broke. The bull fell at Cayetano's feet as he stepped back to honor it with a bow.

He cut two ears and a tail for the second bull. It was the third time a tail had been awarded in the history of the

Madrid ring. The *"Olés!"* had slapped at the sky the way a giant's hand might pound a bass drum which would need to be as big around as the arena. Twenty thousand white handkerchiefs were agitated. The second bull had been so tremendous in its valor that it was given three vueltas of the ring, pulled from its horns as it lay on its side, by a team of union mules.

On his first bull Cayetano had been encouraged to take two vueltas, but after the second bull he had given the mob such emotion that the vueltas were urged on him, one after another. Cayetano and his peons strode around the full turn of the arena with that slow-motion, long-stepping run of a triumphant matador, a gait used only for vueltas and presumably designed for vueltas, which resembled ballet masters pretending to be circus horses.

The crowd cried out for his immortality; it sang that he was numero uno of all of the matadors of the world. It cried *"Olé tu madre!"* and threw watches, flowers, cigars, shoes, brassières, hats and skins of wine into the ring all of which the cuadrilla threw back after belting the wine as they stood in the exact center of the world.

The duchess was standing as he came past Tendido 10 and the end of the fifth and last vuelta. Her eyes were shining with being a Spanish woman who had seen the most Spanish beauty and knowing that she would soon be a part of this physical hymn. She was all he could see in a ring filled with twenty-two thousand people. Although he seemed to slow down as he passed, he did not stop. He saw her smile, as she remembered Ibanez' gambit, and slip her wedding ring from her finger, run a tiny handkerchief through it and throw it into the piste. He scooped it up as he ran by. Against all custom, he did not throw it back into the stands.

He was dressed and standing in the patio de caballos outside the chapel before she could get there because the crowd had been so great, refusing to leave such a scene of its triumph too quickly. For some reason, the crowd did not molest him with its adoration. It parted respectfully and gave him free way. Perhaps with a shared eye it knew that it was seeing and, because of other miracles passed that afternoon, felt it was in the presence of a god and goddess.

El Meson is about four miles out of Madrid on the Burgos

road. It has outdoor tables, wine in pots, and a big view of the Sierre de Guadarrama. The duchess drank white Puerto Rican rum over ice cubes with a little water, which is for little children if you remind the child to stop at four of them.

They talked for a while, with their heads close together. He stared at her, suddenly popeyed at the realization of what was about to happen to them, unable to believe it. She began to giggle at the look on him, reading it easily. He kissed her then. It was the first time he had ever kissed her. They stood together motionless, welded, their tears reflecting the sun as a statue, safe within a fountain, cloistered in a green garden behind a high, cool wall, can reflect the sun.

Bourne, in Paris before that memorable Sunday, sat facing Jean Marie and Eve in the salon of their apartment on Rue du Boccador. It was on the ground floor. It had a tiny garden in the back and an ancient cellar for storing wine, or gold coins, or for growing mushrooms. It had been rented furnished from a French family then in Kwangchowan. He paid ninety thousand francs a month for space which cost his landlords forty thousand francs a year but, as rent went for furnished apartments off the Avenue Georges V, they began a bargain.

Bourne explained his analysis of the unexpected situation and the conclusions he had reached with the regard to the recent business reverses they had suffered.

"Now, understand me, I don't say that Chern knew that his principal was going to hit us. On the other hand, for all we know, Chern may be the principal. We'll find that out this evening, or at least we'll start to find that out this evening."

"What do you mean, start to find out?" Jean Marie, who had been in filthy humor all the day, suddenly asked.

"I mean it may take some time," Bourne answered lightly. "He'll undoubtedly have to be persuaded to talk."

"Suppose he won't talk?"

"Oh, for heaven's sake, Jean Marie," Eve exploded, "stop looking as sinister as Jean Gabin in a *policier*. You know you'd faint if Chern as much as yelled at you."

"Why should he yell at me? I won't be asking him the questions, Jim will. The more I think of this entire outrage, the angrier I become. I feel like filing my teeth to sharp points and biting this damned Swiss as he comes through the door."

"It's just terrible, that's what it is," Eve said, combing her hair with vicious swipes.

"And I repeat—suppose he won't talk?"

Bourne said, "I am going to proceed in this meeting as though we have already granted the fact that Chern will not talk or tell us anything. I think we must plan as though he either will not or cannot tell us anything because it is possible, after all, for him to get hit in the small of the back by a taxi on his way here and we have to be ready for contingencies like that."

"How?" Jean Marie demanded.

"That merchandise is worth a lot of money. We have to find out if it has been sold as soon as it has been sold, or more importantly we have to rig it so we find out as soon as it's offered for sale. This isn't going to be flash and run. There'll be a lot of haggling over those pictures. If we connect everything up right we can be there before they close any transfer."

"But how? Who do we ask all these questions?"

"Crooks. Fences and thieves."

"But we don't know any crooks."

"Then we'll arrange to meet some. But first let's organize the legitimate side."

"Would you like some coffee, Jim?" Eve asked. "Jean Marie?" They both declined.

"The art business is like any other business," Bourne said. "Let an art dealer sneeze in Rome and a dealer in Amsterdam catches cold. If these three pieces are out and circulating, looking to catch some money, the news will be felt somewhere in the legitimate market. And that's your job, Jean Marie. You'll cover London, Amsterdam, Berlin, Geneva, Paris and Rome during the next week. You'll chat with the active dealers and you'll ask them to contact you if they hear of a Velázquez or a Zurbarán or a Greco becoming available. When they ask you which ones you're interested in you'll show them the picture from the Dos Cortes catalogue which I'll have cut out of the book and pasted on stiff cards. These pictures haven't been seen out of Dos Cortes in two hundred years or something so the dealers

85

won't catch on that they're hot. They'll figure you are a legitimate buyer or acting for a legitimate buyer. I doubt that even one of them will be sharp enough to spot these as Dos Cortes masters, but the pictures are so great they'll remember them real clear and if they get a rumble on them it figures that they'll contact you if only to get the bidding started."

"That won't do any good."

"I didn't ask you."

"But, Jim—the maniac we took this job from is obviously not a man who is going to sell the pictures. He's obviously some kind of an art nut. Why waste all that time and money traveling around Europe."

"We don't know that. We don't know if the person who had us hijacked is a man or a woman, a professional criminal or an art nut. I never told you but I had figured out an entirely different kind of a dodge as The Market for these paintings before you came in with the Chern wrinkle, so for all we know this one has figured out a wrinkle or two on his own. We know he can figure real good because he certainly figured rings around us. Now please, Jean Marie. No arguments. There's just one boss on this job and that's me."

"Then we are no longer a democratic group?" Jean Marie's feelings were hurt. "I have joined an army, is that it?"

Eve looked at him stonily. "This never was a democratic group, and you've probably thanked God for it every night in your prayers."

Bourne said, "Do you want to hear the rest or do you want to go home and pack and start for London?"

"I will hear the rest," Jean Marie said loftily.

"All right. Thank you." Bourne turned to Eve. "We'll need a well-entrenched, well-organized criminal contact in Spain. That shouldn't be too hard to set up."

"Shouldn't be too hard?" Jean Marie was incredulous.

"Aren't you glad this isn't a democratic little group?" Eve asked him.

"Call Frank Renaro, the publicity man over on Rue Stockholm," Bourne said to Eve. "You remember him. He handled both of Jean Marie's shows for us."

"Oh, I remember him all right," commented Eve in a sardonic tone, but she made no comment beyond that.

"Renaro knows Spanish criminals?" Jean Marie was shocked.

Bourne ignored him, or didn't hear him. He concentrated on Eve and the problem at hand. "Ask him to call the editor of *The Revealer* in London. It's a Sunday paper. National circulation and lots of dirt. If Renaro doesn't know somebody on the paper he'll know some British newspaper guy who does. Have him set up a meeting with the editor, Sam Johnston, for you tomorrow if possible. *The Revealer* has syndicated the memoirs of every top hoodlum in England and they have a man who knows every one of them like a brother."

"Would he know Spanish mobbies, too?" Eve asked.

"No, but it's like any other business. The English hoods have to do business outside the country from time to time. Perhaps a top British thief might not know a Spanish thief directly but he'd know a French thief or a German thief who could set up a Spanish boy."

"Why go all the way to England then?" Jean Marie shrugged patriotically. "If we have more influential crooks in France why not make the arrangements in France?"

"That makes sense," Eve said.

"I just think there is something much more reliable about a hoodlum who works year in year out to build his reputation up to a position where *The Revealer* will be interested in his memoirs. A man like that is likely to be far more of a romantic than any of your grubby French thieves, and therefore much more likely to cooperate with our requests. I ask you—if you were a literary gangster and a beautiful, mysterious young woman came to you and asked for a Spanish contact, wouldn't you cooperate?"

"Yes, I suppose I would."

"Of course you would! A setup like that would have all the makings for a really first-rate chapter in your memoirs and you know it. You'd have to cooperate!"

Eve asked, "Does that go for the editors of *The Revealer,* too? I mean, they've spent years conditioning these mugs into the literary frame of mind. Why should they just turn one over to me?"

"You are absolutely on the right track. One of the reasons I adore you is because you always ask exactly the right questions."

"As opposed to me," Jean Marie asked tartly.

"A few years ago, just after a film festival at Cannes, some people from Hollywood were staying at Cap Ferrat and I got some shots of them. Not what you're thinking. It's just absolutely top stuff—intimate, informal stuff of two people who make it a point to be photographed as infrequently as possible which makes it the kind of a layout which would be pure gold for Sam Johnston of *The Revealer* and which would render him delighted to see that you are introduced to the elite of hoodlumry because that will be your stated fee for the pictures and he's a professional Scotsman."

"Shouldn't I have a reason for wanting to meet English muscle?" Eve wanted to know.

"You are a lady novelist. A condition like that can explain any difficulty."

Eve stood up and said she'd get started by calling Renaro and asking him to lunch if she could find a pair of iron pants. She walked into the bedroom and shut the door. Bourne slapped Jean Marie on the back as he crossed behind him to the kitchen saying, "Let's have some coffee." Jean Marie got up to follow him.

"Do you want me here for the meeting with Chern?" Jean Marie asked.

"Solidarity is in order."

"Then you want me here?"

"It's up to you. Some pretty rough stuff may be necessary."

"That is exactly how I feel."

"Then you'll be here?" Bourne handed him a steaming cup of black coffee.

"Yes. Five o'clock?"

"Right." Bourne walked back into the salon with his own cup of the stuff.

"I'll be here," Jean Marie said again. "Then I'm going to get a nine o'clock plane to Geneva. Then I'll swing through all of them to Rome."

"What happens after Rome?"

"Go straight to the hotel in Madrid. Then we'll pool what we've been able to find out and see what we'll want to do next."

"All right."

"Let Lalu know where you'll be staying."

"Yes." Jean Marie walked away and stared out at the little garden in the back. "You know something, Jim?"

88

"What's that?"

"I wasn't so upset yesterday. I mean those copies to me were no different from a few hundred other copies I had made and, after all, from my end I couldn't feel bitter or outraged the way you could because I couldn't get the sense of having been directly violated. You know? Like if I had been there, I could have felt that way. You know what I mean?" Bourne nodded. Jean Marie's eyes were troubled. "What I mean is, they shouldn't have killed that fellow. That's what has me so upset today."

Eve had lunch with Renaro upstairs at Le Tangage and let him pinch her twice, then bore down heavily with a salad fork when he tried for her thigh under the table. Neither of them spoke of the other's tactic. Renaro made a sound like an ancient Chinese as the fork dug into him. It started with a sound something like *Aaaiiii,* then segued into the first person pronoun beginning his next sentence. "Aaaaiiiii certainly will be most happy to help, Mrs. Bourne. Your husband and I have had a wonderful association."

She left for London on the four o'clock plane because of the seven o'clock appointment Renaro had made for her with Sam Johnston, editor of *The Revealer,* at the Ivy on West Street in London. Renaro had walked with her, chattering away, from the restaurant to the Hôtel California on Rue de Berri where he left her with Buchwald and Nolan, newspaper and airline peons respectively, who were at a chessboard in the bar, while he went off to telephone a pal on *The Revealer.* When the call and the arrangements had been completed he took her out to a cab, explaining the action. After they had been gone five minutes Nolan asked Buchwald who was the beautiful broad with Renaro. Buchwald looked up at him from the chessboard as though Nolan had been chewing cocoa leaves. "What beautiful broad?" he demanded querulously.

Lawyer Chern was prompt. He arrived at Bourne's at one minute to five o'clock, beaming. Bourne showed him into the long living room where Jean Marie sat glowering. Chern crossed to shake hands with him briskly, not noticing the dourness.

"Well! I take it you were able to find some Spanish

masters, hey?" He rubbed his hands and grinned some more.

"Sit down, Mr. Chern," Bourne suggested. Chern sat down and crossed his legs precisely, arranging the crease in his trousers with a certain degree of conscience.

"You got the paintings—or a painting?" Chern asked, directly this time.

"Yes."

"Good. Oh, that is good. On which list?"

"Schedule A."

"Oh, splendid! That is splendid."

He looked ingenuously from silent Jean Marie to silent Bourne. "May I see them?" They didn't answer right off so he added, "Oh would you prefer to wait until the formal transfer at the bank?"

Bourne cleared his throat nervously. "As a matter of fact, Mr. Chern, we *had* three of the paintings in our possession but at the very last moment before we were to have left Spain, they were stolen from us."

"I don't understand."

"I say we *had* three paintings listed on Schedule A but they were stolen from us just as we were leaving Spain."

"What is this?"

"Yes. They were."

"But how could that be? You mean you had the paintings but that you do not have them now?"

"Right."

"How could you wire me to rush to Paris then? I mean if there are no paintings to transfer how could you put me to this expense and inconvenience? I am a very busy man, Mr. Bourne. This is intolerable!"

"We were naturally chagrined at the loss of the paintings. In fact, we still feel quite ugly about the entire thing and we had hoped you could help us," Bourne said politely.

"Help you? How could I help you?" Chern's eyes narrowed.

"It is clear when one studies the matter that you and your client were the only people who knew that we would have the paintings, Mr. Chern."

"Are you accusing me?"

"If I haven't, I will, Mr. Chern. Be sure of that. And bring the tone of your voice down, please."

"Yes," Jean Marie agreed, "please modify the tone of your voice. It is quite unpleasant."

"I shall do more than that," Mr. Chern stated flatly. "I shall refuse to stay here and be insulted." He got up and strode across the room. As he passed Bourne, Bourne hit him with a heavy right hand. It was unexpected. Chern had no notion to prepare for it so he fell heavily into the fireplace with a clatter of brass andirons and lay there quite still. Bourne went to the low table in front of the sofa and saw to the tea saying, "I hate this kind of thing but because of motion pictures it is one of the few methods one can use, particularly in crime, to convince a man that one is in dead earnest."

"Ah, he's such a stuffed shirt anyway," Jean Marie said.

Bourne filled a cup for Jean Marie and one for himself. They sipped in silence until Chern stirred. He sat up, although still sprawled, rubbed his jaw, and stared at them with sort of an amazed fear. "You hit me," he said.

"There can be no doubt about that," Jean Marie said.

"Will you have some tea?" asked Bourne.

Chern got slowly and ungracefully to his feet. "Yes, thank you," he answered thickly. "I don't mind if I do." He sat down, reached for a napkin which he spread on his knee then accepted the teacup from Bourne.

"What is your client's name?" Bourne asked conversationally.

"I have no idea and that is the truth, Mr. Bourne. The bank contacted me on the client's behalf. I have never met the client and I have never known his name."

"That's too bad."

"What do you mean?"

"Mr. Chern, either you or your client have very neatly swindled us out of three hundred and thirty thousand dollars, which is shocking. We were deliberately sought out to do all of the painful work then we were fearfully duped. Only you and your client knew we were working on the assignment. I must keep repeating that. Furthermore, a professional criminal would not have stolen the paintings from us while they were still in Spain because of the peril involved in getting them out of Spain, if indeed they ever intended them to leave Spain. What the hell, Mr. Chern, did you expect us to just forget the whole thing? It's not only the three hundred and thirty thousand any more. We have been grossly insulted, and a man has been murdered."

Chern went white. "Murder? Who? Who was murdered?"

"The man who was employed to steal the paintings from us was murdered the following night, the night before last, according to a cable I received yesterday."

"My God, this is terrible!"

"It certainly is," Jean Marie said with bitterness.

"You must see our point," Bourne told Chern. "First off, we have to determine that you, yourself, were not the client. That could be, you know."

"It could be, but it isn't."

"Don't act. You could have designed the entire undertaking yourself, you could have organized Mr. Calbert and myself, as you did in truth, while pretending there was an imaginary client. With the plane connections between Zurich and Madrid you could have done all of the rest."

"The bank can establish the fallacy of that immediately, Mr. Bourne. They will tell you that I am not the client."

"I have never given you my present name, either. I gave you an entirely different name. The cable I sent to you yesterday was signed with the different name. Yet you call me by this name. And I was recognized in Madrid. Also my associate, Miss Lewis."

"I had to protect my client. I had you followed to Paris. I had your pictures taken as a matter of routine. It was my duty."

"You are now an accessory before and after the fact of murder, Mr. Chern."

"I am not, sir!"

"Will the bank reveal the name of your client?"

"I doubt that very much. In fact, we all know the answer is no. You know Swiss banks as well as I do."

"I agree that they would not reveal the name to me. But you are a lawyer practicing in Zurich. You must have done a good deal of work with the bank in the past because they chose you to represent this anonymous client so vitally interested in Spanish art."

"They know me, naturally."

"And I say that when you, a responsible Swiss attorney, go to a Swiss bank which has charged you with representing a principal who has turned out to be a thief and a murderer, they will tell you the name. They have a responsibility to you, Mr. Chern. And you have a responsibility to us."

92

"I am sorry, I cannot agree. I could go to the bank and I could talk myself blue in the face. They will tell me that I cannot charge a man I do not know, cannot identify, and cannot prove exists, with a murder and a theft. They will tell me that a bank cannot be concerned with the personal, peripheral activities of anyone."

"Do you agree that you have a responsibility to us?"

"I do not. As a legal agent I drew up an employment agreement between you and my client. At no time had I any responsibility to you."

"You agree that you have a responsibility to observe the letter of the agreement?"

"I do."

"When will my good will deposit of one hundred thousand Swiss francs be returned to me?"

"When I have filed with the bank and the bank has advised my client that you wish to withdraw from the project."

"I should imagine he would give me permission to withdraw. After all I was helpful to him."

"You read the agreement before you signed it."

"And do I get the remainder of the expense money?"

"I repeat, Mr. Bourne. You know the agreement. You have not delivered a painting. Therefore the remainder of the expense money will not be paid."

Bourne grinned sardonically: "That means your client has acquired a Velázquez, a Zubarán and a Greco—peak works of each master—for fourteen thousand two hundred and thirteen dollars and thirty-two cents."

"You have an excellent memory," Chern said in sincere praise.

"Yes." Bourne closed his eyes and rested for a moment.

"About forty-seven hundred dollars apiece," Jean Marie said. "Hah!"

"That is not my affair," Chern said stiffly.

"Then you must be persuaded to make it your affair," Bourne said.

Chern placed the teacup carefully on the low table. "How do you mean persuaded!" he asked anxiously.

"Exactly what you are thinking," Bourne answered gravely.

"But, Mr. Bourne, you *know* Swiss banks. The protection of the anonymity of their clients is their great hallmark."

"The protection of a murderer?"

93

"They have protected genocides! A Swiss bank is a building and vaults and locked books! Personalities do not exist for Swiss banks."

"How did you correspond with your client?"

"I wrote to the bank."

"To what name?"

"I wrote to Mr. Pierre Traumer referring to an account number. Return information would come through Mr. Traumer."

"What account number?"

Bourne stared at him until he took out a small book and read off the number which Bourne noted in his own small book.

"Have you been paid?" Bourne asked.

"Yes. I was also to have received a certain bonus if the paintings were any of those appearing on Schedule A."

"So you were cheated, too. Well—I can see that we could discuss this for many hours, even days, and not get anywhere," Bourne said, stolidly, getting up, and causing Jean Marie to notice again what a huge man he was. "Mr. Chern, I have decided to lock you up in the cellar of this house. There is a water tap down there, but——"

"No!" Chern made that word into a terrible sound. It was such an agonized no, such an hysterical objection that Bourne and Jean Marie exchanged quick glances, then Bourne continued, "I am going to keep you down there for three weeks or so and then we can——"

"Mr. Bourne, please! I beg you! I fear rats greatly. And darkness. I had an experience during the war. I have not always been a Swiss. I was in the German army. Mr. Bourne, no! You cannot! I can do nothing to help you. I know nothing. You must see that!" The words jammed and crowded out of him. He could not back away any farther because the wall was pressing him behind and Bourne towered in front of him. He began to talk unevenly again but the sound was cut off when Bourne's hand closed over his mouth; gripping cheeks, mouth and jaw in a huge vise, the other hand sinking into the material of his right trouser leg and lifting. Bourne carried him like a sack, out of the room. Chern's china-blue eyes stared at something an eternity away as he disappeared. Jean Marie, watching, shivered.

All Bourne would say in reference to the incident when

he returned from the cellar was, "I have never seen a man so afraid of the dark."

"I don't much like rats, myself," Jean Marie told him.

Mr. Sam Johnston, editor of *The Revealer*, turned out to be a jolly man who had a lovely time living, in fact, a lovely time just breathing. He had khaki hair and purple cheeks through which the tracery of tiny crimson veins could be seen. Eve fell quite in love with him within the first fifty seconds at the Ivy, a carved mahogany restaurant, even though he was some forty years older than she.

He liked the photographs Bourne had sent along, explaining how tired he got of the steady run of pornography which crossed his desk, pictures all right for English Sunday publication, but impossible to syndicate on the Continent or anywhere else in the world. He bubbled that the world rights to these photographs would bring a pretty packet, and that in three or four months she would indeed have a surprise on her hands when the first accountings from the sale of the pretty pictures came in. It was a confusing kind of an oration until she remembered Bourne's designation of the man as a professional Scotsman and realized that he was doing this delightful waltz to prevent her from thinking of making a claim for immediate payment. It was merely his way of determining whether she was amateur or professional.

She thought he would cause her to be beatified when she told him that she wanted no money at all for the pictures then thought she might be the death of him from sudden stroke when she said she had an entirely different kind of a fee in mind. He recovered his joy at once however when she explained that she merely wanted to meet a distinguished British criminal, through *The Revealer* staff, and that would be her fee.

He patted her hand and said that he could arrange everything. He told her that Merton, his crime editor, would grumble and carp at sharing his contacts with anyone, because, after all, criminals were Merton's profession and a wonderful living it had been for him for twenty-six years, what with the tastes of the English reading public, but he was sure he could arrange everything for her.

He did not ask her why she wanted to meet a leading English criminal. He took it for granted entirely that all

visiting young women would head directly for crimina
leaders upon entry into any country. He did ask whethe
she leaned more toward meeting a top murderer or a
champion thief. She told him that her preference was to mee
the very top echelon of highly organized general crime
professional, diversified crime which covered a wide area o
enterprise. He understood at once.

"I should think somebody like Jack Tense would be wha
you'd need," he said thoughtfully. "He's a leader. We've
serialized him four times in all. We've done 'Race Course
Gangs' with him. And a series on safe cracking, which he
did a lot of when he was first starting. Then we did six
instalments on 'King of British Crime Bar None' over hi
name, sort of an autobiography; then, of course, he's pub
lished his recommendations on juvenile delinquency with us.'

"He sounds exactly right!"

"Yes. I think he is."

"Would you say he had international connections?"

"Oh, definitely yes," said the jolly editor. "He was very
very big during the war. Spied for both sides and made a
fortune. Would have been knighted, except for his record."

"My!"

"You know, that might not make a half-bad series. 'Crime
Is An International Business,' I'd call it."

As it turned out, Mr. Merton did raise cain about being
asked to share a contact as lucrative and as important as
Jack Tense. First he claimed that Tense wouldn't talk to
anyone but him, which Mr. Johnston had characterized as
sheer nonsense. Then he offered someone named Albert
Nickels whom Mr. Johnston said was nothing but a common
slasher. Then he claimed Tense was out of the country, an
allegation which he didn't even bother to refute when he used
the excuse that Tense was working on a book and that if
he were to take time out to talk to every Tom, Dick, and
Judy who came along he'd never get the work finished. There
was more talk like that, but when he'd felt he'd made his
point he finally relented with the proviso that in the event
Eve ever wrote anything concerning the encounter it could
not be offered for sale without first being sent to Dorrance
Merton of *The Revealer* for first refusal and with the further
understanding that he had the full right to edit all of the copy

and to pre-empt any or all of it for British publication without payment to Eve.

"Would that include fiction?" Eve asked innocently, "or only material which would be of interest to your newspaper?"

"Most definitely fiction!" Mr. Merton exploded. "Any kind of fiction, first and foremost. My dear Sam, if this young woman has fiction in mind out of this proposed meeting with Tense I am afraid I will have to warn him of her intent."

"But it is not my intent. I merely asked. Besides I won't be with Mr. Tense for more than a half hour. After all, I couldn't get very much of a novel out of him in a half hour, now could I?"

"I don't see why not," Mr. Merton answered hotly. "I did his 'King of British Crime Bar None' and his recommendations for juvenile delinquency without seeing him at all."

In the end it was all straightened out with Eve agreeing to every condition Mr. Merton had made. Merton called Jack Tense and made an appointment with him for the Red Giant pub in Belgravia Mews for two o'clock the following afternoon. The Red Giant is a simple workingman's pub run by a handsome Irish fellow who sings when feeling spirited. It is difficult to reach because of the Jaguars and Bentleys which sprawl all over the Mews, driven there by the Red Giant's simple workingmen customers.

Eve sat behind a table in the pub with Jack Tense beside her and they both sipped ale. Tense was a slender middle-aged man with fearfully hard dark eyes and a wrenched pale mouth. He wore a Tattersall vest which held a heavy gold chain to match many of his teeth. His hair could have been arranged with machine tools. He did not believe a word of Eve's story about being a lady novelist, and in every way did his best to cooperate in no way at all, most indirectly and enigmatically.

At last, when it seemed as though he were going to leave in the next instant, she decided to be more explicit with him.

"All right, Mr. Tense. Here it is. We got away with three Spanish paintings in Madrid and we were hijacked the day the paintings were to leave the country to get the money."

He smiled for the first time. "That's more like it, ducks," he said, signaling for two more ales. "What kind of paintings?"

"Masters."

"Genuine?"

97

D

"Quite."

"Worth how much?"

"That depends on who bought them."

"I know."

"About fifty thousand quid," she lied.

"And now you need help."

"We're Americans. We don't know anybody in Spain who could run this down."

"Who's we?"

"My husband and I. Since we were hijacked in Spain they must be meant to stay in Spain because why should anyone take the risk of getting them out of the country when we were going to take them out anyhow and they knew it."

"You think they'll turn up in Spain then."

"If it was a professional job. Nobody would steal paintings worth this kind of money just to look at them. They have to sell them somewhere, and when they do move with them the Spanish underworld has to know about it."

"You're a smart girl figuring this out and getting to me like this."

"My husband has the brains."

"Why isn't he here?"

"He's running down some other leads."

"No duplication, I hope. One doesn't want two lads on the same errand."

"No duplication."

"I know the operation in Madrid and Barcelona. Very political-minded crooks, they are."

"I go to Paris tonight to meet my husband. I expect we'll be in Madrid by tomorrow night."

"I couldn't move that fast. One can't do these things by wire, you know."

"Of course you can."

"Well, maybe I can. But there'll be certain expenses involved."

"Of course."

"About a thousand pounds."

"Are you crazy? For sending one wire then going back to sleep? Come off it!"

"Of course if you knew how to do it yourself you could get it done for nothing, couldn't you?"

"Look, Mr. Tense——"

98

"Call me Jack. Everybody calls me Jack."

"Look, Jack—I'll make you an even better deal. How would you like to get five per cent of the fifty thousand quid we'll get when we pick the paintings up again?"

He laughed with genuine enjoyment. He had a high-pitched, womanly laugh. He was really greatly amused by her offer and at last had to dab at his eyes with a handkerchief. He didn't bother to answer her with words.

"We just don't have a thousand pounds," she said.

He didn't answer her but sipped at his ale still smiling warmly over that percentage offer.

"How much in cash?" she finally asked him. He grinned at her and patted the back of her hand. "I haven't laughed like that in years. How about dinner tonight?"

"I told you. I'm leaving for Paris."

"Change your plans. We can have dinner together at my place. Just the two of us. We'll have a fine time. Then, at breakfast tomorrow morning we can talk about a revised estimate on the fee."

"On whose fee?"

"Why, bless your heart! My fee!" He smiled at her with delighted eyes as fondly as if she had been his own.

"That's good. I'm glad you didn't have my fee figured at any thousand pounds." She glared at him so indignantly that he began that shrill laugh, which was not unpleasant, and which was even more boisterous this time. He pounded the mug on the table to emphasize his pleasure. When he calmed down at last he had to dab at his eyes again.

"What a chapter it would have made," he gasped, "if you had only come along. Merton would split. Intrigue, sex, the Spanish underworld, great masterpieces, oh, he'd love it, Merton would, and I think we ought to write it anyway. Look here. When you get back to Paris will you send me your photograph with a passionate inscription in your own writing. Something like—'To Jack, my masterpiece—You gave me my castles in Spain.' Then sign it with your full name. Any name."

"Why?" she said, genuinely puzzled.

"*The Revealer* will need illustrations when the chapter comes out. 'Crime Is My International Business'—how's that for a title?"

"My picture?"

"Well, I suppose not. Then send me any pretty girl's picture you happen to come across. That's not asking much, is it?"

"Plus how much cash to find me some friends in Spain?"

"Ah—make it fifty quid."

Jean Marie's inquiries drew blank after blank with dealer after dealer in country after country, but each one of them greatly admired the reproductions from the Dos Cortes catalogue. Out of the twenty-seven dealers he spoke to in seven countries, fourteen identified them as from the Dos Cortes collection, which would be a surprise to Bourne, although none of them had ever seen the originals. They told Jean Marie that if such paintings showed up they would surely advise him but that he would have to take his place in line with a few hundred others, and he would have to have more money than a bank, which depressed Jean Marie.

The dealers in Geneva, London, and Rome, once the original topic had been exhausted, which didn't take long, persuaded Jean Marie to allow them to represent his work in their markets. He had not traveled at all, being a Parisian, so he was extremely gratified to learn how famous he had become in the art trade. He made several promising arrangements. By the time he had left Ciampino for Madrid he had apportioned all of his leftover canvases to dealers in three cities on a consignment basis and life once again began to take on that rosy glow which had been tarnished by the news of the murder of Señor Elek.

Jean Marie reached Madrid two and a half days after Bourne and Eve; just in time for the party which the duchess gave to celebrate the arrival of the newlyweds.

To establish the shy ambiance of newlyweddism, Bourne had waited in Paris for Eve to return from London, and sent a cable to Cayetano in Barcelona which read: FEEL LIKE AWFUL SNEAK BUT MARRIED IN PARIS TODAY TO WONDERFUL GIRL RETURNING MADRID TOMORROW NOTICE YOUR SCHEDULE TAKES YOU VALENCIA THEN THREE DAYS PAUSE BEFORE JEREZ SO HOPE WE WILL SEE YOU BLANCA MADRID BEST BOURNE.

Chern had been a bit noisy what with pounding on the cellar door for more than an hour in the early evening, but it was a thick, ancient door and his voice could not be heard, just distant thuds which gradually weakened and then stopped altogether. Bourne had left a flashlight in there with him so that he could find his way to the water tap. He had decided that it would not be unhealthy not to give him any food; that conversely it might be very good for him to fast for a sixteen to twenty day period.

When Eve got to Paris the evening before the morning they left for Madrid, he decided not to mention Chern's presence in the cellar because it would disrupt her ease and since she never went near the cellar unless she were alone and looking for cognac, he decided that the whole thing would be better overlooked. She had asked him how productive the meeting with Chern had been and he had told her that it had yielded nothing, which was the truth, and that Chern had been indignant over having been brought to Paris on a wild-goose chase, which was strictly accurate as well.

Eve returned on a wave of triumph. The most shining result of her journey had been two very elegant French-women stopping her in the hall of the Savoy to ask her where she got her wonderful clothes; secondly she had accomplished her primary mission of establishing a crime cartel, and, in glorious addition, she had succeeded in finding a copy of Robert Graves' *Antigua, Penny, Puce* on Charing Cross Road.

She told Bourne it was a pity that he had formed such a rigid policy about refusing to fraternize with other criminals because Jack Tense had definitely been a Warner Brothers hoodlum by J. Arthur Rank. They had ended famous friends and he had driven her to the airport in a robin's egg blue Rolls almost as big as a Staten Island ferryboat. He was at work even then having a poll taken of London's fences big enough to handle a deal like three Spanish master canvases and he had assured her that he would jolly well know about it, and that she would be informed forthwith. Bourne became apprehensive. He had not rehearsed her on what to say for receiving follow-up information, but she reassured him blandly. Tense would contact her through the Spanish contact who was to reach her through the key desk of the Hotel Autentico which was just off the Calle de Toledo in Madrid, on the Calle de la Cava Baja. She told him proudly that the Spanish crime executive whom Tense had found for her was actually the board chairman of the most effective operation in Northern Spain, meaning all but Andalusia. His drop name would be Enrique López and he always appreciated it, Tense had said, if all exchanges, as far as operationally possible, could be done with innocuous notes through the key desk at the Autentico. Tense had guaranteed that no one could dispose of the paintings in the Spanish underworld without Señor López knowing about it, if López sent out the word that he wanted to know about it, which he most certainly would.

Bourne was as pleased with her as if she had won the Women's Singles at Wimbledon, but there was very little that she did which did not please him. If she had returned from London to report that it would not be possible to arrange for a Spanish contact he would have accepted that and would have made other arrangements, because part of his love for her was in the unending growth of the conviction that her judgment was impeccable and that her loyalty to him and to their life together an expanding thing of unmeasurable proportions.

They spent the evening at home. Bourne read and smiled over the Graves book. Chern remained utterly silent. Bourne had taken the precaution of shutting the two doors leading to the pantry which held the cellar door, but twice during the evening he had gone to the kitchen to pretend to fetch a drink of water and not a sound could be heard. Eve packed their trunk and their suitcases, darned socks and pottered generally wearing a breath-taking french-blue house coat over skin as though it were a Mother Hubbard. She seemed entirely oblivious of the effect her extraordinary figure produced in that slashed sheath until Bourne was forced to comment on the effect, to which she had replied, "Why don't you do something about it?" So he did, striking a decisive blow for Togetherness.

Later on, while he was back at his book and she back purring over her darning he reminded her that it was essential that she remember that they had been married that afternoon, because they would be entering Madrid as bride and groom. She nodded. He said he had known she wouldn't mind it, so he had had a new marriage certificate made so that the servants at the hotel could find it and spread the verification. She told him that marrying him had given her three lives and four identities, had transformed her into an active, exciting community of people which was something few women in the world had ever had and that she was grateful for it and

102

that she loved him and that she would always love him. He could not do any wrong with her. He was truth for her, which is what everyone seeks, she said.

For ten minutes or so he conjectured aloud as to whether or not Señor López could have been the man who had hijacked them. It seemed to be a thought which gave him comfort if only because it gave their villain a shape, and a place in space. Gradually he proved why that condition would be entirely unlikely. All at once she began to weep. She was sitting on the edge of a hassock when it started. She tried to stifle the sound. He didn't talk. He didn't ask why she was crying, knowing that she had an excellent reason to weep if she wept. After a while, it was over.

"I dread going back to Spain."

"Why?"

"I'm not sure why. I only know that there is something very wrong about this whole thing."

"It's the first time for you. There is always a strain the first time."

"We don't want those paintings if that man had to kill to get them."

"What man? We don't know it was a man."

"You know what I mean, Jim."

"Killing is a terrible thing," he said, "but people aren't to be feared just because they kill. Stupidity, not invincibility, makes a killer. He just didn't know what else to do. The murder of one man has no connection with the life or death of another."

Eve got up and went into the bathroom. He could hear the water running while she washed her eyes. She closed the bathroom door, then he heard water running from the shower. He went back to his book. After forty minutes or so she came out again wearing a pale blue nightgown and a pretty, filmy robe. She sat down opposite him and spoke in an even, friendly voice all of the thoughts she had been preparing and editing as she had bathed and perhaps for some time before that.

"Jim, you know I'm not advocating a return to government by women's intuition, don't you?"

"You can if you want to, there's nothing wrong with that."

"It's just that—well, for one thing there's the duchess."

"Yes?"

"I have to say this sometime so I'll say it now and get it out of the way. I can't accept the duchess's friendship. I don't like the feeling of hypocrisy. It makes me feel cheap and sick. We have exploited her and stolen from her."

He snorted. "It's about time you brought that up."

"Please, Jim, let me finish. There's Dr. Muñoz, too. I cannot be natural with a man whose trust we have used so that we could steal with less risk from people who trusted us because Dr. Muñoz trusted us. And your friend, Cayetano Jiminez; your very dear friend, and you his, and yet we stole from the woman most important to him." She leaned back in the chair.

"Finished?"

"Yes."

"I am not reproaching you."

"I understand. I was not reproaching you. I only said I would rather not go to Spain and face those people."

"Eve, what business was your father in?"

"He was an insurance broker."

"You've carried different kinds of insurance, haven't you?"

"Yes. Of course."

"For example—did you ever carry a floater policy?"

"Yes."

"Ever lose anything after you had the policy?"

"Oh, a camera, once, I think."

"How much was it carried for in the policy?"

"I don't remember for sure. About two hundred dollars. Why?"

"You reported the loss right away?"

"Yes."

"When did the insurance company pay you?"

"Why—about five months later."

"How much did they pay you?"

"They wanted to replace the camera with another used camera, but I decided I'd take the cash. I think they paid me ninety-five dollars."

"Not two hundred dollars?"

"Well, you see it was a used camera. It had depreciated."

"But when you bought the policy you thought the camera was insured for two hundred dollars? It said in the policy that the camera was insured for two hundred dollars?"

"Yes."

"Your father was able to face you though?"

"I don't understand."

"What business was your grandfather in?"

"Jim, what are you trying to prove?"

He held up his hand for an instant. "In a minute. Tell me."

"Well, he's been in the restaurant business for nearly fifty years. He owns the Huxley chain."

Jim exploded with a guffaw then subsided into a grin. "You mean the chain that bought all of that meat during rationing without giving up any rationing stamps while tens of thousands of hospital cases needed meat like that and couldn't get it, and old people and all sorts of folks like that."

She dropped her eyes and flushed.

"He was still able to face his family and friends and customers after the newspapers had finished disgracing him, wasn't he, honey? But he was exactly like everyone else in this world. There is an area of business and an area for friends. They cannot overlap. If they were to overlap it would be like putting Saint Francis d'Assisi in charge of the Roman games; it just couldn't work. It would be too moral, too Christian for our times."

He pulled his chair over closer to her and took both of her hands in his hands. "Good heavens, there are thousands and thousands of examples wherein the area of business must be separated from the social, fraternal world. There is hardly a business in existence today which does not practice cheating and dishonesty; and if we are to accept degrees of dishonesty, then we must make allowances for honest criminality, like yours and mine. There is absolutely no doubt about our dishonesty, no shadings or degrees, so there may be no possible doubt about our complete honesty, either."

He pulled her head to his and kissed her with rough passion, then held her head to his with his enormous hands.

"Business is a form of hunting. It's shooting for the pot in modern terms, isn't it? It one's dearest friends walk across one's hunting grounds they can get shot, can't they? Furthermore, for all we know, the duchess or Cayetano or Victoriano Muñoz may have been our hijacker. They are far more likely candidates than Señor López or Lawyer Chern. The duchess has perfectly good copies hanging now in her ancestral halls. She, before anyone else, could offer

the originals for sale because she is the ultimate authenti-
cator. Victoriano Muñoz is art-crazy and on Spanish art
is paranoically insane. Cayetano, for all I know, might be a
big-time thief for the thrill of it, he does everything else
dangerously. But forget that. You have been trained to
view crime as immoral. I have been forced to the conclusion
that almost all business is immoral, and certainly all religion.
I lived with that for a long time and then I moved over into
criminal operations and lived with that for a long time and
I say that there is no right and there is no wrong and there
is no shape nor beginning nor ending. Where does the definition for stealing illegally end and the definition for stealing
legally begin? I am you and you are me and what can we do
for the salvation of each other? That is all that matters.
Stealing canvas and paint and wood from the stone wall of
one of the nine houses of the Duchess of Dos Cortes is not an
unkindness nor a sin, but to turn my back on her, to run and
hide because of that canvas and paint or for you, my wife,
to say that you cannot face her and accept her friendship
would be an unkindness and therefore a sin because of all
the things men give and take from one another there is only
one sin which is punishable and that is unkindness."

"How long will we stay in Spain?"

"I have not decided."

"Must we stay on until you find out who stole the paintings from us?"

"Those paintings represent an enormous amount of
money."

"Must you always think first and last about money?"

"It is you who always thinks of money!" He flared up,
his face reddening. It was an intolerable area.

"If the money represented by the paintings leads us on
and on into other things, perhaps into violent things, will
you allow that there is the possibility of one more sin exist-
ing, the sin of the love of money, my learned Cardinal?"

"Sarcasm is not necessary," he said sullenly.

"Answer the question."

"Which part of the question?"

"Both parts."

"I have already been led to a violent thing."

"What?"

"It is a sin, yes."

106

"How many sins will make you safe or get you enough money, then?"

"Eve, listen to me. The lease on the hotel has just under ninety days to run. We will go to Spain and I will try to find the paintings and if I don't find them by the time the lease has expired we will leave Spain or we will stay in Spain as you elect, but I will have finished with those paintings. Is that acceptable?"

"I'll accept it because I have to."

"All right, then."

"Jim, why did you accept this 'new' sin as a sin so readily? You contradicted yourself."

He was puzzled. "What new sin."

"This new sin of violence," she said.

"New sin?" He snorted. "Violence is only childish unkindness." He got to his feet. "Come on. Get dressed. This is our last night in Paris for God knows how long. Let's walk up to Fouquet's and watch the world go by."

The town house of the Duquesa de Dos Cortes overlooked El Retiro where God sat on a park bench under the shade trees fashioning houseflies and dreaming his terrible dreams. The duchess insisted upon giving a gala party in honor of the wedding, three days before, of her friends, Mr. and Mrs. James Wallace Bourne. Seventeen servants polished glasses, roasted birds, shined silver, skated on rags over waxen floors, chilled wine, dampened down cigars, sang horrendous flamenco, and were happier than they had been for years and years because the duque was dead, dead, dead, and the soul of their darling duchess had seemed to soar.

The duchess and Cayetano had two days off from the bulls. They were en route from Valencia to Jerez de la Frontera where he would fight in two days' time. They had drifted on a cloud from Medinaceli to Zaragoza to Barcelona to Valencia and now, six bulls later, they were absolutely at the top of their form, dedicating, commemorating and entertaining their dear friends, en route to more of love and art in the south.

The duchess didn't talk to many people any more and many people didn't talk to the duchess as a result of her revolutionary activities on behalf of the king, her formation of the cooperatives, her contempt for widowhood, her flaunting of a bullfighter and a variety of other reasons so that the guests who were assembled were very pleasant company indeed.

Among those present were Jean Marie Calbert, the brilliant new French painter who had been discovered at Bourne's hotel and invited; Cayetano had invited his protégé, a dashing, young novillero named Victoriano Roger who was a lawyer but who was too sensible to stay with that trade, Cayetano said; the other Victoriano, Dr. Muñoz, Marqués de Villalba, arrived early wearing a black tweed dinner jacket with satin lapels and a peony in his buttonhole. He explained the flower, which he had had bred for boutonniere use, to the bride telling her how he absolutely adored color and underscoring that she could be sure that he was not one of those who would attempt the weight, in color tones, of a fleshy peony against a background of mohair or silk, which was why his jacket was made of tweed. He told her severely that a fitness in some things lays the road to a fitness in all things, then he asked her how long Bourne had been her lover before they had married, if they were truly married. She told him, somewhat expressionlessly, that they were really brother and sister which caused him to suck air sharply between his clenched mouselike teeth then to compliment her on her sense of the decadent. She yawned widely, looked down at him, then turned away to find Jim. His face got very red.

Because Monsieur Calbert had accepted, Representative and Mrs. Pickett had been invited, for new, important painters of any nation made the congressman happy and Mrs. Pickett was sure to enjoy the cold wine. Sir Kenneth Danvers, the famous British photomicrographer of the insect world, danced through the evening with Miss Doris Spriggs, a beautiful insect cataloguer, singing two or three hundred songs of all nations. At one o'clock in the morning a troupe of gypsies swept in with guitars and firecracker shoes and iron palms and a flamenco was started from which the night never recovered, losing joy to the day.

Off and on the population of the party swelled and shrank and swelled again from fourteen to sixty-four people, levelling off at about nineteen, counting Mrs. Pickett who really should have been counted out; all of whom had Dublin thirsts and the glazed intensity of Glaswegians on New Year's Eve, which is enough party spirit to strike terror to the heart of Tamerlane. The fact that four-fifths of the guests were Spanish helped this effect immeasurably. They drew energy from the music, from the gypsies who were acting as though they had just awakened from a rest of seven months of hibernation, and from an undoubted tonic called *sangria*, which went on to become the people's choice, made up of red wine, champagne and cognac with a little lemon for the teeth.

Neither Bourne nor Eve could ever remember such a perfect party where everyone seemed endowed with love and joy, after Dr. Muñoz had taken the Picketts home, and everything that had happened to all of them so worth celebrating.

Before the flamenquistas had arrived, Dr. Muñoz took Bourne aside and told him that he had been put off for the last time, that he understood things like marriages and journeys to Paris had to take precedence over the mere requests of one's old friends, but that he would not take one more postponement of Bourne's visit to his new flat. Surely Bourne would bring Mrs. Bourne, as delightful and beautiful a young woman as he had ever met. Bourne would. And perhaps he would bring the stimulating French painter, Monsieur Calbert, as it was quite possible that the Picketts would drop by. Bourne would. Very well then. The following Saturday, which was three days away, at seven o'clock. Dr. Muñoz had a lot of new things which made him very proud of Spanish art and he wanted Bourne's forthright opinion, no hemming and hawing, about each one of them because, as Bourne well knew, he valued his opinion very highly.

When he broke the news of the engagement to Eve the following day she kicked a hatbox clear across the room in a vile temper. Bourne told her that these were the things one did, that was all, and that he was sure that if they ever got back to the States she could get even through invitations from some of her friends.

The duchess approved of Eve exceedingly, and Eve approved of the duchess even more than that. Eve was a smashing hit with everyone there, but the duchess was particularly pleased with her because she had lived for five days in dread since they had received Bourne's cable: to her Bourne had been the most discriminating of men so it seemed like some kind of justice that he would select something bovine and shrill to marry. The duchess ended the evening as she had started it, hugging Jim and hugging Eve. And she told them that because they were all together, she and Cayetano, Bourne and Eve, at the moment of greatest happiness for each of them and all of them, they would be friends for the rest of their days, sharing all that there was to share. She became very serious. She took Eve's hand, then put Jim's great hand on top of that, then Cayetano's, then her own at the summit. She looked from face to face in the soft light of dawn which had been the legacy of the wonderful night, her eyes shining then running over with tears. She took her own hand off the top of the pyramid pact then kissed Cayetano's hand, then Jim's hand, then Eve's hand with the humility of a great lady.

Time never cheats the great. Time is living and life is only time in motion, fast or slow. The duchess simply did not bother to make the unimportant moves, so that when she chose to move she endowed that space in time with greatness. Eve felt exalted and cleansed. Bourne felt stronger and more tender. Cayetano, who was the truest receptacle of all the duchess would ever feel again, felt loosed among angels.

That night, Mr. Pickett wrote a letter to Arthur Turkus Danielson, the hard-hitting editor of *Art, Things and You,* the dominating art weekly in the United States and one which even Mr. Pickett had only cracked twice in a long life given to art then over a matter of eight-year intervals. He wrote very slowly. Every word would count with Danielson and nothing got by him. What a man, Mr. Pickett thought with a sideways wag of his head at the thought. He had discovered Blore in a junkshop, ten years after the painter's sad death, and had found immortality for him also beginning with that day. He had come out fearlessly against the shockingly dark backgrounds utilized by Titian and by so doing had driven down the values of all Titians throughout the world by over three per cent and the losses had stayed in that cellar for over six months. Mr. Pickett could not be sure how much Danielson knew about the painters of Spain, past and present, because Danielson was not a man who would talk to contributors face-to-face, preferring the letter method, but from the notes they had exchanged Mr. Pickett knew the editor's comprehension of the subject to be more than sound, in fact in several instances almost echoing two of Mr. Pickett's books on the Iberian world. "Dear Mr. Danielson," he wrote. "In a setting suggesting the middle ages I have made a discovery which is destined to thrill the world. It is one which I humbly offer to *Art, Things and You* for final evaluation and stentorian announcement. If that sentence seems vainglorious to you, Mr. Danielson, then what I am about to set down will shatter and stun. In a canvas to be called I hope, from this day forward, The Pickett Troilus, I have discovered the presence of two great brushes and two great palettes. I will frustrate you no longer. One canvas, two immortal masters. One painting, two great painters. You are saying, 'Who are these painters? What is this painting?' I am sure, sir. Upon my twenty-seven years of authority in the field of Iberian art, as author of three books which teach the art of Spain in the schools, colleges, universities and ateliers of the Western world, I pledge to you that the superb Trolius, the property of the Duchess de Dos Cortes, was painted by Diego Rodríguez da Silva y Velázquez *and* Peter Paul Rubens!" Mr. Pickett paused again, baffled and annoyed over whether it was Peter Paul or Paul Peter, chewing in the end of his pen. "One moment, sir!" he wrote on. "Within this communication you will have found a stout brown envelope containing three photographic slides. Project these slides, Mr. Danielson, and when you have seen with your own eyes what I have claimed, then return to this letter and read my documentation which will make the art story of the year." Mr. Pickett took a fresh piece of paper and, setting down as a heading the words THE PICKETT TROILUS, he began to write his monograph.

Mrs. Pickett called out from the bed, "How long are you going to sit there with the light on, you fat son-of-a-bitch? Are you writing to some sailor? Why the hell couldn't I have stayed at that party if all you were going to do was come home here and write all night with the light on, for Christ's sake!"

111

"In a minute, darling girl. In a minute."

"In a minute, my foot!"

"Have a drink, sweetheart. I'll be right there."

"A drink of what, you silly bastard?"

"There's a pint of bourbon in the night table drawer."

"Oh. Thank you, dearest."

The message left by Señor López with the key man at the Hotel Autentico read: NADA. VUELVA USTED DENTRO DE DOS SEMANAS LOPEZ, in heavy, black crayon on the back of a sheet from a German desk calendar of 1943. Señor López had made his canvass and had nothing to report. Tense was efficient. López wanted her back in two weeks. López was thorough. When she did go back in two weeks, Eve decided, she would leave a note asking to see him just to satisfy herself on what he had done so that Jack Tense could say he had earned the fifty pounds and because she had promised a written report to Tense so that Mr. Merton would have more material to fill out the chapter. Before she had left him, Tense had agreed that if "Crime Is My International Business" were ever sold to films Glynis Johns would play her part. "You'd make three of Glynis Johns," he said with deepest admiration, but he'd agreed.

It was a beautiful day so she decided to walk home. Thinking about what a sweet, old thing Jack Tense was she stopped off at SEPU, Madrid's five and ten cent store equivalent on the Avenida de José Antonio and bought a picture of a stereotypically beautiful, middle-European film actress with leaded eyelids and a mouth like a broken doughnut, for five pesetas. At the General Post Office she autographed the portrait for Tense writing *For Jack, who gave me Spain, with the memory of fire, Marianne Pickett,* then slipped it into the stout envelope and mailed it, care of *The Revealer,* London.

Bourne had been mistaken about Dr. Muñoz' new apartment being on Calle Fortuny. It was on the extension of Fortuny, Calle Amador de los Ríos, directly opposite The Jockey, a formidable restaurant.

Dr. Muñoz, looking shorter than usual and altogether less attractive to all of them, was bubbling with good spirits when he met them at the door of the apartment which took up the entire top floor, waving the houseman away then shooing the three guests ahead of him to a very small, very comfortably furnished bar with enormously broad and high windows, high enough to overlook the Paseo de la Castellana and out toward Las Ventas.

En route from the main floor to the bar he kept starting them and stopping them to look at a piece of carving here or a small painting there. Everything was done in breathtaking good taste, which for some reason, probably for reasons of personal revulsion for the doctor, they found surprising.

"For a man who is always crying poverty you live pretty well, old boy," Bourne said, trying for some fake essence of camaraderie.

"My dear boy," Muñoz said, "when I refer to poverty, naturally I speak of relative poverty. After all, if Goya hadn't cost my family almost everything there would have been very few people richer than I in all of Europe. What will you have, Mrs. Bourne?"

"Sherry, please." Eve had perched herself on a high bar stool at the end of the bar near the window. The two men leaned on their elbows upon the bar between Eve and the doorway under the immediate scrutiny of the cat Montes who faced them from a place among the bottles, while the host stood ready for anything behind the bar, a corkscrew in his hand.

"Sherry? Come, come, come, Mrs. Bourne. That won't do at all. I have put in a huge stock of whiskeys for you. Rare bottles like bourbon which only Congressman Pickett could possibly hope to get in Spain. Impossible to get. Very American. Won't you have a glass of bourbon?"

"Sherry, please." He seemed shot down in mid-air. He swallowed hard then addressed Jean Marie, pouring a small glass of sherry for Eve as he did.

"M'sieu Calbert? Quinquina? Amer Picon? St. Raphael?"

"Byrrh, I think."

"Oh." He looked distressed. "I find I don't have any Byrrh. What a pity! And I was being so very French when I prepared all this for you." He looked at Jean Marie hatefully, his face like a little fist, his pencil-line mustache like the seam in a dark, clenched glove.

"I'll take a Dubonnet then," Jean Marie said pleasantly.

"A Dubonnet?"

"Dubonnet is very French," Jean Marie said.

"Of course it is. But I haven't put it in."

"Then give me water. Your Madrid water is marvellous."

"Thank you. But you are sure you won't have a Quinquina, Amer Picon, or St. Raphael?"

"No, thank you. Water will be fine." Dr. Muñoz poured
the water. His hand shook slightly.

"Jim," he said briskly. "What will you have?"

"Anything, Victoriano. Anything at all."

"No, no. Jim! Please I insist! You must have what you
want. Perhaps some vodka. The Jockey gets me Iron
Curtain vodka from Poland. Marvellous stuff. Or Drambuie.
Oh my, yes. There's something *really* smooth."

"You should do television commercials, Dr. Muñoz," Eve
said.

"Pardon?"

"I said you have a wonderful voice for television."

"Ah. Well! Thank you, my dear. Now then, Jim. What
will it be?"

"Vodka, I think. I'll try vodka with a little ice." Dr.
Muñoz had that in front of him in a jiffy. Eve asked him
what he was going to have. He explained that he didn't
drink or smoke then flashed his puerile smile. They all settled
down to awkward talk.

"I've read a great deal about your work, M'sieu Calbert.
Wonderful things."

"Thank you, sir."

"I don't paint myself, but I do pride myself that I am
something of a judge of painting. I hope you concur, Jim?"

"Indeed you are, Victoriano."

"Are you interested in art, Mrs. Bourne?"

"Avidly."

"By the way," Bourne put in, "you mentioned some new
pieces you'd picked up. We're looking forward keenly to
seeing them."

"Muchly," Eve said.

"Later. I shall be certainly honored to show them to you
later. A friend is stopping by for just a moment to pick up a
book. He won't stay but a minute, then we shan't be interrupted."

"What are your new pieces, doctor?" Jean Marie asked sleepily.

"Paintings. Spanish paintings. I'm really so anxious for Jim to see them before I show them to Mr. Pickett."

"Mr. Pickett?"

"Mr. Pickett is *the* authority on Spanish art," Bourne told him. "He was at the party the other night."

Jean Marie turned to Eve. "Am I thinking of the same man?"

"Probably."

Jean Marie shrugged. "Then I guess we were talking about French art. But that's not his field."

"Are you enjoying Madrid, Mrs. Bourne?" Dr. Muñoz darted away with the conversational ball.

"Very much."

"Is it your first trip?"

"No. No, I was a newspaperwoman here, Dr. Muñoz. I learned Spanish here."

"Well! You speak Spanish!" He spoke to the others generally. "We really should speak Spanish, you know." Dr. Muñoz spoke perfect English with a marked British accent. "Do you speak Spanish, M'sieu Calbert?"

"After a fashion. My French is much better."

Dr. Muñoz looked at him strangely for that remark. "Naturally," he said, then, brightening, exclaimed, "Well, why not?"

"Why not what?" asked Jean Marie.

"Why not speak French?" He spoke to Eve. "Do you speak French, Mrs. Bourne?"

"As you wish, doctor. Any language at all."

He bit his lower lip and blood rushed into his face again. He was saved by the doorbell. He excused himself, in French, and hurried out of the room.

"I just may slug this cat," Eve said.

"He is certainly awful," Jean Marie acknowledged. "My God, Jim, how long do we have to stay here?"

"We leave after we admire his new pictures," Bourne said, sounding a little sore. "And I do mean admire. Get with it, Eve, for Christ's sake. It's a job. You've had worse jobs."

"I'm sorry, darling. I will. I can't get started but I will."

They heard Muñoz approaching with his guest, shooing him along. He very nearly pushed the man into the bar. The guest happened to be the chief of customs at Barajas Airport

115

who took one look at Eve then smiled as if he had invented false teeth. "Señorita Quinn!" he cried, pronouncing it Keen. "What a wonderful surprise!"

Dr. Muñoz was covered with happy confusion. "You know each other? That is marvelous!" They were all speaking Spanish now. That is, those who could speak.

"When did you return?" the chief asked Eve and Dr. Muñoz said as if it were a witty joke, "Señora Bourne, may I present Colonel Gómez, chief of customs at our Barajas Airport?"

Bourne looked suddenly at Eve. She nodded slightly.

"Señora Bourne! Well! That was sudden, wasn't it?"

Eve moved in hurriedly, but very smoothly. "You must have been my good luck token, Colonel. He isn't Spanish but he lives in Spain." She hastened to explain almost everything to her husband. "The colonel and I have sort of a secret, darling. But I *can* tell you that we were discussing marriage and its blessings exactly ten days ago, the day before I met you."

"Secrets, hey?" Bourne managed to boom that out, as square as a box.

The colonel laughed with delight. "Nothing serious, I can assure you, sir. But charming. Very, very charming."

Dr. Muñoz crowded Jean Marie up to the colonel, holding him firmly by the elbow, with Jean Marie unobtrusively fighting to get free. "Colonel, this is M'sieu Jean Marie Calbert, a very promising French painter." Jean Marie glared at him.

The two men shook hands, while Dr. Muñoz hastened behind the bar to fetch Colonel Gómez a sherry. The colonel beamed on the newlyweds. "So you met in Paris nine days ago. Oh, I like that very much. What a successful ending to a tour of Europe."

"To a tour of Spain," Eve corrected him gently, then, holding her glass high, "To Spain," she said as the colonel received his glass from Dr. Muñoz. Everyone but the marqués drank the toast because he didn't drink, but he stood at flag attention and looked very silly.

"How did you two happen to meet?" Dr. Muñoz asked. "After all, my colonel, you are very much of a bridegroom yourself." They all had a nice, false, hollow laugh over that.

116

"Señora Bourne came to Spain with a very good copy of a Velázquez which I was permitted to register."

"Really a good copy?" Muñoz asked. Jean Marie glared at him.

"I don't mind telling you," said the colonel, "that it was so good we not only checked this young lady's routing in Spain, but we made it a point to call the owner of the original before Señora Bourne was allowed to leave the country." Jean Marie beamed. Bourne sat up a little straighter. "A mere formality, I assure you, señora. I like to do my job well. No offense meant."

"I forgive you," said Eve smiling charmingly. Her forehead was moist all along her hairline. Beads of sweat, sweat like the sweat in the taxi on the way to the airport when she had last seen the colonel, began to form from all around her ears. She could not look down at her dress, afraid it would be marked with those enormous circular splotches again.

"That good a copy of Velázquez? That's marvelous. Where did you get it, Mrs. Bourne?" Muñoz asked.

"In Paris," she managed to say.

"They have some excellent copyists in the Rue de Seine," Bourne said quickly.

"As a matter of fact," Eve said, "that's just where I got it."

"Will you be staying in Madrid, Señora Bourne?" the colonel asked.

"I live here now," she answered. "My husband is in business in Madrid."

"I've been here for over three years," Bourne said.

They chatted about housing and the climate for ten minutes or so and Eve's fear gradually subsided, although she could not have told what she feared. The colonel then bid everyone farewell, telling them how pleasant the surprise had been and pleading with Eve that they must all arrange to meet really soon. Eve took his wife's telephone number. The colonel asked her permission to tell his wife the secret. Eve managed to blush and nod virginally. The colonel left.

"A very good man," Dr. Muñoz said. "Regular tiger about the law, though. Relentless and all that." He had gone back to English. Bourne insisted harshly that they be allowed to see the doctor's new acquisitions as they had promised Nicky Storich that they would stop by for cocktails and time was running along.

117

"Very well," the marqués said. "I understand. Though I'll wager you won't want to run right along after you've seen these beauties."

They followed him out of the room, turning right into the corridor. Dr. Muñoz fumbled with keys then unlocked the tall, exquisitely carved double doors which were bracketed by dim lights at the end of the windowless hall, saying, "This is a very thrilling moment for me." As both doors opened they could see the brilliant sunlight streaming into the room through the large windows, but Dr. Muñoz leaned into the room and snapped on a light switch. He stood back then and permitted the others to precede him into the room.

They moved forward, or shuffled in boredom, then they came up short, perhaps four paces within the large, long room, staring and shocked. There were three brilliantly illuminated paintings on the walls. They were the Zurbarán, the Velázquez and the Greek from the Dos Cortes collection. Eve made a sound far back in her throat and slipped limply to the floor.

Dr. Muñoz fired a troubled exclamation and scurried from the room. Bourne sat on the floor and held Eve's head in his lap, rubbing her wrists as a woodman would start a fire with two sticks. Jean Marie stood open-mouth and motionless, staring at the pictures. The only sound was the metallic tapping of the marqués' little shoes as they hit the tiled floor of the corridor rapidly. He hastened back into the room carrying a bowl of tiny ice cubes, cubes which looked small enough to have been frozen in a honeycomb.

Bourne thanked Muñoz formally, scooped up a handful of ice and pressed it into the back of Eve's neck. Her eyelids moved, then opened. She was staring directly at Dr. Muñoz.

"Did you have the paintings taken from us?" she asked.

"Yes."

"Did you kill Señor Elek, too?"

"I had to," Dr. Muñoz answered. "You've no idea what a little adventurer that man turned out to be. He tried to blackmail me. It was all too fantastic and preposterous. Would you like a cognac?"

"Yes, please."

Dr. Muñoz darted out of the room again and rushed down the hall like Carroll's White Rabbit on his way to a prefrontal lobotomy. Eve said, "You've come to a murderer, at last, Jim." He looked down at her, but did not answer.

"What do we do now?" Jean Marie asked. "This man is so bland he almost makes me feel as though I should thank him for showing us his beautiful paintings."

Bourne signaled Jean Marie to help them to their feet. He sat Eve in a chair as though she were a rag doll then walked to the window to stare sullenly out at the Plaza de Colón and the National Library. Eve looked at his back anxiously then to Jean Marie who shrugged, then to Bourne's back again.

Muñoz nipped into the room carrying a silver tray holding four balloon glasses, at shoulder height on the tips of his fingers like a comedy waiter in a revue sketch, carrying a bottle of French cognac in the other hand. He set the tray down on the low table, which was ringed by comfortable chairs, and began to pour the cognac saying, "Please sit down. Be comfortable. We have a great deal to talk about."

Jean Marie sat down first and took up a glass. He held it in both hands, inhaling the fumes. Bourne did not move, or turn away from the window. The back of his neck was turkey-red. Eve sat with great care; the way a very fragile, old lady would sit. Her face was startlingly pale. She stared past Muñoz at her husband's back, knowing that he was fighting to hold his temper and that he could not trust himself to speak.

The large room was furnished in the Moorish style; with a lot of reds, a lot of leather, and a lot of cushions. The three paintings were magnificently displayed at exactly the proper eye-level, each one flooded with bright, frame-contained light from a ceiling source. Jean Marie seemed to find it difficult to stop staring at them. Muñoz seemed to gain warm pleasure from watching him stare.

"There are paintings one can build a room around," he said blandly, wiping the spittle from the left corner of his mouth, "and there are paintings one can build a house around. These, one builds one's life around."

Jean Marie made an involuntary sound, not unlike a snort of contempt, but did not speak in answer. No one spoke, but Muñoz accepted their sullenness. He made himself merry and livened them by so doing. "And so we meet again, M'sieu Calbert?" Bourne spun around.

"Again?"

119

"We undertook several art transactions in Paris during the German occupation," the marqués explained.

Jean Marie spoke up immediately. "I never knew his name until today. Or that he was Spanish. Who asks questions like that? He hired me to copy. I copied. He paid." Bourne turned away again and stared out of the window.

"Dear friends," Muñoz orated, "please listen to me. If you believe that I have brought you here to crow over you, you are wrong. Please try to remember that whereas you had planned your robbery for a mere year or two, I have been planning mine for my entire life. Please forgive me for causing you such disappointment. I really mean that. I have asked you here because I need your help."

"My God, what a man!" Jean Marie said. "He does us out of all of the French francs in Spain then wants a little favor!"

Bourne turned again. He tried to talk but his voice sounded strange and choked. He coughed and started again. His voice wasn't normal yet, but he had control of himself. "I want a letter to go to Traumer Frères now, instructing them to release my escrow funds."

"I will," Muñoz answered. "At once."

"Now! Now, goddammit!" Bourne shouted. "We've been cheated out of a profit on this thing so far, but I'll be goddammed if we'll operate it at a loss!"

"As you wish," the doctor said. He rose and moved out of the room, rapidly but with dignity. "I will write it now and you may mail it. You are entirely right."

"Are you going to bargain with him, Jim?" Eve's voice was strident. "He's a murderer. Let him haggle things out with the police."

"He's also crazy," Jean Marie said.

"Shut up, both of you! We've been cheated out of a lot of money and nearly three years of work. I cannot and I will not be a chump for this foolish man. And don't talk to me about murder! We can't bring Elek back and there'll be time enough after we dispose of these paintings."

"You heard him say he killed Señor Elek!"

"Eve. Please. This is no time for a hysterical argument about morals. We'll hear what he has to say and we'll move when I decide we know what we're doing."

"Jim, we've come to a murder. By our direct actions we have made a murder possible. We don't want to be dragged any farther. I'm not hysterical. You're looking at me and you know it. That's what sin is, Jim. If we go any farther doors will close all around us and we'll never get out."

Dr. Muñoz came back into the room carrying a sheet of letter paper and an envelope. He crossed the room and handed the note to Jim. "Having a family argument?" he asked. "Does not mama love papa?"

Eve looked at him as though he were a swarm of locusts, seen through glass. "We were discussing my suggestion that you be turned over to the police to be tried for murder, you creep," she explained with a reasonable voice.

The marqués, in his turn, snorted in contempt. "Is that letter satisfactory?" he asked Bourne. Bourne nodded, folded it, inserted it into the envelope and sealed it.

"What do you want, Victoriano?" he asked.

"I feel that with all this bold talk about giving me to the police perhaps it would be best if I first tell you what I have and then what I want. It will put an entirely different complexion on things. You must know that I have a case against each of you. For M'sieu Calbert's sake, I want to point out that I have a case against his wife."

"One moment, my friend. My wife has nothing to do with any of this."

"I have, of course, an open-and-shut case against your wife, Jaime. Colonel Gómez is a dedicated civil servant who has befriended your wife to be cruelly deceived by her. Beyond that single instance, she has violated many points of the Spanish law and I am certain that I could arrange to keep her here, in prison, for thirty or more years."

Eve's face was bloodless, but she was lively in her disapproval of the doctor. "I don't think you can operate that cool. You think you have this on us. We have a murder on you."

"No you have not, Mrs. Bourne. I can prove. You cannot. And as far as M'sieu Calbert is concerned, well! There is no doubt there. He will be greatly admired by the court and the press for the quality of his work but, if I choose, he will die in prison in Spain." He grinned at Bourne sillily. "And as for you. Ho-ho! Do you know that I have infra-red photographs of you in the very act of stealing these paintings from Dos Cortes? You'll need two lives to give to the Spanish government."

121

"I suppose you've considered the rather distressing thought that if you turn us in," Bourne said, "you'll have to give up these paintings and that we will most certainly implicate you."

"Of course I've considered that."

"And?"

"Jaime, I am a grandee of Spain, in Spain. You are foreigners and in your case, Jaime, and your wife's, I contend that when your passports and other papers are placed under the scrutiny of your own Federal Bureau of Investigation, with whom our government works on a daily basis, they will prove to be spurious. Oh, there is an entire chain of circumstances which would render you helpless to involve me," he crowed.

He poured cognac into Eve's glass, into Jean Marie's and into his own. Bourne had not touched his.

"Don't you see?" he continued. "I am not trying to bluff you. Look here. I am ready to go much farther to convince you. I see it this way: No one likes me so anyone would believe very nearly anything about me if I were charged by an unimpeachable source." He held up his finger. "I said, *unimpeachable*. Also, everyone knows the lengths I would pursue to possess a certain masterpiece of Spanish painting because I am considered crazy on the subject of my family and the wrongs which were done them. Well, perhaps they are right. I care about masterpieces of Spanish painting because they are one of the ancient rights and possessions of my ancient family which I, myself, have the power to restore. Therefore, and here at last I am getting to the point, if you force me to turn you over to the police and to the state— and I do not want that—I will so do this in a manner which will reveal as the leader of the band of thieves who have stolen these three paintings, so that we may be tried together and so that I may testify against all of us to insure maximum sentences for each of us, including your wife, M'sieu Calbert, when our absolutely certain conviction is secured. That is how serious I am."

By the time he had finished, Bourne's face and Jean Marie's face were glistening with sweat. Jean Marie's hand also trembled as he leaned forward to take the bottle to the glass again. Eve sat erectly looking like a classical ivory carving. Muñoz fumbled with his wrist-watch band, which seemed a bit tight.

"Victoriano," Bourne said, leaning forward as though he were selling insurance, "let's start at the beginning. I'd like to get everything as clear as possible."

"By all means, Jaime. You must."

Bourne spoke deliberately, with some effort, thinking of each word just before he chose to speak it. "You wanted these paintings for what you considered overpowering reasons. You have known Jean Marie for some time. It is possible that he told you of my plans for Spain."

"Think it through, my friend," Jean Marie said. "This one doesn't have much money. Your way I could have made more money than any of us have ever seen."

"In any event, I haven't seen or communicated with the man since nineteen forty-three," Dr. Muñoz said.

"All right," Bourne acknowledged. "In any event you found out what I wanted to do just about eighteen months ago, because that was just about when you began to seek me out after the weekly concerts at the Royal Palace to discuss art."

"Yes. About the time you began to meet Madrid society."

"And to discuss art with you."

"I am still astonished at what you know and feel about our art."

"Yes," Bourne answered. "And more so now than ever. Once you knew we had started, and I assume that you knew this in detail from Lawyer Chern, it was simple to keep a watch on his studio and to know the dates of the transfer of the copies and by which frontier. Because you knew which copies had been executed, you knew which originals would be stolen and where they were hung. Each time I took an original from Dos Cortes you were among the guests."

"That is all quite true, as you say it," Dr. Muñoz told him. "However, I was rather proud of the way I wangled the great Homer Quarles Pickett to Dos Cortes to give his solemn judgment on all three copies never realizing he would exceed himself to the point of finding a bit of Rubens in the Velázquez."

"That was really droll," Jean Marie said. "My God. That was really comical."

"Killing Señor Elek—now that was *really* droll, if you appreciate the droll," Eve said. The marqués pretended not to have heard her, but he flushed. He decided he had to

123

answer her. "I killed him because he gave me reason to kill him. He tried to blackmail me."

"You would have killed him anyway," she said with a harsh voice.

He stared at her. His face hardened. "That is true," he said.

"I don't want to discuss that now," Bourne said loftily. "You have the paintings. The dream of your life hangs in a locked room. The affair is finished. There are no loose ends. There are only blank walls for those of us whom you have cheated while the others do not even know that their property has been stolen. The risk has been run, the deed is done. You not only have your paintings, but you are safe."

"And all done rather cleverly I thought."

"Indeed, cleverly. Brilliantly."

"It is good of you to say that."

"Not at all. Then—not because of vanity but as a part of the plan from its beginnings, because you telephoned me to come here for tea not forty minutes after my wife had left for the airport thinking she had the three paintings in that tube. Why? That is incomprehensible to me."

"Entirely. I have never been so baffled," Jean Marie said. "Did you really think you could not be killed and the paintings taken from you?"

"You hear, Jim?" Eve asked. "A theoretical murderer is here with us. We are making progress as I said we would. Theory and practice. Interest is the trigger. Cause and effect."

"I cannot agree with you less, M'sieu Calbert," Dr. Muñoz interrupted enthusiastically. "You people are not suited for killing. You are all thought, no passion. You would have contempt for a man who would kill for anything he could just as well steal if he put his mind to it. Am I not right, Jaime?"

"I haven't thought about it."

"I think you are wrong," Jean Marie said slowly. "There is a lot of money involved here. I think I could kill you if I had a plan. And I may get a plan."

"No, no," the marqués rejoined good-naturedly. "Your wife is implicated here. You don't know whether or not I would have given some lawyer or some banker the entire story with all the evidence in a sealed envelope and that sort of thing to be opened in the event of my unnatural death et cetera, et cetera. And, furthermore, you will never see these paintings

124

again. They will come down when you leave today and where they go no one but I will know and that is not one of the things anyone could make me reveal. No, I am master here and Mrs. Bourne knew it long before you men knew it. There is nothing you can do but study hard what I am about to instruct you."

"What do you want us to do?" Bourne asked Muñoz.

"There is one more painting I must have."

"Ah."

"I do this for my family. Please see that. It is not for myself. I am content to live here within a mile of the greatest Spanish painters in the world, but the injustice done to my family is another matter entirely. We go back beyond Pedro of Aragon. We are a very old and extremely important line which has been cruelly and unnecessarily humiliated."

"What is the other painting?"

"I must tell you in my way." He paused to insure against interruptions. "If it may be said that my family fell from their high places on any particular date, that day must be the second of May in eighteen hundred and eight. On the second of May, the Spanish people decided to resist the forces of Marshal Murat, the Napoleonic commander, and under him Colonel Grouchy and Captain LaGrange. We, my family that is, had decided to cast our lot with Napoleon and his brother which we did only, I most solemnly assure you, to help Spain. You know what Godoy was. Ferdinand was as stupid as his father and as vicious as his mother. We were rich and powerful. We needed no privileges Napoleon could give. What we did was a deeply patriotic thing. I have been over every single document again and again which attests to every motivation of my family at that time, until my head swims. What we did we did to bring Spain to Europe." He was pleading with them for understanding and for retro-active approval. "We did what we did to make Spain a modern country, abreast or ahead in the march of new commerce, of new expansion, of new bases of world power and if it would have meant accelerating our country's dying, with the rest of the world, it would have accelerated her living far more."

Bourne seemed to have encountered an enormous immovable fact; a huge, melon-shaped, rank-smelling, pulpy fact which he could neither climb over nor walk around; yet a fact so dismaying that he could not believe it as it stood before him, not merely overwhelming him, but threatening him.

"Do you mean," he asked Muñoz slowly, "are you telling us that, is this painting which you say you must have, could that painting be Goya's 'Dos de Mayo,' which is now in the Museo de Pinturas del Prado?" Bourne had taken each word out of his disbelief as deliberately as a housewife unpacks a paper sack filled with grocery items.

"Mon dieu! Get the handcuffs!" Jean Marie moaned.

Dr. Muñoz acknowledged neither the dazed question nor the outburst. He went on. "The painter Goya was the key factor in my family's humiliation. He had become a police informer for Ferdinand. He continued as an informer for Joseph Bonaparte. When the French left he became an informer for Arthur Wellesley."

"Arthur Wellesley?" Jean Marie asked blankly.

"The English general. Later the Duke of Wellington. Crashing bore."

"Oh. Yes." Jean Marie stared at Eve and shrugged.

"When Ferdinand returned to the Spanish throne, Goya had used up all trust," Muñoz said. He had informed on all sides for all sides. The king moved to prosecute him. He bargained to save himself with a dossier he claimed to have assembled on my family. A deal was made. They let him leave the country and he went to die in Bordeaux and my family was stripped."

"Victoriano?"

"Yes, Jaime?"

"Are you going to tell me that you want Goya's 'The Second of May'?"

"Yes." Muñoz nodded. He was calm, reasonable, even judicious in his manner.

"The painting is in the Prado."

"I know that."

"It is eight feet high and eleven feet wide."

"I certainly know the painting. You surely aren't going to give me a short talk on Goya's painting, are you?"

"It can be done. That's what I am giving you this short talk on. It is impossible to do. Do you understand me? Victoriano, it cannot be done."

"Jaime, please! You haven't even thought about it."

126

"I don't have to think about it!"

Eve put her hand on her husband's forearm. "Jim, don't bargain. He's crazy and he's a murderer, and there's nothing he can do to us."

"What do you mean, Eve?" Jean Marie said quickly.

"We'll tie him up and be out of the country before he can find a traffic cop. And when his servants untie him he'll think twice about throwing away these paintings."

"She's right, Jim," Jean Marie said to Bourne. Bourne looked calmly at Muñoz for the answer.

"She's right as far as she goes, M'sieu Calbert," Dr. Muñoz said patiently, "but to give you a convincing demonstration of my sincerity, I'll tell you what I'll do. I'll have your wife arrested tonight by the French police, which I had intended to do all along if any of you attempted to leave the country."

"I tell you to leave my wife out of this, Muñoz. If a minute of my wife's life is disturbed I will make you very sorry."

"But, sir!" Dr. Muñoz protested. "That will be too late! Your wife will already be in prison. I have been able to arrange with some very important friends in our Ministry of Security here to ask the Sureté in Paris to detain Madame Calbert for questioning by Spanish experts with regard to other mysteries caused by the disappearance of great pieces of French art twelve years ago."

Jean Marie sat quietly, everyone watching him. He gulped the cognac and poured more. He turned toward Bourne, staring at his chest, not his eyes or face and said, "Tell your wife to stop her talking. Is she trying to hound Lalu? We must do what he says and stop all this talking and talking. It is *my* wife who is theatened."

Everyone seemed to stand at once. Dr. Muñoz said, "You run along now. I know you are tired and that you have a great deal of thinking to do. Please call upon me for any help I can possibly give, and let's have lunch very soon to talk things over." He shepherded them along the corridor. "Don't do anything foolish, I implore you. Spanish law is inordinately severe on charges like these. I did not exaggerate when I outlined my frank interest and intentions. Who wants to die, I ask you that? Particularly in a dungeon."

He slipped ahead of them and opened the front door. They passed out of the apartment silently. They did not wait for the lift to come, but descended the stairs, passing from his view.

The duchess was splendid naked in a square, sunny room in a graceful building which watched the sea from the outskirts of Jerez de la Frontera. She had a red rose in her blondined hair, her feet were propped up on the bedstead at the foot of the bed and she was laughing like an alto saxophone. She was the incarnation of the great tart of all the world; generous, lewd, safe, irresistible and unresisting. Cayetano sprawled across the bed, as naked as money, talking rapidly and interrupting his own talk with grins, flashes of teeth, and bolts and bursts of laughter. He shifted his position, north by northeast, bracketing her beautiful head with his elbows and staring deep, deep down into her eyes. She stopped laughing but she still smiled; for carnal is as carnal does. It was a different smile and it sent electrical jolts up into her belly. Her eyes closed to slits until just glitter came out of them. She stared up at him, not speaking, and dared him to do again what he thought he had not had the strength to do. Her breasts which had waited so long for all of this and more of this and more than this, for the over and over and over and over of the lifetime of this and more than this, pushed up at him. He stopped grinning. She stopped smiling. Her mouth loosened from its moorings in propriety and fell open. She made a glorious sound.

The next evening Jean Marie walked the short distance from the hotel to the General Post Office and called Lalu in Paris from a telephone booth because his experience with all past telephone operators in hotels had convinced him that it would be madness to expect privacy in a telephone conversation from one's own room. He spoke his especially soft, musical French into the telephone within the booth and told Lalu that Bourne's friend had liked his work very well and that he had offered so much money for a portrait of himself that Jean Marie had decided to stay on in Madrid to paint it. No, he would not say how much over the telephone. He would be in Madrid for at least a month. The weather was beautiful. It was not Paris, but it was an enchanting city Even she would love it. He liked it himself. He wanted her to come to Madrid. Never mind the expense! Lalu, darling!

Stop fretting about the expense! Little cabbage, the fee for this one portrait would be the biggest fee he had ever made. Little mouse, the tour of the European dealers had been an enormous success, as he had written to her. *Sacré bleu!* He wanted her to have a change. *Alors!* Would she visit her aunt in Bayonne if she would not come to Madrid? Would she please stop this constant resistance about expense? He should not have telephoned? A letter would have said what he had wanted to say much better and be much, much cheaper? All right! That was enough! He was no longer suggesting, he was commanding. She would get out of Paris before tomorrow evening and she would visit her aunt in Bayonne until he told her to go back to Paris. No, nothing more! He hung up feeling very proud of her. He had a wife who looked after his substance. No frivolous waster, his Lalu, like others such as Eve Bourne with her two new dresses since arriving in Madrid, having a trunk full of perfectly good dresses as it was. Lalu knew the value of money.

He squared his shoulders and made his way out of the building, then crossed to sit upon the *ramblas* to drink a coffee and watch the lively crowds; not as lively as in Paris, but very lively; and the pretty girls, who while not as pretty as the girls in Paris, were very pretty. They floated past like noisy flowers talking harshly and incessantly from their rifled Spanish throats, some with happiness like a newly struck match in their faces, others busy upon the deep study of their own pride in its visible extension. They walked their backs, shoulders, throats, chins and eyebrows as the people of other nations might walk their dogs or children for a short while through a soft, warm and gentling evening which shuffled a packet of endless hours and dealt them out toward the next day. The incessant and harsh voices of the women, the rudeness of the trolley bells, the shrill repetition of the word *lotería* over and over, like identical lush flowers upon invisible wallpaper, the boasting horns of the valorous cars, the rake and rapping of the men's high, hard heels upon the pavement, and the endless, multiple octaves of talk, talk, talk upon his ears soothed Jean Marie, who was very much a city man, and more and more allowed him to shift the new problem presented by Dr. Muñoz to Bourne. Jean Marie explained himself to himself as only a student of what could be seen and felt. Bourne was the thinker. Bourne was the

129

E

man in the present who coped with the future, but he was irritable at having begun to think of Muñoz again. It bothered him. It spoiled the evening.

At long last, made possible by rehearsals of a lifetime in sidewalk cafés, he finished the tiny cup of coffee and crossed the Paseo de Calvo Sotelo to walk slowly up the medium hill of Calle Alcala. When he reached the hotel he found Bourne far back in the corner of the room marked American Bar, sitting at a table and sipping on a whiskey. Jean Marie sat down beside him, motioning the waiter away.

"You figuring everything out?" he asked.

"I was thinking how much I hate to be handled like an amateur, not to say a chump. The risks are so heavy in this business that it is an absolute law that the price has to be right."

"Can the painting be stolen?"

"I think so. I must think more about it."

"You think now he will pay us to get the Goya for him?"

"He wants that Goya more than salvation. As you saw he is not less than insane in that area. No matter how much he threatens, I'm not going to do this piece of work for nothing." He worked on the whiskey for a moment. "We'll wait a few days then we'll talk with Victoriano some more. We're not being unreasonable, you know. Right is right, and he's got to be made to see that."

"See what?"

"We are entitled to an equity in this transaction! He thinks we can get the Goya. And maybe we can. I won't say yes, I won't say no, but I will say absolutely to the man who will put his name on the dotted line and guarantee a fair fee for our labour and for the risk we will run."

"Sign? He'll never sign. What are you talking about?"

"He wants the Goya so much that he won't move on any threats if I tell him we can get it. He'll listen to reason. If we get him that Goya I want those three paintings back, free and clear. That's what we came to Spain to get and that's what we're going to get."

"I think he'll agree," Jean Marie said. "I feel that the way you feel it."

"Yes. I do, too."

"And you know what else I think? I think after we get those three paintings back that he should be killed. I know

130

you're against that kind of thing, and for that matter, so am I, of course. But he's unpredictable because he's crazy. We don't want to have to try to go through life expecting that one to drop police on us from every rooftop. Seriously, Jim. I think he should be killed."

"Yes," Bourne said. "I do, too."

The next morning Eve was awake and out of bed when Bourne opened his eyes in the calamine blue room with sharp white carpets and the doric-formed, lemon-chrome drapes which stood as frivolous, tall sentinels on either side of an enormous opera-pink bed. Months before, awaiting Eve's arrival, Bourne had had the room redone down to matchboxes. Jean Marie had composed the colors, Bourne had allotted the spatial elements and the over-all effect reduced Eve's size to the size she had cherished since she had been a child, to the daintiest, most feminine, and helpless illusion of the sometimes useful, most times useless ancient illusion of a woman. When viewed by the chambermaid the bed seemed as big as a badminton court, but when their large frames lay across it, the bed seemed a normal size. Bourne was as big as a mausoleum and he had always maintained that on Olympus the cupids would have played handball up against her fine behind.

Eve sat at a severely practical dove-white table containing just about as much blue as the breath of frost, writing with a ball-point pen which was one end of the world's most vulgar, mail-order, long, white, furry feather, a wedding present from two nuns to whom she had once loaned five thousand lira at an airport in Milan after they had learned they had left their purses in Turino.

Bourne felt himself being pulled out of the hopelessly deep well of delayed sleep by a rope of light and sound which was fastened tightly around his forehead.

"Whatta you doing?" Bourne asked thickly.

"Writing to Jack Tense."

"Wha'?"

"It's only fair that I call him off. And I've done a note for Señor López."

"You're right." He swung himself awake, getting his legs out of the bed and his torso upright. His face looked like a used dumpling. It was squashed and bloated and seamed

131

in all of the places where it should not have been. It wasn't so much that he looked old. He looked sick. "I couldn't sleep," he said, as though apologizing for this new face which he had not yet seen himself.

"I know," she said, and went on writing.

"Whatta you mean, you know? You slept like a snake inna warm pail."

She didn't answer. Suddenly he decided not to brook her not answering. "Answer me I asked you a question. What the hell is the matter with you?"

She turned rapidly in her chair and moved out of it at him crying, "What the hell is the matter with YOU, you foolish, doomed man?" She came out so fast, like a good, rough fighter from a corner of the ring, that he flinched at the ferocity of her action because he had hardly heard her words. Her ferocity contrasted markedly with the way, in spite of her destructive manner, her terrible anger and her near hysteria, she could keep her voice down, and the way, in spite of his demonstrated anxiety, he could maintain the low level of his own voice when he answered. It was the empty politeness of people who had died more slowly than other people by living their lives in hotels.

Her voice clawed at him. "Don't tell me you can't sleep! You will not dare to tell me you can't sleep you grotesque son-of-a-bitch because you know why you can't sleep and you've become too spineless to change it." The words were bitter and her voice had pain that was worse than pain because it contained the realization that she could not respect the man she must love, and that of the two, from man to woman, respect was the greater need.

"What's the matter, baby? I don't understand," he said, but he understood. He knew that the unit of contempt had displaced the unit of regard and that only he could make the exchange again.

"Let's talk some more about you with your dowdy clichés like 'honest dishonesty' and your father the immoral money-changer. Does your father work with murderers?"

"Now, just a minute, Eve. I've spent nearly three years on this project and I have a ri——"

"You invested a lot of money, too, didn't you?"

"You're goddam right I invested money. A helluva lot of money and I have a ri——"

132

"You fool. Bosh to you, you square!" She turned her back on him and went back to her chair, back to the desk. She put her face in her hands. "You know, Jim, I don't know what to do. I can't stay here. I can't go. I thought I understood you. I really believed that the only way you could find some kind of dignity for your starving, resentful soul was by stealing. I—I believed that and I thought you believed it. And I thought I understood you when you talked about no right and no wrong and the unlikely possibilities of relative morality and all the jargon like that, the way you talk. But you're just a cheap merchant with his hand in the till. You're just your father's son grubbing out money and keeping a double set of books who would even bargain with a murderer for an edge."

He forgot the hotel whisper. "What the hell do you think this is, Gilbert and Sullivan? *The Pirates of Penzance?* Would you enjoy thirty years in prison?" he shouted.

"Don't shout. You know better. Then use your head. You're a smart man, Jim. You're one of the smartest men anyone ever knew. Use your head. Get Lalu to Switzerland or to Greece. One cable will do that. Hire a ship or a rowboat at Malaga, and we'll be in Tangier. Then we'll join Lalu wherever she is or Jean Marie will join her, and we'll go anywhere we want to go in the world. This man can't touch us, outside Spain, and he'd be afraid to touch us inside Spain. If I can think of that to get away, do you possibly think you can possibly tell me that you didn't think of it?"

"Yeah. I thought of it."

"Then who is singing the *Pirates of Penzance*? Who crumbles then under the fear of thirty years in a Spanish prison?"

"Ahhhh, for Christ's sake, Eve," he said. "I'm entitled to get those three paintings back. I worked and I have to get paid, one way or another. I don't blame you for feeling queasy. You're a woman. I will never blame you if you want to get out, and I'll get you out and you're right, he can't touch you once you get out. And now that we have everything right out in the open, I want you to go. I couldn't bear it if anything happened to you."

"What do you think is happening to me now, my darling? You look at me and tell me that I'm upset and that you cannot understand why I am upset. You understand! But

133

you understand money more! You need money more than you need me and that is what is happening to me." She slammed her hand down upon the top of the desk. "Muñoz killed Elek. He killed! He threw a knife into the throat of Señor Elek and he stopped his life with it. But you are not intimidated, you are fearless. You cannot be pulled down and stained by this; you are aloof. You want your merchandise returned to you, and what does it matter if there is a little blood on it?" She stared at him piteously. "Jim, Jim, Jim!"

She went to him and clutched his upper arms, her body away from him, the top of her head pressed into his chest. She did not weep but keened tonelessly over the death of her joy.

Cayetano Jiminez sat, drinking beer and recalling paradise, in the citron sunlight on the terrace of the outdoor café opposite the great mosque-synagogue-church in Córdoba, talking earnestly with the manager of his career from the beginning, a rumpled, bald, sad man who had managed his late uncle, killed at Santander the year before Cayetano had started.

"A lifetime is enough to give any profession," he said gravely. "You cannot tell me I have not spent all my life with the bulls."

"No."

"Also, you have my two brothers. Curro looks very good. Better than I did at nineteen."

"Yes."

"I want to get married. It is my right."

"Yes."

"This is no business for married men, especially happily married men."

"No."

"I took my *alternativa* in Madrid during San Isidro eleven years ago, so it is the neat and complete thing to finish in Madrid during San Isidro, so give me your blessing."

"You have my blessing wherever you go," the sad, small man answered, "but you belong with the bulls."

Bourne paid the cab driver then walked unhurriedly from

the pavement of the Paseo del Prado to the columned entrance of the Museo de Pinturas. He nodded to the guard at the door on entering and walked directly forward to the staircase which ascended to a point opposite the entrance to the Sala Velázquez one floor above.

As he moved slowly along he remembered the pleasant shock which had engulfed him on the day when he had seen the Prado for the first time. It had been like the discovery of a new world. It was the perfect hall of paintings; not perhaps so inclusive of all schools of painting as the National Gallery in London or the Louvre in Paris, he thought, but in its own distinctive way, as a gallery of superb paintings brought together by a group of collectors with individual taste, it had no equal in the world. It had begun in the eighteenth century as a museum of natural history. Maria Isabella of Braganza, queen to Ferdinand VII, had turned it into a gallery for royal pictures. Gradually the great paintings of Spain had been added from the Royal Palace in Madrid, from the Escorial and the Casita del Principe, then La Granja, Aranjuez, and in legacies from the great families.

Bourne entered the Sala Goya; octagon in shape, well-lit from the ceiling and smelling of furniture polish and floor wax. He stopped walking in front of "The Second of May," but did not look at it until he had checked the stop watch in his hand and had noted the ensuing time against a column of figures representing other time trials over the same course. He stared up at the enormous canvas; eight feet high by eleven feet wide; with its six dead showing and hundreds to come, with its action of desperation ; knives into French Mamelukes, split Zouave over white horse's rump, baggy red pants and turbans against peasants who needed haircuts badly, only two men's blood and one horse's blood focusing the composition of the picture. He turned about and walked away from it the way he had come, nodding, in passing, at two guards as he went.

At the curb of the Paseo del Prado he consulted his stop watch again, set down the numbers on a sheet of paper in his small, clear hand, then hailed a taxi.

There was no more light in that room than there is in a womb. Eve sat up in the great bed and, groping, took Bourne by the shoulders in her powerful hands, and shook him.

135

"Jim! Stop it! Stop it!" She took a clump of his hair and wrenched it, then shook his head with it.

"Aaaah!" He bolted up. "Eve! My God! What is it?" She snapped on the light. He stared around the room. She slapped him with her full force across the mouth and knocked him back into the candy-pink linen which covered the headboard. "What did you do to Chern?" she demanded to know. "You tell me, Jim! What did you do to Chern?"

"I-I-I——" He let the words fall back into his throat. His right hand pushed at the dirty stubble on his chin. It gripped his cheeks to keep his face from falling apart. His eyes were not nice to look at. She hit him again.

"What did you do to Chern?"

She had hit him very hard. He seemed dazed.

"Talk to me! Tell me!" Her voice was brutally harsh.

"I locked him in the cellar at Boccador."

"You locked——"

"You remember we were talking in the Tuileries? We were talking about what we should do to make Elek talk?"

"When did you lock him in?"

"I don't know. I can't—the day you went to London. Yes. I can't get him out. Muñoz. They'll take Lalu."

"We've got to get him out."

"I can't think any more. Jean Marie is a painter and he isn't supposed to think, but he thinks. I'm the planner, but you think of everything. If I could sleep, I could think."

"He's been locked in for nine days."

"Nine days."

"What are you going to do?"

"I can't figure. I'm in a fog. I can't figure it."

"We've got to get him out."

"I know. But I can't get him out. I can't call some casual friend. I can't call the police. Lalu is absolutely no good for this."

"Why can't you call the police?"

"He has plenty of water. Nine days isn't much only he didn't do anything and he shouldn't be in there."

"We've got to get him out. She hit him on the thigh with her balled fist with all the force she could muster, with a vicious, punishing, chopping club. He grunted sharply, then to increase his own sense of pain and her own tangible anxiety he said, "He was terribly frightened when I put him in there.

136

Something happened to him in the war. Rats and the dark. I never heard a man so scared as Chern. I got him down there and he——" Bourne could not allow himself to finish the sentence, watching his wife's face.

"Call the Paris police," she snapped.

"Now, just a minute, Eve——"

"Are you looking for murder? If you keep looking you'll find it."

"The police will trace the call. An international call is the easiest thing for them."

"Ah, Jim. You'll tell them that you're the managing director of this hotel. You'll say that you've just opened a letter which could not have been left by accident on your desk in your office at this hotel and which tells of a man being locked in the cellar at 97 Rue du Boccador in Apartment 3 for nine days without food. They'll ask you your name and you'll tell them your name and anything else they want to know except what you have to conceal."

"They'll have us by the throat with the apartment. My God, Eve, we live there."

"The apartment is in my name. In my old true name. That girl has disappeared and no one living can find her, including herself."

"Do you think Chern is going to dust off his clothes, thank the police for their services and refuse to divulge how he happened to be shut up there? The Paris police know their business. They'll climb him until he'll be happy to tell them how he got there."

"Chern lives, like you, for money."

"Eve, for crissake——"

"Shut up. Chern won't tell them the time or press any charge or admit they found him there until he presses you to find out how much money you have for him to make up for the inconvenience."

"Eve, please, don't say things like——"

"Don't touch me, you money-simple merchant. Call the French police!"

Bourne didn't move, then breathing heavily he leaned across the huge bed and took up the telephone.

Teresita, the night hotel operator, answered. He told her to call the Palais de Justice in Paris, office of the chief of detectives. The recurring lack of sleep, his wife's savage grief,

137

the hollowness he felt inside himself, the indulgence of searching across a continent for an instrument of contrition, all must have dulled him because he forgot the lesson he would have taken and underscored under any other circumstances; the lesson contained in his betrayal by his senior, executive employee, Señor Elek.

Teresita told him she would call Paris immediately, then call him right back. He hung up to wait; to sit on the side of the bed, his back to Eve, his bearlike hulk hunched over in despair.

Teresita, having disconnected with Bourne, immediately dialed 34-78-92 which was the telephone at the new apartment of Dr. Muñoz. The marqués answered with the first ring. Teresita explained what Señor Bourne had told her to do. Mr. Muñor thanked her sincerely for the service she had done and told her that when she awoke the following evening to go to work a handsome reward would be awaiting her in her mother's hands. She suggested that if he preferred to leave the reward in her mother's hands would he please seal it in an envelope, or if it was all the same to him would he leave such an envelope with the waiter, Jorge, at the Café Werba on the Calle de Bravo Murillo. He agreed with pleasure he said, and would attend the waiter, Jorge. She thanked him. Dr. Muñoz then suggested that she call him again in ten minutes then ring Señor Bourne as though she had called Paris then connect him with Señor Bourne. She told she would do that. He reminded her to be sure to show the long-distance call in her log, in fact later on in the morning perhaps she could call Paris so that Paris charges would eventually come through. She said she would.

Teresita waited ten minutes, then she called Dr. Muñoz, then she rang Señor Bourne.

Bourne spoke into the phone using his middle belly-tone voice, a timbre employed throughout the world by public relations experts and confidence men. *"'Allo?"*

"I have your Paris call, Señor Bourne."

"Thank you."

"'Allo?" Dr. Muñoz came on, using a high-pitched voice. *"Le palais de justice ici."*

"'Allo?" Bourne answered. *"Je veux vous faire savoir un crime, s'il vous plaît."*

"Un moment, m'sieu," Dr. Muñoz replied. He put his hand

138

over the telephone mouthpiece and sat very still in the over-stuffed chair, looking very strange under his cloth mustache cultivator. The cat Montes tried to walk across the taut telephone wire from the receiver to Muñoz' ear, but he fell, grabbing at the wire with his forepaws, swinging like a trapezist for a moment then dropping to the floor. Muñoz counted to fifteen, took the telephone up towards his face again, then reconsidered and counted up to forty-five, then released his hand from the mouthpiece and spoke, this time in a deeper voice.

He came on as Detective Sergeant Orcel. Bourne, with his good citizen's voice, dutifully reported the case. Dr. Muñoz took down his full name and address with grave grunts, utilizing a real pencil, real paper, and real writing. He thanked Bourne. Bourne thanked him. He told Bourne, *"Je serai sans doute forcé de vous déranger encore, mais alors peut-être pas,"* and hung up. Then Bourne hung up. He felt greatly relieved. After a little while he slept for the first time in many nights. His wife held a small towel to her face as she lay on her side along the edge of the bed as she wept silently. She would not let him find a pillow stained with her tears.

Early the following afternoon, upon the long, dark-wood Moorish table of Dr. Muñoz, Bourne unrolled the large sheets of architectural paper which contained his own precise diagrams of the Sala Goya, the Goya floor at the Prado, and the street floor leading to the Paseo. His jacket was off, his sleeves were rolled up; a pencil was stuck behind his ear. He seemed too large to be a grocery clerk, too immaculate to be a shipping-room boy, so he most resembled an advertising agency account executive ready to pitch. Dr. Muñoz helped this illusion with his air of stifled eagerness, as though he were a prospective client whose packaged twenty-five-cent cancer inducer was about to be forced upon a nation. The cat Montes, a taffy sculpture, sat erectly and listened with the expression of a junior executive who will go far. Bourne sat on the corner of the table, swinging one leg, boyishly and informally, facing Muñoz, friendly and relaxed. The marqués gave him his complete attention, pince-nez glittering. It was a moment replete with tranquilizers.

"I've given your whole proposition a good deal of

139

thought, Victoriano," Bourne said judiciously, "and I personally think it makes one helluva lot of sense to talk about the fee structure before we get down to the brass tacks of talking about the job." He spoke English because he felt much more solid and square in English.

"The fee?" Muñoz was baffled. "The fee is your freedom."

"I know that you know that we have the necessary know-how, Victoriano," Bourne said. "And I tell you this flatly. We will not undertake the project without payment. I mean that."

Muñoz shrugged. "I could never pay your prices, Jaime. I'm not a poor man but I'm not in your class either."

"That remains to be seen. And I'd like to point out that no matter how you look at it the risks on this kind of thing are very great. I mean that."

"If you are saying that you might decide not to do this job because the fee wasn't right, believe me, my friend, the risks would be one bloody awful lot greater," the marqués said earnestly. "Prison must be a godawful thing for men of our age."

"Do you honestly think we should take these risks after three years of time and money and other risk without any fee whatsoever?"

"I haven't expressed myself either way."

"Do you honestly think you are giving us incentive to solve this problem by refusing to discuss a fair fee?"

"Refuse? We are discussing it!"

"All right. Name the fee."

"I'm not a storekeeper. Tell me your fee!"

"I want the three paintings of Dos Cortes. That's my fee."

The marqués shrugged. "Do you think you can get the Goya?"

"If certain peripheral problems are met. And in comparison to my central problem, these little marginal problems are nothing."

"Let me hear your plan to get the Goya then I will answer you regarding the fee."

"That wouldn't be good business. The plan is everything. Almost anyone could take the Goya if they had this plan."

Dr. Muñoz smiled his hopelessly banal smile. "I don't think so," he answered.

"Hombre, if I'm caught nobody will ever see me again. I'd be safer trying to steal the British crown jewels."

"I should hope so."

"Well?"

"All right. I will pay you the three paintings if you get me the Goya." He pulled a chair away from the wall and carried it to the center of the room to sit down, facing Bourne. "What is your plan?"

Bourne again became as confidential and businesslike as an insurance salesman. "First, we will need a permit from the Director of the Museo de Pinturas so that Jean Marie will be allowed to copy in the Prado."

Muñoz made a note with a gold pencil the size of a carpenter's nail on a small leather-bound pad. "Nothing difficult there," he said. "So you are going to have him copy 'The Second of May' in the Sala Goya and switch paintings."

"No. He will copy 'The Second of May' at the hotel. It cannot be done at the Prado because no one is permitted to copy in actual size."

"But I don't understand. What do you want the permit for!"

"We will come to that. Get the permit in the name of Charles Smadja. He is a widely known copyist of the masters who is now on his annual fishing dredge off St. Raphael, Jean Marie tells me. The Prado people can check the name with the Louvre, if they choose."

Muñoz wrote the name down, pausing to verify the spelling. "I was aware that copyists worked in the Prado all the time but I did not know that they needed a license," he said.

"Make a note to point out that M'sieu Smadja has been commissioned by very dear friends of yours, in Paris, to copy three Spanish masterpieces."

"Three?" The marqués' eyebrows shot up. "Three? Mother of God, Jaime, do you propose to pick up two for yourself?"

Bourne laughed as though he were really enjoying himself for a moment, but it didn't last long. "No. Nothing like that. But we must provide Jean Marie with material for conversation with the guards so that they will become quite accustomed to him sitting there day after day in the Sala Goya. He will paint a triptych; three paintings on one canvas in the manner of a *trompe l'oeil* which gives the absolute illusion in miniature of 'The Second of May' exactly as it hangs against its background in the museum, flanked—and I mean actually flanked—on the left by Goya's 'Milkmaid of Bordeaux' and on the right by his own self-portrait. One of those interior decorator ideas."

"As I remember the 'Milkmaid of Bordeaux' is on the right of our big canvas."

"No. To the left. It is as though your family were looking out of the big one. To *their* left."

"Ah, yes."

"The important thing is that the canvas on which Jean Marie will paint his clever triptych will be very nearly exactly the identical size of the canvas holding 'The Second of May.'"

"I'm not sure I follow, but why not exactly the same size?"

"For this reason. Jean Marie's master copy of our Goya will fit exactly inside the mother frame which will be the triptych. It will be virtually impossible to detect the second canvas packed inside the first unless one knows where to look. When we take the real Goya down from the wall, and put the copy up, the real Goya will be housed, tightly locked, behind the *trompe l'oeil* which shields it in the mother frame."

"Oh, I say. That *is* amusing. Oh, I like that!"

"I should think so. It solves nearly everything."

"You said nearly everything."

"As quickly as possible, tonight if you can get it from your friends at the Prado or from the Instituto de Cultura Hispánica, we must have the best color transparency in their files on 'The Second of May.' Try to get the largest size which should be about ten inches by eight inches, Jean Marie tells me."

"I'll have it at your hotel tonight if it exists."

"If it doesn't exist you must arrange to have it photographed. But it will exist. It will be in the files." Bourne continued, noting the marqués' excitement, "Jean Marie works fast. He painted that Velázquez"—he gestured to The Pickett Troilus hanging on the Muñoz wall—"in two days. We'll use the rest of this week on our Goya. He's looking forward to it. He's been with it at the Prado for the past

142

two days and he's straining at the leash to start to work."

"You wouldn't rather have him work with a photo-graphically sensitive canvas?" the marqués asked cautiously.

"I would not. This isn't a coloring contest. It takes great art."

"It was only a suggestion. Please proceed. I am extremely pleased with what you tell me so far."

Bourne propped his charts up against a makeshift pile of books on the table and assumed a lecturer's manner. "Follow me closely, if you will. Every morning, beginning next Monday morning, provided you have secured his permit—"

"He shall have his permit," Dr. Muñoz interrupted.

"—Jean Marie will enter the Prado through the gate on Calle Ruiz de Alarcón, trundling this huge canvas on which the *trompe l'oeil* will gradually be taking shape, upon a little double platform, supported and carried forward by roller skates. He nods to the guards with whom he will make it a point to become more and more friendly each day. Occasionally, he will do a portrait sketch of each of them, in pencil, as he takes the cigarette breaks with each one, away from the public halls. Every time he moves with his little trundle cart his copy of 'The Second of May' will be locked inside the outer, mother frame holding the canvas on which he paints. If a guard should decide to help him push it the guard will be familiar with the exact weight."

Bourne took on the unctuous self-confidence of a medi-cine show pitchman as he traced Jean Marie's course in and out of the Prado, day after day. "He will trundle in each morning behind his permit and trundle out each night for two full weeks right up to the Feria of San Isidro when we will take the Goya for you."

"Ah, San Isidro. Much diversion. Very good, Jaime. Very good."

"Well—not quite, but I'm happy to see that you are right with it."

"What do you mean?"

"In a minute. We'll stay with the sequence for the mo-ment. I propose that we take the Goya on the first Tuesday of San Isidro which will be May 12th this year, at some time between four and five in the afternoon after the bull fight has started and still close enough to closing time at the Prado so that Jean Marie can wheel the original Goya out in the mother frame before any remote, almost impossible off-chance that the copy could be discovered and the alarm raised."

"Of course. Any day you choose. Naturally!"

"And so comes my third and most important request and one which you have actually, in a way, anticipated."

"I did? Well! What was that?"

"You must provide us with an extraordinary diversion. You must cause something to happen which will stand the entire city on its head for not less than twelve minutes and eighteen seconds."

Dr. Muñoz' interest was rapt. "What kind of a diversion?" he asked.

"Something completely grotesque. Something shocking. Something which will spread like wildfire across the city."

"But why do you need it? If you tell me why you need it, then I will understand it better."

"Well, look here, old man—if you give me the kind of a diversion I must have the news will reach the guards at the Prado as soon as it reaches the cafés, the vaults of the banks, the hospitals, the ear of Generalissimo Franco because this is an excitable, and very talkative city of gregarious, inter-dependent people. If it is the diversion I must have the guards who hear it first will call all the other guards because everyone must get an enormous sensation out of spreading such news until little knots of Prado guards will be totally engaged—shocked, voluble, gesticulating, entirely abnormal for as long as it is possible to engage the total attention of adult humans. I need eleven minutes and eighteen seconds and will gratefully accept the gift of sixty seconds leeway."

Dr. Muñoz got out of his chair with extreme excitement and interest. He scooped up the yolk-colored cat Montes, and cradled him at his bosom, releasing chorded purrs. He walked to Bourne and leaned over close to him saying, most earnestly, "But what kind of a diversion? You have thought about this. You must have something vaguely appropriate in mind."

"Only vaguely appropriate," Bourne answered. "I leave this to you because really a Spaniard must design this thing. He must know to the last nuance what will explode like a shell in the midst of Madrileños. When it hits you you will

144

know that this is exactly the right diversion for the job. You feel what I mean?"

"Yes. Oh, yes. Definitely. But perhaps you can give me an example. Perhaps one suggestion."

"Oh something like turning a fire hose on a bishop while he is saying high mass—"

"*Madre de Dios!*"

"—or shooting a bull with a machine gun during a *corrida*. Something, as I said, grotesque or repellent, but definitely something completely shocking."

"Ah. Ah, yes. Of course. I see now. Hmm. Let me think about it. Put it entirely out of your mind. I will deliver to you a splendid diversion. Oh, yes. I'm sure of it now that I understand it."

"It is the most important single part of the plan. The rest is plain arithmetic. We begin with the time and motion studies tomorrow morning. We'll go through the drill of taking one painting down and putting the other one up over and over again, so many times that it will ultimately become pure reflexive action." Bourne took on the huckster's flashing eye, his roguish smile, his braying voice and incipiently untrustworthy expression. "The rest is semi-automatic. Let's say that the diversion is timed for twenty-six minutes past four on that Tuesday afternoon. Jean Marie will be in the Sala Goya finishing the copying of the *trompe l'oeil*. I will stroll into the museum through the Paseo entrance at five minutes past four. I will walk leisurely to the Sala Goya, arriving in front of 'The Second of May', at sixteen minutes after four o'clock. I ignore Jean Marie. He ignores me. At four thirty-one or four thirty-two, no later, I should hear the shout which means your diversion has taken place and has spread across the city. If there should be anyone in the gallery with me at that time I will shout the diversion at them, pointing away from the Sala Goya. Jean Marie will repeat this in another language, pointing off. They will move. Then I will remove the Goya, with Jean Marie's help, and hang the copy. The original will snap into its place behind the *trompe l'oeil* under the mother frame. I will saunter off to the other side of the Sala Goya. Jean Marie will continue his copying of the triptych. I will make my way out of the main exit at four fifty-two. At three minutes before five the guard will come to Jean Marie to announce closing

145

time, to tell him the shocking news of your diversion, and Jean Marie will trundle the huge mother canvas which carries the Goya beneath it, out of the Sala Goya, past the guards who wave good night, as he has been doing every day for three weeks. To tell the truth, Victoriano, the world may never discover that 'The Second of May' has been stolen."

"Then what do you do with the Goya?" Dr. Muñoz asked politely.

"I exchange it for the three paintings from Dos Cortes."

"Ah. Yes. I see," replied the marqués.

Jean Marie completed the copy of "The Second of May" in five days, one-quarter and Dr. Muñoz, viewing it, wept at its sweep, beauty and utter authenticity.

Bourne had conducted two drills a day for nineteen days with Jean Marie. They were engaged in drill number thirty-nine. They began at seven thirty in the morning, each morning, after which they would breakfast and Jean Marie would stroll off with his trundle cart to the Prado to begin his long day's work which was having the effect of dazzling the guards with its wizardry.

They worked in the salon of a large apartment on the top floor of the hotel. The furniture of the room had been pushed to one side and covered with bed sheets.

A large frame containing a blank canvas had been hung on a wall of the room, at the same height from the floor as was hung Goya "Dos de Mayo" in the Museo de Pinturas del Prado.

Jean Marie sat in a canvas-back chair in front of a large empty frame which held no canvas but which framed air. He had lost nearly fifteen pounds. He was haggard and sick-looking. He sat with his hands in his lap, staring disconsolately at Bourne, who stood staring at the empty canvas hanging in the frame on the wall, talking in a low, even voice to Jean Marie while he clearly was calculating something else entirely.

"Jean Marie," he said clearly but with remote preoccupation, "please continue to have confidence in me and what I have to say to you. You can forget your nerves. What you think you are going through is the same thing encoun-

146

tered by film stars when they undertake to become stage actors. I mean it. They make themselves sick imagining what will happen when they make their first entrance from the wings and have to face that sea of live faces. As the time grows shorter, as the rehearsals continue, just as our own rehearsals are now continuing, their panic grows like a mushroom in a damp, dark cellar." Bourne's voice had taken on a cadence. It was soothing. It was insistent, and different from any other voice he ever used. "But they do make their entrance on opening night and, once they are on, they don't have time to be nervous because the director has given them so many things to do with their hands and with their bodies that once they are out there, they have neither the time nor the mental room to be nervous. The same goes for you. Identically the same applies." He walked to Jean Marie and put a hand on his shoulder. "Move over," he said.

"Move over?"

"Get out of the way. Get up. I want to start you counting this morning. I'll show you."

Jean Marie got up and moved aside. Bourne sat down. "This is all you have to do," he said reassuringly, his voice massaging the atmosphere. "I nod to you. You stand up." Bourne stood up. "You move to your position at the far corner of the Goya frame. One, two, three, four, five, six, seven, eight." Bourne paced to the position counting each of his steps in French as he went. He stood motionless at the far corner of the frame, looking serenely across the room at Jean Marie. He motioned to him to take that place. Jean Marie moved in and stood where Bourne was standing. Bourne moved to the directly opposite corner of the painting.

"Now, I will make my first moves. I take my bolt cutter. I snap the lower holding pins. One, two." He snipped at imaginary bolts. "I take out the folding stepladder. I set it against the wall. I climb the ladder. One, two and three. I snap the top holding pin. One. I step down the ladder. One, two and three.

Bourne looked over at Jean Marie expectantly. "Now we reverse positions. You walk close to the frame. I walk in the outside lane. All right. Count as you go." Bourne started forward on Jean Marie's first count. They changed places and were in position at the count of six. Jean Marie held firmly to his side of the frame as though supporting it. Bourne repeated the identical moves he had made on the other side, bolt cutter, stepladder and counting, but this time he supported the painting with his shoulder as he made the last snip, having snipped from top to bottom on this maneuver. "All right! The painting is free. We move it, walking backward, counting together. One, two, three, four, five, six, seven, eight." They had reached the empty mother frame with an imaginary painting. "In she goes," Bourne said. Each man slid his end in. They moved crab fashion, pushing it into secure place for the length of the frame, pushing air, rehearsing and pretending.

"Now, all we would have to do would be to hang your copy in the place of the original and the job is done. Nothing to it. All you had to do was to be able to count to twenty-seven. There is absolutely nothing else you have to do but be able to count to twenty-seven. I merely have to be able to count to forty-six. It's that simple."

"I know," Jean Marie replied wearily. "It is simple. You have made it wonderfully simple. But I am an artist not a thief. I am a highly imaginative man and I get nervous when I think about it and I can't stop thinking about it. I want to vomit when I think about it too long, and I live in fear that I will start to vomit while we are in the middle of the job. And I can't sleep. The more I don't sleep the more nervous I get. I was not born to be a thief. It is that simple."

"Perfectly natural. After all, I'm not a nerveless man, Jean Marie. In my own way I am a highly imaginative man too."

"I realize that, Jim. Please—there is no doubt about that."

"And I know as well as anyone that the part we call living is the internal life we have, the life of reflexive feeling, the poet's side of us, the ground on which all of our wars are fought." His voice stroked at Jean Marie. "Because I understand this I seek to bring order to the external life, the less important part of life because it is not life but rather the time-motion plasma which supports the internal life, where we truly live, as a river supports a cork as it bobs and moves along the endless stream from birth to death."

"Yes," Jean Marie hummed. "I can feel what we see and what you say."

Bourne made his voice a shade more monotonous and a
148

beat slower. "Feel what I am saying to you. Absorb it into your innermost mind. When we finish the next drill, the second counting drill, number forty, you will go to your room and you will lie down and rest. While you rest you will think about what I have been saying and you will see the truth in it. You will see the strength you have been given to do this thing. By counting to twenty-seven, by reducing the entire action to twenty-seven simple movements you will have found complete external order. The external in order, the internal life cannot be confused or troubled. Your imagination cannot carry you away and weaken you with insomnia and nausea. Twenty-seven simple moves outside your mind and body. Twenty-seven. Only twenty-seven. Feel it as we do it again. We will go through the real drill this time. We will actually take the frame down, move it into the mother frame, and hang your copy on the wall. Then it will be all over. Make yourself ready. Think only of the count. You are exhausted but you will be refreshed if you think only of the count. Only twenty-seven numbers. We start now. When I nod to you we start." He nodded.

Jean Marie got up from the canvas chair and began his cross to the corner of the painting. "One, two, three, four, five, six, seven, eight." He was in position.

Bourne inserted the bolt cutter behind the frame and began his own first pattern. "One, two." The metallic clicks were sharp and clear as the cutter went through. Bourne removed the collapsible ladder from under his coat. "One, two," he said, his face serene, his manner relaxed and unhurried.

Jean Marie stared at him, impatient to begin his count again.

Just as Saturday is the best day for the West End of London, because London is a walking city and Saturday finds it deserted, and Friday is the best day nearly anywhere in the United States cities because it is payday, Sunday is a great day in Madrid. The people all go to church so dress their best to uphold themselves among the others. After church, to put these clothes to total use and to employ the tonic spring most fully, they stroll or march or walk, depending upon individual personalities. A favorite course is the Paseo de la Castellana which is bounded on the

149

north by Conrad Hilton and on the south by Cesar Ritz. It has two beautiful plazas of its own, and shares two others with relatives. It has tall trees, thickly leafy. It has the most luxurious, restful sidewalk cafés in the world, contained in peace as though conscious of the need to restate man's humanity to man.

On the Sunday before the Tuesday which stood like a mountain in her mind, Eve sat beside Bourne in a straw easy chair before a breakfast table on the *ramblas* of the Paseo de la Castellana, drinking coffee early in the morning rich with sunshine. The *gran paseo* of well-dressed Madrid, rich or poor, had begun, and the word Sunday in Spanish has the onomatopoeic ring of the gayest bells: Domingo!

Eve had climbed out of the squalor of her fear. She had told herself that she was resigned to what would happen and she believed she had pushed her fear far enough back into her mind to misplace it if she needed to start to look for it again. She sipped her hot coffee and enjoyed the marchers until all at once it came to her that she was seated at the intersection of Calle de Zurbarán, and the millrace of acid fear began again.

The erosion had gone far enough that she did not think in terms of Muñoz any more, only of Bourne and herself. Two nights before he had struck her with his broad hand, knocking her across and over the broad bed and leaving the marks of his fingers under the make-up on the side of her head because she could not stop pleading with him to get out with her; she had had to start all of it all over again. He knew whenever she started, that if he walked away, then ran, she would walk then run after him, saying what she must say. Before he had hit her Friday night he had told her, "I don't have a woman to bring me trouble," because man has never perceived that is the only reason why God gave him woman, to make him trouble and to stir him to glory from among the sun-warmed beer cans of his ego.

On the Sunday morning, on the *ramblas*, she started blandly enough. She said, "What is the flaw which makes criminals, do you think?"

"Resentment in the mild cases. Then maybe fear, called by them contempt, in the major cases."

"Contempt of what?"

"Birth, I guess."

"Station at birth?"

"No, no. Just having been born without having been consulted. That simple *gaffe* on somebody's part has caused some of the world's great rages."

"I agree it could frighten everyone who thinks about it long enough, if they were silly enough to spend their logic retroactively, but certainly not every criminal thinks of it."

"Thinking doesn't come into it. They feel it. They are afraid of being left behind in some awful, unknown night. They are afraid of the scorn of working with all the others who are willing to work because they think honest work can make one faceless and being faceless, not findable, not identifiable, and therefore more easily left behind. It's hard times. It isn't helped much to call it contempt when you feel a fear like that."

"Do you feel it?"

"I have felt it."

"Do you feel it now?"

Bourne seemed to study the lace mantillas of two beautiful silver-haired ladies who walked away from them. Eve followed his gaze and was fixed by their carriage. For no reason she thought of the Spanish School of Riding at Vienna, and realized that she had become a student of the Spanish School of Walking in Madrid.

Bourne began to rumble on against her question. "You know, I've read over and over again about the relief supposedly felt by many criminals when they are finally caught and sentenced and imprisoned. And I have read the nonsense that they had unconsciously wanted to be punished and had necessarily arranged the pattern so that they would be punished. That's a lot of stuff."

"Is it? I don't think it is."

"Well, you've never studied it and you don't know what the hell you're talking about anyway. *I* think that criminals need to be caught and sentenced and imprisoned, not to be punished but to be loved. It is an ideal arrangement for those with blind psyches. They can keep their contempt and their fear as coffins to sleep in yet still able to accept the loving attention of the rest of society within the definition of honorable bounds. The pursuit by society of the criminal takes a keen interest of the most personal and overt sort. The majesty of the impersonal grief felt by society

151

when they must shut away another creature or, sometimes, kill him for his own good is grief nonetheless and grief may only emerge from deep loss. The solicitousness of society as they house, feed, clothe and re-educate their frightened brothers is a mark of love. It's all an enormous process of love made insane and bringing pain instead of hope with its fulfillment."

"Do you include yourself in this—this frightened fraternity?"

"No."

"Why not? You steal for a living. Stealing is the most literal kind of taking, if we are going to theorize, yet every teacher worth remembering has taught that the only real need is someone else's need, that only if you give can you get."

"A man must tell a story with his life and the story must have order, that's what reason is. That's how I want to live it. My reason, to show you that I know exactly what the hell you are talking at all over again and to prove to you that I no longer resent it, my reason in this Spanish chapter of the story I'm telling with my life is that I have put nearly eight per cent of that life into getting those paintings. That's an imperative reason. If I negate it, I negate myself."

"Bosh," she answered.

"What?"

"I was merely commenting that you were making noises like a stuffed male."

"Ah, sometimes I'd like to whack that smug superior look of yours right across the street, you semantically inhibited, Scotch Calvinistic bitch."

"You call that cursing?"

"Well, what are you talking about with that stuffed male jargon?"

"Because reasons mean nothing," she answered. "Don't go leaning on reasons. Reason is nothing. Meaning is what a life has to have."

"Now, what the hell, Eve! Why do you always have to argue like this? Meaning and reason are the same thing."

She looked at him as though she would have hit him with the coffee pot joyously. "Jim, my dearest Jim," she said. "That rotten, little son-of-a-bitch Muñoz told us his reason for killing Señor Elek, but the reason had no meaning. His life has no meaning, only reasons. His reason for living is to justify his ancestors, some people he has never seen and cannot prove existed, therefore they can have no meaning. Because he exists only on reasons he cannot feel love; only pride, and pride has no meaning because it is merely vanity felt from doing one's best and when it is vanity felt from the best or worst done by some people one cannot prove existed, then it is utterly without meaning. But we love. You love me, I know you love me. And I love you or I would have left you for what you are but I cling to you and hope for you for what you are. Only that has meaning. Not paintings or profits. You can't pull paintings into your internal life, that peace or war you always talk about, that battleground within yourself; but you can take me there and I belong there, Jim. I have a right to be there and I beg you, Jim, to slug Muñoz and let's get the hell out of all this pain."

He sat staring at his hands which rested in his lap as though the final answer lay in them. It was a long time before he spoke but he did speak, softly and carefully. "Eve, you feel fear for us, and I say it is unreasonable. In my whole career I have never seen a job which will play out as smoothly and as safely as this one. I cannot throw three or four or five hundred thousand dollars away because you have developed a case of jitters. If you could prove that there was the possibility of harm to someone anywhere in any part of this thing, I would listen to you and I would take you away from here. But it is harmless and it will be sensationally profitable and for Christ's sake stop looking at me as though all of these dull, business reasons had something to do with my not loving you because you know goddam well where we stand on that question but I will state it again so that it becomes clearer than clear. I have never loved anyone else, I am incapable of loving anyone else and I will never love anyone else through all of my lifetime."

She leaned across and kissed him on the cheek and made her peace.

Each pair had so looked forward to seeing the other again that, although they drove in from different directions, their cars each slid into the parking slots in the Plaza de la República Argentina in front of the Commodore restaurant at exactly the appointed hour, two forty-five, which put them into an even more euphoric mood, if that were possible. The manic state, while totally unexpected for the Bournes, was habitual with the duchess and Cayetano.

The ladies ascended in the tiny elevator, operated by a small boy with bright red hair, freckles and a scarlet suit with shining brass buttons.

The men climbed the short flight of stairs. They all sat at a large round table overlooking the courtyard, beside a wide-open window, and ordered martinis con vodka as thought it were part of a special ritual in a special shrine. The air shimmered with manic angels. The duchess spoke Catalan with Señor Torte, the keeper of the keys, and three long-aproned waiters stood by warily lest ice cubes show signs of melting.

Cayetano observed that it seemed a sad thing that in a world so filled with facile lyricists, no one had ever written a song to the first martini con vodka at any luncheon. Eve told him she had once sung a dirge following the fifth martini con vodka.

"No dirges," the duchess admonished, "as I am thinking in terms of two hundred violins and estragon sauce and because I have an announcement to make." She lifted her own martini con vodka and told them that she and Cayetano would be married in Madrid on the concluding Saturday of the Feria of San Isidro, however banal that might sound. There was a storm of handshaking, kissing, backslapping, martini gulping, and an orthodox number of tears were contributed by Mrs. Bourne into a small handkerchief she always had with her in the event of such announcements.

Bourne rushed one waiter off for another round of martinis and another waiter for two magnums of iced champagne. They left at top speed but Señor Torte, the keeper of the keys, came right back to Bourne to check whether Bourne had really meant two magnums. Bourne discovered that he had not meant magnums, he had meant bottles, but he appreciated the idea of two magnums so much that he persuaded Señor Torte to allow the order to stand.

Eve wanted to know *where* they would be married in Madrid, as if that mattered. She asked the question with that sense of desperate urgency women can get about such things

154

and the duchess took the cap off the tension by stating that they would be married in her late husband's home on Alcalá and Lagasca because it would please the servants so. She told them that, except for themselves, she had decided to invite no one below the rank of bishop. Cayetano said he had decided to invite no one below the rank of picadores above the age of fifty because in that way, although none of the picadores would be likely to get any more religion, it would be a marvelous social opportunity for the bishops.

The actual ceremony would be at some church, the duchess supposed, so as not to shock the servants who, excepting the Bournes and Cayetano, would be the only real friends she would have left when this news came out, but most certainly the reception would be at her late husband's house and she would ransack every one of her houses for every known portrait of her late husband to be nailed to the walls of the reception room to increase everyone's sense of fun.

"I feel so good," the duchess said, "that I wish I could hire an entire regiment of Scottish bagpipers just to walk through this restaurant once, playing something awful. You look very thin to me, Jaime."

"That may be," Bourne answered, "but whatever you've been doing, you've never looked so wonderful." Then he seemed to hear what he said and started to blush.

"Stop that kind of talk, Jaime," the duchess said, "it embarrasses Cayetano."

"I haven't got the strength left to be embarrassed and I'm only a boy," Cayetano told him.

"Just for that you get no more marzipan," said the duchess just before finishing the martini before her. "Now that we're back here I can't tell you what a marvelous feeling it is to get away from Madrid if only because one doesn't run into Picketts."

"One doesn't say one runs into a picket," Eve corrected, leaning forward so that the waiter could set martinis down. "One says one runs into a fence."

"Eve just made a joke in English, darling," the duchess told Cayetano.

"Have you seen the Picketts?" Bourne asked. "I thought he'd be back in Washington by now."

"Have we seen the Picketts?" Cayetano rolled his eyes. "To be perfectly frank, only one. The large one."

"You mustn't tease about him, Cayetano. He is so desperately earnest, the poor man," the duchess explained to all of them. "He is obsessed with his discovery of this—this Rubens trace—in the Velázquez. It is all very sweet, really. He came to see me to ask whether I would have any objections to allowing the press to refer to the painting as 'The Pickett Troilus.' I don't know what he would do if anything ever happened to that painting. He apologized to me for having hired a firm of propagandists in the United States and a firm in London. Whatever for? I asked him. He told me this was the biggest single event of his life finding the coincidence of the two masters on the one canvas and that he must move to secure this authority everywhere, that it would make him the great Spanish art authority in the world if it were handled with discretion and tact."

As the duchess spoke Eve had seemed to stop the transit of her martini con vodka in mid-air, then to return it to the table, careful not to take her eyes off the duchess. Bourne sat very still but gave no other sign that the duchess's appeal had reached him.

The duchess continued. "Some American picture magazine is flying photographers here from Lausanne, or anyway one photographer, and Mr. Pickett pleads with me to simply throw open Dos Cortes to him, and while he was there someone from the Duque de Luna's office at Tourismo called and made the identical request for some German photographer who is coming down for a magazine in Munich and I decided then and there to tell them both that if they would take their pictures all at one time, or at least all in one day, I would permit it so I suppose the picture press of the world will shortly be publishing pictures of Mr. Pickett, Señor Velázquez and Herr Rubens shaking hands at the net. In the meantime it's all for the great cause so cheers for art and the Picketts and culture generally and will one of you darling men please make discreet inquiries as to what the hell happened to that champagne?"

At that instant, through the doorway across the dining room, Señor Torte appeared, driving the magnums before him and, in no time at all, thoughts of drinking brassy stuff

156

like martinis con vodka were spent in memory. Señor Torte enquired at exactly the right moment whether they would like to order food and Cayetano requested that he prepare anything at all in the style of S'Agaro, the meeting place of the great and near great on the Costa Brava, because that was what he had been instructed to say, he told the duchess.

"Who instructed you, lamb?" the duchess asked.

"Jaime Arias."

"Oh. Well. Then, yes."

"Who's Jaime Arias?" Eve asked, looking slightly buzzed.

"He's a newpaperman from Barcelona who collects teacups which gets him to believing that he's an epicure, poor man."

"What kind of teacups?"

"The kind with printing on them. Ones which say Hotel Dinkler-Plaza, he actually has one which says that, you know, and the Negresco in Nice. We had a few cups printed for him at Christmas last year because he's a darling man. They say The Kremlin, Moscow, in red. They've become his most cherished pieces although, of course, he keeps them out of sight."

Cayetano said, "This is a week of miracles, really. I ask everyone here. Who is the most improbable Spaniard you can think of who would announce that he was going to attend a bullfight?"

The duchess did not hesitate for an instant. "My cousin, el doctor, Victoriano Muñoz, el Marqués de Villalba." She drawled the name sounding precisely like Victoriano and they all thought that was pretty funny."

"Your cousin?" Bourne blurted.

"Oh, now, come, Jaime! He's not that bad. He just hates bullfights and practically everything else attractive people like."

"I couldn't tell you why I was so surprised," Bourne told her.

"Everyone is related to everyone, really, if you subscribe to that new Adam and Eve theory."

"It is a very decadent thing for the corrida, that Victoriano has decided to attend it.," Cayetano said.

"I begin to get the idea that he is setting a precedent," Eve said.

"A precedent?" cried the duchess. "It is as though Winston Churchill took out Italian citizenship!" She turned to Cayetano, incredulous. "Did I hear you say that my cousin Victoriano Muñoz was going to a corrida?"

"You grasp the general idea," Cayetano told her patting her hand, then thinking better of the whole thing and kissing her hand. "He called me this morning and asked if I would kill in front of Tendido Two next week on my first bull because they were the only seats he could get and he has promised to take Mrs. Pickett and he is afraid she won't last out more than one bull so he wants to make sure of that by making it as awful as possible, he said, with the kill right under her nose, so that she will faint or get sick and they can leave immediately."

"He's certainly a clear thinker, my cousin. Who else do you know who would think his way out of a social trap like that?"

"There's no guarantee that Mrs. Pickett will faint, you know," Bourne said stoutly.

"Oh, she'll faint," Cayetano said confidently. "To help him out I might botch things with the first sword."

"I feel buzzed," Eve said.

"It is the martinis and the wine and the vodka," the duchess said. "One is not to worry, my sweet."

"That is the stand I have decided to take," Eve replied. "Please cause the glasses to be filled with this fine champagne as we have not yet run out of announcements."

The duchess stared at her with joy. Her chin dropped, her eyes popped under the influence of women's telepathy. "No!"

"No, what?" Bourne asked.

"Please cause the glasses to be filled," the duchess said, but as she said it Señor Torte had signaled waiters from fifteen yards away to get with it.

Eve lifted her glass. "I hope you will consider that I am engraving these words for you as I go along. Mr. and Mrs. James Bourne take great pleasure in inviting you to the christening of their first child in approximately five months an announcement which is possible because the child's mother is a tall woman who, up until the present time, is carrying it so well that it shows not more than a pocket watch would show in the evening clothes of Mr. Fred Astaire."

Bourne goggled at her. "What?" he exclaimed.

The duchess filled in smoothly. "You must call him Cayetano. We in turn, to show our appreciation, will call our firstborn Herbert Hoover Jiminez."

"Eve—— My golly—— Well, what wonderful news!" Bourne looked as if he had just finished a performance as the Sorcerer's Apprentice.

"Jaime!" Cayetano protested. "Enough of the little father faces! We have not yet drunk a toast!" He lifted his glass. "To the dear child of the dear Bournes," he said and drank it down. The glasses were refilled.

"To the sweet, sweet baby's sweet, sweet mother!" cried the duchess, drinking it down. The glasses were refilled.

"To the wedding of my friends and the birthday of my child," Bourne boomed and drank it down. The glasses were refilled.

"To The Pickett Troilus and the great deep swoon of Mrs. Pickett!" intoned Eve and drank it down. The glasses were refilled.

"To all of us, each and every one of us, may we love and live forever!" sang the duchess and drank it down. Something in the style of S'Agaro was served and the luncheon got under way.

Tuesday was a model spring day. Bourne and Eve were sipping coffee in the living room of their apartment with the terrace doors swung wide, Eve fully dressed, Bourne in pajamas and robe, when there was a knock on their door. Bourne scurried into the bedroom and Eve answered the knock. Jean Marie came in.

"My God," she said, "you look terrible."

"I feel terrible. Believe me, chérie, I feel one hundred per cent lousy all the way through. It is something I didn't eat, no doubt. Big joke. Something I couldn't keep on my stomach. Do you mind if I try once again with your coffee. I will try not to vomit on your cushions. But the coffee works sometimes. If I could get my hands and teeth on a good brioche I might survive at this time of day. Or a good anything at any time of day. Sweet Jesus, but the Spaniards are terrible cooks. Everyone is mystified why Americans continue to come to Paris when the prices are so high. I'll tell you why Americans keep coming to Paris. Go eat some of this fantastically overcooked, under-flavored Spanish food and you'll know why. Look at this weather. The Spaniards are very strong on beautiful weather. If Americans stayed in France for more than one week they'd see some of the lousiest weather ever manufactured, but Spanish weather is superb. One would think it didn't all come from the same place there is such a difference. Well today is the last day of this madness. The last day. The goddam, bloody very last day. I could not have gone on for one more day. I swear to God and Jesus and the Virgin I could not have gone on. God alone knows whether I will be able to survive today. I don't think I have the strength in my hand to hold the brush to pretend to finish that bloody *trompe l'oeil*. Imagine me being forced to take three entire weeks to finish three lousy Goyas. I could have illuminated a Gutenberg Bible, hand-painted some neckties for the Pope and knocked off four large Breughels in the extra time I've had. Of course, Jim was right. Because I've been mopping and daubing the guards are like my uncles now. That big one who swings in on the relief hitch must eat garlic rubbed with garlic. You cannot conceive of how that man smells. One more little pressure on me, the smell of garlic. Everything is crumbling under this pressure. My bowels, my joints, my sleep, everything, thank God, except my painting. I will never make a thief. The reason that the world is as honest as it is falls under the same heading. The wear and tear of a life of crime is simply too excessive. I'll tell you one thing, if we can get that goddam *trompe l'oeil* out of the country I'm going to hang the goddam thing in my dining room. Jim said I could have it. Not that I need a souvenir of this goddam job. I'll never forget this goddam job and that is for bloody, horrible goddam sure."

Bourne emerged from the bedroom, fully dressed, somewhere in Jean Marie's mid-sentence.

"Hi, kid. Where's Eve?"

"Eve?" He spun around comically, looking, but there was no sign of her. The door to the corridor opened at that instant and Eve entered with a covered plate. "I went down myself instead of calling room service," she said. "Now you sit right down here and eat it."

"Eat what? I can't eat anything. I can't hold anything on my stomach."

"Two nice, fresh brioches. And I happen to have some
160

marvelous confiture. The same brand exactly that Lalu always has for you. And fresh butter. Come along now."

Bourne's face was pinched with anxiety as he read the note from Dr. Muñoz on the heavy, scented paper. He had not been able to reach Muñoz, or one of his servants, on the telephone or at the apartment for the past four days. The note, which had just arrived, had been delivered by hand to the concierge. It said that Muñoz had completed all arrangements for a magnificent diversion which would happen at four twenty to four twenty-nine and three-quarters, give or take a split second, and was written in such a manner as to suggest that the marqués was enjoying a joke against Bourne's outrageously precise time allowances. The note assured Bourne that the diversion would do more than set Madrid on its head, that it was the only possible choice of all possible diversions because it could not fail. The note said that the doctor had decided not to reveal what the diversion would be, that surprises were the spice and all that, and it sincerely hoped that Bourne would be found by the note, in the best of health and spirits and that Dr. Muñoz would be with him, in spirit, throughout the day.

Bourne picked up the telephone beside him and dialed Muñoz' number impatiently once again. The phone sound rang and rang but no one answered. Bourne crashed the phone into its cradle and looked up at the wall clock. It was three twenty-five and time to leave. He opened the top drawer of the desk and took out a small, green, glass vial. He shook two white pills out of it upon the green desk blotter, recapped the vial, then poured a half glass of water from the vacuum bottle which shared the telephone table. He heard a sound at the door, looked up and found Eve standing there. She closed the door behind her and stared him down.

"How come the pills for the easiest job you've ever done?" she asked.

He didn't answer. He swallowed the pills with some water. "Time to go," he said. He stood beside her. She wouldn't look at him. He pinned her arms to her sides and kissed her. She didn't respond.

"I'll be back here at five ten," he said. "Please don't worry." He slid past her, opened the door and was gone.

She walked to his desk and sat down. The ticking of the

161

F

wall clock sounded very loud. She sat and stared at the green desk pad. At four o'clock she opened the top drawer of Bourne's desk and took out the green, glass vial. She tossed two of the pills into her opposite hand and swallowed them without any water.

In the Sala Goya, Jean Marie tried to give the impression of working steadily. He had come back from lunch at three thirty, but he had not been able to eat again. Lunch had started well enough. He had journeyed across the city to Calle Ternera because the restaurant called El Callejon was one of the few which cooked food even halfway appealing to him, but within ten minutes the nausea had returned and at last he had had to hasten deplorably to the facilities where he had retched until his stomach had felt scraped.

Back in the Sala Goya he daubed and wiped but mostly stared at the great "Dos de Mayo." Sweet Christ, the size of it, he kept observing until he could not think of anything but the size of it and what it must weigh until he began to convince himself that his own expert eye had detected a miscalculation in Bourne's design of the mother frame. Sweet Jesus, how could a monster the size of that bloody Goya ever fit into this mignon of a frame he was swatting away at? Christ's thorns, they would be tugging and pushing at the goddam thing without a chance of ever jamming it into the goddam mother frame. Mother frame! Sweet Son of Mary, if a mother ever carried a child this size she'd split open right down the middle. What would they do? They would be tugging and pushing and the guards would walk right into the room and find them. He felt a terrible and humiliating flash of embarrassment to imagine the expressions on the faces of his friends the guards when they discovered that he had betrayed their trust. He actually had to close his eyes as he thought of that. He forced himself to think other less embarrassing thoughts. Was he ever to see Lalu again? He thought of the silent peace in the galleries of the Louvre and of the Musée Delacroix and the ten and the twenty and the thirty of the other galleries of Paris he had copied in. So much repose in that life, so much assurance. It was like living a life in a chair sled moving along a gentle slope of virgin snow, well bundled up, moving down toward a small cottage alight with warmth and Lalu. Tiny Lalu, sweet Lalu.

A guard almost caused his death by coming out of nowhere and touching his shoulder. Jean Marie thought he heard himself scream then he heard the guard apologize for jolting him while he was lost in a reverie of art. It is my fault, Jean Marie thought, I should have smelled the son-of-a-bitch. Sweet God, they had rubbed garlic into his hair today. The guard was anxious about Jean Marie because he was perspiring so ; he was sure that Jean Marie was running a body fever. He urged that he leave and go home and purge himself. Jean Marie explained that it was merely a mild stomach upset, that it would pass, and that at the moment he was immersed in thinking a most difficult problem through, so that he could not possibly go home. This sent the guard away, awed and respectful.

The white Mercedes moved along Lagasca slowly, the duchess seated in it, quite alone. She stayed on Lagasca until Padilla then turned right, balling along until Silvela then crossing into the Avenida de los Toreros. She made the long curve above the Plaza de Toros, then down to its level, driving in between the two parking lots, to the corner of the smaller lot, directly opposite the gateway to the Patio de Caballos. A small, one-armed Civil War veteran with a patent-leather visor on his cap held the space for her by sitting on it.

She had driven along the only relatively clear route in the city. The feria was under way and it had been slow-moving. The streets swarmed with traffic and traffic police. The cars had moved a few feet at a time while the foot traffic seemed to move faster. She gave the custodian of her private parking space five pesetas. As she walked away from the car a fourteen-year-old gypsy girl carrying a four-month-old baby and dragging a three-year-old child, neither of them wearing shoes, came up out of the ground chanting the song which was the gypsies' vocation, not to say profession, on fiesta days. The duchess was ready. She had a *duro* in her glove which she surrendered willingly.

As she walked two small boys offered to sell her a brightly colored souvenir program which, they explained gravely, walking beside her as she walked, also contained the history of the entire corrida. She thanked them solemnly but refused the opportunity. Three ticket scalpers, one after another, offered her excellent seats in *sombra,* in *sol* and in *sol y sombra.* The excited crowds were everywhere and the sunlight was so thick as to make the world be seen as though through a bathysphere sunk in *goldwasser.*

The noise was a splendid Spanish noise; a gay noise which also packed the authority of *afición,* and the preening self-esteem of many people all together who could afford to secure seats for the corrida during the Feria de San Isidro.

As she walked briskly toward the main entrance, gradually slowed by the thickening crowd she could see the four mounted police sitting like sleepy monuments caught in a flood. Great-busted, matronly women standing over capacious baskets offered single cigarettes for sale, single pieces of candy, single pieces of chewing gum. Impassive, gnarled men guarded stone jugs which had the nozzle velocity of water pistols and cried out with great joy that they were willing to sell a drink to absolutely anyone for fifty centavos.

At the front entrance, the great gateway, the carteles for the day were emblazoned on either side of the arch. She was moving slowly now, as part of the peanut-butter-thick crowd, so had plenty of time to read them as she moved forward. They were printed in red, yellow, blue, brown and white, carried a huge reproduction of a painting of Cayetano in a *pase de pecho* and said:

PLAZA DE TOROS   LAS VENTAS   MADRID
*Grandiosos acontecimientos taurinos
para el Feria de San Isidro
el Martes 15 de Mayo de 1956*

*Las maximas
combinaciónes
Gran Corrida de Tòros
Con superior permiso y si el tiempo
no lo impide se picarán, banderillearán
y seran muertos a estoque*
6 *Hermosos Toros* 6
*de la acreditada ganadería de Don Salvador Guardiola
Espadas*
Cayetano Jiminez
César Giron
Gregorio Sánchez

The duchess saw Victoriano Muñoz five people ahead of

her in the crowd. She called out to him, but the noise of the crowd swept the sound away and she couldn't get his attention. She craned her neck to try to catch a glimpse of Mrs. Pickett, but with no luck and when she looked again for Victoriano he had disappeared into the bull holiday bustle of arms, legs and faces, of olive oil-crusted voices, of dwarfs and children and beautiful women, of the world's richest and the world's poorest pressed against photographers from Göteborg, distillers from Glasgow, secretaries from Winsted, Connecticut, and Arabs from the Riff. She was swept along into Tendido Eight. Three ushers rushed to seat her, causing a bottleneck on the stairs in the chute leading into the stands. She was settled with many murmurs of "*mi duquesa*" in a barrera seat behind the matador's burladero.

Bourne entered the Paseo del Prado entrance of the museum wondering how he could get his hands to stay dry. His mind ticked off each movement and placement which kept him abreast of his schedule. He had the look of a businessman about to go into a meeting in which he will hold most of the power and know how to maneuver the rest. He wasn't nervous, but he couldn't keep his hands dry, which was annoying. He wasn't aware of his jaws being chomped together, grinding his teeth into a vise and depositing lumps at the corners of his face. He wasn't aware that his sphincter muscles had tightened like a imp's fist, or that his throat was dry enough to strike a store match on it, or of the military academy rigidity of his back. He wiped his hands with a handkerchief for the third time within five minutes. His breathing was shallow as he entered the Sala Goya. An Arab in a burnoose and two Arabs in western clothes were standing in front of "The Second of May," silent and studious. Bourne moved to Jean Marie's extreme right to stand at the side of "The Maja Clothed" so that Jean Marie would notice him, which he did, with a terrifying start.

The brilliant sun divided the bull ring into halves, impartially but decisively. On the stroke of four o'clock the bugle sounded the notes which summoned the two *aguacils* into the arena, riding schooled horses, dressed in the manner of sixteenth-century Spain. They galloped across the ring to doff their hats to the president, pretending to catch the keys to the toriles in their hats, as though the keys had been tossed down from the too-distant president's box. They reined away in opposite directions from one another, one riding clockwise around the ring, the other counter-clockwise to meet at the portal where the toreros had formed.

They led the paseo forward. The three matadors followed behind them in a line abreast, with their cuadrillas filing after them. Cayetano, as senior matador, marched on the extreme left. César Girón, cockier than any marcher who has ever strutted, was on the extreme right, his right elbow cocked almost as high as his shoulder as he came across in his own distinctive marching style. Sánchez, heavily handsome, dedicatedly sullen and solid, marched in the middle.

Cayetano wore a suit of burnished silver, the masses of it crusted and heavy, over lavender silk and he looked, perhaps, as blithe, as brave and as beautiful as the duchess thought he looked. They marched as they had taken their lines on the cartel outside the plaza and Cayetano would fight the first bull which Don Savador would send out. Behind the three bravos came forty-two banderilleros, puntilleros, picadores, monosabios and mulillas. Each line as they completed the full cross acknowledged the presence of the president and the matadors moved left to their burladero where Cayetano winked at the duchess but did not move into the callejon to speak to her because he had the first bull. His *mozo de espada* spread his cape before her just as he turned away. His peons took their positions behind the two other burladeros, the bugle sounded, the toril gates swung clear and the bull came crashing out into the ring.

For the same reason that the carteles for this fight had to be reprinted eleven times within the next month to become eventually a standard item for the tourists, no one can say whether it was a good fight, an indifferent fight, a dull fight or a triumph of honor and of skill. Naturally, the newspapers said it was the greatest single *lidia* that Jiminez had ever fought and the people who were there said it was even greater than that until it became tauromaquia beyond the capabilities of any man who ever lived or who will ever live. However, what they said was the only possible judgment.

After the banderillas had been placed, Cayetano walked to the place in the ring beneath the president's box and, with his montera in his right hand, made the formal request of the president to kill the bull. Then he walked in that slow, self-assured way of his for about twenty-five yards to stand directly in front of the duchess. He *brindised* to her with great solemnity, dedicating with the words *"Va por ti"* then breaking into his dazzling, boyish smile looking deep into her eyes and making her feel weak and stirred. He wheeled, tossed his montera over his shoulder into the stands for the duchess, then signaled to his peons to bring the bull from the far corner of *sol y sombra* to the section of the ring directly in front of Tendido Two, far to the left of the duchess. While he waited for them to bring the bull into place for the faena, Cayetano caught Dr. Muñoz' eye, and winked. The marqués grinned happily and winked back.

The magnificent Guardiola bull was an *asarajado* which meant that his skin was as tawny as a lion's. It was an extremely brave bull who charged straight each time the lure called him. It followed the capotes of the peons obediently across the ring and was lined up for the twists of Cayetano's muleta economically and well.

The faena was a blur of movement and sound and pain afterwards; then it became blank to remain blank as though there was no room for it in any of the twenty-one thousand memories which had witnessed it. As Cayetano started his faena with a *derechazo,* which is a natural pass with the right hand and which is extremely moving in its simplicity, Dr. Muñoz left his seat in *contra barrera* and walked to the stairway, immediately behind him, which led to the chute which led to the street. Mrs. Pickett did not seem to be with him. Cayetano, passing the fine bull at the very peak of his art, took the blankets of clear separate *"Olés!"* which slapped down upon his linked passes with blithe pleasure, and grinned with sheer joy through the complete and absolute silence which the twenty-one thousand people presented to him between that organized, deliberate thunder. Everyone was forward on the edge of his seat. The *guardias* at the steps at the mouth of the chute were standing far forward, rapt with the scene of the man and the bull. The chute was covered. The guardias did not see Dr. Muñoz as he passed them nor did they see him as he stood on the deserted steps, the long knife in his hand at his side, looking out at Cayetano from behind them.

Cayetano squared the bull, profiled, then went in to kill,

crossing his muleta and hitting the huge bull exactly true between the shoulder blades. As he was framed between the horns, Dr. Muñoz threw his knife. It rolled lazily through the air, end over end, needing only to travel fifteen yards to hit Cayetano directly between the shoulders. He sagged over the bull as the bull sagged under him, blood leaving both of them in gobbets.

They died together.

At four thirty-six Bourne left the Sala Goya and walked along the corridor. He was half the distance to the nearest guard on duty when he heard a great shout. He stopped. He saw the guard stare straight ahead of him, saw him strain to listen, then saw him bolt and run out of sight. Bourne wheeled and proceeded rapidly into the Sala Goya, shouting in English and pointing over his shoulder. Jean Marie leaped to his feet and began to shout in French, pointing in the same direction. The three Arabs stared at them blankly, startled in a fixed freize, which scattered and ran out of the room in the opposite direction from which Bourne had pointed.

Neither man spoke. They walked to the mother frame and slipped the framed copy out of its hiding place and dragged it to the wall before the "Milkmaid of Bordeaux" where they propped it up, facing the wall. Jean Marie went stolidly to his corner of "The Second of May" as it hung on the wall, counting under his breath as he moved. Bourne waited at his corner. He made the first three snips with his bolt cutter. He set up the stepladder. He climbed the three steps, unhurriedly. He made two snips. He stepped down daintily. He picked up the ladder and moved in the outside lane to Jean Marie's corner, while Jean Marie, counting as he went, moved to his. Bourne completed his work on the far side of the painting moving exactly as he had moved through forty-nine drills, through the precise plans which he had held in his mind and which he had sketched and studied on graphed paper.

The crowd rioted at the bull ring as soon as the realization that what had happened before their eyes had really happened. Two children and one woman were trampled to death; twenty-six persons were injured, nine seriously. Two men, seated sixty yards apart in separate sections of the plaza, had been pointed at as having thrown the knife but miraculously had been saved from the mob by courageous police. Thousands of people looked up at the sky, seeking God, and wept. Hundreds and hundreds and hundreds in every section of the stands stood or sat where they had been and remained there, huddled and numb, staring out at the spot on the sand where he had been murdered, tears streaming down their faces. They stayed there, hundreds and hundreds and hundreds of them, long after darkness came. The Patio de Caballos overflowed with thousands of people just standing in silence outside the chapel where he would be laid. The streets were choked with mobs. Houses, cafés, stores and cars had emptied. People moved through the streets all during the night. They set up a vigil, nine thousand of them, outside the police headquarters. They set up vigils, hundreds and hundreds, outside the neighborhood police stations. Madrid had been canted, her people cascading mindlessly down its sides in a mass, agonized hopelessness of rage and loss.

Dr. Muñoz had told the strict truth in his note to Bourne in saying that it would be an extraordinarily successful diversion.

Bourne and Jean Marie each held the great painting by a corner and by its side as they staggered backward with it to the mother frame. Just as they reached it, two elderly American tourists, a man and a woman, walked slowly past in the corridor outside the entrance to the room and stared directly at Jean Marie, registering absolutely nothing, not even seeing what they saw because they were looking for religious paintings by Bartholomé Estaban Murillo, and passed on.

Jean Marie only knew that they stared at his guilt, had seen him while he stole, had documented his fear and had realized his nightmares. He did not slow down his movement. He did not comment. He merely dropped his corner of the painting and ran. He ran without thought, without hope of escape. He ran and left Bourne and the Goya and the mother frame and the *trompe l'oeil* and the huge identical copy which had so pleased Dr. Muñoz.

Bourne watched him go, but could not cry out after him because he was engulfed with despair. It was as if a chained

169

man sat at the edge of a ferryboat while the wind blew all of his life savings out of a hat at his feet and he could see the money, the green paper money, float down the river toward the sea in the moonlight. But his mind reacted, that motor part of it, as it had been trained to react; his reflexes bearing the fruits of the discipline which he had put himself to over so many years. With his height and because of his great strength, he managed to lift the bottom edge of the Goya into the mother frame, but then it slipped and crashed upon the floor. He lifted again, straining in agony, and got it placed more solidly this time. He pushed one corner home, then slowly traversed the length of it, securing it into the mother frame and this time it held. He tapped it methodically all around its periphery to make sure it was secure, then he picked up his smart, dark blue homburg hat, by Gelot of the Place Vendôme, from the floor and strolled leisurely out of the room, using the exit opposite the one which Jean Marie had run through, wiping his hands on his handkerchief as he went. En route to the gate on the Paseo, he paused with some Swedish tourists to appreciate El Greco, exactly on schedule.

He reached the door of his hotel room at ten minutes after five o'clock. Eve told him Cayetano had been murdered.

By ten minutes after five the police and other security officers had sealed off the Sala Goya and its approaches from the rest of the Prado. The six guards of that wing were lined up against the far wall of that room, faced by nine police officers of high rank. Six extraordinary security officers were present and four representatives of the Instituto de Cultura Hispánica. With them were the Director of the Museo del Prado with two Goya experts. They were grouped about Jean Marie's copy as it stood propped so incongruously against the wall under the great bare spot, looking as though the original had slipped from its moorings and had slid to the floor.

Each of the twenty-seven men in the room were whey-faced with shock and anxiety. The experts had just finished agreeing, as impossible as it sounded, that because of the quality of pigment, the age of canvas, and the wood across the back of its frame this representation before them which had to be "The Second of May" by Francisco Goya y Lucientes was not that painting and while they did their best to cope with this obscene enigma they tried to ask themselves,

170

then the police experts, for the smokiest wisp of an idea as to where the original could have disappeared.

Behind them, at room center, as bulky as a battleship, stood the great false frame which seemed to hold only the triptych of the three copies of the Goyas on a single canvas.

Guard after guard confirmed the story that for three weeks a man known as Charles Smadja had wheeled the great frame into this room, as indeed they had assisted him day after day, to work under official museum permit to copy the three Goyas. They were told to test it for weight, and man after man insisted that the weight was exactly the same as it had always been.

With these points established the police asked the Director of the Museo del Prado who turned to ask his assistant who turned in his turn to ask his assistant to have the museum permit explained. The police learned that the permit had been issued to accommodate Dr. Victoriano Muñoz, the Marqués de Villalba.

The triptych was ordered impounded by the police. A police van carried it to a police warehouse where it was ticketed, crated and wrapped in strong, brown paper. The Goya painting called "The Second of May" was even more concealed from the eyes of its host, the Spanish state.

PART III

Aplomado

The bull is tired. His flanks are heaving and his
breath is short. His speed is cut, but he is determined to use his horns on something solid. He is
beginning to think there is something not quite
right about the lure. He must be killed quickly now,
respecting both his tiredness and his intelligence.

THAT the art of Cayetano Jiminez was as impermanent as
Nijinsky's or Booth's inasmuch as it could live on, in reality,
only as long as an individual physical performance lasted or
as long as the memory of its last living witness, in fantasy,
made it no less a great art and perhaps a greater one for
while their genius had to remain interpretive his had been
summoned out of death, not unlike Picasso drawing in the
air with electric lights in both hands; art only while you
could see it, but undeniably creative.

That his courage had been fixed by the ritual of the corrida, a choreography repeated since the beginning of man's
practice of contempt for death in this form, made it no less
gallant nor less formidable than any other human's explora-
tion into any other unknown. The term unknown throughout
man's fix in time has been framed within the relatively
known, while the unknown hinted at by death has been
obfuscated by the wishful thinking or threats of priests and
bounded on all sides by the unseen visions of basilisk saints
and the professional conjectures of martyrs.

What follows appeared on the leading page of Spain's
national newspaper on the day following Cayetano's death.

*   172   *

*The shocking and senseless murder of Cayetano Jiminez in
the full light of day within the arena of the Plaza of Bulls
of Madrid yesterday closed a glorious cycle and presented
the memory with an accumulation of feats, of enobling
passion, of art and wisdom, in all of which he played a leading role. Cayetano Jiminez was above all else the dominating
figure, the axis of an epoch, the antenna around which
revolved the turbulence of the fiesta. To trace his memory
is both easy and complicated. It is easy because to some it
would be enough to say that he was the greatest fighter of all
time. It is complicated because to characterize him in every
moment of the evolution of his art and in every trace of his
style is a project more than arduous. His outstanding quality
was without doubt his vocation for the profession to which
he gave himself without reservation from the time he was
thirteen years old, as his illustrious ancestors had given on a
like basis for the past one hundred and twenty-three years of
the corrida. This was the killer of bulls who passed rapidly
through the arenas, obtaining the highest consideration that
any master could dream of, to die grotesquely as though
death had donned the ruby nose of a clown at a murderer's
hand at the age of twenty-seven in his full glory, without
knowing the pain of failure, without showing the slightest
symptom of decadence. It can thus be said that however
heinous his passing and however exemplary his life, his death
was transcendent in its completion of a cycle without a fault,
with mythical perfection.*

Bourne could not seem to unclench his fists or to unknot his
jaws when he was not speaking. Eve could not seem to take
her eyes off Bourne. Her beauty had been paled by the shock
of the news of Cayetano's death and more so by the raving,
drunken, mumbling, guilt-ridden, immobile, grief-ripped
Bourne it had produced. The paleness she emanated was
contrasted and colored by the gray-greenness of her large,
dismayed eyes ; by her glistening, full, red mouth and by her
lush, shining body under the green Japanese kimona which
she held around herself loosely, partially open over her
nakedness. She sat there trying to will Bourne to look at her
body. She wanted to make him use her body as an anodyne,
to drive himself into it so that the pain and growing hopelessness could be driven out of him.

Bottles, ice buckets, glasses, pitchers, cigarette stubs, snarled used cigarette packages, thick smoke, broken fragments of food and wet heat pocked the room. Bourne had slumped forward into the unapproachable drunkenness of an enormous man, his hands dangling between his legs knotted into fists at the level of his ankles, his meaty shoulders low, his head sunken into his chest, staring at the floor. Whenever he spoke brokenly about the duchess or Cayetano he had to shut his eyes.

It was nine forty-five of the morning of the first day following Cayetano's murder. For the two hundredth time Bourne mumbled, "I didn't know. I didn't know."

Eve moved slowly across the room. The robe fell open. She stood directly in front of him, then she sat on the sofa beside him and pulled him over to rest on her.

"It will all be settled today," she said, "you'll settle it all today."

"But I can't find him!"

"We'll find him. You'll see. We'll find him today." Bourne had telephoned Muñoz nearly forty times in fifteen hours but there had been no answer.

Eve turned his head with her right shoulder and with her right hand urged his face into her breasts, offering them as sanctuary.

"I was only trying to get what was mine," Bourne muttered. "I worked for three years for it. How could I know what he was going to do?"

"You were right, darling. You did right."

"That butler fills the door and keeps saying 'no, señor, the duchess is not here' when all the while she's writhing on a bed upstairs with the cords of her neck bursting from her throat while she says the word why over and over and over again."

"You'll see her today. And you'll see Muñoz today. You'll drag him to Blanca and you'll make him tell her what he did and make him tell her how you didn't know," she crooned.

"That's what I'll do. That's what I'll do today." He struggled to get up, but she held him close to her. "I'm going to get dressed now."

"Sleep first," she said. "Go to sleep, my dearest, go to

sleep." He lay still upon her and she began to pray that they could both be turned to stone.

Not only the Spanish press saw the truth in Cayetano from the perspective of his death. *Time*, the American news magazine, recorded his passing with these words:

North Americans would never be able to comprehend, because in this one area they had become the Carrie Nations of the SPCA, why men wept in the streets of Spain, or why holy candles burned in private houses in Peru, or why tens of thousands of Mexicans went into mourning, or why movie theatres in Venezuela were packed to show, again and again, newsreels of a man whose name most North Americans had never heard. Throughout that world plain people felt they had lost one who had given them, not delight, but a grim, transcendent excitement ; a pageant of death, and of courage, death's enemy.

The duchess sat in a straight-backed chair looking into the darkness through the open window and across the Retiro into the third morning after that afternoon. She had not slept. She had hardly stirred. To force her servants to leave her alone with her past she would pretend to sip the broth which they had brought and pretend to eat. Her black eyes were more protuberant in a bony, haggard face.

Many people had come to the house from Madrid and Spain ; from Rome, from London, from Cannes and Paris. Bourne, desperate with guilt and grief, had been turned away four times. The telephone had rung hundreds of times to be told by Pablo, the major-domo, that the duchess was not there. The cooks wept. The chambermaids wept. The footmen were red-eyed. Josefina, who was Pablo's wife and the duchess's body servant, looked crazy as though she were revealing the face of the duchess's soul while the duchess, having forgotten she had a mind or a body, sat staring out across the night.

As the false dawn of the third day appeared, the day before his funeral, the day before he would be taken far to the south to be buried forever, the duchess was at last able to clutch her mind and her memory leaving the place she sat in and the time she was trapped in and the body in which she was contained with such pain. She became a fussy and finicky
175

curator in dimensional time, shaking the cushions of memory, poking into display cases of sensation and old hurt, sweeping out ropy desires from the far corners of the museum of her life with Cayetano. She had willed herself to become a satellite of her shining past, circling the planet which was her memory; speeding with chilling loneliness through a vacuum, separated from all the substance she ached for by the gravitational force of death.

She became a learned scholar who taught herself her own dreams. She read and reread memory beginning at the afternoon in Sevilla when she had first met him, and devoured each nuance of their exchange as the light of her need struck it, going over the minutes of her life with him as some other marooned scholar might read and reread the pages of the single book he had salvaged from a wrecked ship.

She had held so strongly to the fleeing life as it had fled. Now she struggled to lock it within herself after it had flown. Reason had no part in this. Need was all and everything. She concentrated upon the state of oneness with the immediate instant she and Cayetano had shared, allowed one instant to cross her grateful memory at a time; one memory at a time, one pearl becoming a necklace, the necklace combining into one pearl; each instant brief and evanescent, not measurable in time and, being timeless, becoming eternal as well as instantaneous.

Time had no relationship to the new reality which trembled at the timeless instant of her evoked perception. The rest of the time continuum which had happened and was even then happening to all others beyond herself and Cayetano, became unreal figments of imagination.

She would begin to read her book in her memory in Sevilla, reading slowly, savoring each gesture and touch, hoarding the growing sharpness of tactile sensation, finding wondrous new meanings each time, never tiring of the story any more than a child who, to itself, lives it forever, would tire of a haunting fairy tale. Each time she went through the book she always went through from start to finish, never doubling back when she reached a snag but making a note to investigate that snag or new memory or blank space the next time she started from the beginning of the story to work her way to the ineradicable end.

On the morning of the third day something had happened

to these sequences. She grew more and more puzzled then confused each time she reached the last fraction of the story. There was one puzzling inconsistency which kept striking out at her, which kept interrupting the even flow of her narrative to herself. She tried to push it out of her place in time, but it must have been wrapped in her sanity. It would not leave.

In her mind, the only reality, it was that sunny, loving day when they had all met for luncheon at the Commodore. She started this sequence again, against all rules, as one would start a home movie projector at a favored place. She and Eve Bourne were riding in the tiny elevator with the small red-haired, freckled page boy. They swept into the dining room, and she noticed the golden-brown murals showing the horse-men and the hunters this time.

She relived the movement and sound of the luncheon with happiness. She loved the Bournes. Eve was a beautiful, warm and genuine girl. Jaime was good, solid and dependable, with a brilliant mind. They gave love to each other and to their friends. Cayetano had felt it and he had loved them too. She watched Cayetano and heard him talk. The great glacier which was growing to be a large blocking mass each time began to form.

"This is a week of miracles, really. I ask everyone here. Who is the most improbable Spaniard you can think of who would announce -that he was going to attend a bullfight?" She heard herself reply, *"My cousin, el doctor, Victoriano Muñoz, Marqués de Villalba."* She had imitated Victoriano's voice and everyone had laughed merrily.

She pulled herself forward through what had happened and what was happening again. She saw Cayetano lean over and kiss her hand, and her left hand opened beseechingly as she relived the sensation. Then he said in a voice which had become louder and louder and louder each time he said it again, *"He called me this morning and asked me if I would kill in front of Tendido Two next week on my first bull because they were the only seats he could get and he promised to take Mrs. Pickett and he is afraid she won't last out more than one bull so he wants to make sure of that by making it as awful as possible."*

It had been as awful as possible.

Some voice began to shout questions at her from a great distance within her head. Why had Victoriano agreed to go to any corrida? What about Mrs. Pickett could have persuaded him to overcome such a tremendous, cherished prejudice? He had contempt for Mrs. Pickett. He had never spoken more than ten words to her in any given day at any time they had been thrown together. If she had caught fire before his eyes he would have rung for a servant to help her to put the fire out, no more. Why would he take such a woman to the corrida when he detested the corrida to an even greater degree than he felt indifference to the woman? The sound, disembodied and nonexistent then, which had come from a radio in an automobile which had passed under her open window during that first night after that afternoon came up to her now and entwined itself around Victoriano, and Mrs. Pickett, and herself. The sound was a radio voice which told with mournful wonderment that at the instant of the death of the great Cayetano Jiminez, Francisco Goya's great masterpiece "The Second of May" had been stolen from the Prado. She did not know, nor would she have cared, that that was the only announcement ever made about the theft of the Goya, that the story was killed forever within eight seconds after that announcement by highest order and all inquiries blandly denied, the denials saying the announcement had never been made ; denials by the radio, the press and the government and most of all by the Prado.

Jean Marie, locked in the suite where he had copied the Goya, dreamed that one brutalized *agent de police* had him by the hair, another by his right arm and both of them kept striking him with large riot sticks quite like the riot sticks the gendarmes had used on the Place de la Concorde during the Stavisky riots when he had been a boy, as they dragged him through black, frightening gates of what he was sure could only be a prison.

At eleven forty on the morning of the fourth day which was Saturday, the day of Cayetano's funeral and the day which had been set for his wedding, the duchess's servants sat, silent and expressionless, in the foyer of Dr. Muñoz' apartment. When they heard his key scratching into the lock Pablo arose and opened the door, surprising him.

"Eh!" Dr. Muñoz exclaimed, while the cat Montes stared at the two servants from under his arm, more surprised than

178

he, his eyes more demanding of an explanation. "Ah. Well. Pablo. Why are you here? And Josefina. Did the duchess send you? Of course. Good heavens, has there been more bad news?"

Josefina stared at him malevolently. Pablo stood aside, clearing the entrance. "My duchess waits for you in the salon, marqués," Pablo said.

"The salon! Well! How long has she been waiting, for heaven's sake?"

Pablo took out a large, gold pocket watch and snapped open the case. He studied it carefully. "Eighteen hours and forty minutes, marqués," he said gravely.

"What? What the devil has happened?" he said sharply. He stared at Pablo then at Josefina but got nothing. He moved rapidly across the foyer and down the corridor to the tall, arched doorways which led into the Moorish room. He hesitated at the closed doors, biting his lower lip nervously and pill-rolling his fingers on the balls of his thumbs. At last he turned the latch and entered.

The duchess sat, facing the door, framed by the light which filled the sky beyond the large windows behind her, erect in one of the high-backed, heavy council chairs. Involuntarily, the marqués glanced up at the paintings which were illuminated on the wall.

The brilliantly colored carpet beneath his feet seemed as soft as sand. He could not remember sensing that before. Everything which he had ceased to be aware of in that room seemed now to take on deeper dimensions. The lights flooding the paintings shone more brilliantly as though caught in the lights from the eyes of the Archangel Michael. The atmosphere between himself and the duchess seemed pelagic. He knew he must not shout but he feared that no sound could be heard this morning in that room.

The duchess watched him come in as one looks at a bellman whom one has been told approaches with a message. She saw him as he was on that day, at that instant, not as she had always seen him: an extension of their childhood, as a somewhat pitiable, resentful child held together with the wires of his pride and with the strength of his forefathers' failings. All at once she was saddened to see that he was a comically effete man wearing, not clothes but some kind of flagrant plumage as he peered forward through himself as though he

179

were standing well behind himself. His greased hair shone like stars reflected in soup. His poor mustache seemed like the vibrissae of a spaded mouse.

His crenelated mouth moved without opening.

"Good day, Victoriano. Did you have a pleasant journey?"

"Journey? What d'you mean?"

"You've been gone for four days the porter said so I called that nice Castanos man at the Comisario de Policía and in no time at all they were able to tell me that you were in Santiago de Compostela."

"Oh. Yes. Wonderful place for a rest, you know. Great peace. That sort of thing."

"Indeed, yes."

"I hope you have been comfortable here?"

"Thank you, Victoriano."

"If there is anything you need——"

"Nothing, thank you."

He took a deep breath and let it out slowly. "Blanca, I can explain the presence of these paintings."

"Sit down," she said. "Here." She touched the heavy council chair beside her. He seemed to need to think about that for a moment but then he walked to the chair uncertainly and sat down.

"Pablo!" the duchess called out in her strong, sweet voice. The man appeared instantly in the doorway. The duchess turned to Dr. Muñoz and said, "You will think I have simply taken over your house."

"It is your house, my duchess," he answered gallantly as Pablo crossed behind him and brought a loop of strong cord over his head and bound him to the chair, across the chest, torso, legs then one arm. The duchess watched with the amount of simulated interest one consumes watching someone else's child play a short piece upon the piano. The marqués neither cried out nor spoke while he was being bound. When Pablo had finished, and he did a rapid and thorough job, he stood silently by, waiting for further instructions from his mistress. "Thank you, Pablo," she said and he left the room.

Muñoz tried to appear as natural as possible under the conditions but above all tried not to look at her. His right arm was free. He lifted it slowly and regarded it as though it were a new object, strangely shaped, as though it were something he had once read about but had never seen. The cat

180

Montes walked up his bound left arm, across his shoulders, then down his fragile chest on the right side, to settle down for a splendid sleep, after a long journey, in his lap.

The duchess, wearing black, sat with her hands in her lap, in repose. Her hair looked like what is left on the ground after a fire in a cornfield. Part of it was yellow and part of it was black. Her popping eyes, black and congenitally intense, watched him serenely. She wore many rubies against the black. At last her long white fingers moved, discovering him, and she began to speak again quietly.

"I telephoned Mrs. Pickett. She told me she had not been to the corrida with you."

"Blanca——"

"I was surprised to learn, as you will be I know, that she had never been to a corrida and yet it always seems to me that when she isn't hinting at what men would secretly like to do to her she talks about nothing but bullfighting. It must still remain a romantic thing to her, like jousting or falconry."

"What I insist upon establishing here and now, Blanca, is the fact, the simple fact that——"

"I cannot explain to you why those particular words of Cayetano's about your attending last Tuesday's corrida stayed in my mind."

"Did he mention that?"

"He made it very amusing, as usual. He told us how you had called him and had so urgently requested that he kill the first bull in front of Tendido Two just to get the agony over for Mrs. Pickett that much more quickly."

She looked at him brightly. She had so much pain in her eyes. He moved as well as he could tied as he was telling himself that he must never look into her eyes again or he would never be able to sleep again. He shut his eyes for an instant trying to project his consciousness forward to some impossible moment of sleep. "Would you mind if I smoked?" he heard his cousin say.

"Blanca——" He started and stopped. "Nothing in this world is certain. That is to say at the last moment Mrs. Pickett decided not to go to the corrida."

"Ah, that explains it."

"Yes. Yes, of course."

"But when I saw you outside the plaza you told me she
181

was with you." This wasn't true, of course, but she wanted to hear his answer.

"I couldn't have."

"You did though."

"Actually I didn't hear a word you said over the noise of that awful crowd. I just nodded, I suppose, or said something inane. She wasn't with me. She called at the very last moment and canceled everything."

"Then I must be mistaken."

"You most certainly are, Blanca dear. But no harm is done where none is meant."

"The old sayings are the best." The duchess flipped at the silver lighter in her hand and lighted the long cigarette she held between her square white teeth. She assayed a smoke ring and, in the stillness of the air in that room, no opened doors, no opened windows, it evolved beautifully. "When I spoke with Mrs. Pickett this morning she told me that you have never invited her to a corrida. She didn't even imagine that you would want to invite her anywhere. Not at any time. She told me that she hadn't spoken with you since you drove them back to Madrid from my place and that was some time ago."

"That is outrageous!"

"My questioning her?"

"How could she dare to tell a lie like that?"

"Breeding, I suppose," the duchess said. " 'No manners, no conscience' is a good old saying, too." She puffed at the cigarette and touched the ruby pendant hanging at her white throat.

"She must be mad. You will certainly admit that she behaves like a madwoman."

"Do I behave like a madwoman?"

"Of course you don't." His constant movement under the ropes in the chair had gotten his left shoulder quite low and he seemed unable to right himself again, but he was careful not to move too noticeably and call attention to it.

"Why did you go to the corrida last Tuesday, Victoriano?"

"Why did I go?"

"Come now, pet. Please don't tell me now that I didn't see you outside the plaza."

"Of course I won't, but I'm not sure I understand the question."

182

"Forgive me. I asked you that because there is no Madrileño more famous for his detestation of the bulls than you."

"Now, one moment, Blanca. Just one moment. I want this to be clear now and forever——"

"Forever." She tipped her head back to stare at the ceiling. "If someone could only tell us how long is forever."

"Pardon?"

She looked at him again, but he looked away quickly. "Nothing," she said. "Go on."

"You've been asking me some extraordinary questions. And not only to me, Blanca." His voice had the aggrieved indignation of a pupil who has been unjustly told he must remain after school. He looked piercingly at her right shoulder and indicated that he would not tolerate this sort of thing, even from her.

"One question."

"Ask me anything. You *know* you can ask me anything," he replied.

"Why have you not made any mention of the somewhat unusual, not to say eccentric, fact that my servant has entered this room and has trussed you into your own chair?"

"I—what is there to say? It is all most embarrassing. I mean, if I were to acknowledge this condition you speak of, I said to myself, I should be required to become very angry with you, Blanca. We are old and dear friends. I mean, since childhood. I could not under any circumstances, that is to say I thought that——" With his free right hand he brushed confusedly at the empty air.

"You thought that you would deserve what would happen, whatever happened. You felt such guilt under my gaze that your guilt expected punishment."

"Blanca—I only knew that when you saw these three paintings you would reach the conclusion that I had stolen them from you. I decided at once that you had taken this unusual means to question me about the paintings and I could not fathom why you insisted upon dwelling upon the idiotically unimportant point of whether or not I had taken Mrs. Pickett to the corrida last week."

"Not last week. Last Tuesday."

He licked his lips to dry them, but his tongue was dry. "Stealing paintings such as these would be a most serious charge," he said staring at the intense patches of light on the walls and trying to will her mind away from talking about that afternoon. She turned with his glance slowly, seeming to move out of politeness rather than an appreciation of art.

"You stole these paintings from me?" She seemed utterly surprised. She rose from her chair and walked close to the Zurbarán to study it intently for a moment. "Why!" she exclaimed, "this is a painting from Dos Cortes!" She sidled along the wall to the Velázquez. "Upon my word I believe this one is The Pickett Troilus!"

"The—what was that, Blanca?"

She wheeled to gape at him. "You stole these from me?"

"Is that not what you had decided?"

"To tell the truth, Victoriano, I have had so many things on my mind that I have never thought of these paintings at all and I have been sitting here for some time. Did you say you stole them from me?"

"I have nothing more to say."

The duchess walked to consider the Greco, her back to the marqués. "If I were to turn and look at you," she said, "I know I would find your face set into that stupidly stubborn look you used when you were a boy and had been outwitted and bewildered, that hopeless look which means that you have decided that you will say nothing more even if it were to mean your salvation."

"I am sorry, Blanca," he answered stiffly.

She walked to the fireplace and took up a poker from among the fire irons. "I know, for example, that even if I were to swing this iron back and crash it with all my force into the bone of your lower leg then to swing it back again and bring it with even more force to crush your kneecap, that even then you would not talk about this matter of the paintings because you have set your mind and that is the way you are."

"That is the way I am," Dr. Muñoz answered simply.

"Then I am helpless."

"I do not know entirely what you wish to learn from me but as regards those paintings I have closed my voice."

"I plead with you," she said languidly looking closely at the brushwork of the Greco, the marqués ten feet behind her.

"Forgive me. I cannot."

The duchess sighed and strolled to the long table which
184

stood against the far wall. It was ancient and possessed Spanish history in its joints. She slid the drawer of the table open and removed a pair of shears. They were long and heavy.

"Your resolve batters me," the duchess said. "I am helpless in the face of your will power." She turned with the heavy shears in her hand.

"Thank you, Blanca," Dr. Muñoz said briskly, if not indulgently. "I am happy that you can see it as it is. Now, cut these cords with those shears, my dear, my circulation is growing sluggish. We will speak of this no more. The incident will be our secret."

She walked across his gaze, which followed her. She pulled a leather-backed chair out from the wall and dragged it to a place directly in front of the Greco which was hung in a direct line with the marqués' vision. She stepped up daintily to stand upon the chair saying, "I have known of the iron nature of your character since you were a little boy, Victoriano. I know I cannot cope with it. I admit defeat."

"Why are you standing on that chair?"

She raised the points of the closed shears over her head, bringing them close to the face of the central saint in the painting. "I am going to destroy these paintings," she said with detachment.

"Blanca!" he screamed. "No! Stop! Blanca! That is the work of El Greco, the great and immortal El Greco!"

She lowered the shears. "Will you answer all of my questions?" she asked.

"Yes. Please step down. Put the shears back in that table drawer, please. You cannot know what this does to me."

"Can you mean that your iron resolve has melted?"

"Yes. Step down, Blanca."

"How can I be sure? Perhaps I should destroy just one painting to demonstrate my sincerity." She made as if to turn toward the canvas again.

"Blanca I have completely changed my mind! Please step down. Now. Step down, Blanca."

She stepped down. She walked slowly to the great table, opened the drawer and returned the heavy shears to their place.

"Who would have dared to think that you would ever have relented?" she asked and sat in the chair next to the marqués,

185

crossing her legs. "You are really very, very chivalrous you know, Victoriano, to have changed your steely resolve so quickly, a position from which wild horses could not have dragged you."

He fought not to look at her. His free right hand dragged at his collar. "I am always happy to advise you," he said. "Surely you know that. I value your friendship highly."

"Who stole the paintings for you? You have neither the intelligence nor the character to accomplish such a thing." He flushed with fear because the charade was over. He had known her for such a long time, through many reactions, in several circumstances when she had been parted from something she had honored, loved, or valued. He began to breathe heavily, but he could not look into her eyes.

"That is true. I did not steal the paintings. Your friends obliged me—Mr. and Mrs. James Bourne." As he said the names he wished he had not said them.

She struck heavily at the arm of his chair with the poker in her hand, splintering the wood as he drew his right hand away. "Don't lie to me! Don't lie more than you have to me!"

"It was not a lie. It is most difficult to believe but it is true. He is a professional thief. She is his wife. She brought the copies to him from Paris where Calbert painted them. He never knew I was interested. My own participation, quite unknown to him, was to bring Expert Pickett along on the last foray to verify the copies."

She had grown very pale. She closed her eyes and did not seem to breathe. "I feel sick," she said. She had been balancing herself on a thin, high wire above the crocodile mouth of catatonia. The wire seemed to have been heated white-hot, sending shocking pain through her. She felt herself toppling as the crocodile grinned then all at once she was able to steady herself upon her hatred and her desire for what was right which was only as thick for grasping and steadying as one line of printing which said, an eye for an eye and a tooth for a tooth. The future became as clear to her as it had once been seen by an old gypsy woman who had told her own fortune with a pack of Tarot cards, had paused to peer through the light of a kerosene lamp in the woodshed of a farmhouse, confirmed what she had seen and cut her own throat. While the duchess groped for the railing which would

186

support her, Dr. Muñoz, who loved her on his own terms, spoke quietly. "It was an impersonal thing, Blanca," he said. "When Bourne met you he had no way of knowing how dear you are or that he would come so quickly to love you and respect you deeply. Try to see him in a different word because thief is a word which can trap you. He had worked everything out on scale drawings with time and motion studies and a thorough investigation of how he would market the paintings after he had acquired them. Why, he spent just over three years on this one project of overtaking those masters. Some time after he had settled in Madrid he had discovered the paintings of Dos Cortes in a book. Then, afterward, he asked if he might meet you, if he might see the paintings. He played the role of an art lover most effectively, but he wanted to test his paper plans against the actual conditions at the castle. This man, I tell you this, Blanca, and plead that you believe me, would never have been able to bring himself to hurt you. To him, these were paintings hung too high in semidarkness on a wall in a house which was seldom lived in, and not any part of you. Not in any way any part of you. He stole those paintings from that house and I had them stolen from him."

Muñoz felt free for what he had said. He felt that he wished he could be alone now and analyze what he had said because something in those words or the way he had felt when he had said those words had well, not lifted his spirits, but had made him feel good enough—good enough to be a friend of Blanca de Dos Cortes. He saw at once that he had caused himself to have pride in himself and it was an enormous discovery. He saw, running parallel to that astounding, cosmic fact, that he had never explored that area of his life but that he had only used a pride, which was a word and perhaps rightfully confused with the pride that is self-respect, with pride in his family. Supported by the cords around his small body, he literally let himself go into this new, stunning sensation. He could not think of what he might do for Blanca next. Blanca was the key to pride in himself, the start of what could be many rewarding experiments. Pride was his word. It was Spain's own word. After so many years this new revelation of pride had been given to him. He was charged to learn exactly what it could mean. He wished he could be alone, that Blanca would go now, so that he could get to work and run down the sound answers. He thought it was some form of telepathy when she started to talk again.

"I'm sure you're very proud of yourself for having said that. You have as much pride as any man I have ever known or read about, Victoriano. To me it is unnatural, but I do not pretend to have your view." She spoke slowly. She had just lost her last two friends whom she had loved. They were dead. She had mourned for them for a moment and now she must return to her tasks and get her work done. "Your pride is based entirely upon the past which to me, and I say only to me perhaps, is an unpleasantness like having a picnic in a cemetery."

He wanted to cry out that she was wrong. That may have been the case but that she misunderstood the boundaries of his feeling. "Nonetheless," she went on, "no form of this protective pride, the touchy, face-losing-face-saving kind has any place between you and me. That has been acknowledged throughout our lives."

"I agree, Blanca. I have never feared that you would scorn me."

She burst with the bitter words. "Then why didn't you say you wanted those paintings from me! Did you believe I would have refused you? You know that I know that Spanish painters are a great part of your most abnormal life, but if I had known that you had needed them like this!" She stared at him in despair but he would not look into her eyes. "You could have had them for use in your lifetime. And you know that! Why did you want them stolen from me?"

"I needed them. I needed to use them to do something."

"What did you need which they would trade for? What did you have to have which no one had the power to give you, but which you decided you would have to take, no matter what pain you caused? What was it? Tell me what it was, Victoriano."

"The attack upon the Mamelukes in the Puerta del Sol."

His voice was quiet but it had filled him with great pride. The first kind of pride, the pride in his family. If he could only regain for a moment that thrilling pride of self so that he compare them, just for the moment, then later sit before the fire and think about it.

" 'The Second of May'? The Goya?"

"Yes."

"From the Prado?"

"Yes. For my family. I wanted to possess that symbol for the honor of my family for what that man and that day had done to my family." He drew his voice down into decorum. "Essentially, Blanca, we have spoken of the condition many times."

"I know." She drew her hand across her eyes and he looked up at her lovely face quickly as she did so, fearing no risk, then looked away. She had been the good friend of his life. She had never ceased to protect him. No matter where, she had always defended him, and now—he could not grasp what had made him want to cry out piteously— the light had gone out in her eyes. Her soul had died. He looked at her hands, reposed in her lap against the black of her mourning, as she spoke to him, almost absent-mindedly.

"Two things were repeated over and over, until I had to do something about them. He was dead. There is that word 'forever', which you used. He is dead forever. God gave me a way to return to him. I wanted to stay there, but two things, little things, stopped me."

"Forgive me, Blanca. Please forgive me."

"The Seine was eleven silver lakes, to him, caught between the bridges. The air in London was wet, he said, and it washed the past away. Madrid was the center of the universe and therefore not as important to lovers as Sevilla where no one needed to be so self-conscious. He was dead. The first lever which began to pry me out of my mind and memory was the wonder of why you would take Mrs. Pickett anywhere and, of all places, to a corrida. The other came to me from a radio which was in a car which passed under my window on the Alcalá. I heard it because it said his name. His name came up to my ears and the radio said that he had died at the very instant that the Goya had been stolen from the Prado. The Goya, you have always said that someday you would possess." She looked at him sadly and with pity. "You didn't get it, did you, Victoriano?"

"No. I didn't get it. Or rather Bourne didn't get it. Almost. I almost had it, but I didn't get it."

"It must be a bitter disappointment to you."

"Well, nothing else really interests me very much."

"You'll never have another chance."

"No. I suppose not."

"You killed Cayetano to draw attention away from the activity at the Prado?"

"Yes. I'm sorry, Blanca. That was the way it was."

"Who else was with Bourne?"

"The French copyist."

"M'sieu Calbert?"

"Yes."

"I want you to telephone them now and tell them to come here. At once."

"What good will that do? What can a lot of talking accomplish?"

"Do as I say." She pushed the telephone across the low table, stopping it at his free hand. "Was Mrs. Bourne connected with the Prado operations?" the duchess asked.

"No. But if she had been, instead of that ——"

"Call Bourne."

The marqués took up the receiver of the telephone and put it on the table. He dialed the hotel number. He picked up the receiver again and held it to his head. "Señor Bourne, please," he said into the telephone. He waited. "Jim? Victoriano Muñoz here." He flinched while a gabble of furious voice escaped from the instrument. His face colored and hardened. "All right," he said sharply, "if you want to talk so much come over here. Immediately. And bring Calbert with you." The crackling, furious, distant voice continued but the marqués slammed the receiver into its cradle. "They botched everything, after I gave them everything they asked for, and now they are the ones who are angry," he said indignantly. "This is really too much, I must say."

The duchess stood up. He sat there as though being tied to a chair in his own house were a natural thing.

"Am I to remain trussed up like this while those men come over here to whatever pointless discussion you have in mind?"

"Thank you for calling, Victoriano," she said.

"Not at all," he replied, and unconsciously his eyes lifted and he looked directly into hers and he saw what he had done and understood it for the first time.

"Goodbye. God have mercy on you." She struck him heavily across the crown of his skull with the heavy iron poker. There was a popping sound. She hit him twice more, swinging slowly. She dropped the poker from her gloved hand to the floor beside him. The exhausted cat Montes did not awaken. She turned away from the man-into-corpse as formally as a movement in a folk dance and walked to the window which led to the terrace. She opened the catch in the door and went out upon the balcony to look down over the wall. She stared down impassively at the Calle Amador de los Ríos. In ten minutes or so, Bourne's car turned into the street on two wheels from the Calle de Fernando El Santo to stop directly in front of the entrance to the Muñoz building.

The duchess went back into the Moorish room, closing the door of the terrace carefully behind her, paying no attention whatsoever to the body which was slumped in a mess tied to the chair. She moved the telephone to the other side of the table and dialed.

"Police? Police, come quickly, come quickly," she said into the telephone. "Dr. Muñoz, the Marqués de Villalba, is being murdered! The men are still in there. Quickly! Number four Calle Amador de los Ríos. Dr. Muñoz."

She replaced the telephone and moved swiftly out of the room and along the corridor. As she crossed the foyer, Pablo held the door open for her. "It is done," she said. "The others will be here shortly."

She left the apartment. Pablo closed the door. She went down the stairway quietly just as Bourne and Jean Marie reached the top floor in the elevator, needing to pick her way with great care because she was blinded by the tears in her eyes.

Homer Pickett fairly burst into his suite at the Palace Hotel waving a copy of a different picture magazine in each hand and grinning rapturously at his wife who had been rubbing a product called *Splendor* into her face.

"Both of them! Both of them!" he cried out. "And both in color! 'The Pickett Troilus.' They both say it, just like that. I'm bigger than Berenson right now. All I need to do is follow up this advantage and I tell you, Marianne, I'll *stay* bigger than Berenson."

Mrs. Pickett walked to him rapidly, curlers in her hair over a smart, black sheath dress by Balmain. "My God, Homer, did they run any of those pictures of me?"

"I'll say they did. Well, the German magazine did anyway."

"The German magazine!" She took both magazines away from him and threw the American magazine on the sofa, seven feet away. "Well what the hell good is that? Who reads the German magazine except a lotta goddam Germans?" She flipped through the pages rapidly. "Where? Where is it?"

"Here." Mr. Pickett tried to grab the periodical from her, but she swerved away. "Let me have it," he said. "Page seventy-eight. There. Look at that color reproduction."

"Where? Where am I?"

"Right there. Down in the corner."

"Aaaah!"

"Doesn't that Velázquez look marvelous?"

"Marvelous? What did that little son-of-a-bitch do to me? Why didn't you tell me my hat was practically over my chin? I look like a goddam drunk."

"Look here. Read this caption."

"Read the caption? I'll sue the goddam magazine."

"No, no. Here. Look. The Pickett Troilus. A painting by Velázquez is called 'The Pickett Troilus' in the public prints."

"The public prints! A goddam German magazine."

"No, no. In both of them." He scampered to the sofa and scooped up the American picture magazine and broke it open uncannily at exactly the right place for the layout, having clipped the pages together. "The title of the *entire goddam article* in this one is 'The Pickett Troilus.' Did you ever *dream* of such a gasper? Do you realize what this is going to mean to Arthur Turkus *Danielson*? I'll bet right now that he tries to make me sign for a *minimum* of six pieces a year and a coast-to-coast lecture series. Oh, I tell you! These public relations firms are worth every cent they cost."

"I suppose you're happy and proud about that picture of me?"

"Lecturing is like the best part of life in Washington, hon. It's one long cocktail party day after day with all kinds of people pressing up close and asking thousands of questions."

"Incidentally, what about Washington? How can you talk about a lecture tour? They'll hand you your head."

"Never mind. It'll all be handled. I take care of the party and the party takes care of me. I guess I'm entitled to a little sick leave. How would you feel about a lecture tour?"

Mrs. Pickett sat down in front of the large mirror and

192

began to massage her face again, her neck protruding far forward, her nose almost touching the glass as though she had reached the terminal in progressive myopia in trying to study each pore in her face.

"*Look* at these layouts! I wonder if I shouldn't hop over and show these to the duchess."

"Uh-uh." Mrs. Pickett shook her head vigorously into the mirror.

"It might cheer her up," Mr. Pickett said speculatively. "After all they *are* her paintings and I do feel I owe her something. If she's kinda down in the dumps because that fighter was killed maybe that's what I should do."

"I wouldn't, Homer," Mrs. Pickett said. "I talked to her on the telephone yesterday morning. Nothing in this life'll ever cheer up that woman."

Mr. Pickett sat down on the bed beside his wife's bench, his weight pulling him down and down into the mattress, until his eyes sank below the level of Mrs. Pickett's. He cleared his throat. "I know this *could* sound actually *ghoulish* in a way, and I *certainly* wouldn't say it to anyone else but *you*, Marianne, but her connection with that bullfighter and the paintings at the same time and the way he was killed just as they announced I had discovered The Pickett Troilus, you might say, you know it *could* be just the kind of thing which could absolutely *make* this lecture tour."

She thought that over for a moment or two. She stared at him soberly in the mirror. "I suppose you're right, hon," she said wrenching a metal curler from her hair. "In fact, now I think about it, I know you're right. The art jazz is all right for snob appeal in the lectures but that under-a-bush-with-a-toreador stuff is what they really want to hear."

"I'll ask the Press Officer at the Embassy to get me some pictures of both of them," Mr. Pickett mused. "The newspapers here must have plenty of them."

In the four days which had transpired between Cayetano's death and the equally abrupt passing of Dr. Muñoz, Bourne had tried to accomplish three things all at once. He had searched unceasingly for Muñoz. He had sought, with desperation, to find the duchess. He had done his best to cope with Jean Marie who had fallen into nervous collapse after the attempt in the Sala Goya in the Prado. While he had

193

been away from the hotel he had had Eve telephone the Muñoz flat every half hour. He had driven to the Muñoz aparment every three hours to pound on the apartment door after ringing the bell and himself into a frenzy and eventually to agitate the building porter to the point where the violence could be assuaged, but never undone, by money. He had haunted the outside of the house on Calle Alcalá, pacing like a distraught animal, pleading with and futilely trying to bribe the butler, Pablo. He telephoned Dos Cortes twice a day and had called twice in three days to her farm in Andalusia.

His huge bulk absorbed alcohol so much per pound then so much more per pound. He talked to himself while he drove from the hotel to Muñoz', to Alcalá. "What can I tell her? How can I prove it to her? Didn't know. Gotta see. What am I going to do? Muñoz. Find him and drag him. Muñoz. Where is he? Blanca, Blanca, Blanca."

He kept Jean Marie locked in the large suite on the top floor where they had run their drills. When Bourne left him sitting on the edge of the bed with his face in his hands, whimpering, Bourne wanted to run and hide until it could be all over and all of his friends could be well and safe again and then he would remember that Blanca could never be either well or whole again and the crazy circle of running and hunting for Muñoz would start all over again so that he could be saved from his guilt and so that when he was saved, he could begin to try to think how he could help again.

On the morning of the fourth day after that afternoon, Bourne and Eve attended Cayetano's funeral to look for the duchess. The body had been lying in state on a catafalque in the church of St. Rose de Lima since the morning of the second day. Fourteen thousand people had moved past the bier in twenty-four hours.

After the requiem high mass had been said the body was carried in its silver casket to the soot-black hearse which would lead the cortege from the church to the railroad station where the coffin would be placed aboard a special train and taken for burial in Sevilla. The bright, blue-domed day, the thousands upon thousands of milling mourners, the over-powering and pervasive odor of the heavy flower pieces, the smiting music, and the desperate fruitlessness of trying to find the chief mourner who wasn't there worked upon Bourne's fatigue like a nightmare. He could not connect the
194

long, silver box with the grinning, easygoing Cayetano. In the weary wrangle of his mind he kept seeing a huge cigarette box for the desk of a giant of dreams. He could not transpose himself into the collective grief of the crowd because they were celebrating a formal, respectable, solemn mass grief while his was a frantic thing like a live rat sewn into the stomach of a basket case.

He moved through the church continuously before, during and after the ceremony, oblivious of the rite, searching for the duchess. At the moment the silver box was being carried down the aisle of the church, she was seated in the Moorish room of the Muñoz apartment waiting for the marqués to arrive, enjoying a discussion about the *calamares* of Valencia with Cayetano in her memory.

As Bourne looked for the duchess, Eve followed him, listening to the prayers around her and wishing that she knew how to say them. He ended standing next to the camera crew of the government No-Do newsreel, peering into the crowd as though he himself were a camera. Eve led him off to their car. He sat, heavily and silently, in the front seat. She slipped behind the wheel and leaned forward to open the glove compartment to take out a flask of brandy. She unscrewed the top of it and passed it to Bourne.

"Thank you," he said thickly, and took it.

The crowds were thinning out. It would soon be possible for a pedestrial to move in the direction of choice rather than being taken wherever the crowd wished to move.

Eve held his left hand in her hand, across her thigh. "Let's go home now, Jim," she said and the pleading she tried to control seeped through the words. "Let's try to rest, sweetheart."

"I'd just like to stop at Muñoz' for a second."

"We'll call him the minute we get home. It's the same thing."

"No, baby. I have to stop by Muñoz'."

"You can't go on like this, Jim." The words were infected with hysteria.

"I'd stop if I could," he replied dully. "I can't."

A white-helmeted traffic policeman appeared on Eve's side of the car and asked them politely if they would please move the car along, that this was a difficult morning for traffic. Eve moved the car along the Paseo de Santa María de la

Cabeza. Bourne looked glassily at the buildings as they went past, exhausted. The car crossed the Plaza of Charles the Fifth and entered Retiro Park at its southwest corner. Eve drove slowly.

"Will we be out of this after you find both of them?" she asked.

"I don't know."

"Will you try to sleep when we get home?"

"All right."

"If we are out of this I am sick trying to think of how we'll handle Jean Marie."

Bourne said, "I thought maybe we could drive to Irún then load him with sedatives. We could hire an ambulance and take him over into Hendaye as a mental case."

She swerved the car into a parking space, a nose-in space, and stopped short. "You've been thinking about getting out. Oh, Jim. Oh, Jim, I love you!" She picked up his hand and pressed it into her lips.

His huge, dirty hand took the back of her head and brought it gently to him. He kissed her softly. "My love, my love," he whispered. "If I can show you once how much I love you!"

"I know, darling. Really, I know."

"The grieving can smother us. Guilt can suffocate us. They keep shoveling it on us. But what must be done has to be done and I'm as proud of you that you understand that as I am ashamed of me that I ever let us come to it." He held her hand tightly, suddenly. "They would have been married today." His eyes were bloodshot in front of this new reminder to twist the knife into himself. There was a dirty stubble of beard on his face. The hand which held her was bound at the wrist by a soiled white cuff closed by gold-encrusted, elegant cuff links. The fingernails of the hand had a high, glossy polish over thick lines of black on the ends of each. There was a sweet, sick smell of ruin coming from him. He closed his eyes. "I think maybe I'm going to be able to sleep," he said thickly. She backed the car into the roadway and they moved off toward the hotel.

An hour and twenty minutes later, icily awake, he unsnapped the lock of Jean Marie's suite and told him that Muñoz had called. An electrical change came over the painter. When Bourne came in he had been sitting in a torn bathrobe over fish-white skin; apathetic and unshaven. The

196

announcement that they were going to see Muñoz acted like a shock treatment. "We must kill the little pig," he suggested brightly. "Where is he? Come, come. Let's go and kill the little pig."

Bourne dragged him into the bathroom, pulled the robe off him and forced him under alternating hot and cold showers, which Jean Marie did not seem to feel. "How can he have the brass to telephone you?" he kept saying, and, "What new kind of doom does he offer us this time?" When they left the hotel, mere minutes later, they were both quite clean but they badly needed shaves. They were in front of the Muñoz building just about twelve minutes after Bourne had taken the Muñoz call. Jean Marie could have been slipping into a relapse. Bourne held his arm, fearing pneumonia and cursing himself for having given him the bath. They moved rapidly from the car, into the hallway, into the waiting elevator. Bourne punched the top-floor button savagely. The lift doors slid closed. "I want you to sit quietly, Jean Marie," he told the painter. "You have nothing to think about. I'll handle everything that has to be done."

"Sure. Sure. What are you going to do?"

"First he's going to sign a paper confessing that he killed Cayetano then I take him to the duchess."

Jean Marie started violently. "Cayetano? That young bull-fighter? He killed Cayetano?" His conception of the trouble he was in began and ended when he had dropped the picture frame in the Sala Goya of the Prado. Bourne looked at him as though he had stepped out of a time machine from the turn of the last century. Jean Marie pulled at his lapels and the car went up steadily. "What has that killing got to do with us? Is it connected with the Goya? Jim! I'll never see my wife again. I'll never see Lalu." He began to cry helplessly. Bourne shook his head, took a deep breath, and rocked him with a slap across the face. The doors slid open at the top floor of the building. Bourne pushed Jean Marie ahead of him and looked for the door-bell. Pablo opened the door instantly, not waiting for the ring. Bourne neither looked at Pablo, nor did he recognize Josefina. "Dr. Muñoz expects us," he said. "Take us to him."

Pablo led them down the corridor to the high, double doors. He opened one door slightly, let Bourne push his way past and through with Jean Marie behind him. When they

197

were in the salon Pablo closed the door and locked it from his side. He returned slowly along the corridor to take up his station at the front door.

They stared at the sickeningly battered head and the slumped body. Jean Marie bent over and picked up the bloodstained poker from the floor.

"My God, my God," he moaned. "What a terrible mess. We've got to get out of here."

"Come on!" Bourne said, wheeling toward the door. They were bewildered to find that they had been locked in. "The door is stuck," Jean Marie said. "What a time for a door to be stuck."

"It's locked. We've been locked in. I don't know what the hell this is all about, but we're locked in," Bourne said dazedly.

They heard many heavy voices beyond the door, at the end of the hall. The police station was two hundred and eighty feet away on the Calle de Fernando El Santo. They came down the corridor noisily, moving fast. Bourne could hear the key turn in the lock and the lock snap. The police burst into the room, registered its contents in one professional, collective glance then unhesitatingly beat Bourne and Jean Marie senseless with weighted leather billies. The time was five minutes after noon.

When Eve had been sure that Bourne had fallen into a deep sleep that morning she left on tiptoe out of the apartment for her regular Saturday morning appointment with the obstetrician. She returned to the hotel at twelve twenty-five. Bourne was gone. She called the desk and inquired whether he had left a message, knowing with falling heart that he had taken up his compulsive search again. The desk told her that Señor Bourne had gone out of the hotel in a great rush with Señor Calbert and had left no message.

She let herself sink down on the edge of the bed while her mind wove patterns of conjecture. She had not seen Jean Marie since Tuesday, four days before, but Bourne had told her that he had grown worse if anything and last Tuesday he had been a reed-voiced, shaking stranger. News must have broken. It had been electric enough news to reactivate Jean Marie, so it must have something to do with money, his panacea and denominator. She never knew the bloodthirsty

198

side of Jean Marie because that was his fantast's side allowed to be seen by very few but Bourne and scattered astonished prostitutes. He had often mourned that good character when interchanged for bad was not a ball, round on all sides with the weight of its love and dread distributed evenly throughout the mass.

Eve knew that the departure of the two men would have to be connected with Dr. Muñoz. If the duchess had called Bourne would not have taken Jean Marie with him, and nothing else but Dr. Muñoz could have persuaded both men to leave the hotel.

By three o'clock she was concerned enough to think of telephoning the Muñoz apartment, but she didn't. She had her lunch sent up to her terrace and occasionally, as she tried to eat, when she thought she heard Bourne's car stop in front of the hotel on the street below, she would get up nervously and try to peer down through the treetops, seeing nothing familiar.

Out of necessity she began to concentrate on the negative aspects of the duchess. She began to convince herself that her husband was so affected by the duchess's lot that she, Eve, must hold the duchess's fate at an arm's length never to be touched by it. If she began to feel Blanca's grief for Blanca's life she would be trapped, she would need to offer up sacrifices to stave off that grief. Her husband was the only sacrifice that grief would accept. She had to be taken if her husband were taken because she could not conceive of living without him. She railed at herself to reject the duchess. She was a housefly whose wings had been pulled off; she was insignificant except to herself; she did not exist where Eve and Bourne existed. She focused her concentration on the naturalism of Blanca's life: the woman had a record of sadness the way a habitual felon had a record of crime or a baseball player had a batting average. In twenty-nine years she had managed to find nine weeks of complete love. She was predisposed to tragedy and though Eve warned herself that she must deplore this the way women in fashionable restaurants deplore starvation overseas and urge their escorts to put coins into labeled tin collection cans outstretched by other fashionable women, she had need to find strength to protect herself and her husband from allowing themselves to propitiate that grief by giving themselves over to this stricken woman's terrible predilection.

199

She nearly ran, she strode so rapidly toward the bath, stripping her clothes off. She stood under the shower and turned on the full force of cold water. She gasped as it hit her, and kept gasping, but she stayed under it. She stayed under the icy water for nearly five minutes until she felt cold to the bone and had to get out. As she dried herself she felt far away from the duchess's problems and most dispassionately objective about her husband. She decided she would have to get him out of the country, cutting short his martyrdom, either by persuasion or threats or, if need be, in that ambulance he had summoned up, heavily drugged as he had so patronizingly planned for Jean Marie, to cross the border at Irún as a mental case.

At four twenty-five, the telephone rang. Eve ran across the room and snatched it to her ear. It was the duchess.

"Eve? This is Blanca."

"Blanca! Darling, where have you been? We've been imagining the most terrible things." She began again to feel the need for absolution from Blanca, as Bourne felt it, with staining force.

"Forgive me, my dear."

"We were at the funeral. We looked for you everywhere. Oh! Oh, Blanca!"

"Yes. It is terrible."

"If there were only some way we could——"

"I would like to see you."

"We've been desperate to see you. Jim *must* see you."

"May I come round?"

"Yes. By all means. Or we'll come to you. Whichever is best. Oh, Blanca. Forgive me for crying like this. It can't help you. It can't help Cayetano. Blanca, what are we going to do?"

"I'll be there at five-thirty, Eve, darling. Don't cry. Please don't cry for Cayetano any more."

The Cárcel de Carabancheles was the biggest jail in Spain and it suffered transient boarders only, in the outskirts of southwestern Madrid. In the warden's office of the jail three four-men interrogation teams of police under Captain Isidro Galvan were assembled in an extraordinary session which included the Director of the Prado Museum, the Under-Secretary of the Foreign Office representing the Institute of

Spanish Culture, the Superior Chief of Madrid Police, the chief of the Police Commissariat and, seen for the first time in their lives by eleven of the policemen assembled in the squads present, the Minister of Government himself and the Director-General of Security. Such an excess of seriousness made large, cold lumps seem to form in the stomachs of the men.

The Minister spoke. In his face and his voice a considerable amount of strain was evident. It could have been that, for several days, the focus of government had been directed wholly upon him and upon his ministry. His talks stressed that, under any conditions, the painting known as "The Second of May" by Francisco Goya which was presently "missing" from the Prado, had to be recovered without fail and at the earliest instant.

The Minister spoke from notes which had been well formed. First he understated the necessity of overtaking the painting because it needed no emphasis, every man in the room was a Spaniard. He filled in details of the background of Victoriano Muñoz, his family and his family fixation which had been long forgotten by most society. He advised them that Victoriano Muñoz had secured a transparency photograph in color from the Institute of Spanish Culture of the painting itself only two weeks before the disappearance of the Goya. He told them that through friends in the government—everyone in the room understood this thoroughly and did not judge it for in Spain nothing can be accomplished toward good or evil unless it is done through friends— Victoriano Muñoz had secured a license for his friend, purportedly a painter named Charles Smadja who was a famous French copyist and who had been authenticated within the past twenty-four hours as never having entered Spain at any time of his life, to work as a copyist in the Sala Goya of the Prado. All day-duty guards at the Prado had positively identified an equally well-known French copyist named Jean Marie Calbert as the man who had worked at copying in the Sala Goya entering and leaving the premises by use of the permit issued to Charles Smadja. The chief conserje at the hotel in which Jean Marie Calbert had resided in Madrid attested to having used his passkeys to examine the contents of an unused apartment on the top floor of the building, during the absence of Jean Marie Calbert from the hotel, and discovered a full-scale copy in progress of the Goya painting now missing together with projection equipment for viewing the color transparency. The hotel in which Jean Marie Calbert resided was and had been under lease to James Bourne for over three years. Two guards at the Prado had identified Bourne as having spent considerable time in the museum, particularly the Sala Goya prior to the disappearance of the Goya and on the day of its disappearance. The Federal Bureau of Investigation of the Government of the United States had identified Bourne's fingerprints as being those of one Robert Evans Cryder last known at the time of his death in an automobile accident in London, England, when he had been a captain in the U.S. Army assigned to the Cryptography Section of Supreme Headquarters Allied Expeditionary Forces. The Passport Division of the United States Government showed the passport in the name of James Bourne to have been a forgery inasmuch as neither the photograph nor the expiration date matched the Cryder data. Both prisoners had consorted with Victoriano Muñoz. All three were acquainted with and had been the guests of the Duchess de Dos Cortes, owner of the paintings by Velázquez, Zurbarán and El Greco found on the premises which had been occupied by the murdered man. In the statement by the duchess, as she had identified the paintings as having been hers she said —the Minister nodded at Captain Galvan who nodded at Augustin Termio who took out his notebook, opened it to a place held by a rubber band and, clearing his throat carefully first, began to read. He had never been in such exalted company in his life and he was scared to death.

"Question: Can you identify these paintings, my duchess? Answer: They are paintings which hung—which should now be hanging—in the castillo at Dos Cortes. Question: Did not the duchess notice that they had been taken? Answer: Somehow a substitution has been made. Paintings which are identically like these paintings are hanging at Dos Cortes at present. This is not like Dr. Muñoz. I am mystified. Question: Can the duchess clarify her last statement? Answer: Yes. You see, Dr. Muñoz has always been intensely interested in all Spanish paintings but he has said so many times that the only painting he would ever wish to possess for himself would be 'The Second of May' by Goya." Augustin Termio snapped his notebook shut and stood at attention. Everyone

202

else ignored him. The Minister asked for the statement by the porter in the Muñoz building to record a condition which had arisen after the Goya had disappeared, despite the fact that the men had been close friends before the disappearance of the painting. Captain Galvan nodded at Emilio de los Claros, a sergeant who had been in far more distinguished company than this and for a considerable period of years. He became the embodiment of crisp coolness, disdaining to address the Minister but reporting directly to his superior officer upward in a direct and dizzyingly altitudinous line.

"Statement by Ignacio Flan-Torres de Francisco, building porter at number 6 Calle Amador de los Ríos." The sergeant flipped open his book, giving the impression by so doing that he was a Black Belt in Judo, and read in a harsh, flat voice. "Oh, yes. That's him all right. That is his picture all right." The sergeant paused, looked up and stared hard at Captain Galvan. "He refers to a photograph of James Bourne, sir, known now as Roberto Eva Cryder." The sergeant returned to his reading. "I tell you I was frightened of that man. He came five or six times a day to the building. Sometimes he appeared late at night or early in the morning. He would shake the whole place with his fists as he beat on the marqués' door. He would curse in some foreign language and kick at the door, may his soul rest in peace. I have never seen such a violent type and I thought it was a lucky stroke that the marqués was away."

The Minister told them that Dr. Muñoz had been at Santiago de Compostela for four nights and three days visiting his confessor and spending most of his time praying at the cathedral.

The Minister told them that beyond a doubt they were assigned to a case which called for the organization of evidence which would lead to the conviction of the person or persons who had murdered Dr. Victoriano Muñoz, the Marqués de Villalba; however, as had been indicated by his presence there and by the statements made, that a most vital concern in this work was the recovery of the Goya and that a clear connection had been established between the two cases. He did not wish to interfere with police routine, but evidence which had come to his attention indicated that the prisoner Jean Marie Calbert would be the most vulnerable because of reprisals against his wife, presently a resident of

Paris, which could be brought to bear by the French public and French justice and that he would appreciate it if they would begin the interrogation of Calbert at once. He said that they had sufficient evidence against Bourne's wife to arrest her but for the present he considered that she could be more useful to them while at large inasmuch as it was possible that she could direct them to the Goya.

The Minister had become paler with inner tension as he talked. The Under-Secretary, whose brother was a doctor, diagnosed him as an actual or incipient ulcer man or a sphincter grinder. The eyes of the men staring at the Minister, as though they could see each word as it left his mouth, became larger and darker in their intensity. They were all clear on all present meanings. The man who found the Goya could jump four ranks. The man who found the Goya could be transferred to wherever his whims would like him to go, within reason. The man who found the Goya would have the protection of the highest figures in the government, and would be marked for all the better things. In short, the men of the teams were shaken with awe in having been called to the presence of a State Minister, the Director-General of Security, the Chief of the Commissariat of Police, the Superior Chief of all Madrid Police, an Under-Secretary of the Foreign Office and the Director of the Prado Museum, but they appreciated it very much and were eager to get on with their work.

To curb the higher enthusiasms, Captain Galvan put the questions for all of them.

"There are many, many methods of questioning prisoners, your excellency," he said in a straightforward manner, "and I wish to assure your excellency on behalf of myself and my men that, as indicated by the information which you have so skilfully gathered and so fortunately provided us, one or the other of the prisoners, if not both, will undoubtedly reveal where the Goya will be found."

"Bear two things in mind, Captain Galvan," said a short, pale man, who wore heavy tortoise-shell glasses and who stood at the elbow of the Minister. "First, the prisoners must be in a condition, following your questioning, to stand public trial in approximately two weeks if that can be arranged and I am sure it can be. Second, they are foreign nationals who are principals in a case which will undoubtedly attract the attention of the foreign press."

"Yes, your excellency."

"Are there any more questions?"

"No, your excellency."

"That will be all," the Minister said, leaving the room followed by full entourage including all present but Captain Galvan and his teams.

Both prisoners were reported as having fully regained consciousness and having eaten at two fifty-three ayem, so Galvan and four of his young men decided to start in on Jean Marie first in a squad room which had windows at the ten-foot level. They sat around him in a semicircle, except Galvan who paced most of the time. A male stenographer worked in the corner of the room, behind Jean Marie.

He had been provided with an armchair with the leather rubbed glossy but the benzedrine which he had been given in the coffee he had been served with the meal he had had when he came to, made him seem even more French than ever. He could not sit still and requested permission to pace about with Captain Galvan the way important businessmen sometimes conduct crucially important meetings while walking ten or so miles around a golf course. Galvan said he would be happy to have Jean Marie join him. He hoped silently that the prisoner had not been drugged too much because too much could make any of them begin bawling like a baby for no accountable reason and a benzedrine crying jag was almost impossible to stop.

Pacing with a high step, as though he were dictating to his aide-de-camp, the Marshal Ney, Jean Marie began to unwind by talking. He used the word gentlemen frequently, almost as punctuation.

"Let there be no mistake, gentlemen," he said. "Whatever we have done which could be considered as illegal I am absolutely ready and willing to admit to you. You will say that such an offer on my part, gentlemen, is most generous but I reply that I have great respect for your organization, that I wish to conceal nothing, and that I wish to get all unpleasantness over with."

Jean Marie had no conception that he was being held for murder. He did not associate himself with the death of Dr.

205

Muñoz. Somewhere in his disturbed, sensitive, shaken mind he believed that he was being questioned and held because he had dropped the corner of the painting by Goya in the Prado and had run ; a misdemeanor.

"When the confession is typed I will read it and if it is as I will tell you now I will sign it without delay," he continued after a complete turn of the room with Captain Galvan while he allowed them to consider the magnanimity of his offer. "But one fact must stand absolutely clear and apart, gentlemen. I had absolutely nothing to do with the murder of Cayetano Jiminez or of that insane little insect Muñoz or that hotel fellow, what's-his-name, Señor Elek." As far as the listening police were concerned, cases were about to be cracked right and left but the listeners showed no expression. Captain Galvan stopped pacing in tandem with the prisoner and moved next to the stenographer as though to test the acoustics in that part of the room.

"Neither I nor my friend Señor Bourne had anything whatsoever to do with those murders. Is that quite clear? If so we may proceed from there."

"That is entirely clear, Señor Calbert," Captain Galvan said blandly and imperturbably. "Please proceed. Please tell us the entire experience with all of these masterful copies of masterful paintings from beginning to end."

"Ah, you have seen the copies then?"

"Formidable, señor."

"Thank you, thank you."

"We would like to hear all about them."

Jean Marie sat down in his chair, and pressed his hand to his forehead in order to help himself think better. "You see, gentlemen," he told them, "some time ago, well over a year ago, my colleague and partner Señor Bourne came to me in Paris and began to talk to me about various methods by which we could substitute the copies of the paintings of masters for the original masterpieces." He turned to the stenographer behind him. "Do I speak too fast for you?" he asked.

"No, señor," answered the stenographer. "Please continue as you will." He told them everything he knew most accurately but he was merely baffled when they pressed him about the Goya. The Goya was in the Prado. Had they not heard him say that he had seen the people staring at him and

206

that he had dropped the corner of the painting and had fled the room? They could certainly believe that he hadn't run off with their Goya. He was happy to see that he had convinced them after such a long night because, in his mind, that attempted but unsuccessful contretemps in the Prado was the reason why he was being held.

Approximately four hours later at six o'clock that morning, Captain Galvan joined the relief team of two men and a stenographer in the room with Bourne. He nodded pleasantly as he came in but Bourne looked back blankly, fatigue showing in every excrucited muscle of his body.

Bourne's face was bruised on the forehead just under the hairline beside the left temple and his right cheekbone was split and badly swollen where the arresting officers had hit him. The stubble was longer and filthier, his eyes blearier, his hands dirtier. The elegance of the tailoring of his jacket and shapeless, soiled trousers seemed comical on his hulk. The jail clock he kept staring at mentioned six ten ayem or peeyem, he didn't know which. It was a diffident kind of a clock. Time has very little authority in jails.

"Anything new?" Captain Galvan asked his young men.

"Nothing, sir. He says he will talk after he has been able to see his lawyer."

"These American criminals come complete with lawyers. It is a result of the cinema."

"Yes, captain."

"Who is his lawyer?"

"He has asked permission to see the Duchess de Dos Cortes, captain. So that she may recommend a lawyer to him."

"He'll have a crowded cell if he keeps these requests up," the captain said.

"Yes, captain."

"He's good and tired, isn't he, the poor fellow?"

"Yes, captain."

"Good. Read this to him." He extended a typed copy of Jean Marie's statement. "That should wake him up." The young officer thanked the captain and settled down comfortably near Bourne's left ear and began to read in a clear voice which was well under a shout. The captain lighted a cigar and sat down with his chair tilted against the whitewashed

207

wall. "Termio, please!" he remonstrated from his place sixteen feet away. "Not so loud!"

"Yes, captain." Termio modulated and Bourne seemed to be listening carefully.

"Would you care to initial that?" Galvan asked Bourne when the reading was over.

"No. I mean, I cannot until I have been permitted to consult a lawyer."

"Where is the Goya?"

"Ask me later."

"When?"

"When you're ready to make a deal."

"No deals."

"No Goya."

Captain Galvan motioned the two policemen out of the room. "That's all. This man needs sleep."

"Yes, my captain," Termio said and they vanished. Captain Galvan strode heavily to the nearest chair and pulled it by its back near Bourne while he talked easily. "What is this talk about deal, anyway? Perhaps I misunderstood your meaning, Señor Bourne." He grinned with vintage cynicism.

"I am very tired, captain," Bourne said, "and I am not able to think clearly but my feeling is that after our innocence has been established, after the trial, that all we will owe you then will be a few relatively minor charges such as illegal entry, false papers and the theft of paintings which by now have already been returned to their owner, the duchess, and I think probably since you won't burn so much to see justice done that you might send my wife and Calbert and me over the frontier in exchange for giving that Goya back to Spain and the people of Spain and that is what I had in mind when I used the word deal." Bourne fought to focus. Each word he had managed to say had emerged from him, alone, as one unit, not as a part of sentences. There are people who learn to talk like that in Speech Defect classes and people also talk like that when they lie on the sand on the French coast after they have swum the Channel. Bourne fell asleep sitting up. The captain sighed and went out into the corridor. He called Augustin Termio who came running. The captain's hand stopped him halfway. "You have fifteen minutes to get this man awake and keep him awake," he said.

"Yes, my captain."

"Do you realize that you are the only man in the company who cries out yes, my captain after every sentence I utter? No! Don't answer. I am going to have a bit of breakfast. I suggest you get the surgeon to this man with some efficient restoratives. You will call me when the man has been refreshed which will not be later than fifteen minutes."

"Yes, my captain."

Good God, the captain thought as he strolled down the hall in the opposite direction, the man must be in love with me. He walked toward his breakfast slowly knowing it would be at least forty-five minutes before he would be summoned.

Bourne was awake again. He felt packed in ice and it seemed as though his head had come to a point. He had the illusion of his vision being fantastically keen, which couldn't be so because the same captain was sitting directly in front of him, obscuring most of what could be seen.

"You fell asleep," the captain said.

"No wonder," Bourne answered.

"Before you fell asleep you were saying that you felt we would be more inclined to make a deal with you after you had been acquitted of the charge of the murder of Victoriano Muñoz because the remaining charges, not being what might be called capital charges, would be more easily overlooked by us in return for your returning the Goya. I think that is substantially what you said."

"Yes. That's about what I've been thinking." He felt like a length of heavy rubber being stretched for hundreds of miles by two planes, each pulling in the opposite direction, each determined not to let go of their end of him. He liked the feeling. His visual clarity was phenomenal. He thought of it as his 6D process.

"Well, I am afraid you will not be acquitted of that murder and this is why. I work backward now. Victim killed with an iron poker. Only Calbert's finger prints on the poker. Next, you and Calbert in locked room with the victim at time of death fixed by the medical examiner." He held up his finger next to his nose. "A locked room. Your connection with the victim in two separate crimes—the Dos Cortes robberies and the theft of the Goya *plus* the death of Jiminez, bless him, and the hotel employee Elek have been confessed to by your associate Señor Calbert. All this while you will be before the court after having been unmasked as a passport forger and an ersatz identity. My dear chap, I don't know what you know about our prosecutors in Spain, but I can tell you that they are very keen fellows indeed and that they will wrap you like a small package and deliver you to the executioner."

Bourne smiled wistfully; ruefully. "If he does, goodbye Goya."

"Irresistible force, your execution. Immovable object, the Goya. I am merely suggesting that you might like to trade your life and Calbert's life for a painting which no matter where you have it you will never see again."

"Captain, you know your business. When I make a deal I'll make it with you."

"And I, Señor Bourne, when I make a deal I'll make it with you. How about now?"

"I want to talk to the Duchess de Dos Cortes."

"Why?"

"I have to—I want to ask her myself if she will be kind enough to find a lawyer for our defense. I wouldn't know where to start to find a lawyer I can trust, and I trust her to know a lawyer I can trust."

"You may be right. She has had more experiences than most duchesses with lawyers and jails." He stood up. He patted Bourne warmly on the back. "I'll see what I can do. I think you got the point." He walked to the door of the room with Bourne's limitless eyes following him. He opened the door, thought of something and turned around. "You did get the point, didn't you, Señor Bourne?"

"The Goya," Bourne rasped.

"Very good, Señor Bourne. You'll get your lawyer." He closed the door just as both airplanes, on either side of the continent, let go of the huge, stretched rubber strip which was Bourne at the same time. He slammed into himself from all sides and collapsed on the side of a mountain.

The duchess was ten minutes late for her teatime appointment with Eve, an exemplary action in Madrid, which brought her into Eve's great, crooning embrace at twenty minutes to six, or while Bourne and Jean Marie were still unconscious at the Cárcel de Carabancheles. She wore black, she had removed the rubies, and she had added a tiny veil which covered the expressions she might have, on the upper part of her face.

Both women wept for a time, truly each for the other simultaneously as they wept for self, then the duchess sat down abruptly and Eve sorted tea things.

"The police called me this afternoon," the duchess said. "My cousin, Victoriano Muñoz, has been murdered."

Eve dropped the empty teacup she held and made an anguished cry.

"Eve! Darling, what is it? I didn't mean to upset you. I had forgotten that you knew him."

"I—we met at your party," Eve said.

"It's all quite shattering. Violence upon violence. Both of them men of mine, you might say."

"It's shocking. Shocking."

"It is far more shocking than you think, Eve. I was summoned by the police to identify the paintings which were hung on his wall. They were my paintings. He had stolen them from Dos Cortes."

"Ah!"

"Is Jaime here? Pablo tells me he had come to the house again and again."

"No. He isn't here." Eve picked up the cup again, her mind still. She set the cup on a saucer and filled it with hot tea. "I had thought he would be back by now. He will be. Any moment. I'm sure." It had happened. Eve, who had thought that she could pull Bourne along with her, stumbling through the stench of unclean bats in the cavern, running through the darkness ahead of a doom, knew it had happened and that he had found the faceless wall he sought and had found someone's death between his fingers as she had known he would find it. She fell vertically into a chair. All the life he had poured into her was escaping from her as though through unstoppable holes in the ends of her fingers; escaping like gas when she held the fingers straight up and escaping like water when she left the fingers fall. It was all over and nothing in the world could threaten her ever again or make her feel that it could have importance.

She sat and she stared and she remembered Bourne in streaks of light which waited for her sight, as the duchess sat remembering Cayetano, each tenderly justified; both ransacked. The tea grew cold.

The telephone rang. Eve, nearest to it, did not hear it. The duchess looked at her wrist watch then rose to answer it as if by appointment. She listened, she spoke, and she listened. She said she would inform Mrs. Bourne and hung up.

"Eve. Eve, dearest."

Eve looked up at her.

"That—a friend who is quite powerful in government called to say—to tell me—to ask me to tell you that Jaime has been arrested with M'sieu Calbert for my cousin's murder."

Eve did not speak. She sat up straighter.

"Jaime wants to see me. Why?"

"He will tell you, I am sure."

"I will call the Minister himself." She went to the telephone and with quick movements dialed a number. She spoke a name into the telephone. She waited, then she began to speak again in a low, rapid voice. Her voice became more and more insistent, then the sentences became shorter, then she repeated only one word. "No? No? No?" widely spaced. She hung up.

"No one may see him," she said. "I don't understand it. That was the Minister. He has done far more difficult things for me in the past."

Eve was at the mahogany bar at the corner of the room. She poured two moderate drinks into two large inhalers. The duchess walked slowly across the room to join her.

"He will have the best lawyer in Spain, of course," the duchess said aggressively. "I will see to that this evening. The lawyer I'll get for him will be able to go in and out of those cells at Carabancheles like a turnkey." She sipped the brandy and openly appraised Eve's haggardness. She did not feel as exultant as she had thought she would feel, but she felt stronger and less lonely as she watched Eve empty of reasons for living.

The government released the story for world-wide publication Monday morning. Pictures of the accused went out with the general information about Bourne and Jean Marie, who was identified as a famous French painter. As edition after edition moved, the Paris papers ran pictures of Lalu Calbert, found in Bordeaux, who was tearfully mystified but sure it was all an enormous mistake, who then suddenly disappeared, the French stringers and correspondents were alerted to look for her in Madrid, at the jail or at the trial.

Since the Associated Press sold color art and photos to about two hundred Japanese papers on a very lucrative basis they needed a color angle fast so The Pickett Troilus became The Velázquez Curse for about four days tacked on to a story which said the great Spanish master who had painted only for Spain had loused up this particular painting good on his deathbed warning all foreigners to lay off. It was called King Tut's Tomb copy in the trade and always sold well so what started out to be a mere merchandising convenience for the Japanese market developed into a really worth-while world-wide sale, particularly to the United States roto outlets and South American dailies because not only was it an art story and therefore one with class for the former but it spelled out a whole Spanish angle for the Latin-American outlets.

Sam Johnston of *The Revealer*, London, squandered an overseas telephone call to talk to Eve from Fleet Street coppering the bet by having the conversation monitored by his office tape recorder, but his questions were gentle, generous, general and innocuous. Mainly he seemed to want to know if there had been any evidence which might indicate that this case was in any way linked with the alleged international art traffic which, it was stated in police circles, was controlled by Jack Tense, Britain's Master Criminal. Straight-faced, Eve went along with the paper's basic policy. She said that if Spanish masterpieces had indeed been stolen from the castle at Dos Cortes and the Marqués de Villalba had been murdered as a result it must be the work of some gang of international criminals because her husband, a respected businessman and pillar of society in Madrid whose reputation was more than impeccable was innocent and that she, wife of the accused, would be grateful for anything *The Revealer* might do to prove her husband's innocence. Johnston asked her if she would face Jack Tense if *The Revealer* would send him to Spain and she replied that she would do anything which could be seen to serve the cause of her husband's vindication and freedom. Sam said he felt he could get something real juicy out of that and he hoped it would help her in every way, because it would certainly build readership for Jack's next series.

Feature writers, magazine people, extra men for syndicates, mail, wire and telephone, stringers covering for the important American news magazines and the Milan weeklies which had abandoned active coverage in Spain, began to appear in

213

Madrid. They looted every nook and cranny of the story, but none of them saw the prisoners. Eve and the duchess were still barred as well from seeing Bourne. Paris *Match* submitted a petition signed by the entire French press corps fruitlessly in an effort to see the man the London and Glasgow papers called "Kithless Calbert," Jean Marie being without attendant kin. Some of the new people began by camping in the lobby of the hotel to bushwhack Eve or tried to push their way into the duchess's vestibule but they were disposed of by silent *policía armada* within ten minutes after the complaints had been received, causing very little outcry over the freedom of the press.

The No-Do government newsreel shot for Spain and also serviced the National Broadcasting Company, the Columbia Broadcasting System, Movietone, British and French Gaumont and the French Pathé reels which was more a matter of monopoly than keen salesmanship. This was redistributed to keys in Europe and on a second-run basis to South America and Asia providing work for planes, people, ticket takers, and workers in film raw stock factories. The scenes photographed showed the outside of the Cárcel de Carabancheles on a sunny day when it looked the most like a glove manufacturing plant, the duchess alighting from her Pegaso and walking rapidly across the pavement behind a high muffler and dark glasses into her house, and close shots of copies of the Velázquez, the Zurbarán and the Greco which were always explained vividly by the beaming Representative Pickett of Illinois and his delightful young wife in several languages.

Mr. Pickett got more over-all space out of the murder than any other element in it ; more than the outside of the jail, more than El Greco, more than the murder weapon, more than the building porter at the Calle Amador de los Ríos, more even than Mrs. Pickett mainly because he was so articulate and available.

He encountered one small squall when a Republican committeeman from Illinois telephoned all the way from the western part of the state and asked him what the hell he thought he was doing when he knew goddam well that Congress was in session. Pickett fired right back that he was cementing U.S.-Spanish relations and that he was proving that there was someone in politics who knew just a little something about how the great Spanish people felt about their great

214

painters, for Christ's sake, and what the hell was this poison pen talk like he didn't know Congress was in session? The boys knew goddam well how sick he was and how he was taking a lot of goddam chances with his health right now in order to make sure that this murdering renegade Bourne didn't bring the entire Spanish-American accord right down on their goddam heads. "Did you ever hold office, you silly son-of-a-bitch?" Mr. Pickett yelled. "Do you know the first goddam thing about practical politics? I tell you one goddam thing you'll know, you silly son-of-a-bitch, you've made one good, solid, lifetime enemy out of Homer Pickett!" He slammed the phone down from shoulder height then crumbled into the chair beside it and mewed at Marianne, sounding like an utterly different person perhaps forty years or so younger than the one who had just belched smoking terror and reprisals into the phone.

"I *hate* to talk like a longshoreman," he almost wailed, "but it's the only language they seem to understand. That ridiculous Al Burgerfolz! I tell you, hon, if it takes my *last dollar* I'm going to have that one drummed out of the party before he gets some idea that he's going to use *his* last dollar first. Oh, how I *hate* roaring like a lumberjack with all those operators listening in. How I absolutely *detest* and *despise* having to justify what is just about the best job of diplomatic front work being done today *throughout* Europe."

"Ah, the hell with him," Mrs. Pickett said. "No matter what he wants to do to you now he can't make it stick. Not any more he can't."

The duchess's life went through an unusual metamorphosis at this time. All at once, she began to cultivate the leading figures of the government most of whom she had rocked with anathema for most of her adult life. She held open house in Madrid. Invitations went out. She spent most of the mornings on the telephone, right up until two o'clock when she had to dress for lunch, with the cabinet, their wives, their under-secretaries and their wives, the ambassadors and their wives plus visiting prelates from Argentina. Beginning at eight every evening her salon would be populated for the cocktail hour. The duchess crackled and charmed and shocked and titillated very nearly every guest just as though she had always admired and envied each one of them.

At the dinner party following the fourth reception she had succeeded in having the rule reversed which said that neither Bourne nor Jean Marie could have visitors. She also made a fast friend of the Acusador Fiscal who would try the case for the state.

The warden arranged for Eve to see Bourne in a large, square room which was empty except for two chairs. Two *guardias* brought Bourne in, then left them alone. They sat in the chairs and looked at each other. She offered him a cigarette which he refused. She put them back in her purse without taking one for herself.

"It happened just about the way you said it would," he said.

"That doesn't matter."

He felt the value of what she had given him, all at once, as a boy sees the value of the dead bird in his hand which he has just shot. In turn, he had bequeathed to her an anvil of memory, an anchor for a desert. He took her face between his hands and kissed her with longing and regret for what he had not given her. He pulled his chair directly beside her chair, he facing east and she facing west, and spoke almost inaudibly directly next to her ear in an effort to comfort her without comforting the German microphones which he was sure had been sowed in the room.

"We're going to get out of this. I mean it. They are frantic about losing the Goya. They're going to make a deal." He watched her. She turned her head and stared at him, not understanding but trusting. "Don't answer," he said. "Wherever you can just nod. Okay?" She nodded.

"Blanca. Here. Soon."

She nodded.

"We have to go high up. Only one we know they won't double-cross. Okay?" She nodded.

He stood up, moving his chair back to the face-to-face position, and sat down. He held her hands. "No more of this kind of work, afterwards. You can safely quote me that I have decided to retire. We'll open a bookstore in Sweden or a hotel in Switzerland. I've been damned near out of my mind I've been so scared and that's no way to earn a living."

She leaned forward and entwined her arms around his neck.

She rested in his arms, at peace, puzzling the dichotomy of being doomed and blessed for knowing where she belonged. The guards came in and announced regretfully that the visit was over.

Jack Tense called Eve the following morning without mentioning his name but letting his voice identify him and, in his professional fashion, asked her if she expected to be at the airport for lunch that day. Before she could answer he told her it was a very good restaurant and so crowded that "nobody is able to remember seeing nobody." He said at two o'clock she might run into someone with news from home then he hung up as though the telephone booth had begun to fill up with hostile police and troops.

She drove away from the hotel and mid-town Madrid along the only perfect stretch of highway in Spain which is called the Avenida de Americas before it reaches the city line then the Barajas Road after that. It is the highway which takes the most exalted foreign visitors of state into Madrid so it has to be perfect. Illogically, the half mile of road leading into the perfect road from the airport has not been repaved or repaired in man's memory and from its appearance seems to have been shelled regularly every morning.

Tense looked right through her from his place at a table across the restaurant, making no sign that he saw her. He was wearing a popularization of an alpinist's hat with what appeared to be a whisk broom sticking out of the band. She sat down beside him. "You wore the right clothes," he said out of the side of his mouth. "Nobody will remember clothes like that. Good girl."

"If nobody remembers clothes like these I've been gulled out of four hundred dollars," Eve snapped at him which made him shake with laughter until she realized he was back at his pleasure of teasing her again.

"Don't tell me if you don't trust me, and if you do trust me you must be crazy," Tense said, "but what happened with your husband's business affairs?"

She omitted nothing. She spoke with relief. She had someone to unburden upon, and Tense had become one of her three closest friends in the world the day she had first met him. He liked the idea of Bourne holding out the Goya,

217

deeming it to be an extremely professional calculation. She wanted reassurance on Bourne's estimate of the liberating power of the Goya and exulted when Tense told her that there was no doubt but what a deal would be made and the entire matter written off the records once the trial was over. He asked her if she had considered everyone who might want to frame her husband for the Muñoz murder. She could think of no one because there was no one, and her husband was just as baffled as she was.

They had lunch ; paella, wine, flan and coffee. He told her how sentimental Mr. Merton of *The Revealer* had become about her since her husband had been arrested and would be tried on so popular a charge. He arranged all of his sentences so that she would make him laugh with comically affronted reactions throughout the meal. As they were sipping coffee and gazing at each other fondly he asked her if she had been over all of this ground with his friend Enrique López. The question baffled her. It would never occur to her to discuss anything like that with López, whom she had met only in writing, and she told Tense that. Tense explained that López could probably find out who was jobbing her husband. Her lovely mouth formed a perfect O. Tense explained that was what a big organization was for. If López couldn't find out what was happening on the inside of his own opposition he wouldn't be able to stay in business very long, now would he? Eve was startled, confused and very interested to think that there was any chance that she could help Bourne. Tense told her he would talk to López, that he had to pay his respects anyway while he was in the country even if he was there in an amateur capacity as a gentleman journalist. He wanted her to understand that the whole inquiry might come to nothing, that Bourne wouldn't need to know what with that Goya in hand for old-fashioned trading purposes, but a man liked to know who was jobbing him anyway and nothing could be lost by trying. Eve told him that once again she just didn't know how to thank him and he answered that if she really meant that they could go right back to her place and pop into bed because one thing was for sure, her husband wasn't likely to dart in on them. The outraged reaction she flashed at him gave him enormous pleasure.

He insisted that they leave separately. As Eve walked through the airport building she passed Colonel Gomez, chief
218

customs officer. He stared at her, flushed deeply and passed without speaking.

The courtroom in which Bourne and Jean Marie were to be tried in the Palace of Justice in Madrid was one of the most elegant in Europe. It was about forty yards long and about twenty yards wide with a ceiling twenty feet high. It was splendiferously and richly furnished with panels of dark, polished wood on all walls to a height of six feet, surmounted by a princely, rich maroon cloth that continued to the ceiling.

On the wall behind the Magistrates' desk which was made of solid mahogany and richly carved, the royal coat of arms had been fixed signifying that all called to the bar would be accorded the justice of the kingdom of Spain, so designated by its citizens in the public referendum of July 6th, 1947, which returned eighty-two point two four per cent in favor of a promonarchic government. Between the royal coat of arms and the Magistrates' desk stood a large, brass crucifix whose presence made the swearing of witnesses upon the Holy Bible unnecessary.

The Magistrates' desk faced the open end of a horseshoe-shaped dais on which had been placed the desks of the Public Prosecutor, or Acusador Fiscal, and the Private Prosecutor, or Acusador Privado, which were to the left of the direct vision of the Magistrates, and the desk of the Defense Attorney which sat on the arm of the horseshoe to the Magistrates' right hand. The desks of the Magistrates, the prosecution and the defense were three feet higher than the level of the accused who sat at a desk situated approximately between the arms of the horseshoe facing the Magistrates.

Attorneys for both sides had their seats by right and even when addressing the President of the Court did not get to their feet. During important cases, attorneys and magistrates not directly connected with the process were allowed to enter the courtroom and to take such seats as were available at the desks of either the defense or prosecuting attorneys and to remain there as spectators wearing their official robes. When anyone crossed the courtroom at any part of it, passing in front of the crucifix, they crossed themselves or genuflected. At recess times, as the court emptied, it was expected that each spectator would nod in acknowledgment of the President of the Court but in late years the practice had been observed only by visitors from the country districts and the aristocrats and surely never by the newspapermen.

The Magistrates sat in severe, high-backed chairs which were lined with maroon satin, the president in the center. They, as well as the attorneys and the clerks of the court, wore black gabardine robes very nearly identical to those worn at college commencement exercises. A separate black velvet yoke on each hung fore and aft, attached to the robe at the shoulders but not at the sides. Below the waist the robe had eight box pleats which Bourne amazed himself by counting each morning and each afternoon of the trial while the clerk of the court stood and read off the résumé of the proceedings.

All robes were the same, but the magistrates and the prosecutor wore lace at the cuffs of their tight sleeves, while the defense attorney and the clerk of the court wore their cuffs plain. Had there been a Private Prosecutor retained by the family of the murdered man to insure the most rigorous prosecution of the case against the defendants, as was the custom, he would have worn plain cuffs, but the surviving members of the Muñoz family who were then residents of the Canary Islands had no interest in increasing the probabilities of legal vengeance.

The press was admitted to the court, with the general public, after the court had been seated and the attorneys and prisoners were at their desks. No places were reserved for newspaper people. At the opening of each session there was a general scramble by journalists of many lands to secure seats in the front row which had a running table in front of it which could be used as a desk. Photographers were not permitted to work in the courtroom but they made up for that in the corridors.

A dark maroon carpet stretched away from the high desk to where brass posts, joined by maroon velvet ropes, separated the public benches from the trial area. An Usher, wearing a dark suit with brass buttons, stood at the rope ready to lead witnesses from the corridor outside the courtroom into the court. Witnesses were not permitted to remain in the courtroom for any part of the trial, except to give testimony.

The determination of the press to find seats somewhat defeated the hopes of the various sangrophiles and écouteurs among the public who had planned on attending, but as the red-faced man from United Press said, what the hell did they want to squeeze in there for and get pushed around when they could read all about it if they subscribed to a New York paper. This gratuity did not mean, no matter what it said, that the Spanish press suppressed any news of the Bourne-Calbert trial. They gave it, on a standard crime story policy, about the same amount of space that the *New York Times* gave to the Jersey City night court.

The trial was under the protection of a Magistrate President of the Court sitting with two other Magistrates if no death penalty had been requested by the Prosecution and with four other Magistrates if there was a call for judgment requiring the death penalty. There was no jury.

The trial was broken into two daily sessions and most murder trials in Spain have required three to seven sessions because both the prosecution and the defense are required to submit their entire cases in writing to the Magistrates before the trial starts. The briefs are read aloud to the court at the beginning of each trial session together with a résumé of testimony recorded accumulatively at the trial. Both sides have full right of discovery, access to each other's complete cases in advance of trial, including the right to examine witnesses, strategy and physical evidence in the manner in which civil cases are conducted under the rules of the Federal Courts of the United States. The attorneys for each side, in Spanish courts, are required by law to advise the opposing side, through the President of the Court, of any changes to be incorporated so that the opposition may adjust its own arguments to offset evidence or reasoning not anticipated. With all technicians so advised, the trial itself is held to hear witnesses and to proclaim publicly all evidence and all intent which have been placed before the court for judgment.

When the verdict has been reached by a Spanish court the sentence is not passed at the bar but is delivered in writing to the accused in his cell, to his attorneys, to the prosecutors, and to the press.

Eve had walked the seven blocks from Calle de Marengo to the Palace of Justice on Calle de Bárbara de Braganza to stand helplessly before the building unable to enter. She walked aimlessly away from the building until, four blocks later, she found herself at the Calle Amador de los Ríos then backed out again. She walked most of the day, seldom looking up to find herself. At noon she called the duchess but the duchess had been invited to wait in an anteroom, off the court, until she would be called to testify, a deference to her rank as all other witnesses were required to wait in the corridor. At last Eve wandered about and sat within the tiny parklike plaza called the City of Paris at the side of the Palace of Justice then, all at once, worried that she might be telephoned, summoned by some unknown urgency she hastened back to the hotel to cast sidelong glances at the telephone as she paced and fretted.

The trial of Robert Evans Cryder known as James Bourne and Jean Marie Calbert began on a Tuesday morning twenty-six days after the day of the murder of Dr. Victoriano Muñoz, the Marqués de Villalba. The President of the Court, accompanied by four magistrates, entered the courtroom from a door in the rear wall and seated themselves at the long desk with the two high, five-globed lamps. The president leaned forward to the Clerk of the Court and said, *"Audiencias pública!"* in a clear voice. Two attendants opened doors to the side corridor and the procession of attorneys and accused entered. Each prisoner walked between two armed police guards who carried carbines and side arms. They were not handcuffed or shackled. Eight people marched in the procession each to his assigned desk, the guards sitting directly behind each prisoner to which they had been assigned. The attendants opened the doors at the back of the room and the press, with some of the stronger public, boiled in. It was all accomplished in silence which would have been total except for the muffled shuffling of feet. At the instruction of the president, the Clerk of the Court stood and read the case which had been prepared by the prosecution which demanded the death sentence to be passed upon the accused.

The prosecution's case was as long and as tedious as extreme thoroughness demanded. It foretold that it would prove that neither of the defendants were morally competent, that Robert Evans Cryder, known as James Bourne, was in Spain under forged documents and identity, that he had devoted in excess of two years to the planning and preparation of a robbery of certain paintings and of substituting copies for these paintings which had been painted by the co-defendant, Jean Marie Calbert, who would be shown to have been an infamous trafficker in forged paintings for criminal purposes over a number of years. The prosecutor covered every point which had been so neatly set down in the confession which Jean Marie had provided to Captain Galvan plus several other nuts and bolts. The prosecution mentioned Eve Bourne in passing, as the courier who had brought the copies of Spanish masterpieces into Spain through three different points of entry, which was not a crime per se, and stated that the Customs Department would supply further testimony in this regard.

No mention was made of the painting by Francisco Goya called "The Second of May" or "The Attack Upon the Mamelukes in the Puerta del Sol." No mention was made of the murder of Cayetano Jiminez. The Minister of Justice and the Minister of Government had met with the President of the Court and with the Acusador Fiscal and the Defense Attorney and had exposed all of the government's knowledge of the crime involving the Goya and Jiminez together with reasons for bypassing these points at the present and both sides had agreed that justice would be served were the defendants tried for murder without the bulky necessity of bringing in evidence of extraneous crimes. The government's position was that the Goya was merely missing at the present time, and they had faith that, at the right time, someone would come forward to assist them in recovering it. Since the prosecution was willing to concede that this possible area of the case was irrelevant to a successful trial leading to a conviction, the defense readily agreed inasmuch as one more murder and an attempted crime as extraordinary as the theft of a Goya of that nature from the Prado could not enhance his clients' chances. He discussed the matter with his clients before acceding to the request of the government. Jean Marie gave it no consideration and left the decision entirely in Bourne's hands. Bourne thought about little else. This knowledge of the government's interest in painting confirmed that they had not been able to discover the Goya's hiding place nor fathom why a freshly painted duplicate had been found propped up against the wall where the original had been hung. It had the effect of permitting Bourne to watch his own trial for his own life with considerable detachment and without any taint of degrading morbidity and it buoyed up

223

Jean Marie's erratic spirits no end because he had learned that, until the original could be found, his own representation of Goya's conception of the attack upon the Mamelukes would continue to hang in the Prado—until, that is, as an old-time popular song once had sung, the real thing came along.

As the voice of the reading Clerk droned on, Bourne relaxed in his chair, smiling slightly with certain expressed kindliness toward the proceedings. The direction of the brief emphasized that Robert Evans Cryder, known as James Bourne, and Jean Marie Calbert had come to a thieves' falling out with Victoriano Muñoz and had murdered him in consequence thereto. It seemed to express professional smugness that due to Jean Marie's confession, his fingerprints on the murder weapon, and the testimony which would be forthcoming from witnesses who had discovered the defendants an instant after the execution of the murder, the boom could be lowered by the court without any other needless consideration. The statement by the prosecution took up the entire first session. The court was adjourned to meet again at three that afternoon. The judges left the court, then everyone else in the courtroom, including the prisoners and their guards, made their own way out as best they could.

As the armed guard closed in, Bourne signaled to the Defense Counsel who nodded and moved on. The prisoners were taken to separate cells in the basement of the building. The defense attorney, still in his robes, joined Bourne immediately. His name was Rafael Corruno-Baenz. He was a leading monarchist, that is a politician for monarchistic party activity, a friend of the duchess's who was a self-consciously, impatiently brilliant man whose constant quickness darted about to cover up an ugly temper which had been born of almost everyone else's inability to keep up with him. He was still too young to slow down and his political development had been slow because his arrogance had insured resentment, so he had needed the duchess's great, good will among the powers of the Monarchist Party, to be able to continue along with any promise at all.

Aside from a personality and vanity wholly unfit for the most remote practice of politics he was the most successful, most expensive, and best-known trial lawyer in Spain, a country where youth is so poorly served that his feat of pre-eminence was equal roughly to the improbable ascension of a Negro physician to the presidency of the Mississippi Medical Association. Many hands had reached for him before Bourne's arrest. Other cases had been scheduled on court calendars to be tried simultaneously with Bourne's during the time of Bourne's trial. He had taken the Bourne case because the duchess had suggested that he take it.

He was efficient, if not compassionate. He admired Germans for science, orderliness and the military; the British for their literature and for their experience of and with the law although he was mystified by the jury system which left the outcome of their justice at the disposition of the emotions of amateurs-at-law; and those Americans who had retained his services in various capacities, and no others. His feeling for the French deplored the French. For the Italians he had a shrug and a sigh and a harsh noise made at the back of his throat. The rest of the world was made up of fantasts like the communists or non-Catholics like the Swedes and the Chinese, both free to do any horribly sexual thing they wanted without fear of sin. To them went more than disapproval. They got his hatred.

He felt contempt for Jean Marie as a man and as a Frenchman, a man who was admittedly guilty and yet lacking in every feeling for that imperative sense of consequence which defined manhood to Corruno. Bourne, whose physical strength, tailoring, and political connections he envied and appreciated, was a human condition which he had not yet entirely solved. There was a preciseness about Bourne's presentation, he admired Bourne's prehensile mind, but he was not a serious man. He showed no particular sense of the involvement which swarmed around him. He was unaware of sin; legal or moral or spiritual, yet a man who continued to demonstrate a nice feeling for the imperative sense of consequence.

He had been looking forward to lunch, but he knew his duty and knew the almost reflexive requirement of all clients following the first session of their own trials: they invariably found it necessary to be reassured that the prosecution did not have a case which needed to be taken too seriously as promising to advance anything unpleasant. He told them all, naturally, that they were not to worry and they, who had sat there while the Fiscal had sewn them up tightly into a shroud of ineluctible reasoning and evidence, would believe him.

He regarded Bourne patronizingly and, while waiting for the inevitable question, offered Bourne a cigarette, then lighted it for him. He sat down languidly upon the stool in the corner of the cell but when he saw that Bourne intended to remain standing he got quickly to his feet again. Then Bourne sat down on the edge of the bed so Corruno resat himself upon the stool.

"I want to read your brief before you deliver it."

"You what?"

"Why wasn't I shown the prosecutor's brief? You're a legal technician. What the hell do you know about this case except what I tell you? Do you want to argue from the facts or do you want to do legal embroidery?"

Corruno sprang to his feet. "Who are you talking to?" he blazed. "I withdraw from the case and I will so advise the president of the court immediately." He started to leave.

Bourne put his great hand on Corruno's chest and pushed him gently up against the wall of the cell. "Think about it. You withdraw from this case and I tell the duchess that you prepared this case entirely upon Jean Marie's confession to the police and have given me no opportunity of seeing either your brief or the prosecution's, even though his brief this morning contained statements which, if they have been sworn to, constitute perjury and which, if attacked and exploded, can mean acquittal. Is that the kind of a lawyer you are? You want to withdraw?"

Corruno stared down at Bourne's restraining hand and wrist then looked levelly at Bourne. Bourne took his hand away and stepped back. "I'm sorry," he said.

Corruno stared him down then kept looking at him until the violence gradually left his eyes, leaving them expressionless. "Sit down," he ordered. Bourne sat on the bed.

"All right. What testimony?"

"The servants, Pablo and Josefina Soltes, who have been the body servants of the duchess, our duchess, most of their lives for some reason were working at Muñoz on the day of the murder. Nearly everything else they told the police is a lie. The man says he was in the room with Muñoz, bringing him coffee, when he telephoned me to come to see him at once."

"Yes?"

226

"It's a lie. He says that Muñoz came out to greet us at the door to the salon after we arrived, another lie. He says that in fifteen or so minutes our violence and shouting were so much that his wife telephoned the police who came immediately. All lies. The timing of all of it can be fixed by the medical examiner's report and by the time Muñoz' call came through the switchboard at my hotel and the time recorded at the police station which is directly around the corner from the Muñoz apartment and the time of the police arrival. Every one of those times will be a matter of record. The only guess will be the medical examiner's, but it has to work out that his time will fall in with those others because Muñoz had to die between the time he made the call to me and the time the call was made to the police and the arrival of the police."

"This is very, very signficant evidence if it all will hold together, as you say." Corruno had become excited. "But why would the servants arrange such a thing? We must have a motive!"

"I've been thinking about it. A lot of things which change people's lives are done on the spur of the moment. They could have heard him summoning me to a meeting. He spoke with considerable anger. He was certainly in no danger of his life at that moment. I know enough about people to know that he couldn't have talked to me the way he did, if he knew he were about to be murdered. In that hard and arrogant way of his, not unlike your own, he had no intention of dying for many years, believe me."

"I regret my arrogance. It was unprofessional. Please go on."

"Let's say that the servants heard him make the call, and in one of those evil flashes of amateur criminal inspiration killed him, stole whatever they wanted to steal, called the police, and waited for us to walk in to be arrested for what they had done. I tell you the man literally pushed us into that room with the corpse, locked the door after us, and the police did the rest."

"This is all quite worth examining and you may be sure that I will do so most thoroughly. However, I point out that the motives presented by the Fiscal this morning as to why you and your colleague would have killed Muñoz were absolutely impeccable."

227

"Not if the police were to find any of the property of Muñoz in the effects of either the man or the woman."

"That is true. But if such a thing were possible it would not seem likely that such a condition would exist almost a month after the murder."

"We must insist that they be covered by the police. It would take time for amateurs to sell stuff like that. Don't you think that if the timing of the calls held water and if they were caught with stolen property that there would be a very strong case against them?"

"Perhaps."

"And a substantially weakened case against us?"

"Perhaps." Bourne thought of a faceless man named Enrique López. He watched López steal some dark object from the Muñoz apartment. He watched López put the dark object into the pocket of the heavy-set butler, Pablo. He watched the police pounce upon Pablo and his wife almost immediately, then he shuddered and felt nausea and forced his mind to fill and fill and fill with the expanding picture of "The Second of May" by Francisco Goya. He could not explain to himself why he had thought of Enrique López. He knew he had been framed. He knew he hadn't killed Muñoz and that those two servants were the only people who could have killed him, but it struck at him that he was building fright inside this prison and that soon he would begin to agree to anything with his mind to get him out, at bloodying and exiscerating cost to any stranger.

Off somewhere, later, he heard Corruno say that he would have to locate the Fiscal and the Magistrates wherever they might be lunching at once, that changes in briefs would need to be made and an examination of those servants attended to, then the voice had stopped. He was out of the cell and on his way before Bourne was fully aware that he had gone.

He sat in the bed, with his back propped up against the wall, concentrating with all of his strength upon something he remembered Eve telling him about what some psychiatrist had told her years and years before. The man had made much of the point of Eve understanding that she had his permission to think any thought she wished to think or any thought which came unexpectedly into her mind. He had emphasized very clearly to her that only when a thought found action
228

and consequence by being carried out could a wrong, in any sense, be committed which was of course at direct variance with almost all religious instruction and therefore, Bourne reasoned hopefully, undoubtedly true.

He stared at the wooden stool, the bucket and the incongruous, small, and brightly colored rug and thought that if he could talk to Jean Marie he would not know what to say any more than he knew what to say to himself in explanation or apology for what had happened. If Eve had held tightly to that cardboard tube which had contained the three paintings by Velázquez, Zurbarán and the Greek while Elek and the porters had been in her room at the hotel, if she had gripped it tightly as she had checked out that morning he wondered if any of this could have happened. Would Cayetano still be alive? Or Elek and Muñoz? Or, when she had reached the airport would Muñoz have telephoned the police to tell the police that she had stolen national treasure and would try to take the paintings through? Then Eve would have been in jail and that would never have done. He could not conceive of her in jail. All at once he remembered her three passports and her three false names and the Colonel Gómez who had remembered her so well that afternoon when he had stopped by to borrow the book from Muñoz. He knew that she was free because they thought she might, a distinctly unlikely possibility but to any police anywhere a very good one, that she might somehow lead them to that Goya. It was then that Bourne saw where the slip had been made, where the crime had become something less than his sixteen-year standard of perfect crimes. The fault had been with Francisco Goya betraying the Muñoz family in 1810. If that hadn't happened Victoriano would have had no interest in Bourne's work and they would all be free and richer than ever. The trouble with an irrefutable case like that was, one could not plan around it; a cause had to have an effect.

Regret was only worry about the past, but he regretted that because of his sense of propriety which had insisted that they regain the loot from Muñoz and had resulted in Jean Marie living atilt with his normal view. For sixteen years, from before the war in the autumn of 1941 when he had decided what he was going to do, when he had begun to plan his first criminal project, interrupted by the war, Bourne had considered prison as a concrete possibility, as sort of a fine for being caught offside. Prison would be the inevitable consequence of incompetence at his work. It belonged in all of his professional thinking because it was a natural component within the problem of each individual crime he would commit and, in a looming sense, a larger component within the complex of his accumulated criminal accomplishments. Now he was in prison. He could find no incompetence which had brought this clear consequence about. He had acquired the paintings from Dos Cortes with considerable skill. The action had been a business matter well executed. The murder of Gustave Elek marked where business had ended and true crime had begun. If he had only understood the meaning of murder the way Eve had understood it. Because he had not committed the murder he could see no connection of the murder to himself and he had bargained with Muñoz so he could accept the thought of prison abstractly because he had taught himself that if and when he had made a mistake prison was the inevitable consequence and he had delivered that prejudgment wholly unaware of his hopeless inability to understand the threat of true sin, murder and the condonement of murder. The essence of his joy in knowing that the Goya would allow him to escape the punishment which he had earned was that he knew that none of it could ever happen again, that he must end his profession because if his moral judgment was faulty at work such as his he would pay for it in the only way one can pay for any lack of criminal judgment, by dying in prison or under a noose. He thought so deeply and with such focus about himself within this predicament be did not remember to feel sorrow for Cayetano's silence in a silver box under the ground or for the duchess's horror of awakening every morning, of driving herself to live throughout the day then to try to sleep when night came. The disadvantage, when he examined it closely, his mind turned upon his guilt, was that prison, a factor which he had treated with scientific consideration for so many years, had somehow overtaken him and that his misunderstood insensitivity to danger, shown in a murder, had brought him there. So do all stumble when they examine history.

He was notified that the session of the court had been postponed from that afternoon to the following afternoon at three o'clock by order of the President of the Court, at the request of the attorney for the defense.

At ten twenty that night he was told by a jailer that word had been received from the Office of the Minister of Government that an appointment had been granted to the Duchess of Dos Cortes to see the prisoner at seven o'clock the following evening. His analytical, professorial manner with himself dissolved. He was to see her at last, to have a chance to beg her to believe that he had not known what Victoriano was going to do. She would comfort him and tell him that she understood and that she forgave him for any part he might have had in that terrible affair. She would tell him that he did not need to produce Victoriano to swear that he had done that thing without ever telling Bourne. She would look into his eyes, and smile at him, and forgive him, then she would listen attentively and carefully about what she needed to do with the highest officials of government about the Goya and the deal for the Goya so that he could be freed immediately and so that they could all go away from this terrible place of trouble and shame and horror and pain and live happily in kindness to each other.

At three seventeen peeyem the following afternoon when the court had convened, the President of the Court instructed the Clerk to read the argument for the defense. Jean Marie had obtained a sketch pad through the jailer and worked upon it, held in his lap, concentrating and disregarding the developments of the trial. Bourne having rested better than he had in weeks, regarded the scene with vast calm, listening politely to Corruno's brief which he had read at noon. The defense brief was shorter than the case which had been presented by the Fiscal, but excellently reasoned, a condition which reflected credit upon Corruno, who had not slept at all the night before as he assembled its new contents and its syntax.

The defense would prove the improbability and perhaps the impossibility of the defendants' being able to have caused the death of Victoriano Muñoz and in so doing might assist the police in apprehending the actual person or persons who had committed the murder, an opening which was received gratefully by the press in the rear of the courtroom.

231

The defense brief quoted from the brief of the Fiscal as establishing the time of the death of the deceased through the testimony of an expert witness who was to be heard in the court, the medical examiner. The time of the death as so established would be contrasted with the time Dr. Muñoz had made his telephone call to Bourne through the hotel switchboard, with the official police records which would show the time the call had been received summoning them to the scene of the crime and their time of arrival at the scene. In short the defense would reveal, supported by the record, that the time disparities were so great that it would be seen that the murder had occurred between fourteen and sixteen minutes before the defendants could possibly have made the journey from the hotel to the Muñoz residence.

It would be shown that only Pablo Soltes and his wife Josefina were on the murder premises at the time of the death of Victoriano Muñoz by violence which could reveal the possibility that Pablo and Josefino Soltes had perjured themselves in deposing to the Fiscal and the defense would demand that they be produced to confirm or deny their original statements under oath.

"Reasonable doubt. At last an about-face for tomorrow's editions," the man from *France-Soir* said to the man from the London *Daily Post*.

"Reasonable doubt won't help us sell papers," he answered. "A conviction on a couple of servants isn't what the public wants to read. That's a classical anticlimax."

"Not in France."

"Well, after all. Your man is French. You have tomorrow's story all written for you."

The Clerk of the Court read where the defense brief usually would have begun under other circumstances, the description of the exemplary character of the defendant Robert Evans Cryder called James Bourne, which would be supported by laudatory character references from officers under whom he had served in the United States Army. It was known that the defendant had been a respected businessman in Madrid, active in charitable enterprises, a valued member of the most distinguished Madrid society, a musician of talent, a respected scholar in the field of Spanish art, and an excellent horseman. Each of these relative peaks of erudition would be attested to by character witnesses of high station in Spanish life who would testify on the defendant's behalf on a voluntary basis. The defense would show that there was nothing sinister about the false passport and identity carried by the defendant at the time of his arrest, as claimed by the Fiscal, on the sworn records and statements of the United States Army and following affidavits submitted by agents of the Federal Bureau of Investigation of the United States Government, that the defendant, Robert Evans Cryder, called James Bourne, at the conclusion of World War II in England had been struck upon the head in such a manner as to cause severe injury and amnesia in an omnibus accident from which he had been the sole survivor; and that, in the confusion of the rescue, the passport of an accident victim named James Bourne had been retrieved by Robert Evans Cryder from the wreck and that this would be supported entirely by the record which would also show that since 1945 Robert Evans Cryder had been a resident of London, Paris and Madrid believing himself to be James Bourne.

As the Clerk of the Court read on Bourne looked across at Raphael Corruno-Baenz with greatly freshened respect. In fact, he goggled at the defense attorney who happened to look his way at that moment, to nod in boredom. Bourne had stolen the passport from the bus wreck and had planted his own passport on the nearest corpse. He could not imagine what Eve had told Corruno but it must have been a magnificent performance to get that young man to run every official agency source on the accident right down into the record, and he felt a little giddy that two such artists' hands had been at work, Corruno's and Eve's.

The *Time* man told the footless Magnum photographer next to him that they just might see the two defendants sprung. The Magnum man, feeling emasculated without his camera, could not have cared less. He was trying to decide whether he should try to get some shots with a Minox, whether he could get away with it if he did, and if he did get away with it how much money the shots would bring. It was a deadly dull nothing of a trial but that Frenchman was going crazy quietly right before their eyes and some studies of him would sell if he could work fast and if nothing big happened by the last day he would risk it, so he never

233

heard the *Time* man's observation and the *Time* man never knew he hadn't acknowledged it.

The droning seemed to go on without pause then after a while the Clerk sat down and everyone suddenly felt wide-awake again and the president adjourned the court until ten o'clock the following morning.

The duchess came to Bourne's cell, led by the old jailer who had been greatly pleased and greatly honored by her beauty and presence respectively a few years before when she had been remanded to a cell in the building during her trial. They chatted as old friends as they walked along, he walking almost sideways just half a step ahead of her so he could look up at her as they went. Her hair was coming in very black because there was no Cayetano to enjoy it blond. She wore black, and her eyes were dull black.

The old man opened the door of Bourne's cell then scurried away into darkness. The duchess entered, holding out her hand which Bourne took in both of his and kissed. He looked into her eyes and knew what he saw there the way a patient has sometimes read the eyes of a surgeon. He felt himself shiver. He asked her to sit down. She had not spoken and she had not smiled and when she was seated on the edge of the bed, her long, white hands in graceful repose in her lap, she said, "Eve told me you wanted to see me."

"Thank you for coming here, Blanca."

She nodded.

"How is Eve?"

"In good health, I think."

"I have nearly been out of my mind since Cayetano——"

"I, too."

"I want to thank you for finding Rafael Corruno-Baenz and persuading him to take this case."

"I could do no less for you."

"After what happened that Tuesday I went to your house every three hours like clockwork. I telephoned to Dos Cortes and to the south. I couldn't find you. I had to speak to you."

"And now I am here. Or, more to the point, you are here. Speak Jaime."

"When Victoriano was alive, I tried to find him to bring him to you. I wanted to drag him to you to make him tell you."

234

"Victoriano is dead. Whatever you wanted to have him tell me you will have to tell me yourself."

He had tried not to look at her, but his eyes returned to her eyes. As he looked at this friend, he exploded with talk which healed him as it fell upon both of them. As he talked she offered no comment. She did not relent with any facial expression: mild or strong. He sat beside her and held her left forearm with one great hand gripping her wrist, the other clenching at below the elbow as he tried to give her his anguish but, like a child's ball set upon a hill, it came back to him.

"I knew nothing about it. I was involved in it in a certain remote way, Blanca, but I never knew what was going to happen. It could not have happened if I had known. Never. I loved Cayetano as I love you. I had no truer friends than you and I have needed so terribly to tell you *how* I am a part of the cause of your loss, but an unknowing part. Not an innocent part, but I did not know what was going to happen or that Cayetano was in any way involved or that what was going to happen could even touch you or Cayetano. Everything moved in such a way that sometimes I don't know where it started or where it could have been stopped. I stole those paintings from Dos Cortes, Blanca, but I wasn't taking anything from you. I know they aren't important to you and never were. I took some colored canvas down from dark walls, canvases no one ever looked at. But when Victoriano stole the same paintings from me I considered them my property that had been stolen. The thief divested. The thief gulled. The thief self-righteously indignant. The thief at once willing to fall in with the plans of this man he sees as a fool—mind you, Blanca, the man who has gulled him he still sees as a fool, the man who has murdered to get these paintings is still seen as a fool—and then the fool suddenly becomes his master. Eve pounded at me to tell me that I had lost and that if I went along with Victoriano I would be lost, but I wanted my property. The property I had stolen from you."

He stared at her with agonized and agonizing pleading. She turned her head slowly to regard him with an expressionless stare, waiting for him to complete his confession.

"All I could see were the three paintings I had worked three years to get and which I was determined to have. I
235

could get him the Goya. In theory there was nothing particularly difficult about getting the Goya. The human element is another thing, of course. But to get the Goya I told Victoriano I needed some public diversion, a technical balance within the problem. I couldn't do both the diversion and the Goya part of it, and so Victoriano undertook the diversion. Blanca, I knew he was already a murderer. I knew he was a disturbed man, even an unbalanced man, but who—how—was there any way in which to—was there any way to anticipate how insane he was, to foresee what he would do? Do you understand what I am saying, Blanca? I tried to know. For three days before we went to take the Goya I tried to find out what the diversion would be, but he had disappeared. The last time I saw him, which was six days before the day everything happened, I demanded to know what the diversion would be and he told me that he was investigating four alternate diversions and that various factors would prove themselves or eliminate themselves by that Saturday. Saturday was three days before it happened. I tried to force him to tell me but he said what he had was too inconclusive and that I had enough on my mind and that he would tell me Saturday. Then he wasn't there on Saturday. We tried Sunday and Monday, very hard. Tuesday, I went to his house three times and I beat on the doors. I telephoned every hour on the hour Tuesday then it got to be three thirty in the afternoon, and I had to go to the Prado. The point is that if I could have found him and if I could have found out what he intended to do for this obscene diversion it never would have happened. But I didn't know, Blanca! We went through all the motions with the Goya then Jean Marie funked out. It wasn't his fault. It was my fault. He was never meant for that kind of work. I left the Prado and the streets were in a state of nightmare, a state of siege from horror. No one walked, everyone ran. In Spain. People were running and weeping with the sun in the sky. It was like the tenth day of a plague. When I got home Eve told me. She told me. Then I told Eve what the diversion was and I knew what Victoriano had done and I had to find you to make you understand that I never knew what was going to happen. I didn't know what Victoriano was going to do. I couldn't have known because you know I would have stopped him, but he's dead now and he can't tell you that I didn't

236

know, to stand here before you to clear me so that I can be sure that you believe that I never knew what Victoriano was going to do that day."

"But I do believe you, Jaime."

"God bless you."

"I have known for some time. Not as directly as this, of course. But Victoriano did tell me almost everything before I killed him and I could see that he had used you." She was composed. She gave the impression of a cooperative friend helping to clear up a misunderstanding. She stood up, disengaging her forearm from his hands which had suddenly gone limp, and patting him on the shoulder.

"I must go now. You have said everything you wanted to say to me? That was all, wasn't it, Jaime?"

His mind filled again with the liberating vision of the great canvas called "The Second of May" which only he and Eve could ever find and the meaning of the salvation it would bring propped him up, braced him somehow to sit erect and look up at her to say, "That is all. Thank you, Blanca." With a pure mind which had created a pure sin he saw his hope for the purest kind of punishment, but he sent it back into his own mental darkness, identified as a hope. He wanted to lose that hope where it could be found when he could stand freedom no longer and it had to be found. Until that place in future time he wanted to defer the pure punishment, to suffer the memory of her eyes and the sound of her voice, but he had to defer that hope. It was deferred. It remained in a merciful limbo for two full, dimensional seconds until she told him as she passed out of the cell, "Eve told me where we can find the Goya, Jaime. I think they must have it by now. It will be back in its place in the Prado in the morning."

She walked down the long, dimly lighted corridor along the way she had come and her friend, the old man, gamboled along the passageway to meet her. They chatted like old friends as they walked together, he greatly pleased by the beauty and the presence he had known from years before when she had been remanded to a cell in the building during the trials she had stood while she could not bear to remain at large and in freedom without being held within her lover's arms.

It was a warm, sunny day. The terrace doors were open at the Bourne apartment of the hotel. A lazy breeze sauntered through the delicious air to the hassock near the center of the room where Eve sat. She started violently when the telephone rang. When she could make herself move, she answered it. Her right knee struck a small tabouret in passing and knocked it over. She almost lost her balance, but she managed to weave through the bright sunlight and pick up the telephone on its sixth ring.

"Hello?" Her voice was as bright as a child movie star's. It was brighter than the voices of all the salesmen who have ever taken a seven ayem call at a Statler Hotel from the home office.

"Eve? This is Blanca." The voice had urgency and will.

"Hello, Blanca."

"Are you all right?"

"Yes."

"You must listen to me carefully, Eve."

"Blanca?"

"They are going to order your arrest this afternoon. If you stay where you are they will arrest you."

"Arrest me." Eve made an observation which confirmed what she had heard in Blanca's sentence.

"If I could come to help, I would, but I am lunching with the people of the prosecution. You must leave the hotel now."

"I'm drunk."

"No matter. Do you understand me?"

"Yes. Blanca?"

"Don't pack anything. Take whatever jewels or small things you feel you have to take, then walk slowly to my house. They will expect you. Do you understand me, Eve?"

"Yes. Blanca. Blanca?"

"Yes."

"Did you see Jim?"

"Yes."

"Have you begun to buy him out with the Goya? Is he going to be all right?"

"We can't talk now, dear. There is no time. You can't help Jaime if both of you are in prison. Go now, Eve. Start at once. I will be with you and we will talk as soon as I

238

testify this afternoon and you will be safe at my house whether I am there or not. Now, go!" She hung up.

Eve began to move about the room in several directions, bumping into furniture, falling once. She got to her feet uncertainly then pawed about on a closet shelf until she found a large purse, large enough to be standard issue for the visiting nurse service. Clutching the purse, she backed to the bathroom where she held the towel rack on the wall and let her clothes drop, piece by piece, at a heap at her feet. She moved gingerly across the tiled floor to the tub and the shower, the purse hooked over her left forearm, and she was standing under the cold spray before she remembered it. She tried to bend over it with it to put it on the floor beside the tub, gently, but she almost toppled forward so she had to let it drop heavily. She drew the shower curtain then, clinging to the towel rack inside the tub, as she did.

Her reflexes seemed better when she got out of the shower. She rubbed herself violently with the rough bath towel, bringing a high glow to her firm flesh and perhaps moving the alcohol along faster through her bloodstream. She bound her hair under a kerchief which had been hanging behind the bathroom door. She pulled her clothes on, picking each piece up slowly and squatting, not bending, to get it. She took up the purse last and took it to another room to pack it with all of the instinctive items of value. Working like a computer whose tapes had been punched in advance she packed six of Bourne's handkerchiefs, three of his cuff links, four pairs of nylon stockings, two nylon panties, a brassière, Bourne's letters to her, a well-marked road map, her diaphragm and a strangled tube of vaginal jelly, nine small snapshots, two compacts, three lipsticks, two pairs of Bourne's socks and a cigarette lighter. She hooped four jeweled rings on her fingers, snapped two flashing bracelets on either wrist, started to put on a second necklace then dropped it into her purse. She took all of the money which was in the apartment: three hundred and twenty dollars' worth of traveler's checks, six thousand pesetas, seventy-three thousand French francs, a Swiss bankbook, a Tangier bankbook, a New York bankbook, the keys to eight safe deposit vaults and Bourne's lucky Mexican peso which he always forgot to carry. She put her several passports into the great purse. They were made out variously to Eve Lewis, her own

name, together with others borrowed or invented: Evangeline
Lewis, as dopey a name as she could remember reading
anywhere.

She felt bleary again, all at once. She tottered to the bed
and lay face down and concentrated upon remembering
Bourne with her body until she believed she could smell him
there. Her eyes were as dry as a turtle's.

The telephone rang again, directly beside her. She answered
it brightly again, not as brightly as before because she wasn't
as drunk. The unidentified voice was a London voice. She
said, "Hello, Jack," realizing too late that she had violated
his rules. Tense was too absorbed with thinking of how he
was going to say what he had to say to notice this breach
of etiquette.

"Ducks?"

"Yes, this is Ducks."

"I want you to meet me. Straight off."

"All right."

"You know where Velázquez Street is?"

"Yes."

"You know the cafés on the walks in the middle?"

"Yes."

"The one nearest the end towards the Park? The one done
in bamboo? Sort of south-seaish? All right?"

"Yes."

"In ten minutes then. I've talked to our friend."

"Who?"

"My friend. You know, my Spanish business contact."

"Who?"

"Are you drunk?"

"Yes."

"Eve, go downstairs now and stand in front of the hotel.
I'm directly around the corner at the post office. I'll be by
the hotel with a taxi straight off. All right, love?"

"All right. Jack?"

"Yes, ducks?"

"Have you seen Señor López? You know—your friend?"

"Yes, ducks. Now you go straight down and stand on the
pavement in front of that hotel and I'll tell you all about it.
All right, love?"

"Yes, Jack." She disconnected. She climbed blearily to her
feet and balanced unsteadily. She carried the large purse over

her left arm and crossed to the small table near the sunny terrace which held the gin and the ice and the small pitcher of water. She held the gin bottle up. There were about two fingers left in it. She made herself a gin on the rocks. She stared out toward nothing as she sipped it and when it was gone she turned to the door and left the apartment for the last time in her life, testing the latch carefully just as though she were sober and not the wife of the managing director of the hotel.

His taxi rolled up as she came through the front door of the hotel. Tense was just as pleased that no doorman was there to remember whom the boss's wife had gone riding off with. The cab drove to Alcalá then turned right to go up the short hill to the plaza at Puerta Alcalá, swinging halfway around the arch to stop at the Calle de Serrano. Tense dismissed the cab there. After it had moved along, he took Eve's arm and they walked up the gentle hill toward Velázquez, across from the Retiro, passing the house of the Duchess de Dos Cortes on the way.

In a short time they were seated in the café on the Ramblas. Tense ordered three hot, black coffees but what Spanish he had became snarled up with the waiter's conception of that language. Eve straightened them out. Tense had her drink two of the cups of coffee while he toyed with his own. When she finished the second cup he switched that for his own full cup and she sipped on as he ordered two more. Occasionally a trolley car would clang, or the brakes of a bus would hiss at them but mostly it was serenely quiet, warm and wondrously clear, with soft sounds embellished by the soughing of the light wind as it combed the trees. Tense sat enjoying her, apprehensive of her reactions when he would be able to phrase what he had to say, but mainly astonished at what this very nearly unknown girl had done to change his hard-eyed objectivity.

"What did Señor López say?" she asked suddenly.

"Oh. Yes. Well, I saw him two nights ago and I mentioned what we had talked about and he seemed to know what I wanted although he didn't say much, but that's his way. Then a small boy comes to my hotel this morning as I was leaving to cover the trial. The boy had a note for me which says our friend wants to see me. You follow? So I saw our friend." To punctuate, Tense leaned over and touched Eve's bare forearm with the tips of his fingers. He had the traditionally shaped fingers of the storybook safecracker. They were long, slim and finely sensitive. They were extremely clean. "I have been trying to tell myself how to say this to you, ducks. I like you pretty well, you see. López had bad news, ducks. Very bad news indeed."

She implored with her gin-flawed eyes. They pled with him to be mistaken. They urged with all of her need, with all of her weariness with endless trouble, to be mistaken.

"The Government has got the Goya painting," Tense said, dropping his eyes. "They won't need to make any deal any more."

She made a sound which caught in her throat like a bubble scratched by dryness. She looked away from him quickly as though expecting to see hope and deliverance standing across the street. He took her limp, damp hand in his and held it with love, on the table top.

"They had to find it, you know, ducks, what with every policeman in the country looking for it," he said lamely.

"How did they find it, Jack?" she asked.

He inhaled heavily then exhaled slowly, all the way, which is what a sigh is when it functions efficiently, which is to stop life for a fraction of an eternity in anguish. "I don't know what's come over me," he answered. "I wasn't going to tell you, as though you were the one who shouldn't know who your enemies are. But you have to know the same way I would have to know if it was me in your place." He paused in sadness. "It was your friend who told them where it was," he said. "Your friend, the duchess. I don't know how she found out, but it was she who told them."

Eve sat motionless, absorbing the meaning of what he had said then she stood up slowly. "I told her," she said. She leaned over and kissed Tense as he sat in the dappling sunshine. "That's how she found out." She walked slowly away, along the Ramblas toward the park, clutching the large purse. "I told her."

The Clerk of the Court called the next witness, Colonel Gonzalo Gómez, chief of the Customs Service at Barajas.

The prosecutor launched his line of questioning and the colonel testified, somewhat sullenly, that a superb copy of the Velázquez on exhibition in the court had been brought into Spain by Eve Bourne, wife of the accused called James Bourne. He supplied the date of Mrs. Bourne's entry and handed over to the court a certified copy of customs records, which established the temporary importation of the copy of the painting by Mary Ellen Quinn as then represented.

He was asked whether the Customs Service could produce records showing the temporary importation of copies of other paintings such as the Zurbarán and Greco on exhibition in the court. Colonel Gómez produced copies of certificates attesting to such importation at Irún and La Junquera respectively by American citizens named Alicia Sundeen and Thelma Cryder respectively.

The prosecutor asked Colonel Gómez to read the spelling of the name Cryder from the customs department record, which he did. The prosecutor then asked the Clerk of the Court to read the spelling of the name of the accused Robert Evans Cryder to the court, which he did.

"Thank you. Colonel Gómez, under what name did the wife of the defendant enter Spain at Barajas when she imported the copy of the Velázquez painting?"

"Under the name of Mary Ellen Quinn."

"That was the name on the passport which she submitted. Her photograph, of course, was in that passport."

"Yes, sir. I have the records and numbers here, sir." The colonel sounded bitter.

"Colonel, please tell the court how you became certain that Mary Ellen Quinn, who had presented this passport for entry into Spain, was in truth the wife of the defendant called James Bourne."

"I was introduced to Mr. and Mrs. Bourne by Dr. Muñoz."

"Where?"

"At his apartment. I was told they had just been married."

"How long ago was that?"

The colonel told him.

"To your knowledge were the customs officers at Irún and La Junquera respectively, shown photographs of the women who had identified themselves as Alicia Sundeen and Thelma Cryder?"

"Yes, sir."

"Did they identify the photographs?"

"Yes, sir."

243

"Will you tell us who these officers identified?' '

"Mrs. James Bourne."

"I believe depositions were taken to that effect?"

"Yes, sir."

The Clerk of the Court came to the colonel and collected the depositions. The Fiscal nodded benignly to the witness. "Thank you, colonel."

"No questions," Rafael Corruno said. He was not there to defend a woman for illegal entry and there could be no doubt that the copies were in the country so undoubtedly someone had brought them there.

The President of the Court spoke slowly and clearly. "This court orders the arrest of Mrs. James Bourne, wife of the co-defendant, on the charges of illegal entry, possession of forged papers, and conspiracy."

Bourne stared at the floor, breathing heavily, biting his tongue.

"Proceed," the president ordered. The Clerk of the Court rose and called Doña Blanca Conchita Hombria y Arias de Ochoa y Acebal, Marquesa de Vidal, Condesa de Ocho Pinas, Vizcondesa Ferri, Duquesa de Dos Cortes. Within a few moments the duchess had made her way into the courtroom.

"Your name?"

"Blanca de Dos Cortes, excellency."

"What is your age?" The president coughed.

"Twenty-nine years, my president."

"Do you live in Madrid?"

"Yes, excellency."

"Do you know the accused?"

"Yes, excellency."

"Do you swear to tell the truth?"

"Yes, my president."

"Please answer the questions which will be put to you by the Acusador Fiscal."

The Fiscal cleared his throat delicately. His fingers, those ropes with separate consciousness, began to worry a ruler while the Fiscal conveyed his extreme esteem for the distinguished witness by clearing his throat twice more and by moving the black, polyangular hat from one side of his desk to the other. Those extra seats and places at the Fiscal's desk, at the desk of the nonexistent Acusador Privado, and at Corruno's desk had filled with interested, robed men.

244

Jean Marie had stopped his sketching. He stared at the duchess with naked fear. His right hand clutched a blue envelope which he had spoken to Bourne about emptily that morning as they had been marched from the cells to the courtroom. It was a letter from Lalu which told him that she loved him, but that she had been forced to leave Paris because of what had happened and that she knew he would understand that she had to take care of herself. It had been mailed from Paris. He understood without reservation. They had had more time than they had ever dreamed of. So he watched the duchess, fascinated with the doom which had appeared at last, so far from where he had expected to meet it, after promising so very much, so often.

Bourne stared at the floor and tried to concentrate on counting by sevens.

"My duchess," the Fiscal asked, "are the paintings to your left, on exhibit in this court, painted by Zurbarán, El Greco and Velázquez respectively, your property?"

The duchess blinked her eyes rapidly as though not quite comprehending. "Which part of that question would you like me to answer first?"

"I am not sure that I understand your request, my duchess. Shall I repeat the question?"

"No, no. I will try to answer. I believe the paintings are my property, but if they are truly my property they were not painted by Zurbarán, El Greco or Velázquez." There was a hum in the courtroom as though a large generator had been turned on.

It was the Fiscal's turn to blink rapidly. "Pardon, duchess," he said, "but is not the Velázquez the famous Pickett Troilus?"

The duchess looked away, baffled, as though she would be willing to change the subject if the Fiscal would. Mrs. Pickett sat up much straighter. The press in the rear of the courtroom became very quiet. They glanced at one another expectantly.

The president said, "The witness will express herself for the record."

"My president, the first and last time Mr. Homer Pickett was a guest at Dos Cortes he positively identified these paintings as having been painted by Zurbarán, El Greco, and Velázquez. He even purported to have discovered the

245

hand of the Dutch painter Rubens in the second copy of the Velázquez. Foreign picture magazines have been filled with the nonsense."

A stringer representing thirty-one middle western American dailies, including one Democratic and one independent paper in Chicago, decided he could not wait to hear any more and left the courtroom in a rush. Mrs. Pickett watched him go and knew exactly what outlets he represented because he had interviewed her husband twice at the hotel. She got up and made her way slowly across the legs and knees and feet of the row to the aisle. When she got into the open she began to walk more quickly. When the courtroom door closed behind her she was in the corridor, running through the clumps of waiting witnesses to get to her husband before anyone or anything else could get to him, to convince him, to bully him if she had to, that his back had not been broken politically, artistically and most entirely as the lecturer-critic who would rival Mr. Berenson.

The representatives of principal competitors of both of the foreign magazines which had published the nonsense in full color sent assistants to telegraph offices with messages suggesting top priority standby. The American competitor of the American magazine which had proclaimed the Pickett Troilus even went so far as to add the words "practice smiling" on the end of his message, confident that he would never be asked to pay for the extra words.

"Did the witness mention a second copy?" the court asked.

"Yes, excellency. Mr. Bourne had stolen the first copies and had placed them with second copies."

A stout magistrate at the end of the desk to the left of the president scribbled a note and passed it along for consideration. The president read it. "Where are the originals?" he asked, clearly shocked, for the Spanish law and custom on its art treasures was most definite and clear.

"My late husband, the duke," the duchess explained, "had the original paintings removed from the walls in 1944 and replaced by the first copies."

"Where are the original paintings?"

"In Japan, excellency." The duchess was being sincerely co-operative. "They hang in a geisha house in Kobe which was one of my husband's many business interests." The AP man reeled at the bonus he would nerve himself up to ask for, then cut it in half, over the art and features this would move in Japan.

"This was done in 1944? During a war?"

"Oh yes, excellency, if it had not been for the war none of this could have happened. You see, it was through the war that my husband, himself an extremely highly regarded figure in our government, happened to find M'sieu Calbert, the defendant there, who is the supreme artist who has done both copies of all of these paintings and many more." The duchess was sweet and patient with the confusion. She treated all inquiries with the unruffled kindness of a teacher in a nursery school.

"You are saying then, my duchess," the Fiscal said slowly, hoping perhaps to be contradicted, "that the paintings on exhibit in the court were not painted by Zurbarán, El Greco, or Velázquez, but are instead forgeries executed by the co-defendant, Jean Marie Calbert?"

"Yes sir." The Fiscal, as well as everyone else in the forward part of the courtroom, turned to look at Jean Marie who sat in a sick nimbus, staring at the duchess. While all eyes were away from her, the duchess looked into his sunken eyes with her dead ones, and smiled at him in a twisted, vengeful smile which lived for a moment only on one side of her face. Only Jean Marie, Bourne and the duchess were aware that the duchess had struck up the overture to Jean Marie's doom, she achieved it so casually. Bourne, feeling an instant of panic, darted his glance to Jean Marie's pale profile. His eyes were closed. His lips were moving silently and just perceptibly. Bourne felt the cold begin in his middle then spread toward his heart and his head, his loins and his feet. He sat up as straight as a West Point plebe dining with upper classmen as the President of the Court continued his questioning of the duchess.

"The exportation of these paintings to Japan by your late husband, if indeed this be so, is a serious and grave matter. You will please tell the court the fullest background of this occurrence as it happened to the best of your memory."

"I will try to remember everything which pertains to this matter, your excellency," she said. She dropped her head for a moment and swallowed hard. When she spoke her eyes, which seemingly were looking at the president, were looking far, far beyond him at her duty which seemed to hang like some distant star, on the horizon of her days, where she could not avoid seeing it. "In 1942, excellency," she began, "my late husband became a close friend of Reichsmarschall Goering while he was in Paris as a member of the government commission which was so successful in regaining some of the many great Spanish paintings from the Louvre which Napoleon had looted from us in 1810 to 1812. I might say that painting was not the least of the interests which Reichsmarschall Goering shared with my late husband. In any event, my husband elected to remain in France almost throughout the period of the Nazi occupation. Because he was a known art authority who was greatly admired by the most influential Germans from Herr Hitler down, the then Political Commissar of Paris, a gentleman named Herr Abetz who wished to further the interests of his young mistress, brought a plan which had been developed by the mistress's husband, who was the defendant Jean Marie Calbert, to my husband."

Jean Marie's lips were moving silently. The nine journalists representing French news outlets were half out of their seats. They exchanged silent glances and somehow, without speaking, effected a truce which said that one would not leave the courtroom without the others knowing of the departure.

"This plan so delighted my husband, who had an extraordinary contempt for all of mankind and mankind's works which perhaps was what had attracted Marshal Goering to him in the first place, that he brought it to the Reichsmarschall who ordered it put into execution immediately. It was a simple plan. M'sieu Calbert, the defendant, was to have single access to the Louvre and to seemingly unknown art repositories of French art, and was to be permitted to copy what worthwhile paintings still remained from the alleged allotment which the French had claimed to have shipped to safety, so that eventually those paintings which would be exhibited in the Louvre and other French museums would be copies by M'sieu Calbert while the originals would be shipped back to Germany as culture bonuses among the German High Command where they are today. It was the sort of plan which almost exactly described my husband who had been bred to this kind of depravity. I do not know how or where M'sieu or his wife came by it.

"M'sieu and Madame Calbert made a considerable amount

248

of money in this way, my late husband told me. I know my husband paid him exceedingly well for copying three Italian masterpieces in the Reichsmarschall's collection, pieces which were Herr Goering's deep pride and which my husband undertook to substitute because it pleased him to think of the Germans, or anyone else for that matter, worshipping junk. They hang in a geisha house now which pleased him in a reverse way, of course, because mostly seamen patronize the establishments he owns and the seamen think the paintings are cheap copies and no one ever really looks at them, he told me delightedly. M'sieu Calbert's work was so remarkably faithful to the work of the original masters, that it was then that my husband conceived of his geisha plan and when the Germans were forced to withdraw from Paris and the Calberts, for a time, might have been in severe personal trouble, my husband gave them a haven at Dos Cortes where M'sieu Calbert copied every painting we owned. Every painting, on every wall, in every house my husband owned now exhibits M'sieu Calbert's work."

The French press could not wait any longer because the Italian and the British press were starting out of the court at top speed. The rear of the courtroom population seemed to rise as one man and fight toward the two relatively small doors toward the corridor and the street.

"This court is adjourned until ten o'clock tomorrow morning," the President of the Court said suddenly, standing up. No one seemed to know whether the duchess had completed her testimony for the prosecution, but that was no longer of the moment.

If the government could have stopped the news stories from going forward they would have done so, but it was all on the public record and the delay of publication could only last as long as all of the foreign journalists could be detained within the country. The duchess was proscribed by her nation, her society and her community. The Fiscal hurried past her, glancing sideways at her as he went, with eyes filled with horror. Even Rafael Corruno-Baenz went out of his way not to greet her. She had held the sacred memory of one of Spain's greatest aristocrats, a proprietor of the nation, up to public ridicule with the irrefutable authority which she alone possessed. The commoners and the soldiers, the teachers and the bankers, who had taken over the government, as well as the minuscule of persons who actually owned the country were never to forgive her for that.

The prisoners were returned to their cells. The duchess sat alone in the box until the courtroom had entirely cleared of people, then she rose and walked absent-mindedly out of the Palace of Justice and into the street to look for her car and driver, thinking only that she must now face Eve Bourne who had held the matching half of the only truth which would ever be left to either of them.

Jean Marie succeeded in hanging himself just at that time, because the jailer was not there to interfere. He managed it with a bed sheet looped around the bars of the high window in the cell. He stood on the bed with the sheet knotted around his neck and jumped as high in the air as he could go, so that the force of his descent would provide a maximum snap. No one but Jean Marie ever knew whether he died quickly or slowly. The old jailer had been wearied by the emotion of seeing the duchess again so he rested, then he dozed, then he slept, and Jean Marie's suicide was not discovered until the evening meal was served to the cells at ten o'clock that night and, as Spain is a Catholic country, was greatly deplored.

The duchess found Eve waiting in the enormous sitting room-bedroom on the third floor of the house, facing the Retiro, the room in which she had explored her own grief so assiduously. The room was reached by an individual elevator, shafted only for it, which opened through a wall panel and which was an invisible door when not in use. When the duke had been alive she had never entered the room in any other way, always keeping the main door to the room bolted because he had been a man who could become ravening, not to say bestial, from reading the financial page of a newspaper or eating a piece of milk toast.

Although she used the elevator she had had the footman telephone ahead to send a floor maid to tell Eve that she was on her way up because the sight of death emerging from a secret panel was not calculated to be a pleasant surprise for anyone. The duchess had always seen herself as death holding court ; many kinds of death, not all of them as direct as Cayetano's or her cousin's. She was Spain's own vector of catastrophe, she reminded herself as she had grown up. By loving she could maim. By giving she took life; an insight overtaken when she had been very young and her capacity for anguish had seemed romantic.

When she had been a schoolgirl, walled up within the tragedy which had been her family—a father who had become a suicide, a mother who had become a mumbling nun with skin like a baked apple, not to overlook her own saintly husband—she had learned to lean into the perpetual affliction of her life. If the thought of suicide had not disgusted her, if suicide for all others had not been regarded with such cheerful approval by her late husband and if her own death, in any form, did not seem so horrendously passive, she would have undertaken her destruction years past when she had been a schoolgirl who had unschoolgirlish thoughts which conjugated the unpropitious, which had implacably demanded that pain accompany decay. She had sensed long ago that the source of her trouble was that she was too ancient. Victoriano had worn his hoariness as a belled leper goes forth, and with an ineffable sense of design and structure had managed to die of what had made him live. She had, on the contrary, always fought to conceal the headiness of her nine hundred years. She was a grandee of Spain, a cousin of the king as they say, forced to live in part inside the mists of her history where the past was always now, whetting the appetite of pride, well into the mists of history where she was one piece with the men who had written with El Cid and with the hard-mouthed women who had ruled the men until at last she had come to the end of it, an adept at tragedy. She had been toughened to the point where, at last, she lived by it. That was not the case, she knew, with the beautiful and pregnant newcomer to disaster who was waiting for her. The elevator reached the third floor. The duchess knocked softly to announce herself, and opened the door.

Eve sat facing her. Her face was bleak. She was sober. She didn't speak. The duchess crossed the room and kissed her in a sisterly fashion on the cheek, removed her hat, and sat in a chair facing Eve, within two feet of Eve.

"Would you like some hot tea, my dear?" the duchess asked.

"Yes. Thank you."

The duchess rang. "I suppose Rafael Corruno, Jaime's

lawyer, will cross-examine me tomorrow, but I can say with a sense of finality that I have finished my work today. We can leave Spain."

"We?"

"You must leave tonight. As the Fiscal told me they would, the court ordered your arrest today. Do you have an unused passport, that is, a perfectly usable passport?"

"Yes. My own. My real passport."

"Fine. You must take the Daimler which carries a royal crest on its radiator. I bought the thing years ago because it uncomplicated traffic at the feria in Sevilla. And a chauffeur *and* a footman. They will take your passport into the *aduanas* at Irún then you will simply roll across the bridge. No one would dream of stopping that Daimler."

She suddenly peered more intently at Eve. "Have you discovered somehow that I had told the government where to find the Goya which would have freed Jaime?"

"Yes."

"You would have done the same, would you not?"

Eve ran her hand across her eyes then through her hair. She kept her eyes closed when she answered, then opened them. "I suppose I would have," she said.

"Yes. I know you. You would have. It was a thing which the faithful women have to do, my dear."

"Will they kill Jim?"

"No."

"What will happen to him?"

"The timing of the murder which Raphael will present and somewhat support with the records when the defense presents its case beginning tomorrow afternoon will show reasonable doubt, the Fiscal thinks, so Jaime will probably be sentenced to thirty years and a day."

"There is nothing to be done?"

"No, dear."

"Months ago," Eve said slowly, "when we discovered in Paris that the paintings we had stolen from you had been stolen from us, Jim thought of a way to make contact with an organized group of Spanish criminals in case we should need to have means to trace the paintings here. As though it had been an ordinary, simple, clean hijacking operation."

Two servants came in with the tea things on a great cart. Although Eve had been speaking English which the servants would not have understood, she fell silent. The duchess directed operations crisply and dismissed the people. She poured tea and arranged small pieces of the beautiful food on a plate for Eve, while Eve began to talk again.

"The man told me today that you had told the government where to find the Goya. He said he had meant not to tell me who had told, just that the government had the Goya, killing any chance for a deal, but at last he decided to tell me because he said I must know who my enemies were. I walked away from him believing that, then all at once I knew you had killed Victoriano Muñoz and tonight when you inquired whether or not I would have given the government the Goya had it been Jim who had been so senselessly murdered and Cayetano were on trial, I could understand that it would only make everything more hopeless if I saw you as my enemy because I feel with every sense I have that Jim knows what has happened to all of us and that he understands what had been done and why it was done and that he must love you more now for having helped to make you suffer so much. I love you more now because I was part of the cause of your suffering and now I stand beside you with one-half of what I have left. Since we cannot snap our fingers and stop living I must somehow find peace for you and you must struggle to find peace for me, because we will never be able to find it for ourselves, our eyes have gone for that. I believe our eyes were always blinded, as every living being must be blinded in that way of finding hope for themselves because it must be bound up in loving and no one is allowed to love himself so prodigiously. If we had all begun where we are now, knowing that we can only do for each other and that we can have reason to hope in no other way, Cayetano would be alive and Jim would be free but that can't be and we are the only two who are left, and truly the only two who know the secret. When I walked toward your house this afternoon, I knew you knew something I didn't understand because you have known all of these terrible things much longer than me. I knew you had something which you felt compelled to offer to me, the way religion must have been offered when it first began. You didn't know whether I had been prepared enough to be able to accept it and you had no right to foresee that I would know what it was before you brought it to me. We are in one form, body and soul, that everyone must see and agree, but more than that I am you and you are me and what have we done to each other?"

The dam broke within the duchess. The tears she had sought since the terrible days when she had been very young, the tears which had been denied to her through all of the battering came to her now. She wept helplessly but joyously, released and purified, as Eve sipped at her tea and retreated into her bleakness.

She left in the Daimler at two o'clock the following morning. They arrived at Irún at ten minutes after eight. As the seeress had predicted, her passport was stamped with quite some deference and they rolled across the bridge into France.

She had breakfast in Bayonne. While she ate a croissant and drank a café au lait she read that Jean Marie had hanged himself in his cell. She could only remember the words to the Lord's Prayer and since she knew no other she sat with her head in her hands and said the Lord's Prayer once, twice, then three times.

She spent the night in Vendome. She reached Paris quite early the next morning. She had been drinking steadily all the way, but she was not drunk.

The apartment she and Bourne had lived in seemed alien and changed. She needed a brandy. The decanter was empty. She crossed the living room, then the kitchen. She opened the cellar door. A stench assailed her. She looked down. Chern's dead hand reached. His ruined face stared. She screamed. She screamed again. She could not stop screaming.

The Dream Merchants

by Harold Robbins

The Dream Merchants, hailed by the critics as "One of the very few honest novels about the movie business" dissects with intimate precision the glittering, amoral world of the movie moguls.

Here is the story of a man named Johnny Edge. His climb to the very top; the men he trampled underfoot, the women he sacrificed to his greedy ambition, and the celluloid empire he created out of other people's dreams.

The Dream Merchants and *The Carpetbaggers* form two parts of a planned trilogy focused on Hollywood. The third volume, yet to be written, will be entitled *The Inheritors*.

FOUR 4 SQUARE EDITION 6s.